Right as Reign

J.B. VAMPLE

ISBN: 978-1-7374279-4-0 (Hardcover)
ISBN: 978-1-7374279-2-6 (Paperback)
ISBN: 978-1-7374279-3-3 (ebook)
Library of Congress Control Number: 2021913978

Author name: J.B. Vample, 1981
Title: Right as Reign
First edition

Published by: Jessyca B. Vample
Imprint: Jessyca Vample Publishing
Address: PO BOX 21313, Philadelphia PA, 19141
Email: info@jbvample.com
Website: jbvample.com

For Marlene, my dearly departed grandmother. I miss your physical form terribly, but I feel your spirit every day.

Prologue

SITTING ON HER QUEEN-SIZED BED with her back against the plush pillows, Reign Price held her pink and gold ballpoint pen to her spiral notebook. The soft bedroom light illuminated the empty lines as she gathered her thoughts. Within a moment, she began to write:

> *How many times can you say the words "I'm fine" before you believe them as truth?*
>
> *Hell, I've asked myself this question more times than I can count, yet I still don't have the answer.*

The cell phone vibrating on her nightstand stalled her hand. She grabbed it. Clicking the message icon, she read the text.

Sure.

Reign narrowed her eyes at the cold, short reply. Glancing at the eleven o'clock time flashing on the bedside clock, she scoffed. She'd waited nearly three hours for her boyfriend's reply to her 'Hey babe, are we still on for tomorrow?' text. The call she had made to him before that, went unanswered.

"Thanks for taking your sweet fuckin' time answering me," she muttered. Gritting her teeth, she typed out a response.

Okay, see you then. Love you, goodnight.

After hitting send, she waited a moment for a response. When one didn't come through, Reign shook her head. "That's fine," she huffed, tossing it back on the dresser with frustration. Missing the dresser completely, the sleek black phone tumbled to the carpeted floor. She eyed the fallen object with deadpan eyes for a long moment before pinching the bridge of her nose, sighing heavily.

1

Returning her focus to her book, her hand began to glide across the paper once again:

Today, I felt like crying.

Yesterday, I became so frustrated that I wanted to throw something.

Yet when posed with the question, "How are you?" the only answer that I could give was… "I'm fine."

Telling that lie, while holding my true feelings inside, is a habit that I can't seem to shake.

But then again, why would I want to shake it? It works for me.

And what is the point of sharing your feelings if it doesn't change anything?

Telling someone that I'm feeling sad, won't make me any less sad. So, why even bother?

Even when I do try, things don't change. So again, why even bother?

As the neatly penned words filled the page, Reign felt her frustrations come to a head with the sting of tears behind her eyes. Hand still resting on the paper, Reign squeezed them shut, forcing the tears to a halt. "Stop it," she hissed. "Don't let it get to you." Taking another deep, long breath, she opened her eyes. Her tears were gone; her writing resumed.

Despite my logic, I often wonder if this way of handling things is crazy. Is trying to convince myself that I'm okay all the time—that I'm happy—crazy?

I guess the better question would be, is it even possible to be completely happy? Can one be content in every aspect of their life—love life, family, friendships, career—is true happiness even attainable?

I don't have the answer to that question either. Even if I did, I'm not sure I'd really want to know for fear of being disappointed…
Another feeling that's not foreign to me, and yet another feeling that I hide.

2

Setting the pen down, Reign held the book to her face, reading the words that she'd just poured out—her latest journal entry. At thirty-two years old, Reign had written more journal entries than she could possibly count; not that she'd ever tried.

She used them to release whatever was pent up inside of her. The things she couldn't bring herself to speak out loud: her thoughts, her hopes, her dreams, her *desires*. In those moments, her pen became her voice, her notebook a listening ear. Journaling was Reign's solace, her outlet. After every completed entry, she felt lighter—or at least she could convince herself that she had. This evening's writing session was no different.

Eyes heavy, Reign exhaled deeply. Closing her notebook, she placed it and the pen in the drawer of her nightstand, before turning off her bedside lamp.

Chapter One

REIGN JOTTED LINE AFTER LINE into her notebook, pausing only to adjust the rose gold watch on her slender wrist. Shaking her wrist to maneuver the slim time piece back into place, she noticed the time. "Damn it, it's after eight."

She'd zoned out while writing and lost track.

If there was one thing that Reign despised more than time getting away from her, it was having to stop writing in the middle of a thought.

Rubbing her eye with her hand, she stifled a yawn. *I definitely should've gone to bed earlier,* she thought. Work, paired with her late-night journaling session, had her exhausted.

Stretching her neck from side to side, she paused short of capping her pen to glance out her kitchen window, taking in the early morning backdrop—what she could *see* of it anyway. The complex next to her apartment blocked most of her view of the Arizona mountains.

Turning away, Reign reached out to close her notebook, but a beep from her cell interrupted her. Grabbing the phone from the table, she tapped the message icon to open it.

I'm on my way to you. Left my earrings at home, can I borrow a pair of yours?

Reign scrunched her face. "Seriously?" She set the phone back down. "At least say *good morning* first." Rolling her light brown eyes, she reached for a piece of apricot jam covered toast. As she did, her elbow bumped against her mug of coffee, knocking it over.

She bolted from her seat as the warm liquid splashed across

the kitchen table, her open notebook, *and* her clothes. "Shit!"

"What happened? Are you okay?" A panicked voice asked, barreling through the kitchen door.

Reign glanced over, annoyance clear on her face. "I'm fine Mom, I just spilled coffee all over myself."

Approaching the counter, Vivian Price shook her head, grabbing the roll of paper towels from the holder. "You know, you could've reacted to that accident *without* using profanity," she said. "You know how I feel about that."

Reign rolled her eyes again. "While it wasn't my intention for you to hear my profane outburst, *surely* you should know that I curse by now," she ground out. "And trust me, what I just said is *nothing* compared to *other* words that I've used."

Walking to the table with one eyebrow raised, Vivian shot her daughter a challenging look. "Such *as?*"

"Funny, understanding, caring, and kind," Reign quickly answered, tucking some of her bust length curled, dark brown hair behind her ears.

Her mother was perplexed for only a moment before realization set in; she let out a quick gasp, then pointed a warning finger. "Watch it, smart mouth."

Reign chuckled.

Vivian couldn't help but chuckle herself. Her daughter had always been smart—book *and* mouth wise. Tearing several sheets of paper towels from the roll, she began wiping the spilled coffee from the table. Reign placed a gentle hand onto hers, stopping her.

"It's okay, I'll clean it." Tearing sheets from the roll, a small sigh escaped Reign's glossed lips. "I'm so *tired* of this tiny table. I barely have room to do anything but *eat*. I'm always knocking stuff over," she complained, cleaning the mess.

Despite her daughter's protests, Vivian grabbed a dishrag to assist. "Well, hopefully you'll get a bigger one once you find your house."

"Yeah well, a house can't come fast enough. I outgrew this one-bedroom apartment like three years ago."

"I hear you baby," Vivian soothed. "I feel a little bad that I stayed over here last night."

Reign looked at her mother; her brow furrowed slightly. "Why?"

"Because you gave me your room." She picked up Reign's phone, handing it to her. "I told you, *I* would've been fine on the couch."

"Mom, you're sixty, you would *not have* been fine on the couch." Reign retrieved her coffee-stained notebook from the table. "I had no problem sleeping on it. I preferred for you to stay anyway. It was *too* late for you to drive home."

Reign often had visits from her mother, but rarely did they turn into an overnight stay.

"Dear, we only live in Scottsdale," Vivian pointed out, amused. "It's twenty minutes away."

Reign cut her eye. "Still." She held up her book, examining the damage.

Vivian watched with sympathetic eyes. "Messed it up pretty badly, huh?"

Reign sighed. "It's fine. Not like anybody is ever going to read anything written in here anyway." She wiped as much coffee as she could from the sheets, then touched the wet fabric of her dress. "Ugh, I have to go change."

"Well, if it makes you feel any better, you can't even *see* the coffee stain on your clothes." Vivian gestured to her outfit. "All that black you have on."

Reign peered down at her black short-sleeved knee length, fitted dress. "Ah yes, mornings with you would *not* be complete without you trying to talk me out of wearing dark clothes," she jeered. "Like high school all over again."

"I'm just saying, there are so many *other* colors in the world that you'd look so nice in." Vivian shrugged. "One would think that *black* was your *favorite color*."

People who pay close enough attention to me would know that that's not true. Reign eyed her mother—a woman whom she shared the same light brown complexion, dark hair, delicate features and, stunning beauty with. "Mom, I love you and I'm saying this with the upmost respect," Reign began. Her mother stared at her with anticipation. "Lay off."

Vivian waved a hand in Reign's direction. "Okay fine," she relented. "I apologize, I didn't mean to criticize. You look good in anything you put on. Always *have*."

Reign shook her head, amused. Her mother was right. With her tall and toned figure, curves in all the right places, Reign *did* look good in any outfit that she wore. "Thank you," she replied. "But if you *really* want to bug somebody, go bug Cyn about that man's apartment she's spending all of her time in, instead of her dorm."

Vivian gasped. "Your sister is *not* shacking up with some boy!"

Reign raised her eyebrows. "Yeah, okay." She grabbed her pen from the table, then headed for the kitchen exit.

Vivian followed Reign's progress. "You shouldn't lie on your sister."

"I'm *not* lying," Reign maintained.

Vivian shook her head as Reign disappeared into the living room. "Have a good day at work. Love you baby."

"Love you too and don't clean anything else, I'll do it when I get back," Reign hurled back. "Call me when you get home."

Vivian chuckled to herself. "She can't tell me what to do."

"It's about *time*," Marcy Stevens ground out, tossing her hands in the air. She'd grown tired of standing at the bottom step of Reign's apartment complex. "Fifteen minutes is *too* long to have me waiting out here in this heat. You know that brown sugar melts in the sun."

Reign stepped off the last stair. Meeting Marcy's height, her frustration was clear. "It's too early for your complaining, Marcy."

Marcy waved a dismissive hand Reign's way. "It's not, it's *hot*."

Reign shook her head. "I don't know *why* you insist on complaining about the heat like it's not hot *ninety percent* of the time." she said. "We live in *Arizona*; you should be *used* to it by now."

Marcy ran a hand over her hair, then used the same hand to

fan her face. "Trust me, I'm *not*. It's only *May* and it feels like hell," she grunted. "Anyway, did you bring the earrings?"

Reign dug into her black handbag, retrieving a pair of sterling silver hoop earrings. "Do me a favor, give these *back*."

Marcy grabbed the earrings from Reign's hand, placing a hoop into her earlobe. "Why did you say that like I never give your stuff back?" she questioned, offended as she put the other earring in.

"Because you *don't*." Reign threw back. The two women began walking along the sidewalk. "You've been borrowing my things since college, and I have *yet* to receive *any* of what I've loaned *back*."

"And yet you *still* give me stuff when I ask," Marcy countered, unfazed.

"Yeah, I'll add stopping that to my to-do list," Reign sneered, earning a chuckle from Marcy. "Anyway, you *never* walk to work, what made you decide to do it today?"

Marcy adjusted the large designer satchel on her shoulder. Hesitating to speak for a moment, she smoothed her hand down her white sleeveless top. The plunging neckline of the casual top, paired with the yellow floral printed pants, accentuated Marcy's voluptuous figure. "I just… I figured I'd save a few bucks today. The ride shares everyday were getting a little expensive," she finally explained. "And we both know that I don't do buses so…"

Reign continued her stride with Marcy in tow. "Oh okay,"

"But I'll tell you, this will be the first *and last* time I walk *anywhere* that's more than five minutes away," Marcy scoffed. "My pretty feet and these designer sandals were *not* made for it." She gestured to the bright yellow strappy stiletto sandals which displayed her manicured toes. "You like these shoes? I just got them the other day." She gestured to her purse. "*And* this bag."

Reign's eyes skimmed the shoes and matching bag. "They're nice."

Marcy grinned, adjusting the bag once again. "This designer is expensive as hell, but well worth it."

Reign just gave a nod, but did not respond further.

While walking to work wasn't Marcy's routine, it certainly was

Reign's; she lived within a half-hour walking distance from her place of employment in downtown Phoenix. She didn't own a car and unlike Marcy, Reign refused to pay for ride shares to and from work. Besides, she typically enjoyed the moment of solitude before busy days at the office.

Letting out a whine, Marcy paused her steps to adjust her sandal strap. It hadn't even been ten minutes and her feet were already killing her. "Ugh, I don't see how you *do* this every day," she complained, catching back up to Reign.

Reign resisted the urge to roll her eyes. *Please, be quiet.* "I don't mind it," she replied, even toned.

Marcy flung her hair over her shoulder. "Well, *I do.* I need a car."

"Then *buy* one, Mar," Reign suggested, tone not changing.

Marcy side-eyed Reign, making a face. "Girl please, I have a man, I will *not* be paying for my own car." She waved a hand. "No, like these shoes and bag, my car will be a *gift.*"

Reign shook her head but didn't bother replying. She'd known Marcy a long time; her being spoiled wasn't anything new.

The moment of silence lasted for *only* a moment. Looking over at Reign, whose eyes were fixed in front of her, Marcy ran a hand over her hair. "Rae," she called.

"Yeah?" Reign answered, unenthused.

Marcy smiled. "You didn't comment on my new hair."

Reign's eyes widened slightly as she kept her stride. "I saw it."

"I know you *saw* it, heffa, but you didn't *say* anything about it." Marcy flung hair over her shoulder. "I wanted to try this color. What do you think?"

Reign looked at Marcy, fixating on the blond, bust length wand curls on her friend's head. She then zoned in on the smile plastered to Marcy's smooth attractive, brown face. "I umm…" Reign rubbed her forehead. "I'd rather not say," she slowly drew out.

"Come on, be honest," Marcy pressed.

"I don't like it."

Marcy's head jerked back. "Well *damn!*"

Reign shrugged. "Sorry, but I *don't*."

"What's *wrong* with it?" Marcy harped, grabbing a lock of curls.

Reign stared at Marcy's hair. "Is it a wig?" she asked, tucking some of her own hair behind her ear. Marcy nodded. "Yeah, I can tell. It's just not working for you."

Marcy abruptly stopped walking.

Baffled, Reign halted her own steps. She faced Marcy, raising an eyebrow. "Why are you stopping?" she asked, impatient. "If you're going to walk with me, you need to keep up. I have to get to work."

Marcy folded her arms, frowning down Reign's length.

Reign squinted her eyes. "Something the matter?" she challenged.

"I don't appreciate your response," Marcy barked, upset.

A perplexed glare masked Reign's face. "I'm sorry, did you *not* ask me what I thought?" she threw back. "Was I supposed to *lie* to you?" she added when Marcy rolled her eyes.

"Whatever, Rae," Marcy grunted, putting a hand up. "Just because *you* don't experiment with *your* hair, doesn't mean that you get to turn your nose up at me for experimenting with *mine*."

Reign's eyes widened; her mouth opened slightly, but nothing came out. *What in the entire fuck is happening right now?*

Marcy sucked her teeth. "My stylist is booked solid for the next few weeks, so I did this myself, and I *thought* that I did a good job," she pouted. "I felt cute earlier, and now thanks to *you*, I no longer do." Her lip curled in disgust, "Way to ruin my day *bestie*."

Reign's confusion turned to annoyance. Not only had Marcy gotten angry over an opinion that *she asked* for, but now she was throwing herself a pity party and accusing Reign of ruining her day; the whole thing was ludicrous.

Reign shook her head with vigor, an attempt to erase the last few minutes from her memory. "Marcy—I don't have time for this shit, I have to go," she dismissed, sauntering off.

Marcy eyed Reign's departing figure with wide, stunned eyes. "Seriously? You're just walking off without an apology?"

"See you later, Marcy," Reign threw over her shoulder, continuing her quick pace.

Reaching the designated floor, the elevator door opened. Stepping out, Reign's high-heeled pumps clicked along the hardwood floor, her pace quickening. Entering through a set of glass doors, Reign glanced at her watch.

"Yeah, you're late," a female voice said, stopping Reign in her tracks.

Reign looked in the person's direction. "What are you talking about Ava? I've got like ten minutes," she asked the statuesque, dark skinned woman standing a few feet away.

Approaching Reign with two coffee cups in her hands, Ava Williams let a giggle come through. "I know, but for *you*, that's late. You're normally here a half hour early." She handed Reign one of the cups.

Reign gestured to the cup now secure in her own hand; she smiled a grateful smile. "Thank you."

Ava smiled back. "No problem." She pointed to it, "It's a caramel latte."

"You're a life saver," Reign praised, walking towards her office with Ava following in stride. "I spilled the damn coffee that I'd made at home on myself like an idiot. Then I was going to grab some on the way *here*, but I got sidetracked while walking with Marcy—"

"Ugh," Ava grunted, rolling her eyes. Just the mere mention of that woman's name irritated her.

Reign shot Ava a stern look. "Come on now, don't be like that."

"Rae, you already know how I feel about that girl," Ava sneered. "I'm in the office, so I'll refrain from calling her what I *really* want to."

"She's dating your brother," Reign reminded her.

A frown formed on Ava's beautiful face; she scoffed in the process. "Don't remind me." She ran her hand over her black, naturally curly hair that fell past her shoulders, moving a few tendrils away from her eye. "I still have *no* idea what he sees in her."

Reign just shook her head. The bad blood between Ava and Marcy had been brewing since their college years. She had hoped that since they were all in their thirties, the two women would put their differences aside. But from the moment Marcy had begun dating Ava's older brother two years ago, the feud had intensified.

"You're too beautiful and fabulous to be spiteful," Reign chortled, opening her office door.

Following Reign inside, Ava let out a huff. "Fine, I'll stop…for *now*," she promised, standing in front of Reign's desk.

"I appreciate it." Reign set her latte and purse down.

Taking a sip from her own coffee cup, Ava pointed to Reign's laptop. "I saw your email about the two new manuscripts that came in," she mentioned. "Up late again, huh?"

Reign chuckled, "As always." She turned her laptop on. "I was finishing up a sample edit when I saw the confirmation emails from the clients—both are fiction. One needs a developmental edit; the other, a line-edit."

Ava's eyes lit up. "Nice."

Reign smoothed her hands down her dress before sitting. "I'll handle the one that needs the developmental edit."

"I'll take the other. I just finished a project yesterday, so my load is light." Ava smiled. "I commend you for always taking on the hard editing projects. Let's face it, some of the stories that come through here *need* your creative writing mind, and not someone who's simply good with grammar and punctuations."

Reign shook her head. "Be nice," she warned.

"I'm just saying." Ava placed a hand to her chest, "*This* is coming from someone who can't write a book to save her life. But I can correct punctuations and weed out redundancies like nobody's business."

As an English major in undergrad, Ava had excelled in everything her curriculum threw at her, yet creative writing was something that she always struggled with.

Reign on the other hand, *excelled* at creative writing; had since Ava had known her. It was something that Ava had always admired about her.

"I bet you could rewrite some of these books in your *sleep…*" Ava smirked. "Should you ever *get* any, night owl."

Reign chuckled, "Funny."

"You have *talent*, sis," Ava added, proud. "That's why *you're* the supervisor."

Reign offered a slight smile. "I appreciate that."

Upon graduating college with her degree in English, Reign had quickly landed a job as assistant editor for a well-known editing firm. Proving to be a talent in her field—with her exceptional skills, impeccable work, and creativity—she'd been promoted from editor to lead editor in under five years. When her former supervisor retired from the company three years ago, Reign was an automatic replacement for the position. She now successfully managed five editors, including Ava, who had joined the company two years after her.

Reign grabbed her latte. "By the way, that edit you did on that romance novella last month—the author changed the entire story and now needs it redone."

Ava covered her face with her hand, groaning in the process. "God—I hope she changed the name of that *protagonist* while she was at it," she grumbled. "No matter *how* many times she wrote it, I just can't picture the name *Bartholomew* being moaned during those sex scenes."

"Will you *stop* it?" Reign demanded, fighting to keep a straight face.

Humored by her own words, Ava dissolved into laughter.

Succumbing to giggles, Reign pointed to her door. "Go do some work, silly."

Chapter Two

FINGERS FLYING ACROSS HIS PHONE screen, Troy Donovan typed out a text before looking over at the man next to him. "How often do you lift?" he asked.

Chase Williams pulled on his weightlifting gloves. "I try to aim for a couple times a week," he answered, nonchalant.

Troy nodded. "I've been wanting to step my weight game up, but I prefer running."

"To each his own, I guess." Chase placed a plate on the bar. "But you could do *both* if you really wanted to."

Troy shrugged, but didn't give the comment a response. After a moment, a smirk crossed his face. "I'm surprised you're even *at* the gym today. Didn't you just get back in town today?"

Chase cut his eye at Troy. *I really wish you'd stop talking to me, so I can work out in peace*, he thought.

Chase hadn't been to his home gym in a while, due to being away on a work trip. Now back in town, he'd decided to pay the place a visit. He certainly didn't expect to run into Troy; someone whom he wasn't fond of, yet tolerated. "I got back *last night* actually," Chase clarified.

"Oh okay," Troy replied. "You were gone for about two weeks this time, huh? Last time it was what? A *week*?"

Chase fixed Troy with a stern, skeptical gaze. "Why is it that you seem to know every time that I'm out of town?"

Troy once again shrugged, sending another text. "You know the girls talk."

"I guess," Chase dismissed, shaking his head slightly. As a sought-after architect, Chase traveled often for work, sometimes for weeks at a time. He went to place another set of plates on the bar, but the person walking through the gym's entrance caught his attention. "*Speaking* of the girls," he mentioned to Troy, gesturing to the woman approaching. "Here comes one of them *now*."

Troy glanced up from his phone. Seeing his girlfriend, he offered a head nod.

"Hey you," Reign greeted, setting her gym bag on the floor.

"What's up?" Troy gave Reign a quick, one-armed hug, before returning his focus back to his phone.

Reign tightened the cap on her pink water bottle. "How was your day?" she asked Troy.

Eyes still locked on the screen, he shrugged slightly. "It was fine," he blandly returned.

Reign stared at Troy, though he was paying *her* no mind. "Oh...okay," she muttered. She took a deep breath when he didn't speak further. "*My* day was fine too," she hinted. "In case you were thinking of asking."

Troy flashed a quick look her way. "You say something, babe?"

Reign quickly shook her head. "No, it was nothing. Don't worry about it."

Noticing Chase standing there, her eyes widened slightly. In trying to get her boyfriend to engage with her, Reign had unintentionally ignored Chase. She offered him a warm smile. "I'm sorry, hi Chase," she greeted him. "It's good to see you."

Chase had been a silent spectator to their lackluster exchange. When Reign spoke to him, he looked at her, smiling in return. "It's okay," he assured her. "It's good to see you too." He gestured to her black active leggings and matching tank top. "I see you're all ready to work out."

Reign set her water bottle on a bench and adjusted her ponytail. "Yeah," she confirmed. "I missed the gym yesterday because I got off work late." She placed her hands on her hips. "I *refused* to miss today. *Especially* after all the cake that I ate at work earlier."

"Was it somebody's birthday?" Chase asked.

"No, Ava just bought a big ass cake for no damn reason," Reign grunted. Chase laughed. "Chase, your sister is out of her mind."

"*That*, she is," Chase chortled.

Troy shoved his phone into his gym bag before grabbing it from the floor. He placed his hand on the small of Reign's back. "I'll see you later, babe."

Reign looked up at him. Standing at five-foot-eight inches tall, she was used to looking up at Troy's six-foot-three figure. "You're finished?"

"No, I actually never started… Something just came up, so I have to go," Troy explained.

Reign frowned slightly. "Where are you going? You're supposed to help me, remember?"

"I know, but I have something that I need to take care of."

Reign turned away from him, slowly shaking her head in the process.

"Rae, come on don't act like that," Troy said, tone condescending. "I'll see you *later*. We're supposed to be doing this double date thing, remember?"

Reign faced him. Despite Troy's cavalier attitude, Reign had a reason to be disappointed. This marked the third time this week that Troy had blown her off. Yet she didn't want to argue; instead she offered a bitter smile. "Yeah, I remember. See you."

Troy gave Reign's lower back a light tap, then put his hand up at Chase. "See you later, man."

"Later," Chase dryly threw back.

As Troy made his departure, Chase eyed Reign, who was removing hand wraps from her gym bag. Though she'd jerked the items from her bag, hinting frustration, her face was void of emotion. "Everything okay?" he asked her.

"Sure," she abruptly answered, wrapping one of her hands.

"Doesn't seem like it." He leaned against the weight machine.

Reign let out a frustrated huff when she messed up her wrapping. "Damn it!"

Chase held his hand out. "Let me help you with that."

"It's fine, I got it," she bit out.

"Reign," he called, stern.

She looked at him.

Chase stood just as tall as Troy, but that and the fact that both men were handsome, was where their physical similarities ended. While Troy's light brown complexion matched Reign's own, Chase's complexion was several shades deeper. He kept his facial hair short and groomed; Troy elected for a clean-shaven face. Due to his weight training, Chase had defined muscle tone, compared to Troy's slender, athletic frame.

"Just let me help you with it," Chase insisted.

Rolling her eyes, Reign placed the wraps in his outstretched hand. "Okay."

Letting out a slight chuckle, he began wrapping her hand. "Always so stubborn."

"Yeah, I know," Reign agreed, solemn. She exhaled deeply. "I'm sorry, I didn't mean to come off—bitchy."

"You weren't," he promised, fastening it in place before moving onto her left. "So…is everything good with you?"

"Everything is fine," Reign answered.

Chase gave a slow nod. "You remember that I've known you a long time, right?"

Reign stared at her hand as Chase continued to secure it. "Yes Chase, I do."

"Which *means* that I have a pretty good idea when you're downplaying."

Her eyes shot up, holding a narrowed eyed gaze on Chase. "How *was* Georgia anyway?"

Chase glanced at her, then shook his head. "I'll fill you in at dinner later… Nice deflection attempt though."

Reign couldn't help but giggle a bit. "Fine…" Her face relaxed. "But really, I'm okay, it's nothing important. I'm just…a little frustrated because Troy was supposed to help me practice my kickboxing."

Chase frowned slightly. "I don't take Troy for the kickboxing type." Laughter filled his voice, "To be honest, he doesn't look like he can fight at *all*."

"He's *not*, but *I* started again, and he promised to help me practice when I didn't have class. Holding the pads, steadying the boxing bag, and such." She let out a quick sigh. "I know, it probably sounds like I'm overreacting... Apparently I do that a lot."

"No, it *doesn't*, and you *don't*," Chase soothed, finishing up. "You're entitled to feel how you feel."

Reign just shook her head. *Not according to Troy.* She closed and opened her fists a few times. "Thank you," she said, grateful.

"No problem." Chase rubbed his chin. "It's great to hear that you're back at it though. The boxing I mean," he beamed. "You plan on getting into the ring?"

Reign frowned. "*Hell* no. I'm not trying to damage this face."

Chase let out a laugh.

"No, I just got a little bored with my normal workout routine, so I figured I'd go back to it," she explained. "It's been a few years, so I'm sort of rusty."

Chase put a hand up. "I'm sure you haven't lost any skill," he assured. "Once you know, you know."

She ran a hand along the back of her neck. "If you say so," she chortled, feeling a bit better. "Anyway, thanks again for your help." She grabbed her gym bag from the floor. "I better go grab a locker before they're all gone."

"No problem." Chase watched as Reign turned to walk away. "Hey."

Reign turned around. "What's up?"

"I can help you train today if you want."

"No Chase it's fine, you don't have to do that," she protested. "I have class tomorrow anyway."

"I don't mind," he insisted. "Marcy stood me up for *our* work-out, so I have the time."

Reign let out a laugh. "Are you *really* surprised that she stood you up?" she wondered. "Marcy *hates* the gym."

Chase laughed with her. "No, I knew she was only trying to be nice when she offered to join me." He folded his arms. "So, what do you say?"

Reign thought for a moment. "Okay, sure." She adjusted the bag in her hand. "Thanks," she threw over her shoulder en route to the locker room.

Chase gave a nod. "No problem," he repeated, then returned his focus back to loading his weight plates.

Ava sprinted to her door. Snatching it open, she threw her arms around her brother. "I missed you," she gushed.

Chase chuckled. "I missed you too, drama queen," he teased.

Ava broke free and delivered a light smack to his arm. "Don't be an ass, I haven't seen you in like a month."

"I apologize." Chase stepped foot inside his sister's two-bedroom condo, gift bag in hand. "You redecorated," he mentioned, browsing the space.

Ava shrugged. "Eh, just changed some of the colors," she replied, locking her door. "The red accents weren't working anymore." She headed for her light grey couch, picking up a lavender pillow. "Reign helped me pick out the new colors. The lavender looks so much better in here."

"It *does*," Chase agreed. "I saw Reign a little earlier."

Ava looked at him. "Oh yeah?"

"Yeah. Ran into her at the gym."

"You two and that gym," Ava chuckled. "Neither *one* of you need to work out." She placed the throw pillow back in place, then pointed to the bag in Chase's hand. "What's in that bag? Ooh is that for me? If it is, hand it over."

Chase raised an eyebrow at her giddiness. "Are you sure you're thirty-two?"

"As much as *you* are thirty-four," she threw back.

Chase shook his head, handing Ava the small bag.

Ava dug inside, pulling out a small glass paperweight, shaped like a peach. Her eyes glimmered with delight. "Ooh, this is pretty." She bobbed the object up and down. "It'll go perfect on that shelf over there."

Chase took a seat on the couch as Ava placed her gift on the glass shelf in the corner. "Yeah, I saw it and figured you'd like it." He chuckled, "I know how much you love glass objects."

Ava giggled. "I do and thank you, my favorite sibling."

"I'm your *only* sibling," Chase pointed out, amused. Being their parents only two children, Chase and Ava were close.

"How was your trip?" Ava asked. "Did you let Mom and Dad know that you were back?"

"It was good—productive." He ran a hand over his low-cut, black hair. "And yeah, I stopped by the house earlier today."

"When's the next time you go away?" Ava probed, rearranging some items on her shelf.

"Not sure. It'll depend on when a new out of state client hires me," he answered. "For now, I'll be working from my office downtown."

She smiled at him. "Well, it'll be good having you around for a while." His sister headed for the kitchen. "I made dinner, you want some?"

"No thanks, I'm actually going out to eat a little later."

"Oh." Ava continued her journey into her kitchen. After a few moments she returned, plate of food and a glass of lemonade in her hands. She carefully sat on the couch next to Chase. "Where are you going, and where is my invite, rude ass?" she jeered, setting her glass on the coffee table in front of her.

Chase fixed her with a stern stare. "How am I rude when I just bought your spoiled ass a gift?"

Ava flagged him with her free hand.

Chase shook his head. "Anyway, I'm going to this Italian place downtown," he informed. "Marcy and I are double dating with Reign and Troy."

Ava shot a glare her brother's way. "Don't mention Marcy, I'm about to eat."

Chase rolled his eyes.

"*Whose* idea was it to have a double date anyway?" she sneered. "And since *when* do you hang out with *Troy* of all people?"

"I *don't*, and it was Marcy's idea," Chase explained. "She thought it would be fun, I guess."

"Please," Ava muttered, voice filled with disgust.

Chase shot a rigid look Ava's way. "I swear, this animosity that you and Marcy have going on, has *got* to stop."

"I don't have to stop *anything*." Ava dug her fork into her lasagna. "You *know* that I don't like her."

Chase put a hand over his face, shaking his head once again. Like Reign, Chase had been subjected to snide comments from both Marcy and Ava about one another. And like Reign, he just wanted them to get along.

"She's fake, shady, and annoying," Ava bluntly stated. "*And* she's a user. Always *has* been."

Chase squinted, perturbed. "What *proof* do you have that she's a user?"

"*Enough*." Ava eyed him defiantly. "She takes advantage of Reign, and she takes advantage of *you too*."

"No, she *doesn't* Ava, cut it out," Chase demanded. "Now come *on* with this shit, you've known her since college—"

"And I didn't like her *then*," Ava cut in. "On top of everything *else*, she can't be trusted. You should've seen all of the guys that her gold-digging ass screwed and screwed *over* in college."

"I *wouldn't* have seen that because I went to an out of state college remember?"

Ava rolled her eyes. "Irrelevant."

"I didn't know her then, so what you're *telling* me is irrelevant," Chase countered. "We only started seeing each other two years ago."

"Oh please, *that* happened because you were drunk that night, and she threw herself at you," Ava hissed, recalling the night that Marcy had come on to Chase. "*I* was at Reign's birthday dinner too, I saw it." She took a quick sip of her lemonade then set her glass back down. "And that was *after* she caught an attitude with Reign because she felt that Reign wasn't paying enough attention to her… on *her* birthday."

Annoyed, Chase rolled his eyes.

"Marcy is a shitty person, and your relationship *with* her is bullshit. I've told you before, she is *not* it for you." Ava pointed at him. "You've got a master's degree so you're not stupid. *You* know it *too*."

Chase once again rolled his eyes. "I'm out of here," he huffed, moving to stand. But not before sticking his finger in the middle of Ava's lasagna slice.

"Are you serious?!" she shrieked, smacking him on the arm. "That was childish!"

Chase rose to his feet. "Yeah? Stop talking shit about my girl-friend."

Ava frowned at his departing back. "I'm telling Mom."

"Won't amount to anything, I'm her favorite," Chase teased, walking out the door.

Ava gasped loudly. "Just petty, bro!"

Chapter Three

EXAMINING THE MENU IN FRONT of her, Reign ran a hand through her hair. "Anybody recommend anything here?" she asked.

"Try the chicken mushroom marsala," Troy suggested, eyeing his own menu.

Reign made a face. "Babe, you know I don't eat mushrooms."

"Oh yeah, sorry," Troy dismissed. "Well, that's what *I'm* getting."

"I think I'll try that too," Marcy chimed in, closing her menu. "Sounds good."

"It *is*," Troy maintained.

Marcy glanced at Chase, who was still eyeing his menu. "Hon, just get the chicken parmesan, you know that's what you want," she suggested.

Chase quickly shook his head. "Nah, I'm all parmesan'd out. I ate enough of it while I was away."

"You two are about to be all damn night trying to figure out your entrée," Troy grunted of Reign and Chase. He signaled for the waitress. "Let's start with some drinks and appetizers."

After placing and receiving their drink and appetizer orders, Marcy grabbed her glass of apple martini, taking a sip. "This is nice—the four of us hanging together," she said, setting her glass back down. "We should've *been* doing the 'couple' outing thing." She turned to Chase as he sipped his own drink. "We should do another one before you leave town again," she said to him.

Chase looked at her. "Let's just get through *this* one first," he chortled.

"Yo Chase, I don't see how you can leave your woman to go on all these trips," Troy slid in. "You're crazy, man."

Chase narrowed his eyes at Troy. "I'm not crazy, nor am I taking *vacations*... It's my *job*," he slowly drew out.

"I'm just saying," Troy shrugged, nonchalant. "All that time away...you're lucky Marcy doesn't flirt like she *used* to," he laughed.

Reign shook her head, but didn't say anything, still trying to figure out what she wanted to eat for dinner.

Marcy laughed along with Troy. "I was something else, wasn't I?" she recalled.

Chase on the other hand was not amused. He tensed, a scowl forming on his face. "I'd suggest that you concern yourself *less* with what's going on in my relationship," he warned Troy, tone dangerously calm.

"No need to get defensive," Troy goaded. "I was just saying—"

"Just saying *what?*" Chase broke in, staring Troy down.

"Stop it. Troy, stay out of their business please," Reign finally chimed in. Her boyfriend was known for taking digs at Chase. Had been since they'd known each other.

Chase often let the comments slide because of his friendship with Reign. But there were times when his annoyance with Troy was clear—*this* was one of those times.

Marcy put a hand on Chase's broad shoulder, eyeing him. "Pay him no mind, I don't mind your job," she soothed. She turned her attention back to Troy, grinning. "*Besides* Troy, he *always* makes up for lost time when I see him."

Smirking back at Marcy, Troy picked up his glass. "I bet."

Marcy took another sip of her drink, glancing at Reign. "Rae, you're *still* looking at that menu?"

Reign closed it, pushing it aside. "Not anymore, I'm just going to get a salad," she answered, reaching for her glass of white wine. "To be honest, I'm not that hungry."

Marcy sucked her teeth. "Girl, stop showing off. You work out all the time, get some *real* food."

Perplexity masked Reign's face; she set her glass down, not bothering to take a sip. "How am I showing off by not being hungry?"

"Just saying, we *know* you're trying to keep your figure," Marcy harped, rolling her eyes.

Reign held her confused stare, which quickly turned into a glare. "You okay?" she asked. It was more of a challenge than genuine concern.

Troy put a hand up. "Mar, there's no need to come at Rae. You know you look good too," he commented, lighthearted.

Marcy smiled for a brief second, then waved a dismissive hand. "I'm just messing with you girl," she said to Reign. She sipped her drink some more. "Anyway, I think I'm going to change this hair sooner than I'd *planned*." She eyed Reign. "Rae, do *you* have any suggestions on what I should get next?"

Reign sat back in her seat, fixing Marcy with a rigid stare. "No, I don't."

Marcy sucked her teeth at Reign's lackluster tone.

"Why are you changing your hair?" Troy jumped in.

Marcy twirled a few blond strands around her finger. "I was *told* that it looks a mess," she spat, fixing Reign with a disdain-filled stare.

"It *doesn't*. You should leave it," Troy complimented. "I think the color is great." He turned to Reign, who was tucking some hair behind her ear. "*You* should try it; I think you'd look good with blond hair."

Reign eyed him back, frowning slightly. "No, I *shouldn't*," she spat. "I'm fine how I am, thank you."

Chase took a deep breath as he reached for his drink. *Did he seriously just suggest that Reign change her appearance? What the hell is wrong with this guy?*

"What's the attitude for, Reign?" Troy shot back. "It was just a suggestion."

Reign turned away from him. "Whatever Troy," she muttered.

Marcy smirked at Reign, before directing her attention back to Troy. "Anyway, *thank* you for the compliment Troy," she beamed. "At least *somebody* besides *me* thinks it looks good."

Reign narrowed her eyes at Marcy. "If *you like* it so much, then *keep* it," she bit back. She was over Marcy's attitude and the frivolous hair topic all together. "You do not need my approval to make your decisions. Nor do you need my opinions."

"Why *wouldn't* I want your approval, you're my *best friend*," Marcy threw back, flustered. "That, *and* your opinions are important to me."

Reign pinched the bridge of her nose, sighing in the process. *I should've stayed my ass home.*

"Oh, and my *man*," Marcy added. "*His* opinions matter too."

Chase shot a confused look Marcy's way. "I never said that I didn't like your hair, Mar," he said.

Marcy put her finger up. "That's true," she admitted.

Reign folded her arms, glancing off to the side. She was over this date. Both Troy and Marcy were working on her last nerve.

After placing entrée orders, Chase reached for an appetizer. "Reign, how is that realtor working out for you?" he asked.

Troy rolled his eyes as he sipped his beer.

Reign smiled bright. "Oh, she's great. She showed me some nice properties so far," she answered. "Thanks for recommending her by the way."

"You're welcome," Chase replied. "She helped me find *my* house. You're in good hands."

"Rae, I *still* don't know *why* you're in a rush to buy a house," Marcy jumped in, twirling a cloth napkin around on the table. "I say just upgrade to a bigger apartment—but not in that drab building *you* live in. There're a *bunch* of nice ones open in *my* building."

"Because I'd rather spend all that *rent* money on a *mortgage*," Reign explained. "I never planned on living in an apartment forever. That's the reason I even opted for a small one in the *first* place. So that I could save."

"*I* don't *mind* your apartment, Reign," Troy mentioned.

"Well *I'm* over it, so I'm moving." Reign stood firm. "I have an appointment to look at a few places in Canyon County next week."

"Ah, *my* neck of the woods," Chase commented, pleased.

Reign nodded. "Yeah, she suggested the area a few times, so I'm finally looking there," she said. "It's still not far from work...like a thirty-minute ride."

"You don't have a *car*," Marcy pointed out, squinting her eyes.

Reign eyed her back. "Then that means that I'll have to *get* one."

Marcy's brows raised. "Okay Miss Baller. I guess you using *spellcheck* for a living is paying off," she chuckled at her own snide comment. "That money is right, huh?"

Reign gritted her teeth, yet she refused to engage Marcy any further.

Chase side-eyed Marcy, trying to keep his cool. Her nitpicking, childish behavior was wearing thin.

"Plan on moving out of Phoenix, I see," Troy directed at Reign, tone not hiding his displeasure.

Looking at Troy, Reign frowned slightly. "It's *just* thirty minutes away, Troy."

Troy scoffed. "Doesn't matter if it was *two hours* away, it's not like I'm going to be living there anyway," he mumbled.

He hadn't mumbled low enough; Reign had heard him. That was the last straw; this date was over. Standing, she grabbed her purse. "I have to go."

Eyes wide, Marcy let out a gasp. "*Already?*"

"Yup," Reign sneered.

Troy rubbed his face with his hand, sighing. "Babe, just sit down."

"No, I had a long day. I'm tired," Reign spat.

Chase shook his head; he could tell that Reign meant that in more ways than one; he didn't blame her.

"Reign, come on, let's just finish dinner," Troy pleaded, grabbing her hand. "Don't take my comments personal, I was just joking."

Reign jerked her hand from his grasp. "Goodnight," she hurled through clenched teeth, sauntering away.

Marcy crossed her arms, shooting a smug look Troy's way. "Looks like *somebody* won't be getting any tonight," she teased.

Troy rolled his eyes.

Chapter Four

AVA FLIPPED THROUGH THE CHANNELS on her sixty-inch HD screen television, cradling her cell phone between her ear and shoulder. "*You're* home early on this lovely Friday evening," she spoke into the line. "That double date must've ended pretty quickly."

Sitting on her couch, Reign flipped through her notebook. Her phone—on speaker—sat on the end table next to her. "I left early," she ground out.

"You left by your*self*?" Ava frowned slightly. "Troy didn't at *least* take you home?"

"Yes and no, he *didn't*," Reign quickly replied, turning to a blank page. "Anyway, what's up with you, why are *you* in so early?"

"Girl, me being home early on a Friday is nothing new." Ava set the remote on the cushion next to her. "I'm single and you're like my only friend."

"That's a lie, you have at least five other friends," Reign mentioned, amused.

"They're *acquaintances* dear sis," Ava corrected, fingering the curls on her head. "You know I do *not* use the term 'friend' loosely."

Reign chuckled, "That's a shame."

Ava laughed, "Yeah, I know… But in all seriousness, why did you leave early?"

Reign let out a sigh, "I don't want to talk about it."

"Not surprising," Ava replied. "You hardly *ever* want to talk about things that bother you… Been that way since I met you in high school."

Reign sat there silent, staring blankly at the page in front of her.

"You shut down better than anybody I know," Ava finished.

28

Mind wandering, Reign tapped her pen to her chin.

"Hello?" Ava called when she didn't hear anything. "Girl—Are you tuning me out?!"

"Yes," Reign confirmed, nonchalant.

Ava sat up in her seat, mouth gaped open. "I've told you before about doing that shit to me," she huffed. Reign laughed. "Got me talking to myself like a damn fool."

"Sorry, you know my attention span is low," Reign explained, amusement in her voice.

"Yeah, for shit that you have no interest in, I *know*. You think that makes me feel any better?" Ava rolled her eyes when she heard more laughter. "Rude as hell, Price."

"I'm sorry, I'll make a conscious effort not to do that to you anymore," Reign promised.

"Uh huh," Ava muttered, pulling her bare feet up on the couch. "When's the next time you're going to look at a house?"

"In another week or so," Reign answered. "I decided that I want a newly built house. The ones that are in the area that I'm looking at are still in the building stages."

"Ooh, a *fresh* house, I love it," Ava praised. Reign giggled. "Do you want me to go with you?"

Reign removed the cap from her pen. "Sure, you can."

"Cool, I'll bring some wine and we can pretend that it's already yours and toast to it."

Reign giggled, "Sounds good."

Ava scratched her scalp. "Okay luv, I'll let you go. Try to enjoy the rest of your night."

Doubt that will happen, Reign thought. "I will try."

"I'll see you Monday...*maybe*, if I don't call out."

Reign glanced at the phone. "You *do* realize you're talking to your supervisor, right?"

"Huh? You didn't hear that," Ava quickly dismissed.

"Uh huh," Reign chortled. "Later silly."

"Later."

Hanging up, Reign grabbed her mug of green tea, taking a careful sip. Setting the mug back down, she brought her focus back to the notebook in her hand. Staring at the empty page for a few moments, she finally began to write.

She'd barely gotten a few sentences out before a knock at the door interrupted her. Reign glared at the door, but did not move or call out. She just stared at it as another knock sounded.

"Rae…it's Troy."

Reign let out an angry sigh. "Are you fuckin' kidding me?" she grumbled to herself. She had hoped that when she'd left Troy at the restaurant earlier, that he would've taken the hint and not come to her place.

"Babe, I know you're in there. I see the light on. Just open the door please," he begged.

Reign had every intention of leaving him outside. When he knocked again, she rolled her eyes and sucked her teeth, slamming her notebook shut. Tossing it *and* the pen on the coffee table, she rose from the couch and approached the door.

Snatching it open, she came face to face with Troy's hapless smile. "Are you drunk?" she spat.

The smile immediately vanished from his face. "Nah, you killed my buzz when you left." He moved around her to get into the dimly lit apartment.

Reign rolled her eyes as she closed the door.

Troy glanced at the coffee table. "You got that notebook again, I see," he mentioned, voice laced with humor. "What the hell do you *write* in that thing, anyway?"

"It's not important," she grunted, heading back for the couch.

Her hasty journey was stopped by Troy, wrapping his arms around her small waist. He moved one hand down her flat stomach, grabbing the waistline of her leggings.

"Get off." Reign pushed his hands off her. "If you thought you were going to come over here for *that*, you might as well leave."

Frowning, Troy spun around to face her departing back as she

30

moved towards the couch. "Yo, what's your deal?"

"What's *yours*?" she threw back, spinning around to face him. "*You're* the one who's been acting like a jerk lately."

Troy rolled his eyes. "How so?" His tone was mocking. "What, because of my remarks about your little house hunting?"

Reign scowled at him.

"I *told* you, I was joking," he groaned. "You're always overreacting to shit. I *been* told you that you need to lighten up."

Reign ran her hands over her face, an effort to tame her temper. "Troy, you were *not* joking," she stressed. "In fact, *every time* I talk about my *little* house, you seem to get an attitude. Like you don't want me to get one."

Troy tossed his arms up in exasperation. "Of *course* I want you to get one, it's what you *want* right?"

"Okay, then you're not *happy* about it," she amended.

Troy ran a hand over his face, exhaling quickly. "You know what? You're right. I'm *not* happy about it."

Reign stared at him, eyes wide. "*Seriously?*"

"You didn't even ask me how I *felt* about it," he hurled.

"I *did* talk to you about my plans, Troy," she argued. "But you probably don't *remember* because you never listen to *anything* that I say to you. You're always ignoring me—"

Troy put his hand up. "That's not true, cut that shit out," he interrupted.

Reign jerked her head back. "*Wow*, Troy."

"No, *you're* to blame for my attitude. *You* decided to make this major move *without* me," Troy continued. "Didn't ask me shit, didn't consult with me *at all*."

"*Consult?*" Reign shot a puzzled look his way. "You're not *paying* for it, why would I consult you?"

"Oh, I *could*," Troy boasted. Reign rolled her eyes. "And what the fuck do you *mean*, why would you consult me?"

Reign folded her arms, fixing him with an icy stare.

"I'm your *boyfriend, that's* why," Troy harped. "We've been in a relationship for *six years, that's* why."

"Exactly, my *boyfriend* of six years, not my goddamn *husband*."

Troy tossed his hands in the air. "Oh, what? You're gonna pressure me to *marry* you now?" he snarled.

"When have I *ever* pressured you to marry me?" Reign shrilled. "The last time I even *brought up* marriage was like *three years ago* and I simply asked if you saw us *ever* getting married, to which *you* answered 'yes'. But *clearly* you lied."

Troy let out a deep sigh, pausing for a moment. "Look Reign…I didn't lie. I *do* want to get married one day," he said finally. "But marriage is a lifetime commitment…at least it *should* be. It wasn't for my *parents*… I just don't want to go into it—"

"Troy—spare me the excuses," Reign broke in. "It doesn't even matter at this point."

"Look, I just don't see why we can't get a place *together* for a while, *then* talk about marriage," Troy proposed. "Or, you could just move into *my* house."

Reign went still for a moment, fixing him with a flat gaze. "You—you can't really be this dense," she sneered, scratching her head. "What the—so you think, that asking me to put my house on the backburner to move in with you for the sole purpose of *shacking up*, is okay? Is *fair*?"

Troy just rolled his eyes.

She put a hand up. "Fine, you don't want to answer *that* question, well I have *another* one for you, why have you been blowing me off lately?"

Troy pulled his hands down his face in slow dramatic fashion, letting out a groan in the process. "Reign, *please* don't tell me this is about me leaving you at the damn gym earlier."

Reign paused; she clenched her jaw before speaking again. "No, this isn't just about *today*," she slowly drew out. "This is also about the *other* day when I wanted to have dinner with you, the day before *that* when I wanted to see a movie with you—*last week* when I wanted to take that cooking class with you—I can go on."

"I swear to God," he grumbled.

"It's like every time I try to spend time with you—*just* you and I, you find something *else* to do."

Troy clasped his hands together. "Did I *not* just go on this double date that *you* ran out on?" he reminded.

"I said just *you* and *I*," Reign emphasized, angry. "You seem to have *no* problem sharing your time with other people, but when it comes to just *me*, *I* can't get a minute."

Exasperated, Troy held his arms up. "Am I not here *now*?!"

Reign ran her hands through her hair before resting them on her hips. She was frustrated, and Troy was completely missing the point. "Just forget it, Troy," she bristled. "I don't even know why I bother trying to talk to you."

"Yeah, *I* don't know why you bother either," he spat, tone nasty. "You just wind up wasting your time *and* mine."

Reign scowled.

"I *definitely* regret coming over here." He folded his arms. "Not *only* have you killed my buzz, you've killed my libido."

You weren't getting any anyway, you fuckin' asshole. "Whatever," Reign bit out, turning away from him.

"Yeah, *whatever*," Troy snarled. "And stay off my damn case about this 'spending time' shit. I've been busy just like *you*."

She snapped her head back in his direction. "But unlike *you*, *I'm* willing to make time for you," Reign argued. "You can't even give me *that*, and you really expect me to put my life plans on hold for you?"

Troy glared at her. "You'll get my time when I have it *for* you." His tone was full of venom. "Like I *said*, I've been busy."

Reign's eyes widened. Pausing, she gave a slow nod. "Okay," she muttered.

"So, do we have an understanding? Are you done? Is this bull-shit argument over?" Troy mocked.

Glaring, Reign slowly shook her head. She pointed to the door. "You need to go."

Troy ran a hand over his head. *Shit.* Sighing, he took a step towards her. "Rae, I didn't mean to—"

"*Now.*"

"Come on babe." He sighed. "Let's just try to salvage the rest of the evening."

"There's nothing left to salvage. I *said* get out," Reign fumed.

Troy looked hurt. "You're really sending me home, Rae?" He reached for her hand. "Come on babe, I came here to check up on you—"

Reign jerked her hand back, far out of his reach. "I left you two hours ago, and you didn't even bother *calling* to see if I made it home," she threw back. "Stop pretending that you care about me, and get the fuck out."

Scoffing, Troy waved a dismissive hand her way. "Whatever, I don't have time for this dramatic, nagging shit anyway." He barreled towards the door. "And you wonder why I don't want to be around you."

Standing in silence seething, Reign followed Troy with her eyes as he stormed out of the apartment, slamming the door in the process.

Alone again, Reign let out a heavy sigh. Sitting on the couch, she put her head in her hands. Feeling tears prick her eyes, Reign took several deep breaths. "Don't let it get to you, don't let it get to you," she chanted, forcing the tears back down.

After a moment, she retrieved her notebook and pen from the table to pick up where she left off. Holding her pen to the empty line, she hesitated. She was too angry to focus. Frustrated, she tossed the book back down, then got up, making a beeline for her bedroom.

"Do you want some ice cream?" Chase asked from the kitchen.

Marcy, cozy on the couch in Chase's living room, glanced toward the kitchen entrance. "Yes, with chocolate sauce."

"Sure," Chase answered.

Marcy adjusted her position on the couch, smiling up at Chase as he ambled out of the kitchen, two bowls of chocolate drizzled vanilla ice cream in hand. "Thank you, hon," she crooned, as he handed it to her.

Chase sat down next to her. "No problem."

Marcy snuggled close to him while eating her ice cream. "So, tonight was fun, huh?" she said after a moment.

"*Was* it?" Chase asked, eating his own ice cream.

Noticing the brusqueness of his deep voice, Marcy eyed him. "What do you mean?" She dipped her spoon in her bowl. "You didn't have a good time?"

"Not really," he bluntly stated. "Troy's attitude was aggravating." He flashed a stern look Marcy's way. "And so was *yours*."

Taken aback, Marcy put a hand up at him. "Hold on," she charged, brow knitting. "I didn't have an attitude towards you."

"Not towards me, but towards your *friend*, you did," Chase chided. "Reign didn't do anything to you at dinner and you kept poking at her."

Marcy rolled her eyes. "You miss a lot while traveling. Reign and I are *always* like that," she dismissed.

"I've been around enough. No, you're *not*."

Marcy's lip curled. "I sometimes *hate* how much you pay attention to stuff." She let out a quick sigh. "Okay, *maybe* I was a little salty about the hair comment she made earlier," she admitted. "She made me feel like shit, so I returned the favor. See? Good ol' healthy friendly tit for tat."

Chase raised an eyebrow. "If you say so."

"Rae and I are good," she promised.

Marcy returned her attention to her ice cream, quietly eating more. Chase grabbed the remote from the arm of the couch, turning on the seventy-inch LED TV.

Pausing her eating, Marcy looked over at Chase once again. "So…that's nice that you're helping Rae find a house," she brought up.

Chase flipped through channels. "I just offered her a good realtor."

"Still…" Marcy glanced down at her bowl. "Do you really think she'll close on one soon? I mean, I'm sure the housing market isn't that great."

Chase squinted, focused on the screen mounted on the wall in front of him. "I'm sure the housing market is just fine, otherwise she wouldn't be shown so many." Finding a show to watch, he set the remote down. "Why are you asking *me* this?"

"Just making conversation," Marcy answered, shrugging slightly. "*That*...and I guess I'm just wondering why she's so in a rush to purchase a home *right now*. I mean, if *I* were her, I'd wait."

Chase shot Marcy a side-glance. "*I* bought *my* house a few years ago," he said. "If she's ready to buy one, then she *should*. I don't see what the big deal is."

Having begun his career straight out of grad school, Chase had begun making good money in his early twenties. Instead of spending frivolously and living wildly, he'd purchased his ranch style home, paid off his car, and had managed to stack a healthy savings all before his thirtieth birthday.

"I know, but you're a man, you're *supposed* to have one." A grin appeared on Marcy's face. "All ready and waiting for that special someone to move right on in."

Chase raised an eyebrow but didn't say anything.

Marcy set her bowl on the coffee table, then sat back in her seat. Smiling, she delivering a light tap to Chase's forearm. "Hey."

"What's up?" Chase asked.

Marcy grabbed a few strands of her hair, twirling it around her finger. "So...if Reign ends up moving up here near *you*, I won't be able to see her that often," she began, leering at him.

"Why not?"

"Well, because it's a little far—*walking distance* that is," Marcy stated. "It's like a *two-hour* walk...not that I would *ever* walk that far—"

"Whenever I'm in town and you need for me to drive you, I *will*," Chase slid in.

Marcy opened her mouth, but paused for a second. "*Okay*, but what about when you're *not* in town?" She slowly drew out. "I'm sure you don't expect me to plan my visits with my best friend around *your schedule*."

"I'll give you cab money."

Marcy feigned a smile, then wiped it from her face. "Umm… that can get expensive," she shot down. "*I* should know."

Chase rubbed his eyes, letting out a sigh. "I'm sure you have a point in there somewhere, Marcy," he ground out. Having had a long—what he thought to be a disastrous evening—paired with being tired, Chase was in no mood for Marcy's beating around the bush.

Marcy wrapped her arms around his arm, leaning in. "Well… don't you think it would be nice if I had a car?" she asked, hopeful.

"I don't see why you can't have a car," Chase replied. Marcy's eyes lit up as bright as her smile. "Let me know when you're ready to buy one and I'll go look with you."

Smile disappearing from her face, Marcy released Chase's arm and turned around in her seat.

Chase smirked. "Something wrong?"

"Nope, nothing at all," Marcy spat.

"If you say so." Unfazed my Marcy's sudden change in attitude, Chase began watching TV.

Marcy sighed loudly. *Check your attitude girl. You know catching one with him doesn't get you what you want.* Following the inner pep-talk, Marcy cleared her throat. "I have an idea."

Chase grabbed the remote, muting the television. He fixed her with a tired stare. *What are you about to hint at now?* "What's that?"

Marcy opened her mouth to speak, then put a hand up. "Never mind, you're probably going to think I'm crazy."

"I already *do*," he jeered, earning a playful tap to his arm.

Marcy again twirled her hair, grinning at him. "Okay so…you know how you go out of town often, right?"

Chase stared at her. "Right."

"Well, I was thinking, while you're *away*… maybe I can watch your house for you," she proposed.

"My house is watched fine, security system and all."

"Come on, there's nothing like having someone taking care of your home, watering your plants…using your pool while you're away," Marcy claimed.

Chase scratched his head. "Is something wrong with your apartment?"

"No plants, no pool," she quickly countered. When Chase shook his head, Marcy placed a hand on his arm. "*And,* I'll be able to be closer to Rae for a little while."

"You don't even know if she's definitely moving up here," he pointed out. "*She* doesn't even know for sure."

Marcy rolled her eyes. "We *both* know that Reign *always* gets what her perfect little heart desires," she sneered.

Chase tilted his head, squinting slightly. "Do you even *realize* how bitter you sound when you talk about her?" he asked. "At least that's how it comes off to *me.*"

"I'm not bitter hon, I'm happy for her, but back to what I was saying," Marcy hastily dismissed. "But even if she *doesn't* move up here…*me* being here will just make me feel closer to *you* while you're away," she amended. "I mean, while you're in town, I'm here most of the time *anyway,* so it would just make sense, don't you think?" She batted her big brown eyes. "I could just be here *all the time.*"

Chase eyed Marcy skeptically. "You wouldn't be trying to ask me in that not-so-subtle manner to *move in* here, would you?"

Marcy's eyes widened. "No, of *course* not." She scoffed. "I just wanted to house sit for you. *God.*"

"Really?" he questioned, shooting her a knowing glance.

"Why does it seem like you're accusing me of being sneaky?" she bit out. "Like I have another agenda or something."

Holding his stern gaze, Chase slowly folded his arms. "Are you going to tell me what's *really* going on or keep playing these games?"

"Games?" she echoed, offended.

"Yes, *games,*" he stressed. "That mess you do when you have an ulterior motive. Like what you did less than ten minutes ago, when you *tried* to hint that you want me to *buy* you a car."

Marcy rolled her eyes. "Please, we *both* know that your cheap ass won't buy me a car," she spat.

"I'm *far* from cheap."

"With *me*, you *are*." Marcy threw back. "And I don't see what's so *wrong* with me asking my boyfriend for a car." Being Chase's girlfriend, Marcy wanted to reap all benefits of being with him, *including* the financial. She knew that he had the money to spoil her, and he *did* at times, just not as often as she felt that he *should*.

"Marcy, I will not be manipulated into buying you things." Despite defending Marcy's motives to his sister, Chase was no fool. He knew that most women he encountered in the past, once he became established, wanted him because of what they thought he could give them—Marcy was no different.

Chase was all for spoiling a woman, but not if that was *all* that she was looking for from him.

Marcy sucked her teeth, folding her arms in a huff. "Whatever Chase, fine, I'll stay in my *own* plant-less, pool-less apartment while you're gone."

Chase rubbed his face with his hand, letting out a long sigh in the process. "Look Mar, I don't mind doing things for you, you *know* that," he began, tone calm.

"Sure," she grumbled, not bothering to look at him.

"You're welcome to use my car when I'm not using it," he offered. "When I fly out of town, I'll leave you the keys."

She glared up at him. "I'd rather have my *own* car."

Rising from the couch, Chase frowned down at Marcy. "Then *get* your own."

Marcy turned away from him, rolling her eyes in the process.

Chase shook his head at her; he'd had enough nonsense for one evening. Leaving Marcy sitting on the couch, Chase walked off. "I'm going to bed," he threw over his shoulder.

Annoyed, Marcy flopped back in her seat, huffing loudly.

Chapter Five

MOSEYING ALONG THE DIRT PATH, Reign adjusted the earbuds in her ears.

Instead of her routine gym trip early that Sunday morning, she'd elected to take a walk in the nearby park. Along with writing, walking tended to clear her head—something Reign desperately needed.

With so much on her mind, she'd barely slept last night, or the night before *that*.

She adjusted the volume on her phone; the R&B music blared through the bud speakers while continuing her steady pace. Her phone beeped; she glanced at the screen to see a new text.

Sorry about the other night, can I see you later?

Reign rolled her eyes at Troy's message. "Of *course* you'd send a goddamn *text* with that bullshit," she vented to herself. She hadn't seen nor spoken to him since he'd showed up at her apartment after dinner, and as far as she was concerned, she could go a few days longer.

Reign closed the message without responding. Focusing on the song, she tried to let the smooth melodic tunes of her favorite track fill her mind with pleasant thoughts.

Just as her mind began to relax, an incoming call broke through. Agitated, Reign stomped her foot on the ground. "Oh my God, *what?*" she huffed.

She frowned at the name flashing across her screen. Rolling her eyes, she let the line ring a few more times before answering. "Yeah Marcy," Reign spoke, tone lacking enthusiasm.

"Hey…what are you doing right now?" Marcy asked, hesitant.

"Walking, why?" Reign's tone hadn't changed. Marcy was yet *another* person she hadn't spoken to since the disastrous double date Friday evening. Reign wasn't in the mood to chat with *her either.*

"Damn, you sure do get up and get out early, *don't* you?" Marcy's voice was filled with amusement.

Reign peered down at the phone, no sign of humor on her face. It took everything in her not to end the call. "Is there something that you want?"

"Yes," Marcy answered, traces of laughter now gone. "How far are you from Tina's café?"

"Like fifteen minutes, why?"

"Can you meet me for breakfast?" Marcy requested.

Reign let out a deep, quick breath. "I ate breakfast already."

"I bet, but they have *the* best cinnamon rolls and iced caramel latte," Marcy claimed. "We *have* to try them."

Reign stopped walking. She stared at the phone screen, a blank expression on her face. "Cinnamon rolls?" she ground out, tone even. "You're kidding right?"

"No, they really do."

Reign sucked her teeth. *I'm over this shit.* "Bye."

"No, no don't hang up!" Marcy belted out.

Reign let her finger hover over the end button but didn't press it.

Marcy sighed. "Look, I just want to talk to you," she said. "*If* that's cool."

Reign tossed a hand in the air even though she knew that Marcy couldn't see her. She was still irritated with Marcy and didn't necessarily want to see her; but at least she'd *called.* "Fine," Reign reluctantly agreed. "Are you there now?"

"Leaving my place as we speak. Should be there in ten minutes."

Reign turned around on her path, walking in the other direction. "Fine, see you there."

"You're the best."

"Uh huh," Reign grunted before ending the call.

Reign pulled the café door open, scanning the quaint space. Spotting Marcy wave her down from a corner table near a window, Reign headed over.

"Hey," Marcy greeted as Reign sat down across from her. "I ordered you one of those cinnamon rolls and a latte." She pointed to the items sitting in front of Reign.

"Thanks," Reign replied, folding her arms on the table.

Marcy pointed to her own empty plate. "As you can see, I ate mine already," she chuckled.

Reign stared at her. "Um hmm."

Marcy cleared her throat. It was clear by Reign's tense demeanor and stern eyes that she was in no mood for small talk. "Okay, let me just cut to the chase," Marcy began.

"That would be nice," Reign replied evenly.

Marcy nodded, then exhaled deeply. "Listen Rae, I know I came off kind of bitchy to you at dinner the other night—"

"Yeah, what was up with that?" Reign questioned.

Marcy fiddled with the napkin in front of her. "I don't know…" she sighed. "Okay, I *do* know. I was just having a bad day and I guess I took it out on you."

"But you took it out *only* on me though," Reign pointed out.

Marcy looked down at the table.

Reign shook her head at Marcy's lack of reply. "Damn, it was bad enough that *Troy* was on my damn nerves, then *you* went and got on my nerves—"

Marcy quickly picked her head up, eyebrows raising. "What's going on with you and Troy?" she zoned in, fixing her inquisitive gaze on Reign,

"No, we're talking about what *your* problem is," Reign stated. She knew how quickly Marcy could get off topic, and she wasn't in the mood for it. "So, what is it?"

Marcy put her hands up. "Fine." Clasping them together, she sighed yet again. "Truth is… I've been feeling down on myself," she explained. "Have been for a while."

Reign tilted her head. "Why?"

Marcy shrugged. "I just... I feel like my life isn't going how I *thought* it would, you know—"

Puzzled, Reign made a face. "So, your way of coping with how *your* life is going, is to antagonize *me*?" she spat.

Marcy rolled her eyes. "You going to listen or what?"

Reign put her hands up. "Just trying to figure you out, but go ahead," she drawled, sarcastic.

Marcy hesitated; she didn't want to say the words that were forming in her throat. Taking a deep breath, she ran a hand through her hair. "I got fired from my job last week," she revealed.

Reign's expression went blank. She sat there, silent.

"They said that it was due to job performance—it hadn't been good... I had a few warnings before, but I guess they had enough so... They let me go," Marcy continued. "I mean that's *fine*, because like, who wants to do time entry *anyway*. But still...I lost my job."

Reign hadn't planned on offering a response in that moment, but a question popped into her head. "If you lost your job *last week*... where were you actually going when you met me Friday morning?" her tone was even.

Marcy glanced off to the side for a moment. "I was meeting a friend for breakfast at a restaurant—you know that new place they opened near the gallery, right?"

Not so much as offering a head nod, Reign just sat there, staring at Marcy.

"Anyway, that explains why I was dressed up and why I wanted the earrings," Marcy prattled on.

Reign raised an eyebrow. "Oh," she spoke, lackluster.

Marcy frowned. "*Oh?*" she repeated. "Oh? That's all you're going to say?"

"What do you *want* me to say, Mar?"

"More than some damn '*oh*'." Marcy expelled an exasperated sigh. "I mean, I know you're pissed with me, but I need my friend right now."

"Marcy, I—" Reign rubbed her temples with her fingertips. She'd come here to discuss Marcy's unnecessary treatment of her, but Marcy had managed to make *herself* the topic. As annoyed as Reign was, she would put her own feelings aside and tend to Marcy's. "I don't know if you're going to want to hear what I have to say right now."

Marcy gestured with her hand. "I might *need* to hear it, so *say* it."

"Okay." Folding her arms, Reign sat back in her seat. "This is the *third* job that you've been fired from within the past *year*," she mentioned. "And *every time* it's because of your poor performance."

"Okay, so?" Marcy spat.

"*So*, you don't see anything *wrong* with that?" Reign questioned, perplexed. Marcy folded her arms in a huff. "You're not stupid Marcy, so *clearly* your *lack of motivation* is causing you to be bad at what you do."

Marcy glanced up at the ceiling briefly, pondering the words that had just been thrown at her. "Yeah you're right." She flung a hand. "I didn't want to do any of the jobs that I was hired for. I only took them because apparently working is the *adult* thing to do."

Reign's brow furrowed slightly at the lackluster joke. "Don't you think that you should figure out what you want to do and do *that*?" Her tone was stern. "You've been jumping from job to job since you *graduated*."

Lip curling, Marcy squinted her eyes. "Well not *everyone* knew exactly what they wanted to do since birth like *you* Reign," she sneered. "You probably came out your momma's *vag* looking for a book."

Reign pointed at her. "See, there you go again," she said. "You're not happy with your *own* situation, so you get mad at *me*."

Pursing her lips, Marcy looked away.

Letting out a heavy sigh, Reign leaned forward, folding her arms on the tabletop. "Mar... lately it just seems like you have some sort of issue with me, and I don't know why." She looked to Marcy with questioning eyes. "What did I do to you?"

"Look—it's just that you *always* have everything so damn figured out." The disdain in Marcy's voice was heavy; she met Reign with a bitter look. "Like everything just goes according to your plan and *some* of us aren't so lucky."

Reign's questioning gaze turned into a full-on glare. "*Again,* you're mad at me, *why?*"

"I'm not mad at you."

"Yeah, I don't believe that." Reign shook her head. "You know, now that I think about it... This isn't the first time you've acted this way towards me," she recalled, upset. "Or the first time that I've felt this—*animosity* from you. I felt it when I was named valedictorian, when I got my job after graduating, when I got my apartment before you, when I got *promoted*, when I decided to buy a *house*— It's like anything I *accomplish*, you seem to have a *problem* with."

Marcy put a finger up. "Let's get one thing straight Reign, I've *never* hated on you," she argued, offended. "So, don't sit there and make it seem like I'm jealous of you."

Again, Reign shook her head. This time slightly, confusion set in on her face. "*Never* did I say that you were jealous."

Marcy pinched the bridge of her nose; Reign had a point.

Reign sighed. "Bottom line, I've *always* supported you and had your back when needed, but it's not reciprocated," she said. "You're supposed to be my friend Mar, that's not right."

Marcy too let out a sigh. "Okay, okay, you have a point," she muttered. "You're making me feel bad."

"And it's not like shit is just *handed* to me," Reign stressed, ignoring Marcy's comment. "Nothing comes easy for me, I work hard for everything that I have."

"I *know* Rae," Marcy replied, tone softening. "You're not the spoiled one, *I* am... Well, I *was* until I graduated college." Her lip curled as she thought of her past lavish lifestyle. "Parents couldn't *wait* to cut me off. Took the damn car they were paying for, and *everything*." She waved a hand, dismissing the memory and the topic all together. Reaching out, she grabbed Reign's hand instead. "You're right, I'm sorry boo," she pouted. "I never want you to think that I'm not happy for you. I'm just dealing with my own shit. But I should never take it out on you."

Reign took a deep breath. "Okay," she relented after a moment. Marcy worked her nerves at times, but she was still Reign's friend, and the last thing that Reign wanted was a rift in her friendship. "It's fine, we'll move past it."

Marcy gave Reign's hand a slight shake. "And I *do* appreciate how you always have my back. Been that way since we met sophomore year." She smiled, "How many people can say that a roommate they met in college is still their bestie till this day?"

"I could name a few," Reign replied. She removed her hand from Marcy's grasp and folded her arms. "But back to you…in all seriousness Marcy, you're in your thirties. You can't keep losing jobs."

"Hell, I never wanted to work in the *first* place." Marcy examined her long, manicured nails. She chuckled, "I was hoping to hook a jock in school."

Reign ran a hand over her ponytail. "Yes, I remember."

"I didn't care *what* sport he played," Marcy remembered. "Basketball, football, hockey, *whatever*, as long as he was going pro. My goal was to sit my fine ass on somebody's yacht while my man raked in the dollars."

Reign shook her head. "That has always been your aspiration?" she asked, no traces of amusement in her voice. "To want nothing more than to be some rich man's woman?"

Marcy nodded emphatically. "Oh absolutely," she answered without a qualm. "That aspiration is getting my rent paid, honey."

Reign reached for her latte. "*Who's* paying your rent?"

"My man," Marcy boasted, folding her arms. "Shit, now that I think about it, I don't need to be moping about being out of work," she smirked. "That's eleven hundred dollars a month that I don't need to worry about."

Reign took a quick sip of her drink. "What about your other bills?"

"I'm sure I can get those taken care of too." A sly grin appeared on Marcy's face. "I'm *very* persuasive."

Reign shrugged slightly. "All right then, you seem to have it all figured out." She took another sip of her drink, then set her cup back down. "But that's nice that Chase is helping you out. He's a good guy."

Marcy moved her hair over her shoulder, looking away momentarily. "Yeah, so anyway, has Troy ever paid *your* rent?"

"Why *would* he? He doesn't live there," Reign asked, tearing a piece of her cinnamon roll.

Marcy laughed. "Girl, 'cause he's your *man* and should be doing shit like that for you," she stated. "As much money as he has, you shouldn't want for a damn thing."

Reign shook her head yet again, placing the gooey piece of pastry into her mouth.

This was yet another thing that differed between herself and Marcy; Reign was perfectly fine taking care of herself. Sure, with the money that Troy made from his job as a marketing executive, he could be paying her rent among other things. But Reign didn't want handouts from her boyfriend. *Especially* if it would be a substitute for everything that lacked in her relationship.

"What I want from Troy isn't monetary," Reign mentioned after swallowing her bite.

Marcy's eyebrows lifted. "You're still not going to tell me what's going on between you two?"

"No, I'm not," Reign refused. He occupied her mind enough; she didn't need to add a conversation about him.

Marcy put her hands up in surrender. "Okay boo, I won't pry." She had a thought, "Hey, how about we go get our nails done? I need a refill."

Reign held her hand up, displaying her freshly sculpted, painted nails. "Went yesterday."

Marcy poked her lip out. "Aww, I wanted us to go together."

"If you weren't being an asshole, then we *could've*," Reign threw back.

Marcy chuckled, "Touché." She waved a dismissive hand. "Fine, let's go get massages then. I *know* you could use one, all that working out you do." She stretched, "And *I* could use one for all that *persuasive sex* I've been having."

"God," Reign sneered, earning a laugh from Marcy.

Chapter Six

"DAD, YOU SHOULDN'T BE CARRYING all of those bags with your bad back," Reign protested, holding her parents' front door open for her father.

Matthew Price, hands full of groceries, and face dripping with sweat, maneuvered through. "Stop your worrying, I've got this," he grunted, adjusting a few.

Reign shut the door, rolling her eyes in the process. "Mom, your husband is out here trying to be Mr. Strong Man again!" she belted out.

"Matthew, if you throw your back out again, you're sleeping in the yard!" Vivian hollered from the kitchen.

Reign busted out laughing.

Matthew wasn't so amused. He looked at Reign, a stern expression masking his brown face. "You used to be my favorite," he grumbled, prompting Reign to laugh some more.

As her father disappeared into the kitchen, Reign craned her neck. "Mom, do you need any help in there?" she asked.

"No darling, you relax," Vivian retuned.

Reign had no plans to protest. Flopping down on the living room couch, she settled back against the cushions. Having been tied up with a heavy workload over the past two weeks, Reign had barely spoken to her parents. So, when her mother had called requesting her presence for a family lunch, Reign had leapt at the opportunity and jumped in a cab.

Hearing a familiar voice from the kitchen, Reign glanced in that direction. Before she could react, a young woman bolted over to her, screaming. "Yay, my big sis is here!"

Reign let out a shriek as her sister jumped on her, wrapping her arms around Reign. "You knee'd me in my damn stomach!" Reign exclaimed, shoving the laughing woman off.

Cynthia Price giggled as Reign rubbed her stomach. "I'm sorry."

Reign squinted at her. "What was all of that for?"

A bright smile crossed Cynthia's pretty, brown face. "I love you and I missed your face," she gushed, plopping down on the couch beside her.

Reign shook her head with a chuckle. Putting her arm around Cynthia's shoulder, she pulled her little sister in for a hug. "Love you too silly." Parting from the embrace, Reign smoothed her hand down her t-shirt. "How was your semester?"

Cynthia rolled her eyes. "Girl, I'm *not* trying to talk about school right now," she bristled. "I'm sick of those damn professors. I'm so glad to be on summer break."

Reign chuckled.

"I'm *so* serious," Cynthia complained, running a hand through her long, knotless braided brown hair. "Was college this annoying when *you* went?"

Reign shook her head. "*I* actually enjoyed college."

"Ugh, you're such a nerd," Cynthia scoffed. "Still *are*, even in your old age."

Reign frowned at her. "Screw you, I'm far from old."

"Sis, you're in your *thirties*," Cynthia reminded, tone laced with humor.

"Whatever," Reign hissed. "Point is, I'm not old." Being ten years older than Cynthia, Reign had always been subjected to digs regarding their age difference. "Anyway, you have one year left, just push through it."

"I should've never switched majors halfway through. I would've been done in four years, instead of suffering through *five*," Cynthia griped, folding her arms.

"If you keep whining about your twenty-two-year-old, bill-less life, I'm going to tune you out," Reign jeered, earning a snicker from Cynthia. She peered over at the kitchen. "What is Mom making for lunch?"

"Seafood wraps. She's almost finished." Cynthia adjusted her position on the couch. "That is, unless she took a break to cuss Dad out."

Reign giggled a bit. "Yeah, when I got out of my cab, I saw him getting the bags out of the trunk," she told. "I tried to help him, but he told me—"

"Stop nagging him, he's got it, right?"

"Pretty much," Reign confirmed, amusement in her voice. "You'd think after he was forced to retire from the police force because of his bad back, he'd chill out."

Cynthia shook her head. "You're talking about the king of 'nothing bothers me'," she chortled. "Just old, hardheaded, stubborn, and *old*."

Reign couldn't help but laugh; their sisterly critique of their father usually left her tickled. Receiving a hard poke to her arm, the humor quickly left Reign's face. Scowling, she delivered a stinging backhand to Cynthia's arm in retaliation.

"Ouch!" Cynthia yelped, grabbing her arm. "That was childish Rae, I didn't even hit you."

"You poked me for *what*, exactly?" Reign bit out, examining her own arm for a mark.

Rubbing her arm, Cynthia turned her lip up. "You told Mom that I was staying in Mike's apartment, you snitch."

Reign snickered. "*Aren't* you?"

"*No*," Cynthia spat, making a face. "…I chill in *DJ's* apartment now, but that's not the point."

Reign looked confused. "Who the hell is DJ?" she asked. "What happened to *Mike*?"

"I don't like him anymore," Cynthia dismissed. "He scratched me with his toenail that he *refused* to cut, and I had to kick his ass to the curb."

Reign rubbed her face with her hand, trying to keep from laughing. "I swear, you change men like you change your clothes," she said.

51

Cynthia shrugged. "I'm young, might as well get my fun in before I hit *thirty* and become a tied down, book nerd like *you*." She laughed when Reign slowly turned, fixing her with an angry gaze.

"Cynthia, can you bring the lemonade out please?" Vivian asked, setting a tray of food on the patio table.

"Sure," Cynthia complied.

Reign sat down in a cushioned seat, pushing herself up to the table. Taking advantage of the clear day, the Price family had elected to have lunch in the backyard. The large umbrella shielded them from the glaring desert sun.

Cynthia approached the table, setting down the glass pitcher of fresh squeezed lemonade before taking her seat. "This looks good." Her eyes beamed at the seafood wraps, fresh tossed garden salad, and homemade lemon bars.

Vivian grinned. "I sure *hope* it is." She watched with pride as her family piled their plates high with food.

As they began eating, Matthew focused his attention on Reign. "Have you seen any new houses lately?" he asked.

Reign swallowed her food before answering. "I'm going to look at one this week actually." She wiped her mouth with a napkin. "Not going to lie, this whole process is starting to become frustrating," she confessed. "Looking at a bunch of different places—not liking most of them, then having the ones I *do* like sold before I can put an offer in—" She let out a sigh, "I just want to move already."

Cynthia tapped the table with enthusiasm. "Ooh! When you get your house, you should let me decorate my room like—"

"No," Reign shot down, shaking her head.

Cynthia's mouth fell open. "No?"

"No," Reign reiterated.

"No room for your baby sister?"

Reign vigorously shook her head.

Cynthia folded her arms in a huff. "Well damn."

"Cynthia, the language," Vivian chided.

Cynthia tossed her arms up. "Is 'damn' a bad word still?"

Reign snickered at the annoyed look on their mother's face.

Matthew shook his head at Cynthia, then returned his focus to Reign, who was concentrating on her food. "Reign, it's no need to get frustrated over the process," he admonished. "These things take time, and you want to make sure you get exactly what you want."

Reign looked up at him; her posture stiffened. "While I *get* that Dad," she began. "I can *still* be frustrated."

"Just saying," Matthew maintained, stern. He dug his fork into his salad. "It's wasted energy."

Reign nodded slowly, her eyes lowering. "Right," she muttered in a deadpan voice. She grabbed her glass of lemonade. "I'll just suck it up."

Watching the exchange between her father and sister, Cynthia eyed Reign with sympathy before turning to Matthew. She couldn't figure out if his lack of response to Reign's last words was because he didn't hear them, or if he was deliberately ignoring them. Either way, Cynthia wasn't pleased.

"So Dad, when are you gonna stop throwing your back out?" Cynthia asked him.

Her mother coughed as she tried to conceal a laugh.

Matthew glared at his youngest child. "When are *you* going to *move out?*"

Cynthia returned his glare with a taunting smile, "When I'm finished grad school."

"Cyn, I thought you were *over* school," Reign chimed in, reaching for her glass again.

"Oh I *am*, but I'll go *just* to make sure I can annoy Dad by continuing to live here," Cynthia goaded, retrieving the half-eaten wrap from her plate.

Vivian let out a little laugh. "Okay Cyn, leave your father alone," she warned.

"Very well…for now," Cynthia granted.

Reign shook her head in amusement as she went back to eating. She appreciated her sister breaking through the tension and clearing the air.

"Reign, have you dumped that skinny, big-headed boyfriend of yours that I never liked, yet?" Matthew blurted out after a moment of silence.

Reign nearly choked on her food as Cynthia erupted with laughter.

Vivian put her hand over her face, shaking her head.

Chapter Seven

LOUNGING ON A PLUSH ACCENT chair in her brother's home, Ava watched her mother fluff a throw pillow. "Mom, the pillow can't get any fluffier," she teased.

Ellie Williams waved a hand Ava's way. Returning the pillow to the couch, she adjusted a jeweled bracelet on her wrist. Catching a glimpse of her watch, she shook her head. "What's taking him so long?"

Ava examined the gold polish on her manicured nails. "Probably still on that business call."

Ava and her mother had arrived at Chase's home that afternoon with plans of going to lunch with him. But no sooner had he let them in, he'd retreated to his home office to take a phone call.

Ellie strolled about her son's living room, taking in the cleanliness. "I am *so* glad that Chase took after me in the neat department," she praised. "This is the cleanest that I've ever seen a man's home look."

Ava shot her mother a look, raising an eyebrow in the process. "Um, excuse me ma'am, what *other* man's house besides this one and the one you share with Dad have you *been* in?" she questioned.

Ellie pointed at her. "I wasn't *always* with your father, mind your business."

Ava snickered.

Approaching an end table, Ellie surveyed the items sitting on it. Eyes zoning in on something, she squinted. "Hmm," she muttered, picking up the object. "Looks like someone left her ugly bracelet over here."

Ava rolled her eyes. "I'm sure it's Marcy's," she scoffed.

Turning her lip up at the large, red, resin cuff bracelet, Ellie let out a huff. "Lord, *why* is he still *with* her?"

"Ask *him*, because *I* don't understand," Ava replied, placing a hand to her chest.

It was no secret that their mother wasn't fond of Marcy; Ava was glad that someone other than *herself* shared the displeasure.

Before either woman could say another word, Chase emerged from the hall. "Sorry about that. The call ran longer than I expected." Chase smiled, approaching his mother.

Ellie gave him a hug. "That wasn't another call that's going to result in you going away again, is it?" she asked as they parted.

"Mom, don't start," Chase warned, moving to Ava. He attempted to hug her.

Still seated, Ava playfully smacked his arm away. "I don't want a hug, I just saw you yesterday," she joked, earning a laugh from Chase.

Still clutching the bracelet that she'd retrieved from the table, Ellie held it up. With a look of disapproval on her gorgeous, glowing dark brown face, she gestured to Chase with the abysmal object. "Your little girlfriend is marking her territory, I see," she sneered.

Chase shook his head, taking it from her. He pocketed it. "*Snooping again*, I see," he countered.

"I wasn't snooping," Ellie denied.

"Yes, she was," Ava chortled.

Chase shook his head yet again. "And *your* problem with Marcy is?" he asked his mother.

"The girl is *completely* unbearable," Ellie answered without a qualm. Ava snickered hard. "On *top* of that, she's superficial, self-centered and just plain *gaudy*."

Chase pinched the bridge of his nose. "Wow," he muttered. He sometimes forgot how blunt his mother could be.

"Why do you think I don't invite her to the house for so much as *Sunday dinner*?" Ellie continued. "I can't take being in her presence for more than five minutes."

Chase let out a sigh. "I don't know *why* I agreed to you two coming over without Dad here to buffer."

"Dad doesn't like her *either*," Ava joked.

Chase narrowed his eyes at her.

Ellie placed a hand to Chase's cheek, bringing his focus to her. "Chase *please* tell me you don't plan on marrying that girl," she said.

Chase frowned in confusion. "Who said anything about *marriage*?" he asked. "And *why* is this the topic of discussion?"

Removing her hand from Chase's face, Ellie threw up both hands. "I'm just trying to figure out what my thirty-four-year-old son's future plans are, regarding settling down... Hopefully not with *Miss Girl*."

Chase raised an eyebrow. "I'm not planning on getting married any time soon," he assured.

"That's only because he isn't with the right woman," Ava jumped in.

Chase cut his eye at his sister. "Besides, I'm deep into my career right now," he added. "The way that I travel—"

"That's only because he isn't with the right woman who'd make him stay *put*," Ava interjected. "You know good and well there are plenty of projects here in the area that you *turn down* in favor of traveling."

Chase rolled his eyes.

Ava pursed her lips. "Lie if you want to."

Chase glared at her. "You want to leave?"

"Are you going to *put me out*?" Ava challenged.

Ellie pointed at her daughter. "Ava, enough," she demanded.

Ava folded her arms, but kept quiet.

Ellie turned her attention back to her son. "As relieved as I am to hear that you don't plan on making that girl your wife, if you're not dating Marcy with the intentions of marrying her, *why* are you even wasting your time?" she asked. "...and *mine*, I want a grandchild."

Chase threw his hands up. "And here we go with the grandchild topic again," he huffed, heading for the kitchen. He pointed to Ava, "Harass *her* for a grandchild."

"*Hell* no, she'll be lucky if a baby comes out of *this* body before I turn *forty*," Ava rebuffed. "I am perfectly fine being single *and* child free."

Ellie flagged Ava with her hand as she followed Chase into his open concept kitchen. Ava stood up, following suit. "Chase, seriously—"

"Mom," he warned.

Ellie put a hand up. "I'm just *saying*, the time wasted with these pointless—" she paused, pointing at him. "Before it was Marcy, it was Brandie. Before *that* it was Deidre—"

"You're speaking as if I was just *running through* women," Chase argued, cutting his mother off.

"In *high school*, you did," Ava slid in.

Chase shot Ava a stern look. "I ask that anything done prior to the age of seventeen be expunged from my record," he said.

Ava put a hand up in surrender. "You're right, you've certainly earned that."

Ellie shook her head at Ava, then turned back to Chase. "Fine son, I will give you credit, you don't just *run through* women," she amended. "But you have to admit that the *few serious* relationships you *have been* in, have been empty."

Chase rolled his eyes.

"Mom is right." Ava moved her hair over her shoulder. "You started dating Deidre right after grad school. That relationship lasted only a year," she recalled. "Then two years after *that*, you started seeing Brandie—"

"Oh, I remember *that* one." Ellie shook her head. "Brandie was…something else."

Chase stood there, suffering through the commentary. This wasn't the first time that his dating history had been mentioned *or* criticized.

Ava laughed. "Yeah, I wasn't shocked at *all* when that one ended in less than a year," she said. "Girlfriend was—over the top. *Definitely* not the type you could bring to an office function…a family function…outside."

Ellie snickered; the humor soon left her face. "Chase, seriously, you need to stop wasting your time with women who are clearly *wrong* for you," she stressed. "And you *knew* they were wrong, that's why it didn't faze you when the relationships ended."

Chase sighed loudly; he was over this topic. The last thing he wanted a reminder of, was his past failed relationships. He opened the refrigerator. "I'm asking you both to drop this subject," he requested, stern.

Ellie folded her arms, letting out a heavy sigh. "I'll drop it for *now*," she promised. "But just know that this won't be the last time that we have this conversation."

"Great," Chase grumbled, eyeing the contents of his chrome double-doored refrigerator.

Ava sat down on a barstool in front of the kitchen island. "Oh, guess what bro?" she began after a moment.

Chase retrieved a small glass bottle of apple juice, then shut the door. "What?" he asked, unenthused, opening his juice.

"The house that I'm going to look at with Reign this week, is like ten minutes from here," Ava revealed.

Chase's eyes lit up. "Oh really?" He thought for a moment. "It must be one of the houses in the new development."

"Yeah, I think it is." Ava grinned. The sudden change in her brother's mood at the mention of Reign wasn't missed by her.

Ellie smiled. "How *is* Reign?" she asked Ava.

Ava adjusted her gold dangle earring. "She's good, working hard as usual."

"I've always liked her." Placing her hands on the island countertop, Ellie let out a light, relaxed sigh. "Such a smart girl," she gushed. "Good head on her shoulders, a sweetheart, driven, *gorgeous...*" she cut her eyes at Chase. "Boy, how come you never asked *her* out?"

Chase choked on his juice.

"You okay over there big bro?" Ava teased, watching him pat his chest as he tried to regain his composure.

Ellie folded her arms, shooting a disappointment filled gaze her son's way, "Wasting your time with these foolish women, when there's been a perfectly *good* woman in front of you all of this time."

Chase set his juice down as his coughing subsided. "What happened to you dropping the subject for now?" he directed at his mother.

"That was *then*, just answer the question," Ellie demanded.

Chase shook his head. "Reign and I are just *friends*, that's how it's *always* been," he answered.

Ava leaned her elbow on the countertop, resting her chin on her hand. A smirk crossed her face. "*Has* it now?"

Chase narrowed his eyes at her.

Ellie looked back and forth between her children, then fixated on Chase. "That *still* doesn't answer my question," she harped.

Chase put his hands over his face, letting out a groan.

Chapter Eight

REIGN STARED AT HER LAPTOP, sipping her bottled water and reading through a manuscript.

A knock on her office door broke her focus. She looked up. "Come in," she called.

Opening the door, Ava stepped inside. "Hey boss lady, you ready to go?"

"Hey." Reign checked her watch, "Damn, I didn't realize it was five already."

Ava took a seat while Reign shut her laptop down. "How are you liking that new story that came in?" Ava asked.

"It's fine so far." Reign shrugged. "I haven't started editing it yet. Just giving a general read through first."

Ava gave a half-nod. "Well...*I* read it." Bringing a hand up, Ava studied her nails. "You want to know what I think?"

Reign tilted her head. "Judging by your lack of enthusiasm, I'm guessing that your opinion isn't exactly nice."

"You guessed right," Ava confirmed, pointing a finger at Reign. "It's bad—*terrible.*"

Reign grimaced. "Come on now, you know how I feel about attacking a writer's work."

"I *get* it, but no," Ava said, shaking her hand in Reign's direction. "The writer of *that* story needs a *ghostwriter*, because what's written in his *own* words isn't cutting it."

Gathering her belongings, Reign shook her head.

"I sure hope he doesn't plan on *publishing* that mess," Ava jeered.

"Ava, I've told you before, not everybody can execute a story," Reign calmly reminded. "But we *still* need to do the best job at fixing it as we can."

Ava put a hand up in surrender. Folding her arms, she fixed Reign with a stare. "*You* could ghostwrite it, you know," she proposed.

Standing from her seat, Reign looked at her, then shook her head. "I don't write books."

Arms still crossed, Ava stood. "You *do*," she insisted. "I remember those stories and creative papers that you wrote in both high school *and* college, and I *know* you have notebooks full of whatever it is that you keep writing in them, so stop it." Ava cocked her head to the side. "Stop being scared and write these hopeless people's books please, so I don't have to keep forcing my way through these edits."

Reign shot Ava a warning glance. "Stop being rude, and let's go."

Ava chuckled. "Trust me, that wasn't rude. I could've said much worse."

"Yes, I know," Reign said, moving around her desk.

"Okay fine. But just so you know, I *have* had clients ask me about ghostwriting services recently."

"I'm sure you *have*, but this company doesn't *have* ghostwriting services," Reign pointed out, slinging her purse over her shoulder.

Ava grinned. "Not *yet* they don't."

"Tuning you out, let's go," Reign dismissed, walking out of the office.

"And you call *me* rude," Ava hurled at her departing back in amusement.

"Just *think* about it," Ava pressed as she and Reign stepped out of the elevator. "That would be perfect for you."

"Why don't *you* do it?" Reign suggested, traces of frustration in her voice.

"I've told you before, I'm not creative," Ava reminded. "Now if you need me to fix comma placements and grammatical errors once you're finished drafting, then I'm your girl."

Reign just shook her head as they approached the building's exit. Noticing Marcy sitting on the bench near the glass doors,

Reign frowned slightly. She halted her steps, along with Ava. *I wonder what she's doing here,* Reign thought, perplexed.

Marcy smiled at Reign, waving an arm wildly in the process. "Hey girl!"

What the hell is her ass doing here? Ava thought, though on the outside she'd successfully hid her displeasure.

Reign turned to Ava. "Give me a second?"

"Sure," Ava granted, gesturing for her to go ahead.

"Thanks." Reign approached Marcy, who had stood from her seat. "What are you doing here?" Reign asked.

Marcy adjusted the bag in her hand. "Well, I just finished getting my hair done, and since my salon is only a block from here, I figured since I knew you were getting off, that I'd stop over," she explained. Marcy shook her head, displaying the bounce in her newly styled locks. "What do you think?" She smiled.

Reign eyed Marcy's hair. She had swapped out the lace front wig for her own tresses, which had been cut into a collarbone length bob. Also swapped out, was the ice blonde color, opting instead for a warmer shade of honey blond. "It's pretty," Reign complimented.

Grinning, Marcy placed a hand on her head, striking a pose. "You think?"

Reign nodded with enthusiasm.

"Thanks boo." Marcy stuck her hand out, displaying her stiletto tipped red nails. "Changed my nails too. I needed something bold to match this new designer bag that my baby just bought me." She held the small red satchel up for Reign to admire.

"It's cute, really cute," Reign replied. While Reign was happy that Marcy seemed to be in a better mood, she had to cut the impromptu visit short. Reign glanced at her watch. "But look—"

"Come on, let's go to dinner," Marcy cut in, sliding her bag up her forearm. "I'm feeling Thai food."

Reign put a hand up. "I appreciate you stopping by and for the invite, but I can't go to dinner right now," she calmly shot down. "I have somewhere to be."

Marcy was intrigued. "Oh? Where are you going?" She peered over at Ava, who was standing several feet away, looking at her phone. "Is she waiting for you or something?"

Reign glanced at Ava, then back at Marcy. "I'm going to look at a house, and yes, she is."

Marcy's brow furrowed; she folded her arms. "*Why?*" she charged. She didn't understand why *she* was being blown off because of Reign's plans, but Ava was allowed to stick around.

Reign closed her eyes, letting out a sigh. *Here she goes with this shit.* "Because she's going to look at the house *with* me."

Marcy's hand shot up. "Hold up, why did you ask *her* to go, and not me?" she fussed.

Reign looked at Marcy as if she were crazy. "*First* of all, I don't owe you an explanation for what I do and whom I do it *with*."

Marcy rolled her eyes. "Yes, I *know* that Rae, but humor me, please."

Reign tucked some of her hair behind her ears, letting out a quick sigh in the process. "Look, I didn't ask her, she *offered* to come with me, and I didn't ask *you* because I didn't think you'd be interested in going."

"Well why would you think *that?*" Marcy asked, offended.

Reign put a hand up. "Not trying to go there with you right now, seriously," she ground out.

Marcy rolled her eyes yet again. She already knew the reason why Reign hadn't asked her; Marcy hadn't been supportive of her friend's decision. She got it, but she wasn't going to stand by and watch Ava jump in and take her place. "And I'm sure *she* just *jumped* at the chance to tag along with you," she spat out, gesturing in Ava's direction.

Reign sucked her teeth. "Will you cut that shit out?" she demanded. "You're acting like a goddamn teenager."

Marcy made a face in retaliation.

"Now like *you*, she's my friend," Reign reminded. "Been in my life longer than *you* have, remember?"

Marcy smirked. "And yet, I was the *improvement* that your so-cial life needed."

"*Again*, teenage shit, *stop* it." Reign flicked her hand at Marcy. "I have to go."

Marcy grabbed hold of Reign's arm, bringing her hasty de-parture to a halt. "Wait, I want to go with you to look at the house."

Reign let out a huff, "No, you *don't.*"

"No really," Marcy assured her, giving Reign's arm a slight tug.

Reign shot Marcy a cynical look.

"Look Rae, I know that I haven't been supportive, and I feel bad about that," Marcy admitted. "So yeah, I want to go and show my support."

Reign hesitated for a moment, then let out a quick sigh. "Whatever, just don't start shit with Ava."

Marcy held up her right hand. "I'll be on my best behavior. Swear."

"Yeah, that's not helping," Reign jeered, sauntering away.

Ava stared at Reign as she approached. She put a hand up when Reign went to speak. "I heard, it's cool. I'm not thinking about her," Ava said.

Relieved, Reign sighed. "You sure?"

"Yes," Ava promised. "I'm going to support *you*. I'll pretend that she's not even there…which will be easy."

Reign chuckled, "I appreciate you."

Ava smiled back, "You better."

Marcy's eyes roamed as the realtor showed the three women around the house.

"So, as you can see, the living room is equipped with a fire-place, the kitchen has brand-new chrome appliances—"

"How many bedrooms in here again?" Marcy broke in.

The realtor smiled at her. "Three bedrooms, two and a half bath-rooms," she answered. "Kitchen, dining room, living room, den—"

"That backyard is *huge*," Ava bubbled, peering out of the glass double sliding back doors. "You can put an in-ground pool out there."

Marcy rolled her eyes at Ava's excitement. "Rae, this is a big house," Marcy stated. "A *lot* for *one* person. You won't be scared to be in here by yourself?"

"No," Reign replied, nonchalant. "That's what security systems, a baseball bat and my kickboxing lessons are for."

Glancing away, Marcy tucked her hair behind her ear. "Right," she mumbled.

"Kris, you said that they'll put carpet in?" Reign asked her realtor. "I love the hardwood floors down *here*, but I'd prefer carpet upstairs."

"Oh of course," Kris answered, enthused. "If you buy the house, you'll get to pick out the carpet and also the color flooring for the kitchen." She opened the folder that was in her hand, showing Reign. "See, there are several options from which you can choose," she said. "That's just one of the perks of buying a home from these developers."

"That's pretty cool," Ava chimed in, sidling up to Reign. "When Chase bought *his* house, he hated the carpet that it came with and ended up changing it, costed him a pretty penny too. With *this* place, you'll already have what you like when you move in."

"How much is this house?" Marcy asked Kris, completely disregarding the conversation taking place. "It *has* to be expensive."

Kris checked a paper in her hand. "The going price for this home is two hundred and sixty-five thousand."

Marcy's head jerked back, "Well *damn*." She scratched her head. "Rae, can you afford that?"

Reign looked up from the pictures in the folder; she fixed Marcy with a stern stare. "Yes." She was regretting allowing Marcy to come along. Ever since Marcy had laid eyes on the two-story, one car garage, single family home, she'd started in with her discouraging line of questioning.

Ava frowned in Marcy's direction. She was both bewildered *and* annoyed by Marcy's question. The woman's behavior was off-putting, and Ava didn't know how much longer she'd be able to stand it without flying off the handle.

"Marcy, *why* would she be looking at this house if she couldn't *afford* it?" Ava questioned.

"I'm sure she can ask me that herself. She doesn't need *you* as a mouthpiece," Marcy spat, frowning down Ava's length from where she stood, feet away.

"No, what she *doesn't need* is *your* negative ass here," Ava threw back, voice dripping with disdain.

Reign put a hand up. "Hey, not here, not now," she jumped in, her stern tone halting the girls' building argument. She looked at Kris. "Can you please give me a minute to look around some more?"

"Of course, take your time. I'll be out front," Kris obliged, then headed outside.

Collecting herself, Ava pushed some of her hair over her shoulder. She felt bad for engaging with Marcy. Ava had meant what she'd said; she was there to support Reign. "So Rae? What do you think?" she asked, smiling.

Reign smiled back. "I *really* like it." She was bubbling with excitement. "No, I *love* it."

"Yeah, it *is* a beautiful house." Ava glanced around the living room once more. She delivered a tap to Reign's arm. "And you'll finally get your 'writing room'."

Reign chuckled. "I know right?" she agreed. "I'll get to do my writing at an actual *desk*, and not at that tiny kitchen table."

"Yeah, you'll definitely need that desk for all of those books that you'll be ghostwriting." Ava grinned, lightly nudging Reign with her shoulder. Reign just shook her head in amusement.

Marcy was silent as she ran a hand along the mantel above the fireplace. "If you get the house, are you going to put a pool out there?" she asked, cutting into the conversation.

"Probably not right away." Reign shrugged slightly. "I'm not really pressed for a pool."

"Oh, in the event that you *do* decide to get one, let me know and I'll ask Chase who did his," Ava mentioned to Reign.

Reign smiled at Ava. "Thanks—"

"You know Ava, you *don't* have to be so damn hype about everything that she's got going on. I'm sure she'll still sign your paychecks even if you don't kiss her ass," Marcy snarled.

Reign fixed Marcy with a piercing glare. "Marcy, are you fuckin' serious?" she barked.

Marcy was taken aback by Reign's scolding. "What?!" she belted out, tossing her arms up.

Ava folded her arms, her fuming brown eyes burrowing through Marcy. "Did you come up with that amateur comment while your jobless ass sat at home doing nothing all day?" she countered.

Marcy crossed her arms, smirking. "Yup, sat right on your brother's couch, after I got off his *dick*."

Reign's eyes widened at Marcy's lewd retort, lost for words.

Ava's gaze thinned as her breathing intensified. She could've drug Marcy through the entire development by her hair. *I swear to God, I hate this bitch.* "Let me remove myself before I go to jail," she grunted. "Rae, I'll be out back."

Reign followed Ava's progress to the door. She felt horrible. She'd allowed Marcy to insert herself into their plans, and now Ava was upset. "I'm sorry, Ava," she said, sincere.

Ava grabbed the handle, glancing back at Reign. "You don't have to apologize for her." Sliding the door open, she stepped out and shut it behind her.

Remorse fading from Reign's face, she directed her attention to Marcy. The woman was busy examining her nails, a smug, satisfied look on her face. Glaring, Reign pointed to the front door. "*You* should leave too."

Stunned, Marcy eyed Reign with her mouth wide open. "Seriously?"

"*Dead* serious."

Marcy glared back. "That's fucked up," she ranted. "You're quick to jump on *me*, but didn't say *shit* when *she* made that jobless comment."

Reign's eyes expanded in fury. "*You* started with *her*!"

"It doesn't even matter, I—"

Reign put a hand up, silencing Marcy's excuses. "No, I don't care, you will *not* make this about you," she dismissed, agitated. "Take it outside and tell my realtor to come back in here while you're at it."

Marcy sucked her teeth as she barreled towards the front door. "By the way, you had *no* right to tell that girl about me getting fired," she fumed.

"I *didn't*, now get out," Reign hurled at her back.

"Yeah right." Marcy yanked the door open. "Don't bother looking for me after you're finished with your *little house* business. I'll be taking a cab home."

Reign folded her arms, narrowing her eyes. "You could've saved all of that bullshit because I *don't* care," she flashed back.

Sucking her teeth yet again, Marcy stormed out, slamming the door behind her.

Frustrated, Reign shook her head, exhaling loudly.

Within a moment, Kris reentered the house. "Everything okay?" she asked, noticing the annoyed look on Reign's face.

Reign forced a smile. "Yes, everything is fine." She clasped her hands together. "I'd like to make an offer."

Kris's smile was bright. "Great choice," she approved. "I'll make the call."

Emerging from her kitchen with a glass of white wine in hand, Reign was preparing to sit down on her couch and enjoy a movie, when a knock sounded on her door.

Setting the glass on the coffee table, Reign headed for the door. Peering through her peephole, she let out a sigh. She debated for a few seconds before opening it.

"Hey," Troy greeted.

Reign held her arm on the door. "Hey." Her tone was as lackluster as his greeting.

Holding his arms behind his back, Troy shifted his weight from one foot to the other. "Can I come in?"

After hesitating for a moment, Reign gave a slight nod. "Sure." She moved aside, then closed the door behind him. Spinning around, she caught Troy placing a large shopping bag on the floor near the couch. She pointed to it. "What is that?"

"Just a little something," Troy answered, facing her. Closing the distance between them, he held his arms out, smiling slightly. "Can your man get a hug?"

Reign nodded before hugging him. After a long moment, she broke the embrace. She moved for the couch. "You want to sit?"

"Sure." Troy took a seat on the couch next to her.

Troy leered at Reign as she grabbed her glass of wine, taking a sip. "Missed you," he crooned.

Finishing her swallow, she met his gaze, raising an arched eyebrow. "Have you?" her tone was low, even.

"Of course," Troy assured, nodding. He tilted his head when she just stared at him. "You don't believe me?"

She set her glass back down. "It's just that I haven't seen much of you lately."

Even though Reign *did* eventually return Troy's message and had been in communication with him since their argument two weeks ago, she hadn't seen him. Had barely even *spoken* to him. Their communication had been reduced to texts.

Reign couldn't decide which was worse; the fact that she hadn't seen Troy, or the fact that after a few days, she no longer *cared* that she hadn't. She was surprised when he'd called her earlier that day, asking to come over.

Troy ran a hand over the short waves on his head. "Babe, I knew that I was still in the doghouse... I know how you get when you're pissed, so I was just giving you space."

Reign tilted her head, eyeing him sternly. "Troy—you avoided me for damn near *two weeks*," she reminded him. "You barely answered any of my phone calls." She shook her head. "That doesn't seem a bit ridiculous to you? Or were you *so* busy, that you couldn't even *talk* to me?"

Troy let out a deep sigh. "No, that's not—" he shrugged slightly. "To be honest, I just didn't want to argue with you Rae," he admitted. "It doesn't mean that I didn't miss your voice or want to see you... I just didn't want to argue. I *still* don't." He shook his head. "That's not why I came here."

Reign placed a hand to her chest. "*I* don't want to argue *either* Troy, I just—"

"Then let's *not*," he cut in. Reign closed her mouth. "Let's just move forward."

Reign stared at him for a long moment. *How can we move forward if the shit that causes us to argue doesn't change?* But she didn't have the energy for another fight. Looking down at her nails, Reign sighed. "Okay," she muttered.

Troy smiled, oblivious. "So..." he smoothed his hands down his jeans. "The house hunting. How's it going?"

Reign twisted a ring around her finger. "I umm... I actually put in an offer for one earlier today."

Troy's smile grew brighter. "That's great Rae. I'm happy for you."

Reign looked up at him, finally letting a small smile come through. "Thank you." She ran a hand through her hair. "It'll take a few days for me to hear back—I'm kind of nervous."

Troy leaned back in his seat. "I'm sure you'll get it." He paused for a moment; a seriousness fell over him. "Look, I know I haven't been supportive lately and I'm sorry about that."

Reign eyed him intently. "You are?" she asked, a twinge of hope in her voice.

"Yeah." Troy stalled for a moment, sighing. "It had nothing to do with you. I guess I was just feeling left out... That's a big step to take by yourself, you know?"

"Yes, I know," she agreed, softly. "And I'm not saying that I don't understand how you feel but..." she paused. "Given how things have been between us lately—"

"I know, I haven't done the best job at making you feel secure in the future of this relationship," Troy interrupted.

Reign squinted. "*Do* you see a future with me?"

"Of *course* I do." Troy frowned, "You think I've been with you *this* long for *nothing*?"

"I'm not saying that, Troy," she said, calm. "But I have a right to question—"

"Come on Rae, you know how I feel about you," Troy cut in. "You don't have to question our relationship. I'm not going anywhere."

Reign looked back to her hands, twisting the deep pink crystal ring around her finger once again.

Troy leaned forward. "Hey," he said, prompting her to look up at him. "I have plans for us, I promise."

Reign sighed. She wanted to believe him. Even though he irritated her at times, she still loved him; she wouldn't have been with him this long if she didn't. "Okay Troy," she relented. "I believe you."

Troy let out a sigh of relief. "So…is this fight officially over?"

Reign nodded.

"Glad to hear it." He tapped Reign's thigh. "And just to prove *how* sorry I am, I have a gift for you." Troy grabbed the bag that he'd brought in, handing it to her.

Reign chuckled a bit. "What's this?" she asked, peering inside.

"Open it and see." Delight filled his eyes, as he watched her remove a large box from the bag.

Opening the box, Reign's eyes widened. "Oh wow." She pulled out the designer bag. "It's nice."

Troy noticed her tone; it didn't carry the enthusiasm that he was expecting. Most women would have jumped up and down over a bag that expensive. "You don't like it." His tone failed to hide his disappointment.

"No, no I *do* like it," Reign assured. She carefully set the bag on her coffee table. Reign did appreciate a good designer bag; she'd treated herself to one for her thirtieth birthday. But the bright red, oversized tote bag with the popular designer's name largely splashed across the front wasn't her style. She'd never been that flashy—nor had she ever liked the color red.

Nevertheless, she *did* appreciate the thought. Leaning forward, Reign placed a tender kiss to Troy's lips. "Thank you. I appreciate it."

The kiss satisfied Troy enough. "You're welcome," he crooned against her lips. "I have another gift."

Resting her elbow on the back of the couch, Reign leaned her head on her hand. "Yeah?"

"Yeah," he smiled. "A four-day trip to a resort in Sedona."

Reign's eyes widened in delight; she smiled bright. "Really?" she squealed.

Troy adjusted his position on the couch as he brimmed with excitement. "Yup, it's a luxury, all-inclusive resort. It has a spa, a few night spots—it's the perfect couples getaway."

"That sounds amazing," she breathed, putting a hand on her chest. It was the truth; with the tension that she'd been feeling, a relaxing getaway was music to her ears.

Troy was proud of himself. It had been the first time in a while that Reign seemed relaxed. "Can you get off next Thursday and Friday?"

"It shouldn't be an issue," she replied.

Troy grabbed her free hand. "Great... A getaway will be good for us."

Reign smiled at him. "I agree." She squeezed his hand. "Thank you."

Nodding, Troy roamed Reign's figure with lustful eyes. Though she was clad in loose loungewear, Troy was well aware of what lied beneath. Fixating on her lower half, he drew his bottom lip between his teeth. Now that they were back on good terms, Troy was eager to get Reign back in bed. *I'm gonna fuck the shit out of your sexy ass.* "You can *thank* me by bending over for me," he suggested.

Reign's eyes narrowed. "How romantic," she drawled, sarcastic, earning a laugh from Troy.

Chapter Nine

THE LOUD RINGTONE FROM HER cell jerked Reign out of her sleep. She squinted at the clock on her nightstand; six o'clock, it read—an hour before she had to get ready for work. She grabbed the phone, frowning at the caller ID. Sucking her teeth, she answered. "What Marcy?" Reign grunted, rubbing her eyes.

"Boo, I know you're about to get up for work and everything, but I'm around the corner from your apartment and need to use the bathroom," Marcy blurted into the line.

Baffled, Reign pinched the bridge of her nose. "*What?*"

"*Please* buzz me in," Marcy begged.

Dropping a hand over the side of her bed, Reign let out a groan. "Fine." Hanging up, she tossed the phone to the bed. "Yeah, I'm not rushing," she muttered, laying there.

Reign glanced at the empty spot where Troy had slept the night before. She'd heard him leave an hour ago. Rolling on her back, Reign stared up at her ceiling, letting her mind drift.

Last night had been the first time she'd slept with Troy since their fight. Though she was happy that they had moved past their latest argument, therefore reigniting her sexual mood, Reign had to admit that the trysts with her boyfriend left a lot to be desired.

It wasn't that sex with Troy was—*terrible*; he could bring her pleasure at times. But their encounters lacked passion. Lacked attention to *her* needs, *her* body—things that Reign longed for. And while Troy was *never* the romantic type, in the beginning of their relationship he at least *tried*. But somewhere down the line, the effort had stopped.

Reign couldn't remember the last time Troy had kissed her

deeply, the last time he'd touched her sensually, the last time that she had even been *held* after sex—the last time he'd performed foreplay that didn't consist of a few lackluster licks lasting no more than a minute.

She'd never even experienced an *orgasm* with him—neither oral *nor* penetration, though she'd come close a few times in the past. *It's probably my fault. Maybe I just don't allow myself to relax enough. Maybe my body can't have one, unless it's self-produced,* were thoughts that always clouded Reign's mind while a satisfied Troy lay next to her.

Last night's romp had been no different.

Shaking the thoughts from her mind, Reign finally got out of bed. She slipped her pajamas on, then went to the bathroom to brush her teeth and wash her face.

By the time she made it to the door, the buzzer was blaring through the speaker on the wall.

Reign pressed a button. "Yes?" she asked innocently.

"Reign! I swear to God—"

"Stop yelling, hold on," Reign demanded, cutting Marcy's loud words off. Pressing a button, she unlocked her apartment door. Less than two minutes later, Marcy came barging in.

"About time, damn!" Marcy hurled, sprinting for the bathroom.

"You're going to pee on yourself with all that talking," Reign threw back, sitting on her couch.

Reign sat, arms folded and staring at the hallway, waiting for Marcy to emerge. Five minutes later, she did. "Feel better?" Reign asked, unenthused.

Marcy, holding a hand to her stomach, nodded, a sigh of relief escaping her. "Thanks for letting me in…even though it took you *forever.*"

"You're lucky I let you in at *all* after you showed your ass at my house showing last night," Reign bristled.

Marcy ran a hand over her hair. "I didn't *want* to act like that, but you know your little *friend* rubs me the wrong way," she sneered, making a face.

Reign fixed Marcy with a glower. "*First*, Ava is not a child, do not call her little."

Marcy rolled her eyes.

"*Second*, don't blame *her* for *your* fucked up attitude," she chastised, still holding her piercing gaze.

Marcy tapped her foot on the floor. She let out a huff, "*Fine* Rae."

Reign shook her head. "You know what, I can't blame anyone but myself. I should've never invited you," she ground out. "Won't do *that* again."

Even though Ava had placed no blame on Reign for the brief, albeit heated exchange with Marcy, Reign still felt guilty. So much so, that when Reign returned home, she had called Ava to apologize for bringing Marcy along. She knew that having the two women in the same space was a bad idea.

Marcy glanced at her nails, fussing with the jewels on one of them. "Look…I'm sorry okay," she half-heartedly threw out after a long pause.

Reign stared at her.

"*And* I know that it wasn't you who told Ava about me being out of work," Marcy continued, fidgeting with her fingers. "Turns out Chase mentioned it to her. So yeah…sorry."

"Yeah, thanks for that half-assed apology," Reign sneered, getting up. "Show yourself out, I have to get ready for work."

"Rae—" Marcy took a step forward, blocking Reign's path to the hall.

Reign frowned, "What?"

"Are we good?" Marcy asked, hopeful. "Am I forgiven?"

Reign narrowed her eyes, then after a moment, rolled them. *This girl is a mess, but I still love her.* "Sure," she sighed. She shook her head when Marcy clapped her hands. "You're a handful, you know that?"

Marcy giggled. "I do." She followed Reign's progress down the hall. "Hey, can I hang out here while you're at work?"

"No." Reign abruptly stopped, turning around. "*What are* you doing around here this early *anyway*?" she asked, curious. "You never leave your apartment before seven, even when you *were* working."

Marcy scratched her head, laughing nervously. "I umm, I decided to go to the gym this morning, and I must've drunk too much water while I was there," she sputtered. "You know I don't use public bathrooms and your apartment was closer than mine, so I figured I'd stop here."

A puzzled frown fell over Reign's face; she knew that Marcy hated the gym, always *had*. Nevertheless, Reign decided not to dwell. She had to get ready for work. "Whatever," Reign dismissed.

Marcy flopped on the couch. "I'll just sit here until you leave then."

"Knock yourself out," Reign said, walking off.

Grabbing the remote from the coffee table, Marcy clicked the TV on. She adjusted her position while channel surfing. Forty-five minutes into her favorite morning show, Marcy stood up. "I wonder if she has coffee."

En route to the kitchen, she noticed something sitting on Reign's love seat. Moving closer, Marcy fixated on the flashy bag, tilting her head. Hearing Reign enter the living room, Marcy directed her gaze to her.

Reign was dressed, styled, and ready for work. "You look pretty, as always," Marcy complimented.

Reign glanced at Marcy while putting on a pink crystal drop earring. "Thanks."

Marcy gawked as Reign examined herself in a floor-length mirror, fussing over her straightened hair where it was parted down the middle. Marcy ran a hand over her *own*. *Why doesn't mine grow like that?*

Lowering her hand, Marcy shook the envious thoughts from her head. She cleared her throat after a moment. "Hey, I see you got a new bag," she mentioned.

Reign turned around. "I'm sorry, what?"

Marcy picked the red bag up, holding it high. "Treated yourself, huh?" she chuckled. "A celebration gift for finally putting a house offer in?"

Reign shook her head. "Troy bought that for me."

Marcy studied the bag, brows raised. "Oh?"

"Yeah, he gave it to me last night," Reign added, gesturing to it.

Shrugging, Marcy set the bag back down. "Hmm, not surprising. You wouldn't buy something that big and bold for *yourself* anyway," she chortled. "You know how you are, all black everything."

Reign smirked.

"It kinda looks like the new bag that *I* have," Marcy said. "The one that I wore yesterday... I mean, it's *bigger* than mine, but...still."

"Hadn't noticed Mar," Reign replied, heading for the kitchen. "You want anything to eat?"

Marcy was deep in thought and hadn't heard the question.

Reign stopped short. "Mar," she called.

Marcy snapped out of her haze. "Yeah?"

"You hungry?"

Marcy smiled. "Sure."

Reign pulled a bag of bagels from a cabinet, then grabbed the cream cheese and apricot jam from the refrigerator, while Marcy sat at the table.

"So, I take it Troy is back in your good graces?" Marcy began, drumming her fingernails on the tabletop.

Reign placed her bagel halves into the toaster. "Yeah, we're good now."

"That's good." Marcy let out a laugh. "Now you can finally *give* that man some, 'cause I *know* you've been holding out."

Reign shot an amused look Marcy's way. "Whatever."

"Girl, I told you about withholding sex. You know how men are."

"Don't say that as if I use sex as a punishment, because I *don't*," Reign denied. "But if we're fighting, the mood just isn't...*there*." She shrugged, "I mean, who really wants the person they're irritated with, touching them?"

Marcy tucked some of her hair behind her ears. "Me," she answered. "Hell, as long as I get *mine*, I'm good. I don't even have to *look* at him. I prefer doggie style anyway."

Reign shook her head. "Nice Mar, thanks for sharing," she drawled, sarcastic.

Marcy laughed a bit, "I'm just saying." She shrugged, "I'm *always* down for a good fuck… Though I've had some *bad* ones before…in college mostly." She tapped her chin with her finger, recalling some of her less than stellar sexual encounters. She chuckled, "I remember my first fake orgasm. I should've won an *award* for that performance."

Reign rolled her eyes. She glanced down at the ring on her hand. "I refuse to fake an orgasm," she muttered. As soon as the words left her lips, she regretted them. "I definitely did *not* mean to say that out loud."

Marcy squinted her eyes. "*Never?*" she asked in disbelief, ignoring Reign's last comment.

Twisting the ring around her finger, Reign shook her head. "I never understood the point," she answered, honest. "Go through all of that for *what* exactly?"

"To boost the man's ego," Marcy explained, humored. "Sometimes they *need* it."

Reign rolled her eyes again. *I'd rather give myself one after he falls asleep*, she thought but refused to say. She retrieved her bagels from the toaster once they popped up.

"Well, not *all* of us can be so honest." After a moment, Marcy cleared her throat, folding her arms on the table. "So…bet you gave Troy some *last night*, huh?" she pressed. "Especially after he gifted you with that bangin' ass bag."

"We're not *fighting* right now," Reign alluded, grabbing a butter knife from the utensil drawer. "And a *bag* never made me give it up *before*. It had nothing to do with it *this* time."

Marcy leaned back in her seat. "I hear you, boo."

Reign finished preparing her food.

Getting up, Marcy made a beeline for the counter. Eyeing the ingredients still sitting out, she flashed a hopeful look Reign's way. "Are you going to make *mine?*"

Reign raised a piece of bagel to her glossed lips. "There is nothing wrong with your hands," she jeered, taking a bite.

Grabbing the bagels, Marcy made a face when she thought Reign wasn't paying attention.

"Saw that," Reign said, earning a chuckle from Marcy.

As Marcy prepared her food, Reign finished hers. "I swear, I need a vacation," Marcy complained. "A weekend trip or *something*." She looked at Reign. "Ooh, you wanna go somewhere next weekend?"

"Can't, I'm going away with Troy."

Marcy paused in the middle of putting jam on her bagel. "Really? *Where?*"

"To this resort in Sedona," Reign answered, washing her hands in the sink. "Going for four days… I'm pretty excited about it. It's been a while since we went away together."

Marcy nodded. "I see," she muttered, then smiled. "Sounds great."

Reign smiled back, then glanced at her watch. "Hurry up and put that stuff away, I have to go."

"Sure," Marcy mumbled, following Reign's progress out of the kitchen.

Stepping out of the cab, Marcy adjusted the cell phone to her ear. "You know I have an attitude, right?" she huffed into the line. "…Yeah well, what are you going to do to fix it?" She sauntered her way up to Chase's front door. "…No, you need to do better than that." She knocked on the door, then smoothed her hair with her hand, grinning as the person on the other end of the line spoke. "That sounds better… Yeah, I think we can work that out."

She smiled at Chase when he opened the door.

Chase smiled in return, signaling for her to come in.

"I have to go but we'll talk later… Yeah, bye." Marcy ended the call, placing the phone in her bag. She greeted Chase with a kiss on the lips. "Hey you."

"Hey yourself." Chase hugged her. "Who was on the phone?"

he asked, parting.

Setting her purse on the loveseat, Marcy shot him a questioning look. "Huh?"

"I heard your voice before I opened the door," he explained. "You seemed upset."

"Oh, it was just my landlord," Marcy dismissed, waving her hand. "He was replacing the shower heads in the bathrooms and gave my neighbor one that was bigger than mine—I didn't appreciate it."

Chase looked perplexed. "How do *you* know that your neighbor received a bigger shower head?"

"I *saw* it." Marcy adjusted the straps of her sundress. "We're cool, so I've been in her apartment."

"Oh okay." He folded his arms. "Is he going to rectify that situation?"

"Oh, he is," she boasted. "He *better*."

"Good to hear."

Marcy grinned. "Right." She followed Chase through the kitchen. "What were you doing?"

"Just chillin' on the deck," he answered, pausing short of opening the refrigerator. "The sun is setting, so it's the perfect time to be out."

Marcy shrugged, "If you say so."

"You want to join me out there, or do you prefer to sit in here with the air conditioning?" he teased.

"You know how I love air conditioning," Marcy chortled, in return. "But yeah, I'll come out with you." She walked out to his deck, taking a seat while Chase grabbed two bottles of water and some snacks before joining her. He sat in a patio chair across from her.

Marcy looked around, letting out a sigh. "I really don't see how people can sit outside with all this heat." Seeing an insect flying nearby, she scoffed. "And *bugs*."

Chase chuckled. "Well, I'm used to the heat, and the candles that I have tend to keep the bugs at bay." He pointed to the citronella candles on the table. "Besides, it's nice to sit out and look at the mountains." Chase always appreciated the mountain backdrop of his home state. He found them peaceful, and often drove up there just to decompress.

Marcy rolled her eyes. "God, everybody in Arizona is always gawking at these damn mountains," she sneered.

Chase opened his bottle of water. "You don't think they're beautiful?"

She fixated on her nails. "Never got the hype," she said, haughty. "It's just dirt and rocks."

Chase held a skeptical gaze on Marcy for several silent seconds. "Okay," he mumbled finally, then took a sip of his water.

Marcy folded her arms, keeping an eye out for any insects that were bold enough to bypass Chase's candles. "So," she began, after a moment. "I've been thinking."

Chase looked at her but didn't say anything.

"With you being so busy and everything, we really haven't been spending that much time together lately," Marcy continued. "So, I was thinking that maybe we can go away together soon."

Chase glanced up at the sky, pondering her proposal. He gave a nod. "That's not a bad idea."

Marcy clapped her hands in delight. "Great. So, can we go away next weekend?"

Chase winced. "Shit. Sorry Mar, I *can't* next weekend. I have to travel to Vegas for a business meeting."

Marcy's smile faded; a frown appeared in its place. "Of *course* you do," she bristled.

"I know, I'm sorry." His tone was apologetic.

"You can't have the meeting over *video* or something?" Marcy spat. "You mean to tell me that fancy office of yours doesn't have video conference capabilities?"

Chase let out a sigh. "No, I *can't* Mar, not for this meeting. I'm sorry," he said, shaking his head. "But we can go away the *following* weekend."

Marcy sat back in her seat in a huff. "Nah, I'm good."

"What is the problem?" Chase asked, fixing her with a stern stare.

"Your lack of time for me is the damn problem," Marcy barked. "Can't even pull yourself away from your little *drawing* job to take me away."

Chase frowned. He elected to ignore the last part of her snide remark, but the unprovoked attitude, he *couldn't* let slide. "Okay so, out of nowhere you spring the idea to go away next weekend on me, and even though I *can't*, I compromise and agree to the *following* weekend, you're pissed at me?" he summed up. She rolled her eyes. "Are you *serious* right now?"

"It's whatever Chase," Marcy grunted.

Sitting up straight, Chase's frown grew deeper. "I'm not saying *no* Marcy, I just need to push it *back* a week." He was regretting inviting Marcy over; his peaceful evening, after the long day of work, was now ruined.

"I don't want to go the *following* weekend, I want to go *next* weekend," Marcy ranted, stomping her sandal-covered foot on the ground.

He squinted his eyes. "What's so special about next weekend?"

Not having an answer that would make any sense, Marcy turned her head and sucked her teeth.

Chase put his hands up. "Look, I don't know what your deal is, but these temper tantrums that you've been throwing over frivolous things are ridiculous," he hurled. "Your immaturity is irritating."

"Give me what the hell I *want*, and I won't *act* immature and throw tantrums." Marcy eyed him with disdain. "As fine as I am, I shouldn't want for shit and yet, I *do*."

"So, I don't give you anything? Don't do anything *for* you?" Chase challenged, voice eerily calm. "We don't go *anywhere?* I don't spend *any* time with you at *all?*"

Marcy scoffed. "You don't do *enough*," she threw back, tone nasty. "You *really* want to impress me? Spend more money on me. Send me on a first-class trip to an island or something while you're away so I'm not sitting here bored—"

"So this *isn't* about *time*, this is about *money*." Chase's tone had yet to waiver.

She stared him down. "Yup."

Chase raised an eyebrow. "You want money? Find a *career*, instead of looking to me with your damn hand out."

Marcy rolled her eyes. "I don't *want* to work and shouldn't *have* to," she fumed. "*You* work, and you should be *providing* for me. Put me in a house, buy me a car, put money in my bank account every week—"

"You are not my *wife*," he interrupted, eyeing Marcy with a look that mixed perplexity and annoyance. "These are things that I'd do for my *wife*, and the last time I checked, this *relationship* isn't even headed in that *direction*."

Marcy eyed him up and down, frowning. "Wife or *not*, I'm worth *all* that shit. I *deserve* all that shit and you're not delivering."

Chase stared at her in silence, narrowing his eyes. He disagreed; she *didn't* deserve it. "Yeah, you should go," he slowly drew out.

Marcy's eyes widened as Chase rose from his seat. "Seriously?"

Chase rubbed his chin with his hand. "Yes, I'm serious." He moved to the sliding doors, signaling for her to get up. "Come on, I'll take you home."

Marcy's mouth was gaping open; she was truly offended. She and Chase had gotten into it plenty of times, yet he'd never put her out of his house. She hopped to her feet. "You must be out of your goddamn mind!"

"No, I promise I'm in my right frame of mind," Chase threw back, tone calm.

Marcy put her hand in his face. "If I walk out of this house, we're done," she threatened. "I mean it." She stood there smug as Chase stared at her. *Hmm, he ain't crazy. He wouldn't throw all this away.*

"Fair enough," Chase replied after a moment.

Marcy glared. "You're serious? You're really telling me that we're done? That we're *over*?"

Chase nodded. "Yes, Marcy, we're over," he stated. "I wish you the best."

Marcy's eyes nearly popped out of her head. "You're breaking up with me over an *argument*?" she fumed. "Or is it because you can't handle being with a woman who knows what she wants?"

Chase folded his arms. "Whatever reason you tell yourself in order to make you feel better, is fine with me." He refused to be drawn into further drama with her; she'd taken up enough of his time and peace of mind. "But I mean what I said. This is over."

"You son of a bitch!"

Despite Marcy's screaming, Chase maintained his cool. "Let me take you home Marcy."

Marcy gave his arm a hard shove. "Fuck you. I don't need your ride." She jerked the doors open, storming to the living room.

Chase followed Marcy, standing feet from her as she snatched up her purse. "Do you at least want me to call you a cab?" he offered.

Snapping her head in his direction, Marcy flashed a piercing look his way. She flipped him the finger before scurrying out the door, slamming it behind her.

Chase stood there, silent. After a moment, he exhaled deeply. "Bye Marcy."

Chapter Ten

SITTING ON A BENCH, REIGN speared her chipotle ranch salad with her fork. Chewing, she retrieved her notebook and pen from the seat, setting the salad container in its place.

Ditching the office, Reign had elected to eat lunch outside in a nearby park that Monday afternoon. The trees shaded her from the June sun, and she needed the solace to eat and write in peace.

Feeling a warm breeze brush past her, Reign paused in the middle of a sentence, opting to stare at the branches swaying in front of her. She was so engrossed in the scenery that the sound of her ringtone made her jump. Setting the book aside, she grabbed the phone from her purse, giving the screen a quick glance.

"Hi Kris," Reign answered, full of anticipation. The last she'd heard from her realtor was a few days ago, when she was told that the contractors were still mulling over her offer, leaving Reign feeling anxious.

"Good afternoon Reign," Kris's bubbly voice bellowed through the phone. "How is everything?"

"Things are fine," Reign answered. *Come on with the small talk, get to this house.* "Do you have some news for me?"

"That, I do." Kris paused for a few seconds. "Congratulations, your offer has been accepted."

Face lighting up, Reign let out a little scream of delight. "Are you serious?"

"Absolutely," Kris assured. "We just need to get the inspection completed, file everything with the bank, finalize your flooring choices, then we can close."

"How long will all of that take?" Reign asked.

"Thirty days max."

Reign let out a quick sigh; she wished it could be sooner, she was eager to get out of her apartment. But she figured she'd been there this long, what was another month? "Okay, sounds good. Thank you *so* much."

"You're welcome, it's my pleasure," Kris replied. "I will call you back when I have the inspection date."

"Okay, talk to you later." Reign's bright smile remained on her face even *after* she'd hung up. Placing the phone to her chest, she exhaled deeply. "I have my house," she said, aloud.

Her week was starting off on a high note; she finally had her dream home and in a matter of days, she'd be in Sedona spending some much-needed quality time with Troy. Her phone rang once again, cutting into her pleasant thoughts. Seeing her sister's name on the screen, Reign answered.

"Cyn, my offer was approved, I'm getting my house!" Reign squealed. The smile left her face when her sister began to speak; a frown took its place. "Wait, what did you say?..." Reign closed her eyes, letting out a deep sigh. "Shit."

Reign sat at her desk with her face in her hands. She'd retuned from lunch nearly a half hour ago, but had yet to start working again. She had a phone call to make, and she was dreading it.

Lifting her head, she sighed. Gathering her nerve, she dialed a number, placing the phone to her ear.

"Hey," Troy answered.

Reign nervously fiddled with a pen on her desk. "Hi Troy… Umm, do you have a minute?"

"Yeah, I'm just heading out for some lunch." Troy didn't notice Reign's melancholy tone. "You ready for this weekend? *I* am, I've been packed since last week."

Reign pinched the bridge of her nose as Troy rambled on.

"We'll be pulling out early that morning, should take us about two hours give or take."

Reign ran a hand through her hair. "Troy, *about* that," she began. "About *what?*" Troy wondered.

"About the trip." Reign hesitated for a moment. "Babe, I'm so sorry, but…I can't go." She regretted the words as soon as they left her lips.

There was a pause. "What do you *mean*, you can't go?" Troy barked.

"I got a call from my sister a little bit ago… My father was trying to clean the gutters when he slipped off the ladder—he *fell* Troy," she revealed. "He already had back issues and this fall ruptured a disc—" she sighed. "He needs surgery and it's scheduled for Thursday."

"Why *then?*" Troy asked, tone lacking sympathy.

"They said something about wanting the swelling to go down a bit," she tried to explain. "I don't know, but the bottom line is that I need to be here for him."

"Your mom and sister are there," Troy spat. "What's a *third* person being there going to accomplish?"

Reign frowned at his callous words. She figured that Troy would be upset about her cancelling their plans; she felt horrible about having to do it, but he was being outright insensitive. "Troy, you really expect me to leave while my *father* is having *surgery?*"

"What happens *after?*" Troy snarled, ignoring her question. "Let me guess, you'll be spending *every* free moment helping your parents out."

Reign sat there dumfounded.

Troy let out a huff. "Damn it Rae—you were *just* complaining about *me* not having time for *you* and now you won't have time for *me*."

"What the fuck—" Reign had to stop herself; she'd almost forgotten that she was at work. Though her office door was closed, her voice could carry. "I can't believe how you're acting right now."

Troy calmed himself. "Sorry, I didn't mean it like that." He sighed, "It's just that I wanted this time away with you and now… I'm disappointed to say the least."

Reign wasn't interested in his explanation, "I'm *sorry* that my father had an unexpected accident," she replied, sarcastic. "*My* fault."

"Rae, I'm sorry about your father, I really am." His tone was quick, unconvincing.

Reign ran her hand across her forehead. "Um hmm," she muttered, angry.

Troy let out another sigh. "Look, I umm… I shelled out a lot of money for this trip and it's nonrefundable."

Scowling, Reign didn't speak.

"So that being said…" Troy continued. "I'm still going."

Reign's eyes widened in fury. "Wait, you're going to a couples resort by *yourself?*"

"I don't want to waste my money."

Reign slowly nodded her head; she was furious, she was hurt. Her boyfriend, someone who was supposed to be a shoulder to lean on in this stressful time, was willing to abandon her for drinks and a hot tub. As much as Reign wanted to lash out at him, to express just how disappointed she was in him, she knew that there would be no point. It was clear that he couldn't care less.

"Enjoy your trip," Reign spat out through her clenched jaws. She abruptly hung up, not giving Troy the opportunity to say another word.

Tossing the phone down, she sat back in her seat, tears filling her eyes.

This time she couldn't force her tears back down; she couldn't tell herself "don't let it get to you". It had. Covering her face with her hands, she cried silently.

Reign passed through her parents' living room with paper towels and a bottle of wood cleaner. Kneeling before the cherry wood coffee table, Reign sprayed cleaner on it.

Cynthia walked out of the kitchen as Reign was wiping the table down. "Rae, I'm on my way to the pharmacy to pick up Dad's prescription," she announced, slinging her purse strap on her shoulder. "Do you need anything while I'm out?"

Reign looked up at Cynthia with tired eyes. "Yeah, can you

get me something for this headache I can't seem to get rid of?" she requested. "The aspirin that Mom has isn't doing anything for me."

"Sure *can*," Cynthia grinned. "Butter pecan ice cream and rum, it is."

Reign followed Cynthia's progress to the door. "Cyn, you *know* that's not what I mean," she ground out.

Cynthia opened the door. "It's what I *heard*."

Not having the energy to go back and forth with her sister, Reign simply shook her head as Cynthia left. Alone again, she returned to her task of cleaning.

It had been three days since her father's back surgery. He had arrived home that Sunday afternoon to begin his path to recovery. Reign was at the hospital all day during the procedure. While her mother and Cynthia remained the days after, Reign alternated her time between the hospital and her parents' home, trying to get things prepared for his return. Everything from moving furniture around to make room for him to move about whenever he was able to get out of bed, to making sure that the house was fully stocked with food and supplies, so that her mother wouldn't have to run errands.

With the table cleaned, Reign grabbed the vacuum to give the floor a quick run over, when a knock at the door interrupted her.

Peering at the guests through the peephole, Reign's eyebrows raised in surprise. Opening the door, she offered a warm smile. "Hey you two, what are you doing here?" Reign greeted a smiling Chase and Ava.

Chase cradled an oversized gift basket in his hands, while Ava adjusted the yellow bow on it. "Well, when I told Mom about your dad's surgery, she insisted that we hand deliver this gift basket with her well wishes," Ava informed, adjusting the handbag resting on her wrist. "I swear, the woman baked every type of muffin and cookie that she could possibly *think* of."

A softness in her eyes, Reign placed a hand to her chest. "Thank you, we appreciate it."

Reign had informed Ava of her father's surgery, who naturally passed the information on to her family. Both Ava and Chase had spoken to Reign the day of his procedure, then followed up on her father's progress the days following.

"Do you want to come in?" Reign asked.

Ava put a hand up, shaking it. "Oh no sweetie, we weren't expecting to come inside," she politely protested. "You've got enough going on. No need to entertain us."

Chase carefully handed Reign the basket. "You need help with it?" he asked, watching her steady it in her arms.

"No, it's fine, I got it," Reign assured. "Thanks though."

Chase gave a nod. "No problem."

"I thought you were in Vegas this weekend," Reign said to Chase.

"I *was*, but I finished what I needed to do early enough yesterday, so I drove back." Chase replied.

Before Reign could speak another word, her mother walked into the living room.

"Who's at the door, darling?" Vivian asked.

Reign glanced back at her mother. "It's Ava and Chase. They stopped by to drop this basket off for Dad."

Vivian clasped her hands together, her eyes gleaming. "Oh, thank you, how sweet—tell them to come in for a bit."

Reign chuckled, turning back to her smiling friends. She gestured them inside with her head. "You heard the woman, come in."

Stepping inside, Chase retrieved the heavy basket from Reign's arms. "Ms. Vivian, where would you like me to put this?" he asked, polite.

Vivian pointed to the coffee table and said, "On that table is just fine."

As Chase set the basket down, Vivian enveloped Ava in a hug. "Ava sweetie, it's been so long," she gushed, holding on tight.

Ava smiled, hugging her back. "I know, it has."

Though Vivian released Ava from her warm embrace, she still held onto her arms. "It's good to see you."

"You too," Ava beamed.

Grinning, Vivian sized up Chase as he approached her. "Chase, oh my God, have you gotten taller since I've seen you last?"

Chase chuckled, "I don't think so." He hugged her.

"Still as handsome as ever," Vivian complimented, parting from their embrace. She glanced at Reign. "Rae, have you seen how handsome he is?"

"Mom," Reign warned, shaking her head slightly.

Ava snickered at the embarrassed look on her brother's face. Growing up with him, she knew how modest Chase was about his looks, even though women fawned over him *because* of them.

Vivian put her hands up in surrender. "Okay, I'll stop," she giggled. "I'll leave you kids to catch up. I have to go call somebody to go up on the roof and grab the tools that Matthew left up there." She let out a sigh, "I *told* that stubborn man of mine about trying to clean the gutters himself."

Chase took a step forward. "*I* can get the tools down for you."

Vivian quickly shook her head, "No son, I can't ask you to do that."

"You're not asking, I'm offering," he smiled. "Is the ladder still there?"

Vivian nodded, "Yes."

"Then, let's go," Chase prompted, allowing Vivian to lead the way. "If you still need the gutters cleaned, I can do it, just let me know."

Vivian clasped her hands together. "You are a God send," she beamed as they walked out of the door.

Ava stared at the closed door, shaking her head in the process. "I swear, he always has to be the favorite," she jested. Reign giggled a bit. Ava joined her, but her laughter quickly subsided.

Without warning, Ava moved in, wrapping her arms around Reign. Reign hugged her back. "How are you, luv?" Ava asked, holding on.

"Everything is fine." Reign let out a deep breath. "Dad is still his old, ornery self, despite his pain, so I know he'll be fine," she attempted to joke.

Ava released Reign from her embrace; no traces of amusement were on her face, just concern. "I'm glad that your father pulled through surgery, but how are *you?*"

Glancing away, Reign rubbed the back of her neck.

"You're always looking out for everyone, and you never stop to deal with your own feelings," Ava said, sincere. "I know it's hard seeing your parent go through this so, I want to know how *you're* doing."

Reign sighed heavily. Ava was right; she'd been stressed over her father's surgery and now pending recovery. She'd been so consumed with it, that she didn't even get to celebrate her accomplishment of purchasing her home. She was tired and tightly wound. "I'm...I'm fine," she maintained, meeting Ava's worried gaze.

Ava tilted her head; she knew her best friend well enough to know that that was a lie. "Rae—"

Reign lightly tapped Ava's shoulder. "I'm *fine* Ava, really."

Ava let out a deep sigh. "Okay sis, if you say so." She folded her arms. "Have you heard from Troy?"

The mere mention of Troy's name made Reign's jaw tighten. She was still angry with him from their latest fight. "He texted me the other day."

"He *texted* you," Ava scoffed, making a face. "Your *boyfriend* of *six damn years texted* you instead of *calling* you? Hell, forget calling, being *here for* you?" Ava didn't care for Troy, never had. She felt that Reign deserved better.

Reign stiffened. She knew how it sounded. "Yup."

Ava shook her head. "I *still* can't believe he took his ass to that damn resort without you."

"Yup," Reign repeated. "It's whatever, he'd be of no help anyway."

Ava shook her head again, this time vigorously. "*This* is why I'm single," she jeered. "His tires would be slashed by now."

Reign managed a slight chuckle. "Yes, I know." She knew her hotheaded friend all too well. "Frankly, I don't want to talk about him anymore."

"Okay." Ava casually examined her nails. "*Speaking* of people who aren't here for you when they *should* be—"

Reign squinted her eyes.

"Where's *Marcy*?" Ava finished.

Reign folded her arms. "She's visiting her parents in San Diego this weekend," she answered. "Said she needed to get out of town for a bit."

"Um hmm," Ava muttered. As far as she was concerned, Marcy *too* had no excuse for not being there for Reign—especially since the woman was always so pressed about claiming Reign as *her* best friend. "You know Chase broke up with her?"

Reign frowned, stunned. This was the first that she'd heard that news. "What?"

Ava nodded. "Yup." She successfully contained her urge to celebrate, both now and when Chase had revealed the news two days after Marcy had left his house in a fit of anger. While Ava was happy that her brother was finally free of Marcy, she knew that Chase was upset over it. "Guess it just wasn't working between them anymore."

Reign couldn't help but feel bad for Marcy. *I wonder why she didn't tell me.* "Wow… No *wonder* she had to get out of town, huh?"

Ava gave a nonchalant shrug.

Hearing her father's faint voice from her parents' bedroom, Reign glanced in that direction. "I'll be right back, I have to check on him."

Ava followed her progress. "You need me to do anything?"

Reign looked back at her, flashing an appreciative smile her way. "No luv, just make yourself at home," she replied, continuing down the hall.

Chapter Eleven

AVA TIED A GOLD STRING to a large gold and black key-shaped mylar balloon, securing it to the back of a chair. She glanced at a coworker, who was casually hanging gold streamers along the wall.

"Tracy, those are crooked," Ava spat at the stunned woman. She snapped her fingers, gesturing to them. "Come on girl, straighten them out. Get it together."

"Geez Ava, bossy much?" Tracy chuckled, repositioning the streamer.

Ava just shook her head as she tended to the food arranged on a long table. She began repositioning the trays of hot and cold foods, desserts, water, juices, and sodas.

Adding more streamers, Tracy smiled. "Ava your bossing me around *aside*," she chortled. "It's nice that you arranged this surprise shower for Reign."

Ava smiled back. With Reign's pending closing date approaching in just a little over a week, Ava had taken it upon herself to gather her coworkers and higher ups to throw a home shower for her favorite boss. She and the other editors that worked under Reign, Tracy included, had come in early that morning to begin decorating one of the conference rooms. With Reign on her lunch break, they were seizing the opportunity to finish up before she returned.

"She deserves it," Ava proudly gushed, moving some curls from her face. "Buying a home is a huge deal." She put a hand on her hip. "Hell, if a baby and getting married gets you a shower, why shouldn't a *house*?"

Tracy snapped her fingers in dramatic fashion. "I *definitely* hear that." She held an eager hand up in Ava's direction. "High-five."

Ava narrowed her eyes at Tracy. "Girl—just no," she dismissed, earning a loud laugh from another of her coworkers.

Poking her lip out, Tracy lowered her hand.

Ava headed for the door. "Finish up, while I go check to see if she's on her way back," she threw over her shoulder.

With Ava gone, Tracy glanced over at her laughing coworker. "Janet, you did *not* have to laugh that loud," she grunted.

"We *all* told you about trying too hard," Janet shot back.

Reign pulled into the parking lot behind her work building and turned the car off. She had planned on purchasing one after closing. In the meantime, with all the running around she was doing, she had elected to rent a car to get her by.

Reign eyed the lunch that she'd just purchased. Instead of eating, she opted instead to lean her head against the head rest, closing her eyes. She was exhausted. Between work, checking in on her parents, finalizing things with the house, and packing up her apartment, every day was nonstop.

Her phone ringing snapped her eyes open. Looking at the ID, Reign clenched her jaw. Reluctantly, she answered. "Yeah?" the bite in her voice was heavy.

"Still mad at me, I take it," Troy assumed.

"Yeah," she repeated, tone not changing. It had been almost three weeks since their doomed trip, and she had yet to forgive him for leaving without her. The fact that he refused to even *attempt* to understand why she was upset with him, didn't help.

"Rae, you can't keep holding grudges, it's childish," Troy replied, agitation in his voice. "You just *insist* on being unreasonable, and I'm sick of it."

Her eyes widened in fury. "I'm *not* being—"

"Reign, you don't think you're overreacting *just* a little bit?" Troy cut her off.

"*Of course* you'd think so," Reign argued. "When have you *ever* validated anything that I've felt? When have you let me complete a fuckin' *thought*?"

Troy sucked his teeth, "Here you go with—" He let out a quick sigh. "You know what, it's fine. You're right, I'm sorry."

Reign pinched the bridge of her nose. There wasn't an ounce of sincerity in his apology, not that she expected it. This was the side of Troy that she despised; the side that she hoped would *change*. But no matter what she did, or what she said, it hadn't. "Troy... I—" She sighed. "We need to talk."

Troy hesitated. She no longer sounded angry; she sounded indifferent. "Okay," he said finally. "Come over later?"

"Yeah," she agreed, hanging up. She rolled her eyes to the ceiling. When her phone beeped, she looked at it.

Hey Rae, where are you? Ava's text read.

Reign glanced at the time on her phone. "Shit," she hissed to herself. Her lunch hour was moving much too quickly for her liking. She sent a quick reply to Ava, grabbed her purse and lunch from the passenger's seat, and headed inside.

Reign had stepped off the elevator and was making a beeline for her office, when Ava hurried up to her and grabbed hold of her arm.

"Come with me," Ava demanded.

Reign's brow knitted in confusion as Ava tried to pull her along. "Something wrong?" Reign stood there, stiletto covered feet planted firmly to the floor. She raised an eyebrow when Ava gave her arm another tug.

Ava chuckled at her inability to easily move her friend. "*Damn*, you're strong."

"You want to tell me why you're attempting to drag me somewhere?" Reign questioned. "More importantly, why you're not working on those re-edits that I sent you this morning?"

"I started them, you know I'll get it done before the deadline," Ava vowed. Though she was Reign's friend, she never took advantage of that status at work. Reign was still her boss, and she respected that.

"But Dennis called an emergency meeting in the conference room."

Reign immediately looked at her phone. "What? I didn't get an email about that." Normally whenever Reign's manager scheduled a meeting, he sent an email and added it to her calendar way in advance.

"Umm, he *just* called it. Like *right* before you got in," Ava quickly deflected. "Now come on."

Reign was still confused by the lack of notification; worry began to set in as she tried to figure out what the emergency was. *I don't feel like this shit right now*, she thought, walking in stride with Ava towards the conference room.

Reign went to open the door, but Ava quickly stepped in front of her and knocked on the door.

Reign stared as Ava cleared her throat to respond to the person on the other side. "It's Ava and Reign," Ava answered.

Reign slowly shook her head. "You're acting weird."

Ava lowered her head and shook it as she chuckled a bit. "Trust me, I'm aware."

After being given the okay to enter, Ava opened the door.

Before Reign could fully enter the room, she was startled by the loud "surprise" from the room's occupants. So much so, that she backed out of the room.

Laughing, Ava caught her by the arm. "Where are you going? You can't run out on your own shower."

Reign, still in shock, allowed herself to be pulled back into the room. Putting a hand on her chest, she scanned the decorated room full of people. "What is this?" she asked, smiling.

"Your shower," Ava beamed, holding her arms up.

Reign's smile faded. "I'm not pregnant." Her response earned laughter from the room.

Ava shook her head in amusement. "No silly, this is your *house* shower...home shower...party—" she put a hand up. "It's a congratulations party for you buying your home. So, bask in this free food and these gifts."

Reign laughed, then gave Ava a hug. "Thank you, luv."

Ava patted Reign's back. "You're welcome sis. Congratulations again." She parted, "I told Chase to drop a gift off too, but he didn't."

Hand shooting up, Reign shook her head. "No Ava, he doesn't have to get me anything."

Ava's brows raised. "Like hell he *doesn't*."

Reign chuckled as Ava made a beeline for the food.

A half hour into her shower and Reign was enjoying herself; it was a welcomed distraction.

"Reign, congratulations again."

Reign set her plate of food down and turned around to face her manager. "Thank you, Dennis. I appreciate it." She smiled, "*And the gift*."

Dennis smiled back, "Anything for my favorite employee."

"We *all* heard that Dennis," Ava mentioned from nearby.

Reign put a hand over her face, laughing as Dennis shot an amused glance Ava's way.

"I'm not mad, as long as your favorite isn't Tracy, we're cool," Ava joked, then laughed when she caught Tracy's shocked look. "I'm just kidding, Tracy."

Tracy laughed along as she held her hand up for a high five from Ava.

Ava pointed at her. "I *said* no."

Reign shook her head at them, before turning her attention back to her boss.

"I know this should probably wait until after this party is over, but I want to run something by you," Dennis brought up.

"What's that?" Reign wondered.

"In the next few months, I'm going to be implementing ghost-writing services."

Reign squinted her eyes, then nodded slowly. "Uh huh," she uttered. "Can I ask you something?"

Dennis gave a nod. "Sure."

"Was this Ava's idea?"

"Not necessarily," Dennis answered. "She *mentioned* it, but I've been mulling this over for a while now. I just wasn't sure if I was *going* to because we currently only have editors, not *writers.*"

"Okay, so…what changed your mind?" Reign asked, folding her arms.

Dennis rubbed his chin. "You."

Reign furrowed her brow, perplexed. "I don't understand."

"Well, I was looking over one of the books that you recently edited, when I came across a file titled 'rewrites'," Dennis explained.

The confusion didn't leave Reign's face as she tried to remember. After the conversation with Ava about ghostwriting, although hesitant, Reign had taken it upon herself to play with the idea. She'd begun a mock revision of the dreadful book that she was editing.

"Shit," she whispered to herself, putting a hand over her face. After a second, she jerked her head up. "Wait, how did you see that?"

Dennis shrugged slightly. "It was in the same folder file as the edits."

Reign pinched the bridge of her nose and sighed. *How the hell did that happen?* She'd saved that project in a personal folder on her laptop, or so she *thought.* "I apologize for the oversight," she replied, remorseful. "That wasn't meant for anybody to read, I was just toying around with it."

"Don't be sorry, I'm *glad* that I read it—it was excellent," Dennis praised. "I always knew you were talented based on how you edit, but reading a book that you actually *wrote*—Reign, you'd be perfect to take this on."

"I don't know," Reign said, unsure. "I mean, it's one thing to write for myself, but another to write for someone *else.*"

"Reign, I have complete confidence in you and there's so much more money in ghostwriting. I did my research and people are willing to pay top dollar for that."

Reign stretched her neck from side to side. "What would happen to my current position?"

"You'd still manage the editors, but you'd delegate *all* editing work to them. While *you* focus on the writing projects," Dennis answered.

Reign looked away, uncertainty written all over her face.

"I'd of *course* up your salary and will be adding bonuses." Dennis softly tapped her arm. "Just *think* about it," he proposed. "Like I said, I plan on rolling this out in a few months, so if it's something that you really aren't comfortable with, I'll seek outside writers...but honestly, I'd prefer *you*."

"I'll think it over, Dennis," Reign promised.

Dennis gave a grateful nod, before heading off in search of cake.

As soon as he was gone, Ava sidled up next to Reign. "So, what was *that* all about?" she asked.

Reign took one look at the smile on Ava's face and shot her a knowing look. "Don't try it, you heard every word of that conversation."

Ava broke into laughter. "I did," she admitted. "I think you should do it."

Reign didn't reply, though her brow knitted.

"What's wrong?" Ava questioned.

"I *honestly* don't remember saving that document in the public folder," Reign brought up. "I'm always careful when maintaining files. I'd never want to mix something up."

Ava pushed her hair over her shoulder. "Maybe you were distracted or something, it happens," she quickly put out. "No harm done though, right?"

"I guess not," Reign replied, tone low.

Ava smiled. "Good." She tapped Reign's shoulder. "Now stop looking distraught and go get some cake before Dennis eats it all. He's being eyeing it since I brought it in this morning."

Reign giggled.

Reign had just pulled up in front of Troy's three-bedroom, two-story house for their agreed upon meeting. Hearing her phone beep, she looked at it.

Use your key, Troy's text read.

Grabbing her purse from the passenger's seat, Reign retrieved the set of Troy's spare house keys that he'd given to her a few years back. She'd only used them a handful of times.

As she stepped out the car, she felt a pull in her lower back and winced. "Great," she grunted, giving it a rub. Ambling up the path to Troy's front door, Reign let herself in as instructed, tossing her purse on the loveseat. "Troy," she called.

"I'm coming," he answered from upstairs. A moment later, he came jogging down. "Hey." He had a grin on his face.

Reign had no traces of one on *hers*. "Was I interrupting something?" Her tone lacked emotion.

"Oh no, was just straightening up my room." He brushed his hand down his t-shirt. "Making the bed."

Reign raised an eyebrow. *I hope he didn't do that on my account.* "Oh okay."

Troy gestured to the couch. "Sit down," he softly urged.

Reign slowly sat down, grimacing. Adjusted her position, she gave her back another rub.

"What's up with your back?" Troy asked, sitting next to her.

"I aggravated it while I was throwing stuff out in the trash yesterday." She gently settled back against the cushion. "Some old stuff that I didn't want anymore—*heavy* stuff."

Troy rubbed the back of his neck. "Damn, that's a shame."

"It's fine," Reign dismissed, dry.

Troy scratched his head. "If you had asked me to help you, you wouldn't be hurting right now."

Reign narrowed her eyes at him. "Why would I have asked you to do anything for me, after the way that you've been treating me?"

Troy rolled his eyes. "*How* have I been treating you, Reign?" he mocked.

Reign let out a slight chuckle laced with annoyance, "Okay."

"Come on, let's hear it," Troy egged on, gesturing to her. "Just get it out, so you can get over it."

"No, I'm tired of *getting over* it," Reign quickly spat out. "Which brings me to the reason why I wanted to talk. I think we need to—"

Troy's hand shot out, grabbing her own and holding on tight. "Rae...please don't say what I know you're about to," he blurted out.

She huffed. "Troy—"

"Don't break up with me," he begged. When Reign glanced off to the side, he sighed. "*Please* don't. I'll be better."

Looking back at him, Reign shook her head, "You *won't.*"

"I *will*, I promise." He put his right hand up. "Give me the chance."

Reign held a somber gaze on him. "I'm not happy anymore," she said, resolved. "And neither are *you.*"

"Look, I know that we have problems, but I am asking you to not give up on us just yet." Troy squeezed her hand. "Come on Rae, do you *really* want to throw away all of these years?"

Reign stared at him; she was conflicted, and it resonated on her face by way of a slight frown. She didn't understand how she'd ended up where she was in this relationship—unfulfilled and unhappy. She couldn't pinpoint exactly when things had taken a downward turn. In the beginning, they were happy...or what she *thought* to be happy.

Her silence was unnerving him. "We *owe* it to ourselves to stick this out," Troy stressed.

Reign ran a hand through her hair. She wasn't lying; she was no longer happy in her relationship with Troy. But despite how she felt, she didn't want to throw away six years of history. If one more chance would give him the nudge that he needed to be better, she was willing to allow it. But not before she got some things off her chest.

"Troy... I—" She took a deep breath as she tried to gather the words she needed to say to him.

Silent, Troy stared at her.

"I *need* you to understand how I've been feeling about—a *lot* of things in this relationship." She paused, focusing on Troy's face. The look in his eyes—it changed. His gaze had gone from engrossed to blank. Reign knew this look well; Troy was tuning her out.

Nevertheless, she knew that she had to continue. She needed to get what was on her chest, *off*. She took a deep breath. "I just think that in order to give this relationship a fighting chance, we need to—"

Hearing a notification on his phone, Troy picked it up, looking at it.

Reign glared while his fingers moved along the screen. *Is he really fuckin' texting right now?!* "Are you listening to me?" she asked, already knowing the answer.

"Of course, I've been an asshole." Troy's tone was flat as he concentrated on his phone. He finished his text, then set it back down. "I get it."

Reign held her angered gaze. "Do you even *care* about how I feel? At *all?*"

"Sure," Troy replied. His tone was unconvincing.

Rolling her eyes, Reign moved to get up from the couch. "This was a waste of time," she muttered, snatching her purse up.

Letting out a huff, Troy jumped up when she headed for the door. "Just say what you were going to say."

"There's no point," Reign spat, moving swiftly past him.

Troy bolted towards her, grabbing her hand. "Don't leave."

She snatched her hand from his grasp. "Don't touch me."

Troy moved around, standing in front of her. "Seriously Reign, go ahead and tell me all the ways I've been an asshole to you. Tell me how everything is *my* fault. I promise I'll shut up and listen."

Reign scowled at his condescending tone. "Troy, I'm not say-ing that you're always wrong," she argued. "*I* have my faults too, I *know* that. But the difference between you and I, is that when I do something that bothers you, I at least listen to you and *attempt* to change my behavior."

Troy rolled his eyes as she spoke.

"*You* on the other hand make *no* attempts to change," she con-tinued, upset. "You just give me a half-assed apology or dismiss my feelings *entirely*. There is no compromise, and no *effort* put into this relationship anymore." She shook her head. "I mean…do you even *love* me still?"

"Reign, you already know how I feel about you. *Again*, stop with the fuckin' dramatics," Troy bristled, folding his arms. "You're standing here talking to me about what *I* don't change, but *you* have *yet* to change that nagging shit you do."

Reign jerked her head back. "So, me *trying* to express how I *feel*, is *nagging* to you?" she asked, eerily calm. "I just want to make sure that I understand what you're saying."

"Yup," Troy spat.

Reign stared at him, fire in her eyes. Her fists were clenched; she was furious. "Good to know." She grabbed the doorknob, tears of frustration threatening to spill. "I love you Troy, but I need a break from you."

"Reign, wait a minute—"

"I can't," Reign shut down, storming out of the house.

"Babe—" Troy was cut off by the door slamming in his face. Furious, he punched the door with his hand. "Shit!"

Chapter Twelve

CHASE GRABBED HIS CHICKEN SANDWICH, taking a bite, while Ava concentrated on her grilled turkey panini.

"When's the next time you're going out of town?" Ava asked, between chews.

Chase finished his bite. "I'm going to New York in two weeks," he answered. "Will be there for about three weeks, maybe longer."

Ava nodded. "Gotcha." She brushed the fallen crumbs from her tank top. "Still wish you'd just stay local. I mean, you get on my nerves, but I miss you when you're gone."

Chase chuckled, "Stop it, you're just going to miss me paying for our lunch outings."

"*That* too," Ava laughed back.

Saturday afternoon, the Williams siblings were enjoying a quick lunch before heading to the mountains for a hike.

"No but seriously, I don't mind you traveling all the time if that's what makes you happy. *Especially* after that mess with Marcy," Ava continued.

"I appreciate that, but I'm good," Chase assured. "It was just a matter of time anyway, there was no real future there. Marriage was never Marcy's goal…nor was it mine."

Ava tilted her head. "So, you *never* want to get married? Have a family?"

"Of *course* I do," Chase answered. "Just…with the right woman."

Ava nodded in approval, "I hear that." She took a sip of her lemon water. "Are you still going to help Reign move next weekend?"

"Yes," Chase replied, reaching for his cup of juice.

"She wasn't going to ask you, so I took it upon myself," Ava told.

Chase frowned, "How come she didn't want to ask me?"

Ava gave a hard shrug. "I guess she feels weird because you and Marcy broke up. Like she's not supposed to talk to you now or something."

Chase waved a dismissive hand. "Reign can ask me anything, she'll always be my friend," he said.

Ava grinned. "Did you get her a housewarming gift like I told you to?"

Chase made a face. "I planned on getting her one *before* you called yourself *telling* me to do it," he jeered. "Already ordered it." He smiled to himself, "I'm proud of her."

"Me too." Ava took another sip of her drink as Chase went back to eating. "So, how come you never asked her out?"

"Who?" Chase asked, absently.

Ava shot him a knowing look. "Really?" she rolled her eyes at the confusion on her brother's face. "*Reign.*"

Chase wiped his mouth with a napkin. "Ava, like I told *Mom*, Reign and I have always been *just friends*," he pointed in her direction. "You *know* that."

Ava folded her arms, eyeing him skeptically. "*Always?*" she pressed. "Nothing ever transpired between the two of you? Like *ever?*"

Chase gave her a stern look. "*No*," he stood firm. Ava pursed her lips together in disbelief. "Now stop it."

Ava put her hands up. "Fine."

"And even if I *wanted* to ask her—"

"Oh, so you *do* want to?" Ava jumped in, smirking.

Chase narrowed his eyes at his sister. "*If* I wanted to ask her out, *one*, she's in a relationship," he declared. "I'd never go after someone who is committed."

"Troy has one foot out the damn door," Ava scoffed. "She tries to hide it, but Rae is so over his nonsense."

"Still." He paused for a brief moment. "And *two*…I dated her friend."

Ava jerked her head back, her face scrunching in the process. "*So?*"

"*You* wouldn't feel some kind of way if *your* ex-boyfriend asked your best friend out?" Chase put a hand up. "Hypothetically speaking, of course."

"*First* of all, the *only* reason why Marcy clings to Reign as hard as she *does* is because Reign is the only person who *tolerates* her simple ass," Ava sneered. "That girl doesn't even know how to *be* a damn friend, so her trying to claim Rae as a best friend is *laughable*." She moved her hair from her face. "We know who Reign's *real* best friend is."

"I seemed to have struck a nerve," Chase teased.

Ava made a face. "*Second*... Normally, *yes* that would be an issue," she admitted. "However, as previously *mentioned*, Marcy is trash, and you should never have been with her in the first place, so it doesn't count."

Resolved, Chase shook his head. "Yeah, I know," he agreed, sullen. "Not about the *trash* part—you're on your own with that." Ava chuckled slightly. "But...you're right, I never should've gone down that road with Marcy."

Ava nodded in agreement. "What made you finally end it?" she asked, after a moment.

Chase shrugged slightly. "I guess..." He sighed. "I guess I just realized that I'd rather be by myself, than stay in another dead-end relationship."

"I get that," Ava replied, sincere. "I *understand* that." She watched Chase take a sip of his drink. "So back to why you never asked Reign out *before* she started seeing Troy—"

Chase nearly choked on his drink. He composed himself, then fixed Ava with a stern glance while pointing to the unfinished food on her plate. "Drop it and finish up so we can get going."

"Fine," Ava huffed, grabbing the rest of her panini.

Chase looked away from her to the mountains in the distance, letting out a long sigh.

"Mom, do you think that I should take this last year off to help out around here?" Cynthia asked, helping her mother fold clothes.

Vivian shot a side-glance her way. "No, I *don't*," she ground out. "You stay your butt in school and finish."

Cynthia chuckled, "Okay fine."

Hearing a knock on the front door, both women looked up from the couch. "It's open," Vivian called. She smiled bright when Reign walked in. "Hi darling,"

Reign kissed her on the cheek. "Hi Mom." Taking her hand, Reign playfully mushed Cynthia on the side of her head. "Hi to you too."

Cynthia let out a little scream while swatting at Reign. "You're too old to be so childish," she hurled, earning a giggle from Reign.

Smoothing hair to one side, Reign glanced down the hall. "Is Dad up?"

Vivian gave a nod. "Yes, go on in."

Reign went to her parents' room, giving the door a tap. "Dad, it's Reign."

"Come in," Matthew ordered.

Reign entered, immediately zoning in on her father, who was sitting halfway up in bed. "You comfortable like that?" she asked.

"I'm not comfortable in *any* position, so this will do for now," he grunted.

Reign walked over, planting a kiss on his forehead. She pulled up an accent chair, sitting down. "How was physical therapy today?"

"Nothing I couldn't handle."

"Good." She leaned back in the seat. "Maybe in a couple of weeks, you'll be able to walk without stiffness."

"*Hopefully*, because I'm tired of moving around like a damn sloth," Matthew grumbled.

"Yeah, maybe in a couple weeks you'll be *nicer*," Reign retorted, folding her arms. "And be grateful that your injury wasn't much more severe. That you didn't wind up in a *wheelchair*, all because you were being *hardheaded*."

Reign knew that her father was frustrated—she'd been sympathetic, but with everything on her mind, she just wasn't in the mood for his misguided frustration.

Matthew mumbled something incoherently.

Sucking her teeth, Reign glanced off to the side.

Matthew studied her, eyebrows raised. "Something bothering you?" her father asked.

Reign frowned; he'd caught her off guard. "Huh?"

"Is something bothering you?" he repeated. "It seems that I'm not the *only* one in this room with an attitude—yes, you have one," he added when Reign opened her mouth to protest.

Closing her mouth, Reign let out a deep sigh. Her father's perception was correct; something *was* bothering Reign—her strained relationship. Though she knew that the decision to take a break from Troy was needed, it didn't mean that she wasn't hurting. Up until now, she'd thought she was doing a good job at hiding it.

"It's nothing," she answered finally, glancing down at her hands. "Nothing that's worth *saying* anyway... Whenever I *do* say something, it just goes in one ear and out the other."

Matthew fixed his daughter with a stern gaze. "If saying what you want to say isn't going to change the situation at hand, then why would you even *want* to?" he asked. "Sounds like a waste of time and energy to me."

Reign glared up at him. Her father's tone wasn't comforting, in fact it held traces of annoyance. "So, in other words just shut my mouth and keep my feelings to myself," she concluded, agitation filling her voice.

Matthew let out a quick sigh. "Look Reign, I've told you before, wasting energy and dwelling on things does no good," he dug in. "Just suck it up and go about your day."

Reign shook her head, scoffing as she rose from her seat. "I have to go," she bit out.

Matthew followed her progress to the door. "Leaving already? You were supposed to keep me company." He sucked his teeth when she ignored him. "This is disappointing Reign."

Reign grabbed the door handle. "Suck it up, Dad." She punctuated her curt reply by shutting the door behind her.

Passing through the living room, Reign rushed by the couch

where her mother and sister still sat. "I'll see you two later," she threw out.

Vivian glanced up, vertical lines forming between her eyes. "Leaving already?"

Cynthia checked her watch. "Less than fifteen minutes. Dad has set a new record of driving people out of that room," she joked.

Reign jerked the front door open. "I have to finish packing."

"Do you need help moving next week?" Vivian asked at Reign's departing back.

Reign paused, looking back at her mother. "I have helpers for that, but you can help me unpack when I get everything in." That seemed to satisfy her mother, who just offered a smile and a nod. "I'll call you later," Reign promised, walking out of the house.

Sitting on the floor, Marcy grabbed an eggroll from Reign's takeout platter and took a bite, much to Reign's annoyance.

"Why do you *always* have to take my stuff?" Reign complained, closing her half-eaten platter of Chinese takeout.

"Because it's so easy," Marcy joked between chews. She laughed when Reign flipped her the finger.

Reign was spending yet another evening packing up her apartment. She was due to close on her new home in less than a week; it couldn't come fast enough.

In the middle of packing, she'd received a call from Marcy who much to Reign's shock, offered to come over to help. Not long after Marcy arrived, Reign realized that Marcy had *no* intentions of helping.

Marcy finished the last of her food, then handed the empty container to Reign who was en route to the kitchen. "You have anything to drink in there?" Marcy asked. "Not water or any of that healthy juice shit. I mean a *real* drink."

"I have wine," Reign belted out from the kitchen.

"Girl—make sure you get some *liquor* in your new house, or I'm not coming to visit."

Reign emerged from the kitchen, bottle of wine and cup in hand. "Girl shut up. You'll drink what I *have*."

Grabbing the cup from Reign's hand, Marcy sucked her teeth. "Do you have a *wine glass* at least?" she scoffed.

"They're *packed*, so take this plastic ass cup and leave me alone," Reign spat.

Marcy chuckled a bit. "So rude."

Reign grabbed a few glass trinkets from the coffee table, along with a roll of bubble wrap, then reclaimed her position on the floor in front of Marcy.

Adjusting her position on the floor, Marcy glanced at the grooves in the carpet. "*What* happened to your couch and loveseat again?"

"I drug those things to the garbage a week ago," Reign answered. "They were old, and I was tired of them." She shrugged, "I wanted brand-new furniture anyway."

Marcy just nodded as she poured the wine into her cup. She glanced at Reign. "No wine for you?"

Reign arranged the items next to her. "No," she replied, shaking her head. "I'm already tired and wine will just add to it. I have too much to get through."

Marcy glanced at the mess of boxes, plastic bins, and Reign's possessions around the small living room. "I should probably help, huh?"

"*Swore* that's what you came over here for," Reign blandly returned.

Marcy giggled, then gestured to her cup. "I'll help after I drink this." She took a sip. "We should go look at furniture together," she suggested. "*I* could use a few new things my*self*."

"I'll go with you, but I already have what I want picked out," Reign said, wrapping an item.

"Of *course* you do," Marcy muttered. A few minutes passed as she concentrated on finishing her drink. "So…" she began. "How are things with you and Troy?"

Reign kept her focus on the glass turquoise paperweight that she was wrapping. "I don't want to talk about Troy," she shot down, tone dry.

Marcy glowered. "What's up with you?"

Reign placed the wrapped item into a nearby box. "*Nothing,*

Marcy," she answered, tired.

"It has to be *something*," Marcy fussed, pointing. "You *never* want to talk about *anything* anymore."

Reign looked at Marcy, blinking slowly as the woman ranted on.

"Tonight *aside*, every time I've called to talk to you over the past few weeks, you either rush me off the phone, tune me out, or don't answer at *all*." Marcy hadn't intended on revealing her frustration over Reign's recent lack of communication, but having her attempt at girl talk rebuffed was sending her over the edge.

Reign fixed Marcy with an indifferent stare. Marcy had a point; Reign *had* been a bit distant with her. Between her father's recovery, falling out with Troy, and the home buying process, Reign just wasn't in the mood or headspace to deal with Marcy's constant need for attention. "Marcy, I realize that you're used to having access to my time whenever you want, however in case you haven't *noticed*...I have quite a bit going on," Reign drew out.

Marcy rolled her eyes.

"Now, I'm sorry that you feel a way, but everything can't be about *you* all the time."

Offended, Marcy jerked her head back. "I never said that it *had* to be." Nostrils flaring, her eyes blazed with contempt. "I get that you're stressed Reign, but it's no need to be *rude*."

Reign rubbed her eyes. She was too tired to argue. "Okay, Marcy," she sighed.

Marcy too sighed; the tension leaving her face. "But *back* to my initial question." She folded her legs in. "How are things with you and Troy? I mean, are you guys still *good*?"

Reign fixed Marcy with a stern stare. *Why the hell do you insist on asking me about his ass?* "Are things still good with you and *Chase*?" she flashed back.

Eyes widening slightly, Marcy looked away.

"Yeah, you neglected to tell me that you two broke up during the times when I *did* answer the phone." Reign's steely gaze remained steady.

Reign hadn't mentioned to Marcy that she knew of the break-up until now. She'd been waiting for Marcy to reveal the news herself. But it had been a month, and Marcy hadn't.

"You keep pressing me to talk about Troy, yet *you* keep your business to yourself." Reign added, agitated. "Does that seem fair?"

Marcy let out a huff. "Fine Rae. Yeah, Chase broke up with me."

"I *know* that," Reign drew the words out slowly.

"Who told you? *Ava*?" Marcy scoffed. "I'm sure she couldn't *wait* to broadcast that news."

Reign proceeded to wrap another item. "That's not important. What *is* important…" She sighed, her expression and tone softening, "is how you're feeling," she finished, sincere. "Are you okay?" Marcy may have worn on Reign's nerves a bit, but Marcy was still her friend and Reign cared about her wellbeing.

Marcy waved a dismissive hand. "Girl please, yes," she assured. "It wasn't like I was going to *marry* the man."

Reign raised an eyebrow. "So, you mean to tell me that you were with him for two years and you never *once* thought about marrying him?"

"Rae, you know I wasn't trying to be tied down like that," Marcy downplayed. "I just wanted to have fun. *Chase* was fun, we had some good times… He's sexy as hell and the sex was *amazing*—"

Reign put a hand up, cutting her off. "I don't need to hear all of that."

Marcy shook her head. "God, you're such a prude sometimes," she said. "Every time I mention sex, you get all weird."

"I'm *not*," Reign denied. "I just don't need to hear about what goes on in your bedroom. It's none of my business." She placed her wrapped item in the box. "Some parts of your relationship should be kept to yourself."

Marcy tilted her head. "You never *once* wanted to tell me how sex was with Troy?"

"*No*, Marcy," Reign answered, wrapping another item.

Marcy glanced up at the ceiling. "Okay fine, I get it. It *would*

be weird talking about Troy's bedroom game because I know him."
She tapped her finger to her chin. "But what about, let's say…your
first. You wanna talk about *him*?"

Reign focused on wrapping, not bothering to make eye contact with Marcy.

Puzzled, Marcy squinted. "Hmm, I don't think you ever mentioned who your first *was*." She looked at Reign. "It wasn't *Troy*, was it?"

"No, it wasn't Troy," Reign quickly spat out, tone low.

"Oh." Marcy fixed Reign with an intense stare, full of intrigue.
"Did it happen in *college*? If so, who? Do *I know* the guy?"

"Change the subject, please," Reign dismissed.

Marcy shrugged. "Very well." Grabbing the wine bottle, she
refilled her cup. With one long sip, she finished nearly half of it.
After a moment, she tapped her nails on the plastic side. "You want
to hear a secret?"

"It's not about *sex*, is it?" Reign asked, stretching her neck
from side to side.

"No." Marcy looked down at the contents lingering in her cup.
"Well it—" Taking a deep breath, Marcy set the cup on the floor.
"Okay so…I'm seeing someone new," she revealed.

Reign's eyebrows shot up. "Oh wow, really?"

Marcy nodded, enthused. "Yes, and he is *everything* honey,"
she boasted. "Good looks, he's got money, and he *spoils* me with it—
you know my type."

Reign gave a slow nod, "I'm glad that you found someone who
makes you happy."

Marcy grinned. "Thanks girl, he does." Her gaze lingered on
Reign, pondering whether she should say anything more. "Can I tell
you something *else*? …And have it not leave this room?"

Reign adjusted her position on the floor. "Sure."

Marcy placed her hands together as she gathered her words.
"So…the guy that I'm seeing now? …I've *been* seeing."

Reign squinted slightly. "What do you mean, you've *been* seeing?" she questioned. "You mean for the past *month*?"

Marcy bit her bottom lip. "No—I mean that… I was seeing *this* guy, *while* I was…seeing Chase."

Reign gasped out loud, her eyes widened. "What the fuck?!"

Marcy put her hands up. "Now Reign, I know that Chase is your friend, but you *can't* tell him—"

"Marcy—I'm *not* going to tell him, but I'm going to tell *you* that you're dead wrong," Reign chided, upset. "Come on, you were *cheating* on him?"

"I *always* used protection." Marcy's pitiful defense was met with brief silence.

Reign looked at her as if she were crazy. "Yeah, 'cause that makes the situation *so* much better," she drawled, sarcastic.

Marcy lowered her head, shaking it, before looking back at Reign. "You're judging me."

"I'm not—" Reign let out a huff. "I *am*, that's *triflin'*," she condemned. "And this has nothing to do with the fact that I know Chase, this is triflin' in *any* situation."

"Well, it is what it is," Marcy dismissed, throwing her hands up.

Reign fixed Marcy with an intense stare. "How long?" The disdain was heavy in her voice.

Closing her eyes, Marcy ran a hand along the back of her neck. "A year and a half," she answered, reluctant. When she opened her eyes, she was met with Reign's wide-eyed stare.

"*Wow* Marcy," Reign ground out.

"Look— It's not like it was *planned*."

"Not *one* of the excuses that you've given have been valid," Reign argued; Marcy rolled her eyes. "If you started seeing this *new* guy *six months* into your relationship with Chase, why didn't you just break *up* with Chase?" Reign hurled. "Clearly your *everything* was *elsewhere*, why would you stay and *cheat*?"

"Everything isn't as cut and dry as you'd *like* it to be Reign," Marcy bristled. "Some shit is just complicated."

"Bullshit," Reign threw back.

Marcy gave a hard shrug. "What? Are you going to stop being

my friend now?" she hissed. "Is Miss Perfect going to write me off because I've been a bad girl?"

Livid, Reign slammed her hand on the floor. "Don't do that, don't flip this shit around on me." She shook her head, eyeing Marcy in disgust. "Chase is a good man. He *cared* about you—he didn't deserve that shit."

Marcy folded her arms, glancing away, "Look, I did what I did, and I *do* feel bad." Her tone was lackluster. "Despite everything, I cared for Chase too... I still *do* actually, but I can't change what happened and I don't even know if I would *want* to... I'm happy with who I'm with now and I plan on making it last."

Appalled, Reign scoffed. "Did this *new* guy know that you were in a relationship all that time?"

Marcy nodded. "Yup, and he was totally fine with it." A hint of smugness crossed her face. "He had his *own* shit going on, so..."

"Wow," Reign repeated. "You really think that this new relationship is going to last, based off of how it was *built*?"

"It will, because I'll make *sure* that it does." Eyeing the bare ring finger on her left hand, Marcy's lips curved upward. "I might even be persuaded to change my 'no marriage' mindset for this man."

Reign rolled her eyes. "Well, good luck with that."

"I know you don't mean it, but I'll take it," Marcy replied. After a moment, she held her hand out. "Here, let me help you finish."

Reign reluctantly handed the bubble wrap to Marcy. *I can't believe she really did that.* The woman had done some questionable things in the past, but Reign had never imagined that she'd stoop this low.

"I know you're disappointed in me right now," Marcy began, cutting into Reign's thoughts. "But know that I love you and you're not allowed to stop being my friend."

Reign didn't respond, opting instead to glance off to the side.

"Did you hear me?" Marcy pressed, staring intently.

"I heard you," Reign muttered, still focused on the wall beside her.

Marcy gave a slight nod and began wrapping a glass figurine.

Chapter Thirteen

"AND THAT IS THE LAST of the paperwork." Kris smiled, gathering up the stacks of signed documents. She retrieved a set of keys from the table and handed them to Reign. "You are now a homeowner."

Reign clutched the cool metal in her hand, beaming. Closing day was upon her; she'd entered the real estate office nearly two hours ago, and was now leaving with her brand-new house keys and a sense of accomplishment. Both excited and grateful, Reign hugged Kris. "Thank you *so* much, for *everything*."

"You're more than welcome," Kris gushed. "It's been a pleasure working with you."

Parting from Kris, Reign gathered her belongings.

"If you need anything, just let me know. My phone is always on," Kris said as they exited the office.

Reign gave a nod, "I appreciate it." Hearing her phone ring, she grabbed it from her purse. Glancing at the ID, a blank look fell upon her face.

"I'll leave you to your call." Kris handed Reign a folder of housing documents. "Congratulations again."

Reign waved to Kris as she placed the phone to her ear. "Hello Troy," she answered.

"Are congratulations in order? Is it all done?" Troy asked, eager.

"Yes, it's done. I have the keys." Reign had told Troy about her closing date when he'd contacted her a few days ago. Until then, she hadn't heard from him. Not that she *expected* to, given how they'd left off.

"Wow." Troy let out a deep breath. "I umm... I know that things have been strained between us, but congratulations," he said, sincere. "You deserve to have everything that you want."

Reign tried not to, but she let a smile come through. "Thank you."

"When are you moving in?"

"Later today," she answered, heading for the building exit.

"Damn it," Troy muttered.

Reign's brow gathered. "What's wrong?"

"I wish I was able to help you move, but I'm driving down to Tucson to visit my mother this weekend. Leaving in about an hour."

Reign shrugged slightly. She didn't expect his help—she hadn't *asked* for it. "Don't worry about it, I have help," she said. "Enjoy your trip."

"Thank you." He cleared his throat. "If you need some tip money for the movers—"

Exiting the building, Reign tucked the folder under her arm. "I don't. I've got it, but thank you," she broke in.

Troy paused for a minute. "Can...can I come see you when I get back?" he asked finally.

Reign continued her hurried pace to her rental car. "I don't know if that's a good idea, Troy."

"Why *not?*"

"Because nothing has changed, and we'll just end up fighting again." She tried her best to remain calm. "I don't want to do that."

"We don't *have* to fight, Reign," Troy pressed. "Come on, I miss you and I want to work things out."

Unlocking the car door, Reign let out a quick sigh. "I—I can't do this with you now, I have to go," she quickly put out.

A deep sigh came through the line. "Rae..."

"*Yes*, Troy?" her tone was laced with agitation.

"No matter what...you know that I love you, right?"

Reign paused short of opening the car door. She stared out in front of her, sadness consuming her. "I can't remember the last time you said that to me," she said. "I mean...I *really can't* remember. It's been that long."

Troy sighed again. "I know... I regret a lot of shit that I've done…or *haven't* done when it comes to you. *Including* not saying 'I love you' enough."

Reign closed her eyes, briefly tilting her head to the sky. Her day had started out on a high; the last thing that she wanted to be reminded of, was her failing relationship. She regretted picking up at all. "Troy—I have to go."

"Can you just say it back to me please?"

"I *have* to *go*, Troy," she repeated, fighting to keep her building emotions at bay.

"Okay," he placated. "Can I at *least* call you later? To make sure you're settled?"

"If you want." Reign ended the call, not giving him a chance to say anything else. She looked down at the blank phone screen for a moment, shaking her head. Taking a deep breath, she tossed it into her bag and got in the car.

"Are there any boxes left in the truck?" Ava asked, setting a lamp on the living room floor.

Chase walked through the vestibule, cradling a large box in his arms. "Yeah, like three more," he answered, setting the heavy box down.

Reign stepped inside the house, carrying one herself.

Chase headed for her, lifting it from her hands. "I thought I told you to leave the heavy stuff to me."

"And *I* told *you* that I'm stronger than I look," Reign countered.

Chase chuckled a bit. "Not doubting it, but still, let me do the heavy lifting."

Reign put her hands up in surrender. "Okay then. I guess I'll start arranging some things." She folded her arms. "Is that okay with you?"

"Yes, smart ass," he threw back, amused. Reign snickered. "Where do you want this?"

Reign moved around to get a look at the label. "Master bedroom. Upstairs, second door on the left."

"You got it." Chase ambled toward the staircase. "Ava, *you* leave the heavy boxes alone too."

"Bro, you don't have to tell *me* twice," Ava hurled at his back.

Reign shook her head in amusement as she surveyed the cluttered living room. It had been a long day, but with Chase and Ava's help, everything was finally moved out of her old apartment and into her new home. She was sore, she was sweaty, and she'd broken a few nails, but Reign was happy.

"I can't thank you two enough for helping me today," Reign said to Ava, who was busy checking the boxes for labels.

Ava waved a dismissive hand, "Girl, you don't have to thank us, that's what friends are for."

"I get it, but I *am* thanking you and I'm buying you both dinner tonight, so don't argue," Reign insisted.

Chuckling, Ava threw her hands up in surrender. "I'll never argue about food, order away," she replied, earning a giggle from Reign.

Chase trotted down the stairs. "After I bring the boxes in, I'm going to take the moving truck back," he said. "Ava, can you follow me in my car? We can just ride back here afterwards."

Ava stretched. "Sure."

"*I* can follow you Chase, she can relax," Reign stepped in.

"Hush, we've got this." Ava pointed at Reign. "*You* relax, and order that food."

This time, Reign put *her* hands up. "Okay, okay, I'll back off."

As Chase headed back outside, the two women grabbed a few small boxes, carrying them upstairs to the master bathroom.

"You're going to have so much fun shopping for this place." Ava beamed, setting a box on the bathroom floor.

Reign smiled, setting her own box down. "Yeah," she agreed. "I actually started buying little decorative things *weeks* ago."

"That's not surprising, you always plan ahead." Ava shot Reign a knowing look, "You ordered furniture already, didn't you?"

Reign nodded emphatically, "My bedroom set will be here this weekend."

Ava laughed, "Yup, figured."

The women headed back downstairs as Chase was bringing in

the last box. "Truck is empty," he announced.

Reign smiled, but before she could respond, her phone rang. Retrieving it from her pocket, she answered. "Hey Mar."

"Boo! How's the move-in going?" Marcy belted into the line.

Reign rubbed the back of her neck. "Umm, pretty much finished moving everything in. Just putting stuff in the respective rooms now."

"That's great," Marcy paused for a moment. "Listen, I know things left off a bit weird with us last week after—"

"We're fine, Marcy," Reign interjected. Communication with Marcy over the past week had only consisted of a few texts here and there. Though she hadn't told Marcy, Reign was feeling a bit unsettled over Marcy's confession.

Marcy breathed a sigh of relief. "Good to hear. You mean the world to me, so—" she cleared her throat. "Anyway, I had *planned* on coming over this weekend to help you unpack but I twisted my ankle earlier."

Reign grimaced. "Oh damn, that sucks," she said, sympathetic. "Are you okay?"

"I'm fine, but I can't really walk on it, so I'm just going to stay in and keep my feet up for the next few days."

Reign walked into her kitchen, grabbing a take-out menu from the grey granite counter. "Okay, I understand," she replied. "Feel better."

"Oh, I will," Marcy assured. "Talk to you later."

"Later." Reign ended the call, shoving the phone back into her pocket. Scanning the Italian restaurant menu, she stood in the living room entryway. "You guys want anything in particular?"

"As long as I can chew it, I'm good," Ava replied.

Chase, wiping the sweat from his brow with his shirt, was too busy laughing to answer right away. "Ava, what the hell?" he got out finally.

Flustered by Chase's reply, Ava tossed her arms in the air. "What? I'm starving. I don't care as long as it's *food*."

Chase shook his head at her, then looked at Reign. "Whatever you get is fine," he said.

"That's basically the same thing that *I* said," Ava spat at her brother.

"Something is wrong with you," Chase shot back.

Over the next few hours, the moving truck had been returned and the trio had managed to get every labeled box into their designated areas. They were now sitting on the living room floor by the fireplace, enjoying their dinner.

Ava took a bite of garlic bread. "I don't know what it is about this area, but some of the best takeout places are around here," Ava said once her mouth wasn't full. "I need to move up here, for *that* purpose alone."

"You plan on buying a house too?" Reign asked, placing the top on her empty food container.

"Nope, I'm perfectly happy with my little condo," Ava replied.

Reign shot an amused look Ava's way. "Girl, there is nothing *little* about your condo."

"And I plan on *staying* there a long time," Ava chuckled. "I love my place."

Chase drank some of his bottled water. "Reign, now that you're moved in, you need to change your locks," he advised.

Ava gave an approving nod. "Good point."

Reign too nodded. "I'll do that." She let her ponytail down, running a hand through her hair. "I'll take a trip to the hardware store tomorrow."

"Chase can change them for you, he's good at that," Ava jumped in, patting Chase on the arm.

"I can," Chase agreed.

Reign smiled at him, "If you wouldn't mind."

"Of course. *I* was actually going to offer but—"

"You were taking too long," Ava ground out, flagging him.

Reign laughed, then made a move to stand from the floor.

"Shit," she winced, adjusting her pace.

Chase eyed her with concern. "You okay?"

Reign sucked in a quick breath. "My damn back. You were right, I shouldn't have lifted that big box." She grabbed her empty tray, taking it to the kitchen.

She discarded the container, then opened a box on her counter island. As she began removing and putting the kitchen items in place, Chase joined her.

He was content to watch her organize her new space, but when Reign grabbed her lower back, he had to say something. "How badly does it hurt?" he asked.

Reign turned, looking at him. "Huh?"

"Your back," Chase clarified, gesturing. "How badly does it hurt?"

"It's not that bad. I only get the twinge when I make a sudden move," she downplayed. "I'm okay, I'm going to schedule a massage for next week."

Chase nodded. He couldn't help but worry as he watched her rub the base of her spine. "Okay…just take care of yourself."

"I will," she promised, smiling.

Chase smiled back. "Oh," he said, after a moment. "I have a housewarming gift for you."

Reign didn't get to respond because he'd darted out of the kitchen. He walked out of the house entirely, coming back mere moments later holding a bag.

"Thank you." Reign beamed when he handed it to her.

"You're welcome." Chase grabbed his phone from his back pocket, then began scrolling.

Reign set the slim gold gift bag on the counter, then retrieved the item from inside; a smile crossed her face. "Ooh, nice," she said of the bottle of wine in her hand. Riesling—the type of wine *and* brand were her favorite.

He pointed to the bottle. "I know that *champagne* is usually the celebratory beverage of choice, but I also know you don't care for it, so I figured wine would do."

"You're right, I *don't*," she replied, impressed. "I appreciate the gift, that was thoughtful of you."

Chase looked bewildered; he pointed to the bottle once again. "Wait, you think *that's* your housewarming gift?"

Reign glanced at the wine, then back at him, equally perplexed. "*Isn't* it?"

Chase laughed. "No," he answered. "That was just something extra that I picked up for you earlier."

"Oh," Reign laughed, setting the bottle down. "Well, it would've been fine if it *were*."

"No, no, *this* is what I got you." He held his phone out for her to see.

Reign took the phone from his grasp, eyeing the screen. Her eyes widened. "You got me a *desk*?!" she shrieked, marveling at the white wood-stained executive desk plastered on the screen.

"Yeah." Chase couldn't help but blush at her reaction. "A chair too, but that's not in the picture." He shrugged slightly. "Figured you can't have one without the other."

Mouth agape, Reign put a hand to her chest. "Oh my God," she breathed.

It made Chase happy to see Reign excited about her gift; he'd put serious thought into what to get her. "I know how long you've been waiting to have your writing office, so I wanted to make sure that you have the basics."

Reign was floored. She'd told Chase way before she was even able to *look* at houses, that she wanted an in-home office. She couldn't believe that he'd remembered. She stared at the picture; the piece was absolutely beautiful. But after a moment, the smile on her face faded, disappointment taking its place. "Chase…I can't accept this."

Chase chuckled, "Yes, you *can*."

Reign looked at him. "No, this looks *really* expensive, you didn't have to—"

Chase put a hand up. "Listen," he cut in, tone soothing. Reign closed her mouth; she stared at him with wide, shimmering eyes.

"Don't worry about what it costs. I didn't do this for any sort of praise, and you don't owe me anything for it." He put his hand on his chest. "This is just a gift from one friend to another. Because I'm happy for you, I'm proud *of* you and you deserve it."

Reign glanced back at the phone screen, a smile reappearing on her face. Grateful, Reign moved in for a hug. "Thank you so much." She squeezed him. "You have no idea how much this means."

Chase squeezed her back. "You're welcome, I'm glad that you're happy."

"Happy?" She broke from the friendly embrace. "If I could do a backflip—I probably still *wouldn't*, but I'm more than happy, trust me."

Chase let out a laugh, placing a hand on her arm. "I'm glad." Realizing that his touch was lingering, he moved it. He cleared his throat. "It's scheduled to be delivered next week," he mentioned. "I was hoping for it to be here *sooner*, but the desk was on backorder and the delivery time is longer when you have it assembled beforehand—"

"Chase, it doesn't matter when it gets here, I'm happy either way," she cut in, sincere.

Chase let out a sigh of relief.

Reign handed Chase his phone, then retrieved the bottle of wine. "We might as well crack this open." She peered into the living room. "Ava, do you want some wine?"

"Is water wet?" Ava threw back.

As Reign erupted with laughter, Chase covered his face with his hand, shaking his head in the process. "I swear to God," he mumbled of Ava's response.

Reign found the glasses in their labelled box and set them on the counter. As she prepared to pour the wine, her phone rang. "I seem to be popular today," she chortled to herself. The humor left her face when she saw who the caller was. "What the hell?" she blurted out.

"What's wrong?" Chase asked, curious.

"I don't know, this is Troy's mother." Reign placed the phone to her ear. "Hi Ms. Donna," she hesitantly answered. She couldn't remember the last time they'd spoken to one another.

"Hello Reign." The woman's tone held a sense of urgency.

"Is everything okay?" Reign charged.

"I'm sure it is, but I'm just curious, is Troy with you?"

Reign frowned in confusion. "Umm, no ma'am, he's not." She scratched her head. "He's not there with *you*?"

"No, why would you think *that*?"

Reign jerked her head back at the question. "Because he *said* that he was going to visit you this weekend," she informed. "In fact, based on what he told me earlier, he should've been there by now."

"He never mentioned anything about visiting me this weekend, and he hasn't answered his phone all day."

What the hell? Reign was so confused. "Umm, like I said, he's not here with me, but I'm sure he's fine," she said, *despite* her confusion. "His phone probably died or something. He's always losing his charger."

"Perhaps," Donna grumbled. "That boy is always losing things that he *needs*."

Reign didn't say anything, her mind was racing.

"He really said that he was supposed to come visit?" Donna probed.

"I might've misheard," Reign quickly replied. "But listen, I have to go. If I hear from him, I'll tell him to call you, okay?"

"Okay."

"Okay." Reign hung up the phone, setting it on the counter. "What?" she quietly said to herself. *Did he lie? Why would he lie to me about going to his mother's house?* She ran her hands through her hair. *No, that's crazy, he'd have no reason to lie about that. Maybe something happened... What if something happened to him?* Worry began to set in.

"Reign, is everything okay?" Chase asked, cutting into her thoughts.

"Umm..." she didn't want to alarm Chase or Ava, especially when she didn't know anything for sure. "I umm, I have to swing by Troy's house really quick," she said.

"Okay." Chase folded his arms. "Is something wrong with him?"

"I just— I feel like I need to go check on him, that's all," Reign explained. As frustrated as she was with Troy, Reign couldn't bear the thought of something bad happening to him.

Chase nodded. "Okay," he repeated. "Let's go, I'll take you." Though Chase didn't like Troy, he was willing to check on him with her for *her* peace of mind.

"No, I can drive, it's cool," she protested. "I haven't had anything to drink yet."

"Rae, it's late, I'd feel better if I drove you," Chase insisted. "I'll drop Ava off, then we'll go to Troy's, okay?"

Reign nodded after a moment. "Okay."

As Chase retreated into the living room to gather his sister, Reign placed her hands on the countertop. Lowering her head, she exhaled deeply.

Though she was hesitant at first, Reign was relieved that Chase would be accompanying her. She had no idea the type of situation or emergency she could potentially face at Troy's house, nor any idea how she'd react to him being hurt in some way. If nothing else, Chase could get help, if she became too distraught to do so.

Closing her eyes, all she could picture was Troy lying hurt and alone. A heavy, sinking feeling descended upon her.

Please be okay.

Chapter Fourteen

PULLING IN FRONT OF TROY'S home, Chase turned the car off. Still buckled in, the two of them surveyed the house.

"Not one light on," Chase observed. He turned to Reign. "So, what do you think?"

"I don't know," Reign slowly drew out, scanning the area. Something caught her eye; she tilted her head. "Can you do me a favor and pull up a little bit?"

Without question, Chase restarted the car, inching it forward.

"Stop here," Reign commanded. As Chase did so, Reign focused on the side of Troy's house. "Hmm," she uttered.

Chase turned the car off. "What do you see?"

Reign squinted her eyes. "His car is here."

"Are you serious?"

Reign pointed out the yellow sports car parked in the opened, detached garage in the distance.

If Troy's mother calling about his whereabouts didn't worry Reign enough, seeing his car certainly did. *Maybe he was planning on surprising his mom with a visit. God, what if something really did happen to him?* Pulling out her cell phone, she called Troy.

Chase opened his mouth to speak, but Reign put a hand up, silencing him. The phone rang once, then went to voicemail. She jerked her head back, frowning slightly. "If your phone is dead, it goes straight to voicemail, right?" she asked Chase. "It doesn't ring once, *then* go?"

Chase shook his head. "No, if the phone is dead, it doesn't ring at all."

"Yeah, that's what I *thought*," she ground out. She dialed back;

129

this time, after the third ring, it picked up.

"Hey Reign, babe, what's up?" Troy answered. Surprise registered in his voice; he sounded like he was out of breath. "I wasn't expecting to hear from you."

Reign looked toward the house; a light turned on in the living room. She fought the urge to act on her anger. *This lying ass bastard.* "Well, you've been on my mind since we talked earlier, so I just figured I'd check on you now that I'm settled," she answered in her best nice voice, opposite the glare that was frozen on her face. "Wanted to make sure that you got to your mom's house okay."

"Oh yeah, I've been here for a few hours already."

Reign stifled an outburst to his blatant lie. "A few hours, huh?"

"Yeah, yeah, we umm—we're actually getting ready to play a board game now," Troy laughed nervously. "I just ran up from the basement with it. That's why I'm out of breath."

"I never mentioned your breathing, Troy," Reign said, her voice lowering an octave. The more Troy lied, the harder it was for Reign to maintain the "nice" in her voice.

"Oh—right," Troy sputtered. "Forget I said that then."

"Uh huh." Reign's eyes were still fixated on the house. The light turned back off. "Well, I'm glad you made it there. I'll talk to you later, okay?"

"Okay babe, thanks for checking on me," Troy replied. "I'll call you—"

Reign hung up, cutting Troy's words off. She stared out in front of her, seething. As far as Reign was concerned, their *break* was now permanent; this was the last straw.

Chase held his gaze on Reign. He could tell by the tightness in her jawline that her teeth were clenched. Her eyes had narrowed until they were almost slits, and she'd started rocking back and forth—she was furious. "Umm…Rae—"

"He told me he was driving to his mother's house this weekend… He lied to me." Reign scowled. "Why the fuck would he do that? There was no *reason* for him to do that. I didn't *ask* him where he was going, I didn't *ask* him to do anything *for* me. Why would he just *lie*?"

Chase looked on as Reign vented her frustration. He was livid and the frown on his face displayed it. "I don't know Rae," he carefully answered. "Some guys are just…" His jaw clenched, "complete and utter *garbage*." He was utterly disgusted with Troy and sick of his treatment of Reign, but he'd always kept his thoughts to himself. He'd never spoken negatively about Troy to Reign, out of respect for her relationship with him and his friendship with *her*. But if Troy were standing in front of him right then, Chase wouldn't hesitate to punch him in the face.

With haste, Reign dug into her purse, pulling out a set of keys. "I'll be right back."

"What are you about to do?" Chase asked as Reign made a move to get out of the car.

"I'm going to go *check* on him," Reign bit out. Chase gently grabbed hold of her arm, stopping her. "If you don't *get* off of me," she barked at him.

"Look, I don't think it's a good idea for you to go in there right now," Chase argued, unfazed by her angered reaction. "You don't know what you're going to walk into."

Reign snatched her arm from his grasp. "I *said* get off."

Chase jumped out of the car just as she stormed for the front door. He bolted in front of her, stopping her. Cautiously, he extended his arms forward.

"Get the fuck out of my way, Chase," she hissed as quietly as she could. She wanted to sneak up on Troy, not alert him by arguing.

"Reign, I know you're upset—" Chase tried to soothe, his voice almost a whisper.

"You have *no* idea. I'm *sick* of his shit," Reign fumed through clenched teeth. She moved around him.

Chase blocked her path. "Rae—at *least* let me stand by the door while you go in."

Reign was about to reply, when they both heard Chase's cell blare from the car. In his haste to stop her, he'd neglected to roll up his window.

Reign gestured her head in the car's direction. "You might want to get that."

"Shit." Chase took off for the car.

Seizing the opportunity, Reign approached Troy's door. Using her spare key, she unlocked it and pushed it open, then slammed it shut behind her.

"What the fuck?!" Troy hollered through the darkness.

Reign felt for the switch by the door and flicked it on. As bright light filled the room, Reign gasped at the scene before her.

Troy was standing by the couch, attempting to pull his sweatpants over his bare privates with haste. Laying on the couch, clutching a throw blanket to her naked body—was *Marcy*. She and Troy looked even more shocked than Reign.

Reign felt the air being sucked out of her; her blood ran cold as she stood there staring. Leaning back against the closed door, Reign took several labored breaths. She couldn't speak; she couldn't cry.

Troy secured his sweatpants, then put his hands out. "Reign." He took a careful step forward. "Babe—"

With tears spilling down her face, Marcy sat up. "My God, Reign," she sputtered. "I—we—"

Hearing them utter her name was all she could take. Snapping out of her daze, Reign grabbed the first thing that she could get her hands on—a table lamp—and hurled it directly at Troy. Hitting him square in his chest, it sent him stumbling to the floor.

With Troy temporarily incapacitated, Reign bolted for the couch. She jumped over the side of it, landing right on top of Marcy, and began wailing on her with her fists.

Marcy screamed at the top of her lungs, trying desperately to shield her face. Her attempts were in vain; she took punch after punch. "Reign stop it! Get off me!"

Troy stumbled to his feet, then darted over, grabbing Reign off of Marcy. Troy pulled his struggling girlfriend to an accent chair, forcing her down on it. He pinned her arms over her head to avoid another blow.

"Get the fuck off me!" Reign screamed, fighting to get free. Getting a leg loose, she kneed him in the groin.

Troy let out a yelp in pain, but kept her wrists in a firm grip.

Marcy stumbled from the couch. Keeping the cover close, her eyes darted around the room in search of her underwear. Face throbbing and wet, she wiped her hand across it; it came away covered in blood. She was sure her nose was bleeding, possibly even her lip.

Reign continued to scream and struggle as Troy held onto her. "You need to calm the fuck down!" Troy barked at her.

Finding her underwear, Marcy managed to get them on, even though she almost fell while doing so. "Troy, get off of her!"

"I'm trying to keep her from beating your ass!" Troy yelled back.

"Mom seriously, I *have to go*," Chase fussed into the phone. He'd gotten in his car, rolled the windows up, and had been trying to rush his mother off the line since.

"Yes, we'll discuss that later. Bye," he quickly threw out, ending the call. Chase let out a loud groan as he stepped out of the car. Screams were coming from inside Troy's house, sending him straight into panic mode. Chase ran up to the front entrance at top speed and busted through it, practically knocking the door off the hinges.

The first thing he saw was Troy pinning Reign to the chair. Fury in his eyes, Chase bolted over, pulling Troy off of her.

Marcy's eyes broadened. "Oh my God," she muttered in horror.

Chase pushed the stunned Troy, then followed up with a hard punch to his face, sending Troy crashing into a nearby end table and at last tumbling to the floor.

"Have you lost your fuckin' mind?!" Chase erupted, staring down at Troy. "You touch her again and I swear to God, I'll kill you."

Troy just laid on the floor, clutching his face and groaning.

Chase was so focused on Reign's well-being, that he didn't see Marcy standing off to a corner, holding a hand to her mouth. Instead, he tried to help Reign from the chair. "What happened?"

Reign smacked his hands away from her. "Don't touch me!"

she raged, pushing herself to her feet. She was so angry, she could hardly catch her breath.

"Reign what *happened?*" Chase repeated, this time louder. "Did he hit you?" When Reign ignored him, Chase, throwing caution to the wind, put his hands on her shoulders. "Reign, did Troy hit you?"

"Chase—" Marcy managed to get out.

"What?" Chase absentmindedly answered. Looking over to see who'd called him, his eyes widened when he saw her. "Marcy, what the—" he paused, focusing on her lack of clothing. He then looked down at Troy, who was still sprawled on the floor.

Chase glanced at Reign; she looked back at him.

Reign didn't say anything; she *couldn't*. But the pained expression on her face, paired with the tears that had begun to fill her eyes, alluded to what she had discovered.

Chase let out a heavy breath. "God," he managed to get out.

Troy finally managed to get to his feet. "Look man, I don't know what you think—"

Chase lost it. He charged for Troy and the two men fought.

Reign seized the opportunity to run straight for Marcy.

Marcy put her hands out as Reign charged at her. "Rae don't!" she belted out. Seeing Reign's fist coming straight for her face, Marcy tried to grab it.

Reign pushed Marcy's hand aside and delivered a punch, followed by an elbow to Marcy's face, sending her falling into the wall behind her.

Marcy slid down the wall, cradling her face, tears and blood spilling. "I'm so sorry!" she cried out. "I'm so sorry, Reign."

The tears that had filled Reign's eyes began to spill down her cheeks. She tried to control her labored breathing, but she couldn't get a handle on it. She felt like she wanted to pass out.

Putting her hands on her knees, Reign tried her best to steady her breaths. Marcy was her friend; someone who despite her faults, Reign genuinely cared about. Marcy—whom not more than a few hours ago told Reign that she meant the world to her—had performed the ultimate act of betrayal. An apology wasn't going to fix it; *nothing* could *ever* fix it. Their friendship was dead, and in that moment, Reign wanted *her* dead too.

Fury consuming her, Reign bolted up right. Just as she got ready to jump on the injured Marcy, Chase grabbed Reign around her waist, pulling her back.

"Let me go!" she screamed, trying to pry his hands off of her.

"No, we're leaving!" Chase had beat up on Troy enough. He'd had to force himself to stop, or he could've easily killed him. If *he* was angry, Reign's anger was *ten times* worse; he knew that she wouldn't have let up on Marcy. He had to get her out of there.

"Get the fuck off me Chase!"

"I *said* we're leaving." Chase picked Reign up.

"How could you do this to me?!" Reign hurled at Troy and Marcy as she was being carried away. She managed to grab a vase from a nearby shelf and threw it, sending it shattering on the wall next to Marcy. "After *everything*, how could you do this shit to me?!"

Chase held Reign secure in his arms as he carried her out of the house.

Bruised and bloodied, Troy managed to scoot his back against a table. Placing his head in his hands, he squeezed his eyes shut, forcing the tears from them.

Marcy, both hands over her face, covered in blood and shards of glass, cried hysterically.

Reaching his car, Chase put Reign on her feet. As soon as he did, she tried to run back for the door. He caught her around her waist and pulled her back in his arms. "No, no, it's not worth it."

Reign pushed his hands off her. "*Please* let me go back in there," she begged, angry.

"No, I won't." Chase reached for her arm. "You're going to kill someone."

She smacked his hand away as she tried to get around him. "So be it."

He grabbed Reign from behind, holding on as she fought him. "*No* Reign."

Furious, Reign struggled as long as she could, but Chase's strength outmatched hers. Resolved and exhausted, she stopped, secure in Chase's arms. The anger had drained from her; her eyes went blank. As much as she wanted to scream, and cry out…she couldn't. She'd gone numb.

When Chase loosened his grip, Reign jerked out of his grasp and took off walking down the dark street.

Chase went after her. "Where are you going?" he asked, moving in front of her.

Reign didn't answer, she just turned and began walking in the opposite direction.

He moved in front of her again, worried about her mental state. She looked dazed; she shouldn't be alone. When Reign tried to make another turn, he put his hands on her shoulders.

"Get in the car please," he pleaded.

Reign shook her head. "I have to go," she muttered.

"We'll go, just get in the car," Chase urged.

"Leave me *alone*, Chase." Reign knocked his hands down, then started walking again.

Chase put his hands on his head. "Shit." He regretted bringing her at all. He wished that he could've talked her out of coming, or at least *tried*. "Reign, I know you're hurt," he belted out.

She stopped walking, but didn't turn around.

Chase took a careful step toward her. "I know…I *understand*." His tone was caring. "I know you want to be alone right now, but I *can't* let you walk out here by yourself… I can't, and I *won't*." He took another step. "I'll walk *with* you. I'll walk with you all night if I have to."

Reign turned around, looking at him, but didn't speak.

Chase took yet another step, putting a hand out. "Do you want me to walk with you?"

She stared at him. Then after a moment, she slowly shook her head.

"Okay." Chase put his hand down. "Then can you please just get in the car?" he begged. "I'll take you anywhere you want. Just please get in."

Reign stood there for a long moment. She took a deep breath, fighting back the tears. "Take me home," she finally managed to get out.

Chase quickly nodded. "Of course."

He walked alongside her back to his car in silence. He was afraid to speak, unsure of how she'd react. Chase didn't want to upset her; he just wanted to get her home safely. He opened the car door for her, and once he made sure she was secure, got into the driver's side.

Turning the car on, he glanced at Reign; she was staring out in front of her, not saying anything, barely even blinking. He let out a deep sigh, then pulled off.

Chapter Fifteen

VIVIAN WAS STIRRING SAUTÉED VEGGIES around in a pan with more force than necessary, mumbling to herself, when Cynthia checked in with her again.

"I unpacked as much as I could. I just don't know where she wants everything," her youngest daughter said.

Removing the lid from a pot of rice, Vivian let out a long sigh. "Just make sure that everything's organized. When she's up to it, she'll put everything where it needs to go."

Vivian and Cynthia had already made plans to help Reign unpack her house that weekend. What they didn't expect was the news of what had transpired between Marcy and Troy.

Cynthia had received a text message from her sister late Friday evening, giving a short but straight to the point message about what had happened. She'd waited until her mother was awake the following morning to share it. Early Saturday, the two women had driven to Reign's house, electing to spend the night. Now Sunday, they'd done most of the unpacking themselves, while Reign had confined herself to her bedroom.

Vivian glanced at Cynthia. "Cyn, grab some plates out of the cabinet please?"

"Sure." Cynthia did as she was asked. She even grabbed some drinking glasses, setting them all on the island countertop.

"You think she'll eat today?" Cynthia asked, unstacking the plates.

"She *better*," Vivian fussed. "I'll make *sure* of it, even if I have to force feed her." An overwhelming sense of sorrow took over; she put a hand over her face and broke down crying.

Cynthia pouted. "Aww, Mommy."

Vivian sniffled, "I can't believe this. I can*not* believe this." She snatched a paper towel from the holder, dabbing her eyes. "I can't believe they did that to her... My poor baby."

Cynthia put a hand on her mother's shoulder, giving it a rub. "I know." It wasn't shocking to see her mother so distraught over what had happened to Reign. Their mother had always been emotional, especially when it came to her children.

Vivian pulled a pan of baked chicken from the oven. "She's always been good to them. That boy never deserved her. *Never.*" Anger consuming her, she practically slammed the pan on the stovetop. "And that—Marcy—*she* didn't deserve Reign *either.*"

"Mom, I'm telling you now, if I see Marcy again, I'm going to *drag* her," Cynthia fumed. "Troy, I'll run over with my friend's car or something."

Vivian regarded her daughter with a stern look. "Cynthia, you will *not* jeopardize your future over either one of those evil people." She turned the oven off, followed by the gas burners. "Karma will deal with them."

Cynthia rolled her eyes. "Karma takes too long," she grumbled.

Staring at the prepared food in front of her, Vivian shook her head. "I can't even imagine—" She sighed. "Reign's just been up in that room...suffering alone."

"You know how she is Mom," Cynthia sighed. "She holds everything in; that's how she deals with things."

"That isn't healthy," Vivian stressed. "No, she has to let it *out*. She has to *talk*." She wiped the forming tears from her eyes, then grabbed a fork, fluffing the rice.

Cynthia looked at her. "I understand," she said. "But Mom can...can you not get tears in the rice?"

Vivian shot Cynthia a glare. It wasn't the time to try to be funny. "Cynthia, get away from me," she hissed through clenched teeth.

Cynthia quickly backed up. "Yes ma'am."

Sitting on her chaise lounge, Reign reached over, turning her floor lamp on. Though the light illuminating the room was soft, she had to blink several times to adjust her eyes. She'd been sitting in the dark for hours.

Since Chase had dropped her off Friday night, Reign had confined herself to her home. The master bedroom had been her solace all weekend. Aside from Saturday morning when she'd let her mother and sister into the house, and that afternoon when she'd let the furniture delivery people into her room to set up her bedroom furniture, she hadn't interacted with anyone. Lucky for her, her room had an adjoining bathroom, so she didn't have to leave at all.

Reign barely slept. She hadn't cried, she refused to answer any phone calls— She'd just been moving about in a semi catatonic state.

She slowly surveyed her room, eyeing the furniture. The queen-sized four poster bed, dresser, nightstands, bench—all things she had carefully picked out, was excited to purchase—she couldn't enjoy. She couldn't enjoy *anything*.

Reign looked at the notebook resting on her nightstand, staring it down. She hadn't written a word since returning home. She was so consumed with pain and grief, she could barely form a complete thought, let alone a sentence to write.

Hearing a tap on her door, Reign glanced at it, taking a deep breath. She wasn't in the mood for whomever was on the other side. Yet Reign knew that if she didn't answer, they would just keep coming back until she did.

"It's open," she softly called. Reign watched her mother and sister walk in. A tray holding a plate of food and two glasses, one of juice and the other of water, was secure in her mother's hands.

"Hey sis, Mom made dinner," Cynthia announced, gesturing to the food.

Reign looked at the tray; the food certainly smelled good, but she didn't have an appetite. "Thanks, but I'm not hungry," she replied, monotone.

Vivian adjusted the tray in her hands. "Just eat a little bit."

"I'm not hungry, Mom," Reign maintained.

Vivian let out a huff. She understood that her daughter was hurting—she hurt *for* her. But she wasn't going to stand by while Reign refused to take care of herself. "Reign, you *have* to eat something," she pressed. "You didn't eat all day yesterday *or* today. This isn't okay."

Reign rolled her eyes and pinched the bridge of her nose as her mother ranted on.

"Now I *know* you're upset, but I'm not going to let you sit up in this room and starve yourself—"

The more her mother barked at her, the more Reign felt herself about to snap. She rubbed her face with her hand. "Mom, stop. Just stop—" she pleaded through her mother's scolding.

Vivian refused to let up. "No, I *won't* stop it! I'm not leaving here until—"

"Stop it, stop it! Leave me alone! Leave me the hell alone!" Reign screamed.

Vivian gasped. Tears filled her eyes; her bottom lip quivered. Upset, and with the tray still in her hands, she marched out of the room.

Reign felt horrible; she'd made her mother cry when she was only trying to help. "Mom, wait—"

Cynthia closed the door. "She'll be okay, sis."

Reign rubbed her face with her hands, then ran them through her hair, exhaling deeply.

Cynthia took a seat on Reign's bed, facing her.

"I didn't mean to yell at her," Reign said.

"I know," Cynthia placated. "*She* knows. You know how she is, she'll be crying one minute then baking cookies the next."

Reign wanted to chuckle, but couldn't. "Yeah," was all that she could say.

Cynthia stared at Reign for a moment, trying to figure out what to say next. Her sister was looking off to the side, silent. "So… do you want to talk about it?" she began after a moment.

"Talk about how stupid I am? No, not really," Reign ground out.

Cynthia tilted her head. "You're *not* stupid."

"Yeah, I am." Reign folded her arms across her stomach. "I should've—" She took a deep breath. "It doesn't even matter. I don't want to talk about it."

"I understand but…I think that you *should* talk about it though." Cynthia leaned forward. "I mean like…talk about how you're feeling."

Reign glared at her. "*I don't,*" she bit out. "*Talking* about my *feelings* won't change the fact that I was stabbed in the fuckin' back."

"I know Rae, I—"

"Then what are you *asking* me for?"

Cynthia glanced down at her hands. Though Reign had lost her temper a few times, she rarely lost it with *her*. Seeing Reign this upset was unnerving. "I just… I know that you tend to suppress stuff and I guess I get *why*. But this *isn't* something that you should force down." She looked up at her older sister. "You have to *deal* with it."

Reign released a quick sigh of frustration. "I *am* dealing with it."

Cynthia sighed. "I just—"

"What? You want me to cry? Is that what you want?" Reign snapped. Cynthia rubbed her face with her hand. "Well, I'm not *going* to. I don't *need* to. I'm *fine.*"

"You are *not* fine," Cynthia snapped back, fixing Reign with a stern gaze. "And you're not *supposed* to be fine!"

Reign rolled her eyes, looking away.

"*God* Rae, this is not the time to be like *Dad's* stubborn ass," Cynthia argued. "This is not a 'don't let it get to you' moment. Your *boyfriend* and your *friend* were sleeping around behind your *back*. They treated you like shit and you didn't deserve it. You have a *right* to be angry, you have a *right* to be hurt, you have a *right* to scream, you have a *right* to cry— Just do whatever you need to do to get it out." Cynthia's tone was angry, but it was also pleading. "You don't have to be so damn strong all the time. It's *okay* to *feel* shit."

The more Cynthia talked, the more Reign felt her emotions coming to a head. She let out a sigh as she felt tears building behind her eyes. "Can… Can you tell Mom to come back so I can apologize to her?" she softly asked.

Cynthia felt like crying herself; she hated that her sister was going through this. She couldn't tell if she'd gotten through to Reign, but she knew that pushing at her wouldn't help. She stood from the bed. "Sure, I'll go get her."

Reign wiped the wetness from her eyes with the sleeve of her shirt as Cynthia left the room. Within a few moments, Vivian walked in. Reign watched as her mother sat next to her on the chaise.

"Mom, I'm sorry for snapping at you," Reign apologized, sincere.

Vivian tilted her head. "I know baby," she said. "It's okay."

Reign just nodded. She frowned when her mother stared at her, silent.

Without warning, Vivian put her arms around Reign, attempting to pull her in for a hug.

Reign moved her arms away. "No, I'm good." When her mother put her arms back, Reign once again gently moved them down. She even tried to move away from her, but her mother was insistent.

Reign tried to put space between them. "Mom, seriously, not right now." The more that her mother pulled on her, the more she felt herself losing control of everything she was trying to ignore.

"Just come here." Vivian wrapped her arms around Reign again. And still her daughter persisted.

"Just stop, please," Reign begged, voice cracking.

Ignoring her daughter's pleas, Vivian pulled her close once more. This time, Reign collapsed into her arms and burst into tears.

Vivian just held her, rubbing Reign's back as she cried hysterically. Vivian knew that her eldest daughter hated crying and rarely did, but it was something that Reign *needed* to do.

"It's okay baby, let it all out," Vivian soothed, as Reign bawled. "I know it hurts right now, but I promise you that things will get better." She slowly began rocking her daughter. "I promise you, baby."

Ava jumped out of her car, darting up to her brother's door. She knocked several times. When he didn't answer, she reached into her purse for her spare key. Unlocking the door, she bolted in. "Chase!" she called.

Chase walked into the living room, eyeing her skeptically. "Is there a reason why you let yourself into my house?"

"Yes, you didn't answer the door," Ava answered.

"You didn't give me the *chance*." Though Chase was annoyed, his tone was calm.

Ava waved a dismissive hand, "Well, I'm in here now so…" Calming herself, she gave him a once over. Though he *looked* perfectly fine physically, she could tell by the sadness in his eyes that he wasn't. Ava approached, giving him a hug; one that he returned. "I'm so sorry," she said, giving his back a rub.

"Thanks… I'm okay," he replied as they parted.

Ava gave a nod, smoothing a few curly tendrils back into her high ponytail. She remembered the fury that she'd felt when Chase had called her Saturday morning to tell her what had happened. Though she'd honored his wishes not to come to his house over the weekend, it was Monday after work and she refused to honor that wish any longer. She had to lay eyes on her big brother.

"I can't believe—that shit was low, even for *her*," Ava spat of Marcy, upset. "And *Troy*, I can't even— They *both* deserve to burn in hell."

"Yeah," Chase slowly nodded in agreement. Leaning his back against the wall, he sighed deeply. "Out of all the things I imagined would happen when we got to that house… I never imagined *that*."

Ava shook her head, disgusted. "How long has that been going *on*?"

Chase grabbed the phone from his pocket. "According to these text messages that Marcy sent me yesterday…a few months."

"So, she was cheating on *you* with her *friend's man* for several months," Ava scoffed. "I want to beat that bitch's ass Chase, I swear to God."

"She's not worth it," Chase shot down. "Not even a little bit."

144

Ava rolled her eyes, then frowned. "Wait a minute, why the hell is she texting you?" she zoned in. "She's got some damn nerve."

"I don't know, I just started getting all of these 'I'm sorry' messages from her yesterday." A bitter look crossed his face. "She started trying to explain herself, like I give a damn."

"I hope you blocked her ass."

"Her number is definitely blocked now." Chase glanced back towards his room. "I went back and checked my security footage, to make sure she wasn't fucking him in my damn house while I was away." He started getting angry all over again at the mere thought.

Shaking her head, Ava folded her arms. "Triflin' bitch—*both* of them," she huffed.

Chase sighed again. "I know that Marcy and I have been broken up for a month now, and I've been *over* her, but to find out that she was *cheating* on me…" He shook his head, glancing down at the floor. "I'm not going to lie, that shit stings."

"I know. Nobody deserves to be cheated on… *You* definitely didn't deserve that," Ava soothed. "You were good to her, and her gold-digging ass *never* deserved it."

Chase shrugged, "Yeah." He looked back at Ava. "Have you spoken to Reign?"

Ava lowered her eyes. "She…she hasn't been answering my phone calls, but I *did* see her at work today."

Chase frowned. "Wait, she went to *work?*" He thought that she would've taken a mental day; *he* surely did.

Ava nodded. "You know how she is." She directed her somber gaze downward. "But even though she was trying to act like nothing happened—I'm pretty sure that I caught her in her office in the middle of a cry… I know that she's devastated."

Chase closed his eyes. He knew how *he* was feeling; he could only imagine how Reign was holding up. "Damn," he muttered.

Ava's eyes shot back up. "You haven't spoken to her?"

Chase shook his head. "I don't think she'd want to talk to me."

Ava tilted her head. "Why do you think that?"

"I don't know, I guess I'm too close to the situation," he tried to explain. "She doesn't need the reminder."

"Chase, I love you, but you sound crazy," Ava said. "*You* didn't betray her."

"I know, but—"

"Do you *want* to talk to her?"

"Of *course* I do," he assured.

"Then call her," Ava urged. "Or better yet, go *see* her. You're like practically around the corner from her."

"Right," Chase sighed yet again.

Ava patted his arm. "Did you eat today?"

"A little something."

"Well that's not good enough. I'm about to channel Mom and make a big dinner." Ava made her way to the kitchen. "*Attempt* to anyway."

Chase pinched the bridge of his nose. "Ava, don't burn down my kitchen please."

She glanced back at him. "I'll try not to."

Chapter Sixteen

REIGN DELIVERED SEVERAL KICKS TO the punching bag, before working on her punches. She'd gone to the gym after work in hopes of alleviating some stress. But the more she hit and kicked the heavy bag, the angrier she became. She was now an hour and a half into her workout, and she'd worked every muscle that she had. Finally, she decided to stop, afraid of hurting herself if she didn't call it.

Grabbing her water bottle and towel from a bench, she headed for the locker room.

Retrieving her gym bag from her locker, she tossed the bottle and towel inside. As she began to remove the wraps from her hands, she noticed the bruise on her knuckle—a reminder of her fight with Marcy a week ago.

She was so focused on unwrapping her hands, that the locker room door opening and closing went unnoticed. Finally looking up, Reign locked eyes with Marcy standing by the door. Reign scowled; it took everything she had not to lunge at her.

Marcy's eyes shifted under Reign's fiery gaze. She began shifting her weight from one foot to the other. Even from her distance, Reign could tell that the makeup Marcy had applied didn't do a good job of concealing her black eye, swollen nose, or bruised cheek.

"I umm…I saw you working out from the window…and then saw you walk back *here* so I—" Marcy cleared her throat. "I just felt like I needed to talk to you."

Reign didn't say anything, though she secretly cursed the building's design team for making the front windows so large. Reign tossed her wraps in her bag, zipping it with haste; she needed to get out of there.

Marcy carefully took a step forward. "Reign, can we *please* just talk?"

Reign tried to ignore her as she slung the bag's handle on her shoulder, but Marcy kept moving closer, until she was standing in front of her.

Reign went to move around her, but Marcy, desperate to stop her, grabbed Reign's arm. Dropping her bag, Reign snatched away from Marcy. In one swift motion, she grabbed the startled Marcy by the neck and pushed her back into the lockers. Face to face, holding her in place, Reign gave Marcy's neck a squeeze.

"What?! What the *fuck* do you have to talk about?!" Reign erupted.

Marcy clutched Reign's hand, gasping for air.

Reign wanted to squeeze until the life was drained from Marcy, but that would ultimately land her in jail; Marcy wasn't worth that. Reign let her go, retrieving her bag from the floor. "Stay the fuck away from me," she warned.

Marcy, still clutching her neck with one hand, pushed herself away from the locker. "I'm sorry okay!" she bellowed at Reign's departing back.

Reign spun around. "No, you're not," she sneered.

Marcy removed her hand from her neck, placing it to her chest. "I *am*— Rae I— *We* never meant to hurt you."

Reign stared at Marcy in disbelief. "You never meant to hurt me?" Fury filled her eyes. "You never meant to hurt me?!"

Marcy flinched at the bass in Reign's voice.

"Are you fuckin' joking?!"

Marcy looked at the floor.

"You've been sleeping with Troy for over a fuckin' year!" she screamed, causing Marcy to flinch again. "It *was him* right?" Reign's head tilted. "The *man* you were so goddamn sprung over? The one you sat in my *face* and bragged about? The one you cheated on *your* boyfriend with?"

Marcy let out a deep breath as she tried to gather her words.

"Yes— Reign, I—"

"You've been smiling in my goddamn face, pretending to be my friend, and all this time you were stabbing me in the fuckin' back."

"You *are* my friend, I care about you," Marcy vowed, desperation in her voice. "I *love* you. I—I'm sorry. I never wanted you to find out this way—"

"*Please* bitch. I see right through that bullshit apology," Reign fumed. "You can choke on it like I'm sure you do Troy's sorry ass *dick*."

Marcy's mouth fell open at the nasty retort. She scoffed, and all traces of remorse vanished from her face. "You know what? You don't have to worry about what happens with his dick anymore because it's mine now. *All* mine."

Reign smirked. "I knew it. It was only a matter of time before the *real* you showed up," she said. "You've *always* been fake. I should've seen it sooner."

Marcy folded her arms. "I was real enough to take your *man*."

Reign narrowed her eyes. "Congratulations on your fuckin' prize," she shot back, turning to walk out.

Angry, Marcy stepped forward. "I saw him first you know!"

Reign stopped, spinning around to face her.

"When we were at that club that night, I saw him first," Marcy remembered. "*I* was talking to him, *I* was planning on going *home* with him that night, and *would* have, but then he looked past me and saw *you*..." Marcy scowled as the memory flooded back. "Sitting there at the bar nursing your little glass of *wine*, not talking to anybody, looking *completely* uninterested—" She eyed Reign up and down. "Everybody *always* notices *you*. It's been that way since college."

"Marcy, spare me this bullshit." Reign had had enough of Marcy's tirade. "You're so *delusional*. The only person who paid *that* close attention to me was *you*," she bristled. "Maybe if you would've put *half* the energy that you used focusing on *me* and everything that *I* was doing, into your *own* life, you wouldn't be the pathetic bitch that you are *now*."

Marcy clenched her jaw.

Reign shook her head. "It's *clear* now exactly how jealous you've been all this time."

"Yeah, you know what, I *was* jealous of you, so the fuck *what?*" Marcy finally admitted.

"And that was *your* problem, not *mine*," Reign argued. "That didn't give you the right to *take* from me."

"I could never take from you what couldn't be *taken*." Marcy's tone was dripping with venom. "Troy was supposed to be mine in the first place and now he *is*. *I* know how to make him happy, how to *keep* him happy." She pointed to herself, "*I* fulfilled his needs because you no longer *could*."

Reign stood there, seething.

"You're a complicated, closed off bitch Reign, and you *wonder* why he didn't want to spend time with you anymore," Marcy dug in. "*Who* do you think he was spending that time *with?*" A smug look crossed her face. "Funny, I didn't *need* you to tell me how he was in bed, because I already knew."

Reign let out an angry chuckle. "You think you can brag about *sex with him* to *me?*" she sniped. "You forget I know what he *can't* do. So, enjoy faking those orgasms."

"Oh, I have *plenty* to enjoy." Marcy boasted. "I enjoy the money he gives me, the rent he pays, the bags and shoes he buys me and the trips he takes me on…including that trip to Sedona that *your* stupid ass *backed out* of."

Reign's jaw tightened as her frown grew deeper. The more that came to light, the more stupid she felt. From Troy and Marcy disappearing at the same time, to their interactions with each other at group outings: Marcy fishing for compliments from Troy, Marcy constantly trying to get information from Reign on the status of her relationship, her bragging about things purchased for her or money given to her by "her man", but made no mention of Chase's name.

Furious, Reign took a step in Marcy's direction.

The smug look fled Marcy's face, replaced by nervousness. She took a step back.

Fighting the urge to attack, Reign stood there, her shaking fists balled at her sides. *Walk away Reign*, she told herself. Even though she really didn't want to.

Reign stormed out of the locker room, slamming the door behind her.

Reign exited the gym with haste, making her way towards the parking lot walking as fast as she could.

"Reign," Troy called.

She spun around. "Are you *fuckin'* kidding me?" she barked, eyeing him with fury. Just what she needed, to face both Marcy *and* Troy within minutes of each other.

Troy rubbed the bruise on his cheek. He had yet to fully heal from his beatdown as well. He took a step forward. "I know Marcy went in there to—"

"I swear to God, if you come any closer," Reign warned.

Troy stopped. "Okay, but can you just give me a minute to—"

"To what? *Explain*?!" Reign exploded. "*Explain what*? That you were sleeping with me *and* her for over a *year*? It's bad enough that you cheated, but with *her* of all people?" Her breathing became labored. "Not *only* did you hurt me, you *embarrassed* me, you *fuckin'* bastard!"

Troy looked down at the ground in shame.

"All this time you made me feel like it was *me*, like *I* was the problem," she ranted. "Like *I* was being unreasonable. Like *I* was *wrong* for questioning why things had changed between us." She adjusted the bag on her shoulder. "You *begged* me not to break up with you. *Begged* me not to throw away *six years* and all this time you were—" She shook her head in disgust. "If you didn't want me anymore, you should've just let me *go*, Troy."

"This wasn't something that was *planned*, Rae," Troy tried to explain. "I *wanted* to be with you, but you and I were in a bad place—"

Reign's hand shot up, halting his excuses. "You know what, fuck you Troy! *You* put us in a bad place!"

Troy sighed.

"I've only ever reacted based on how *you* were *treating* me," she fumed. "*You* did this."

Troy closed his eyes. It hit him then just how badly he'd hurt Reign. "Despite everything...the last thing I ever wanted to do was hurt you," he said, remorseful.

She shook her head as she tried to keep herself from tearing up. "I can't do this," Reign choked out. "Both of you stay the fuck away from me." She punctuated her warning by walking off.

"I still love you Reign...always will," Troy called after her.

Ignoring him, Reign continued her hurried pace to the parking lot.

Grabbing several picture frames from a table, Reign walked to a shelf in her living room, arranging the pictures of her family. She grabbed a few decorative items, including a house plant and added them to the shelf as well.

After being in her house for nearly two weeks, Reign had finally gotten the motivation to decorate. She hadn't heard from Marcy nor Troy since her encounter with them at the gym a week ago, and she hoped she never would again. As far as she was concerned, they were both dead to her.

A knock at her door put a pause on her work. Reign glanced over at it. She wasn't expecting company; she hadn't had any since her mother and sister had left the Sunday after the incident. Ava had been wanting to come over, but Reign refused to let her. She just wanted to be left alone.

Approaching the door, Reign peered out of the peephole. After a moment, she opened it.

Chase managed a small smile. Reign's face was void of any pleasantries. "Hi," he said.

Reign stepped out, closing the door behind her. "Hey," she replied, tone flat.

Chase took a deep breath; her demeanor was one of the reasons why he was nervous to drive over and knock on her door. He'd tried calling Reign over the past few days, but the calls went unanswered. He couldn't take it anymore; he had to check on her. "I umm, I wasn't planning on staying, I just wanted to check in on you," he explained.

Reign folded her arms. "Okay." Her tone hadn't changed. "I appreciate it."

Chase gave a nod. "Are...are you okay?"

She stared at him for a moment, then slowly shook her head.

Chase sighed. "Yeah, me either," he admitted. "It...it's a hard pill to swallow."

Reign slowly nodded. "Do you know that she was sleeping with him for a year and a half?" She and Marcy were no longer friends; Reign didn't care to keep that secret any longer.

Chase's eyes widened. He looked like the wind had been knocked out of him. "No—she told me it was a few months."

"Try *eighteen* months," Reign bit out.

Chase ran a hand over his hair. "Over half of our damn relationship," he grunted, looking down at the ground.

"Yup." Reign saw the hurt on his face. "You'd already been broken up when she told me. I *clearly* had no idea who it was with." She exhaled deeply. "Nevertheless, I should've told you... My loyalty shouldn't have been to *her*...I'm sorry."

"Don't be sorry," he said, eyes on the gravel under his sneakers. "I couldn't imagine being in your position... I don't blame you."

Reign glanced off to the side as a warm breeze blew past her. "Okay."

They stood in silence for a few moments. The moonlight and the lamp on Reign's front porch illuminated the space. Chase looked up at her. "I'm going to be going out of town tomorrow," he began. "I'll be gone for a few weeks."

Though Reign was full of emotion—hurt, disappointment, regret—her face lacked any of it. "Why are you telling me that?"

"Because I just felt like I needed to let you know why you won't see me for a while," he explained, sincere. "Didn't want you to think that I disappeared on you."

"Okay," she repeated.

Chase ran a hand over his hair again. "If it's okay...I'd like to call to check in on you from time to time."

"That's fine Chase, I appreciate it," she quickly said. "Good night."

"Good night." Chase turned to walk back to his car as Reign went to go back inside. He stopped before he made it that far, turning back around. "Reign," he called.

She looked at him, but didn't say anything.

"If *you* ever want to talk—if you need to vent, yell, cry...my phone is always on," he said. "You can call me anytime and I'll answer."

"Okay..." Looking into his sincere eyes, Reign softened. "You too."

"Thank you." Chase offered a slight wave. "Good night Reign."

"Night."

Chase watched her walk back inside. He waited until he heard the lock turn, then slowly made his way to his car.

Chapter Seventeen

"MOM, I'VE ALREADY TOLD YOU, you guys don't have to do anything big for my birthday," Reign spoke into her phone while typing on the laptop in her office.

"But darling, you're turning thirty-three," Vivian reminded.

"Yes, I know," Reign replied.

"And that is a milestone birthday."

Reign pinched the bridge of her nose. "Mom—*thirty* is a milestone birthday."

"Oh hush, *every* birthday is a milestone birthday, which means that you need a party," Vivian insisted.

Reign rolled her eyes, shaking her head. "No party, Mom." Her fingers flew across the keyboard. "Besides, I don't have enough friends to make a crowd."

Vivian chuckled a bit. "Stop it," she chided, amused. "Okay fine, no party. But would you be opposed to a nice family dinner?"

Reign smiled. "No, I'm not opposed to that."

"Okay great, I'll start preparing the menu." Vivian beamed at the idea.

Reign glanced at her watch. "Sounds good, but listen I have to go okay," she said. "I'll stop by after I get off."

"Child, go straight home, no need to check on us old folks."

Reign laughed, "If you wish. Love you."

"Love you too."

Reign ended the call, placing her phone on her desk. A knock on the door prompted her to look up from her work. "Come in."

Ava entered. "Hey, did you get the email that Dennis sent?"

"You mean the one with the new projects?" Reign asked. Ava

nodded. "I did, I was just about to assign them."

"Okay, good." Ava rubbed her hands together, grinning. "You're giving me the erotica manuscript, right?"

Reign shook her head, amusement on her face. "Don't I *always?*"

Ava pumped her fist in the air. "Yes."

"It's long too. The line edits *alone* will take you at *least* three weeks," Reign said. "I'm sure you'll be happy."

"Happy doesn't begin to describe," Ava joked. "I just hope it's good. My imagination could use some stimulation."

"Lord," Reign muttered.

Ava giggled, taking a seat. "How's the writing going?" her eyes lit with intrigue. "This is what? Your *second* ghostwriting project?"

"Yes, it is. It's going pretty well actually," Reign answered, smiling.

The past six months had been busy for Reign. She was fully settled into her home; she'd even purchased a brand-new car. The company had finally rolled out their ghostwriting services, which she had taken the reins on. Reign had already completed a full novel, and was beginning a second, while still supervising the editing department. She'd gone from thinking that she would be forever tormented by Marcy and Troy's betrayal, to hardly having them on her mind at all.

"The first client that I had, loved what I wrote for her so much that her agent recommended others to me." Reign brimmed with pride. "One of whom is somewhat of a celebrity."

Ava's mouth fell open in awe. "Ooh, can you tell me who it is?"

Reign chuckled, "No."

Putting her hands up, Ava let out a small laugh. "Fine, fair enough." She folded her arms. "See, I *told* you that you'd be good at this."

"I know, I know." Eyes on her screen, Reign's fingers moved along the keyboard. "Oh, and I know it was you who moved that manuscript to the public folder."

Ava's eyes widened. "Huh?" She certainly wasn't expecting to hear that.

Reign fixed Ava with a stern look, folding her arms on the

desk. "You heard me."

Ava let out a nervous laugh. "I have no idea what you're referring to."

Reign's expression had not waned. "Funny thing about documents—you can't see who read it last, but with just a few clicks of a mouse, you can find out who *saved* it last." She raised an eyebrow. "Guess whose name came up when I checked?"

Hiding her face behind her hand, Ava shook her head. *Damn it, Ava!* Meeting Reign's laser-like stare, Ava let out a sigh. "What made you check?"

"I saw that the original file was still in my folder, where I'd *left* it," Reign explained. "I knew I hadn't saved it *both* places, and thanks to the timestamp, I saw that the version in the public folder was saved *weeks* later, so...yeah."

Ava scratched her head. "How long have you known?"

"A while," Reign answered. "I was waiting on *you* to come clean."

"Okay, hear me out," Ava began, holding a hand up. "I only did it because I knew that *you wouldn't.*"

Reign tilted her head. "I'm waiting for the *good* excuse."

"Remember when my laptop was acting up and IT had to work on it, so you let me use yours while you were at lunch?" Ava stammered.

"Um hmm," Reign grunted.

"Well, while I was working, I happened to see your folder open, then saw the document title, so I *opened* it and skimmed the first few paragraphs... Then I emailed it to myself, and read it at home and I *loved* it, and..." Ava paused her rambles, sighing. "Am I in trouble?"

Reign narrowed her eyes. "No," she answered after a moment. "While I can *appreciate* what you did...don't do anything like that again, okay? I'm not a fan of things being done behind my back."

"I understand and I apologize," Ava said, sincere. "*Kind* of... because well, you're making all this extra money now, you're getting famous clients and you'll probably get promoted because you rock as a writer so... I'm *kind* of sorry."

Shaking her head, Reign couldn't help but offer a light chuckle, "Uh huh."

"But you're right, it won't happen again," Ava promised, earning a satisfied nod from Reign. Ava glanced at her watch. "Ooh, it's lunch time." She was more than happy to change the subject. "Do you want to go to the bistro up the street?"

Reign winced slightly. "Sorry, I can't. I actually already have plans for lunch."

"Oh *really*?" A slow smile crossed Ava's face. "Plans as in…a lunch *date*?"

Catching Ava's intrigued look, Reign rolled her eyes. "Stop it, it's nothing like that," she said. "You know I'm not interested in dating again anytime soon."

"I'm just asking—" A knock on the door interrupted her. Ava glanced back at it.

"Come in," Reign called.

The door opened. Ava was pleasantly surprised by the visitor—*Chase*, clad in a grey business suit. Grinning, Ava clapped her hands. "Okay *suit*," she blurted out.

Chase shook his head as Reign busted out laughing.

"Will you grow up?" Chase jeered to his sister.

Amusement twinkled in Ava's eyes. "I'm just saying, you show up here all dressed up, what's going on brother?"

"I had a business meeting today, cut it out." Chase finally looked at Reign, smiling bright. "Hi."

Reign smiled back, "Hi."

"Are you ready?" he asked her.

Reign grabbed her purse, standing from her seat. "Yes."

Ava looked back and forth between them. "Hold up Rae, so *he's* your lunch plans?"

Eyeing Ava, Reign let out a chuckle. "Do you have an issue with that?"

The grin on Ava's face was huge. "No, not at all."

Chase shot her a stern look. "Ava," he warned.

"What, I didn't say anything!" Ava belted out. "I'm just saying that I have no issue with two good friends going to lunch."

Reign raised an eyebrow at Ava; she was acting way too giddy. "Sis…how many lattes have you had today?"

"Three, but that's normal for me," Ava dismissed, waving a hand.

Reign giggled as Chase shook his head. "We should go Rae, we don't want to miss our reservation," he urged, gesturing to the door.

"Right," Reign agreed, crossing the room.

Ava gave Chase a thumbs up behind Reign's back; Chase gave her the signal to cut it out.

Ava flagged Chase with her hand; she had no plans on letting up. She knew that Chase and Reign had been talking. While Chase was away on his business trip for those three weeks, months ago, he and Reign had spoken multiple times a day. When he'd returned, they hadn't slowed down at all.

"So…are you *sure* this isn't a lunch *date*?" Ava teased.

Damn it, Ava! "We're not dating," Chase said as Reign shot a confused look Ava's way.

Ava squinted at her brother. "Um hmm."

"Can we leave now?" Reign asked Ava.

Ava gestured towards the door with glee. "Don't let me stop you."

Flustered by his sister's silly behavior, Chase rubbed his face with his hand. "Little sisters, I tell you," he grumbled, opening the door for Reign.

"I know how you feel, trust me," Reign sympathized.

"Sorry about that." Chase hoped that Ava's antics hadn't made Reign feel uncomfortable in any way.

Reign waved a dismissive hand. "Don't be, I know she's being silly," she assured as she left the office with him close behind.

The waiter approached Chase and Reign's table, setting their entrees in front of them. "Is there anything else that you need?" the man asked, polite.

Reign shook her head. "No, I'm fine, thank you."

"Same here, thanks," Chase added.

Once the man walked away, Chase held his hand out for Reign to take. She looked down at his open palm. "What?" she asked.

"Let's say grace."

A light chuckle escaped her. "Oh, yeah, right." Reign placed her hand in his.

He shook his head in amusement before bowing his head. Chase closed his eyes, saying a short prayer. Lifting his head, he released her hand from his grasp. "Been a while since you've prayed over your food, huh?" he teased, reaching for his glass of water.

Reign made a face. "No, I just haven't held anybody's hand to *do* it." She reached for her fork. "Been eating *alone* if you don't remember."

"Yeah well, that makes *two* of us," Chase replied. Though they had been communicating regularly, it had been a while since he'd *seen* Reign. He was pleasantly surprised when she had accepted his lunch invite. "Thank you for coming to lunch with me by the way," he said, cutting into his food.

"No problem, thanks for *asking* me." She cut into her own meal. "It's been a while since I've eaten lunch outside of my office."

Chase gazed at her. "You're welcome." He took another quick sip of his beverage as Reign took a bite of her meal. "You know I would've... I *wanted* to meet up with you *before* now but...I was giving you your space." He paused for a second. "Figured you needed it."

Reign took a sip of her beverage to help push the food that she'd just swallowed down. "I did," she confessed. "It was..." she sighed, "a *lot* trying to wrap my head around it all at first. I wasn't in a good place and wouldn't have been good company."

"I understand that." Chase empathized. "I'll admit that I was in a bit of a slump too, at first." He set his fork down. "Not about the fact that my relationship was over, because it was over before I found out what she'd been doing but just...*knowing* what she'd been doing—for as long as she *had*... It did a number on me."

Reign nodded slightly. "Felt like a gut punch...followed by a kick to the back of the neck and that's *after* you've been stabbed over and over with a rusty blade and had your heart ripped out and forced down your throat."

Chase stared at her, eyes wide. "Yeah, you *definitely* were meant to be a writer," he chortled. "Hell of an imagination."

"Oh that's nothing compared to what I imagine I'd do to them if I'd never have to face repercussions," Reign casually shrugged. "No, but in all seriousness...it hurt, a *lot*. But I can honestly say that I'm moving on...*trying* to at least."

Chase nodded. "That's good to hear..." He eyed her intently. "Good to *know* because...I worried about you." Leaning forward slightly, he placed a hand on the table. "Still *do*.... like you said, it was a lot."

Reign covered his hand with hers, giving it a light pat. "I appreciate it Chase, but you don't have to," she assured, sincere. "I'm fine... Really."

Chase let out a relieved sigh. "Okay."

Folding her arms to her chest, Reign stared at him, tilting her head. "And what about *you*?" Chase flashed an inquisitive look her way. "Should *I* be worrying about *you* still?" Reign finished. "Are *you* okay?"

"Oh, I'm good," he declared. "Nothing to worry about over here."

Reign offered a nod in return. "Okay."

It was the truth; despite his previous slump, Chase found himself to be quite content over these past six months. Much of which he attributed to *Reign*. Their growing friendship was a welcomed bright spot in his life, though it was unexpected. After he'd left her home that night, though she said that they could communicate, he hadn't expected her to answer his calls, let alone *call him*.

He remembered being on pins and needles every time he dialed her number; he *also* remembered the butterflies he felt when her name flashed across *his* screen. Their brief, occasional phone calls soon turned into *hours* long conversations. With Reign still lingering on his mind long after they'd hung up.

The pleasant thoughts consuming him, Chase found himself staring at Reign as she went back to her meal. Snapping out of it, he cleared his throat. "So," he began, picking his *own* fork up again. "Your birthday is coming up in a few weeks, huh?"

"Yeah, the big thirty-*three* according to my mother," she jeered.

"Do you have anything special planned?"

She shook her head. "No. At least nothing that I'm planning myself," she answered. "My mom is throwing me a family birthday dinner. I'm sure she's not too happy about that. I know that she wants to throw me a party."

"I don't blame her. You *deserve* a party."

"I mean, I get it but..." Reign shrugged again, then looked up at him. "You and Ava are welcome to come to my dinner."

"You sure?" he asked.

"Of *course*."

Chase grinned. "I'd *love* to come to your birthday dinner."

Reign smiled back. "Good."

Chapter Eighteen

REIGN ROLLED HER EYES WHILE waiting on the electronics worker to come from the back of the store. "This is ridiculous," she grunted, glancing at the smart watch on her wrist.

"Why do your parents want to exchange this smart TV?" Chase asked her.

Frazzled, Reign vigorously shook her head. "Because they can't figure out how to *use* it." She let out a quick, audible sigh. "I swear to God, for the past few days I've gotten ten thousand calls from my mother asking me what the buttons on the remote do, and *twenty* thousand calls from my father asking me what Wi-Fi is and why does he need a passcode for something that's in his house."

Chase tried not to laugh, but couldn't contain it.

Reign narrowed her eyes at him. "It's not funny." She put a hand on her head. "I love them, but they drive me up the wall."

"I guess it's a parent's job to pay us back for all of the times that we drove *them* crazy when we were kids," Chase reasoned, humored.

"Please, I was *never* this bad." Reign placed a hand on her hip. "My sister tried to help them, but they got on her nerves too, so she gave up and has been hiding out at her friend's house."

Chase shook his head in amusement.

Reign sighed, glancing at her watch once again. "Well, my stress level is at max," she commented on the reading from the watch screen, shaking her head. "Sorry for delaying our workout."

"Don't worry about it," Chase placated.

Reign had met up with Chase at her new gym for a session. After the previous ambush, Reign had decided to switch to one that was closer to her house.

Not even a minute after she'd arrived, she'd received a phone call from her mother asking her to pick up and exchange the smart television that Reign had purchased for them a few weeks ago.

Chase had offered to tag along to help her load and unload the sixty-five-inch television from her parents' home to the electronics store.

"You're a life saver, because my father actually thought that I was going to allow him to carry that thing," Reign said. "He *just* started being able to move around with minimal pain. The last thing he needs is to aggravate his back again."

Chase chuckled. "Yeah, he almost cussed *me* out for grabbing it."

"He needs to sit down and stop being so damn mean," Reign jeered. She glanced at the worker as he walked out of the back.

"I'm sorry Miss, but we currently don't have regular HD televisions," he informed. "Smart TVs are what's hot right now, so we have an influx of those here at this store."

"Do you know if another location has one?" Chase asked the worker.

Reign put her hand up. "It's fine Chase, we've spent enough time on this." She removed her wallet from her purse, retrieving a debit card. "I'll just take a refund," she told the employee.

The employee nodded, then began typing on the computer in front of him.

Once the transaction was complete, Reign and Chase made their way through the store. "You mind if we stop in the computer section?" Chase asked. "I need to get a new printer."

"No, I don't mind." She moseyed alongside him towards the shelves. "It's the *least* I can do."

While Chase examined several printers, searching for the right one, Reign browsed the computer section.

"Looking to get a new laptop?" he asked her, grabbing a printer that met his needs from a shelf.

Reign folded her arms. "No, the one that I have is good," she answered. "The laptop, the monitor and everything *else* I bought for my home office." She scanned the section once again with her eyes. "You know what I've always wanted though?"

"What's that?" Chase probed, as they made their way to the checkout section.

"A typewriter."

Chase shot a quizzical glance her way. "A *typewriter?*"

She laughed at his reaction. "Yes, a typewriter," she repeated. "An *antique* typewriter, specifically."

"For what?" Chase set the printer on the counter in front of the cashier.

She shrugged. "My grandmother had one," she explained. "She *refused* to get a computer, so that's what I'd write my stories on when I would go to her house."

Handing the cashier his card, Chase listened.

"It was this rustic turquoise color with off-white keys." She smiled at the fond memory. "One day, I accidentally broke the 'r' key. She couldn't find a replacement in the same color, so she got this pretty black glass key where the 'r' was pale pink. She called it her special 'Reign' key." Her smiled faded as another memory filled her. "When she died after I graduated college, I wanted that typewriter... I *asked* for it, but my aunt took it and gave it to my cousin... who sold it." She quickly shook the bitter thoughts from her head. "Anyway, after that, I wanted to get my *own* but—"

Chase grabbed his purchase from the counter. "What stopped you?"

Reign glanced at the ceiling as she thought. "I guess as time went on, it just didn't seem practical," she answered truthfully. "I mean, I'd only have it for memory's sake, but it's not like I can do my *work* on it." She adjusted her ponytail. "Before, I was saving every penny to buy my house and *now* I have a mortgage, a car note, and just spent a ton of money furnishing the place..."

"Nothing wrong with treating yourself, you know," Chase said as they headed for the exit.

Reign shook her head. "I'd rather treat myself to food. It's less money...sometimes."

Chase chuckled.

Ellie pulled a bunt cake from the oven, setting it on a trivet on the counter.

The sweet, familiar smell wafted up Ava's nose. "Is that your strawberry pound cake Mom?" she asked, pouring herself a glass of lemonade.

"It sure is." Ellie shot a quick glance Ava's way. "But it's not for you."

Ava paused mid-sip of her drink; her mouth gaped open. "Mother, I am hurt," she said, feigning offense.

Ellie flagged her with her hand. "It's for my book club meeting tomorrow."

"Very well," Ava relented. "Only because I respect book clubs...*speaking* of which, I just finished editing this book, and let me tell you—"

"Ava, if it's one of those nasty books that you're so into, I don't want to hear it."

Ava busted out laughing. "How do you know what I enjoy reading?"

"You think I never found those books you tried to hide in your room as a teenager?" Ellie scolded. "Just fast minded."

"Fast minded, but never *fast*," Ava chortled. "My body count is *quite* low."

Ava's love of reading had started early in her childhood. She'd read all sorts of books, but once she'd entered high school, she started reading more risqué titles. Once she and Reign had become friends, they frequented the library together, where they'd both racked up their reading count.

Ava laughed, "I remember this one time in eleventh grade, I was walking home from the library with Reign and decided to read a scene from one of those books out loud—"The memory tickled her. "Her face got so red—she was so done with me,"

Ellie shook her head. "You've always been silly, child," she said, earning another laugh from her daughter.

"I know," Ava agreed, sipping her drink.

Ellie glanced over at Chase, who was sitting at the kitchen table, eyeing his laptop intensely. "Son, what's got you concentrating so hard over there?"

Chase glanced up. "Just looking for something," he answered.

"Well even though your face has been stuck in that thing since you arrived, I'm glad that you're here for dinner," she smiled, fanning the steam away from her pound cake. "As a matter of fact, I'm glad that you seem so much *happier* nowadays...*especially* after that whole mess with that—"

"Not worth mentioning Mom, I'm over it," Chase cut in, stern.

Remorseful, Ellie raised her hands. "You're right, I apologize."

Ava sipped more of her drink. *Yeah, I know why he seems happier.* "Mom, did you know that Chase has been talking to Reign?" Ava brought up.

Chase frowned up at her. "You know, your constant reverting to teenaged behavior is worrisome. You should get that checked out," he ground out.

Ava just shrugged.

Ellie lightly smacked her daughter on the behind with a hand towel. "Stay out of your brother's business girl," she warned.

Ava gasped. "Says the woman who prides herself on staying in *our* business."

Ellie shot her daughter a stern look; Ava had certainly inherited her personality from *her*, while Chase was more laid back like his father.

Taking note of the seriousness on her mother's face, Ava decided to back off. "Okay fine." She leaned against the counter. "Anyway Chase, since I brought Rae up, am I riding with you to her birthday dinner next Friday, or do you want me to just meet you there?"

"You can ride with me," he offered, eyes locked back on the screen. "I'll pick you up."

Ava smacked the countertop with delight. "Great, so I can drink."

Chase chuckled, while his mother shook her head.

"Oh, can one of you find out what Reign's favorite type of cake is?" Ellie requested. "I'd like to bake her one."

Ava opened her mouth to speak, but was immediately cut off by Chase.

"Pineapple upside down cake." His eyes never left the screen. Not hearing a response, he glanced up; both his mother and sister were staring at him. "What?"

Amused, Ava threw her hands up. "I'm not saying a word."

Ellie smiled. "Pineapple upside down cake, it is."

Chapter Nineteen

AWAITING HER COFFEE AND PASTRY order at a small table, Reign was jotting down a few words in her notebook. After a hectic morning, she'd elected to take a small break from the office, venturing to her favorite café a few minutes from work.

Though she hadn't missed the midday rush, she didn't mind the extra wait because it gave her a moment to journal. She was so engrossed with what was pouring out of her on to the lined paper, she didn't hear her name being called. The second attempt to get her attention was successful. Closing her notebook and hooking her pen to the cover, Reign slung her purse over her shoulder and went to the counter.

"Sorry about that," Reign apologized to the young barista. "I space out sometimes."

The young lady giggled. "It's okay." She handed Reign her order. "Small caramel latte and coffee roll."

Reign offered a warm smile. "Thank you." Adjusting the items in her hands, she exited the café. Carefully, she sipped her drink as she made the five-minute walk back to work.

"What are you doing back here?" Ava charged, seeing Reign scurrying towards her office.

Reign stopped a few inches from Ava's cubicle, shooting a perplexed look her way. "I still *work* here, don't I?"

Ava giggled. "Yes, I know that silly. I mean, I thought that you were leaving early today."

Reign's bewildered look hadn't waned. "I never said that I *was*."

"Well, you *should've*," Ava threw back. "In fact, you should've just taken the entire day *off*. *Nobody* should work on their birthday."

Reign offered a nonchalant shrug; she had no issue working

on her birthday, though apparently, Ava *did*. "It's not that big of a deal," Reign said. "I can still celebrate my birthday after *five*."

Ava waved a dismissive hand. "Girl, if *I* were you, I would've taken off the entire *week*."

"Well, feel free to do that on *your* birthday," Reign chortled.

"Ooh, I sure will." Ava fluffed her natural curls with one hand. "Oh, and since you *insist* on staying the full day, instead of the team taking you to lunch on Monday, we're taking you *today*, so don't even *think* about arguing."

Reign laughed a little as the other editors poked their heads out of their cubicles, offering animated nods of agreement. "Aww, that's so sweet of you all," she gushed. "And I won't argue, I promise." She headed for her office door. "Let me know if you need me."

Reign entered her office, setting her items on her desk. She sat down to get back to work, when a knock sounded on the door. "That was quick," she chuckled to herself. "Come in."

Ava walked in, a box in her hands. "The mail room just dropped this off for you."

Reign eyed the box. "What is it?"

Ava stared blankly. "Yeah, I never told you, but I have X-ray vision and can see through boxes," she drawled.

Reign retrieved the box from Ava's hands, thinning her gaze in the process. "All of that sarcasm was unnecessary."

Ava smirked. "So was your *question*." She gestured to the package. "Now open it so I can see."

Reign sat the box on the desk, opening it. Eyeing an assortment of red and white flowers in a glass vase, she gasped. "Oh wow."

"Those are pretty," Ava gushed, as Reign removed the arrangement from the package. "I wonder who sent them."

Reign set the vase on her desk. "I have *no* idea." She searched for a card. "It's not like I have any prospects or secret admirers."

Grinning, Ava shrugged. "You just might."

Reign giggled, "Yeah, okay." Reaching back into the box, she pulled out a small white envelope. She opened it. "'Happy birthday,

Rae,'" she read aloud.

Ava folded her arms. "Okay, so it has to be from someone you *know* for them to call you by your nickname."

"Right," Reign agreed. She turned the card over, silently reading the message on the back.

Ava's eyebrows drew together as the pleasant look disappeared from Reign's face, replaced by a mask of anger.

Reign crumbled the card in her hand, tossing it into the nearby trash can. She then snatched the flowers out of the vase, snapping the stems in half before throwing them in the can, followed by the vase.

Ava stepped forward. "Rae what's wrong? Who are those from?"

Furious, Reign grabbed her purse and slung it over her shoulder. "You were right, I should've stayed home today," she ground out, moving around her desk. "I'm taking the rest of the day."

Ava followed her progress out of the office. "Okay luv, I'll see you later," she called after her.

Even though Reign was gone, Ava's curiosity had not dissipated. She moved the broken flowers aside to retrieve the crumbled note from the waste basket, straightening it out just enough to make it legible.

> *Rae,*
> *I know this won't mean anything,*
> *but I just wanted to wish you a happy birthday.*
> *-Troy.*

Ava shook her head in disgust. "Such a fuckin' bastard," she fumed, tearing up the card and throwing the pieces back in the trash.

Cynthia skipped to Reign's front door, cell phone in her hand. "Yes, I just got here...we should be there soon." Hanging up, she pocketed her phone.

She knocked, examining her nails while she waited. When Reign opened the door, Cynthia's arms shot up, as she let out a squeal of excitement. "Happy birthday my favorite, old, big sister!"

Reign narrowed her eyes at the goofy smile on her sister's face.

"Funny," she jeered. "But thank you."

Giggling, Cynthia threw her arms around Reign. "Give me hugs." Parting from the brief embrace, Cynthia gave her sister a on-ceover. "*Damn* you look cute, can I borrow that outfit?" she asked of Reign's form fitting, skinny legged black pants, and black long-sleeved surplice neckline dress top. She'd paired the look with stiletto pumps and rose gold jewelry. Her hair was styled in soft, flowy curls, and she'd added a bit more drama to her otherwise normal makeup routine.

"No, you *can't*," Reign shot down.

"Come on, I wanna see if my boobs look as good in that top as *yours* do." Cynthia put her hand close to Reign's chest.

Reign smacked her sister's hand away. "Stop it," she spat, earning a laugh from Cynthia. "What are you doing here anyway? I was actually on my way to Mom and Dad's for this dinner."

Cynthia grinned. "Oh I know, I'm here to drive you."

Reign fixed Cynthia with a blank stare. "Drive *who where?*"

"I'm driving you to Mom and Dad's for your birthday dinner."

Reign ran a hand over her flat stomach, then glanced over at the crookedly parked car in front of her house. "Whose car is that?"

"My friend's, now let's go," Cynthia urged, signaling for Reign to come on.

Reign's feet stayed planted. "I just don't want to get in that car with you."

Cynthia sucked her teeth. "Don't do that Rae, I'm a good driver."

"According to *whom?*" Reign challenged. "Not the traffic court judge who told you that if you run one more stop sign, he'll take your license."

"Whatever, I stop at every sign now, just get your purse and bring your butt on." Cynthia gestured to the car. "I promise I won't kill you."

Reign made a face at her, but decided that arguing was just going to prolong the torture. In all honesty, Reign didn't mind having a ride. She'd be able to enjoy a glass of wine or two.

"Fine Cyn," she relented, turning back inside to grab her purse.

Cynthia eyed the sparkling rose gold clutch as soon as Reign stepped back out of the house. "Ooh, can I hold *that*, at least?!"

"No, and stop yelling, I have neighbors." Reign locked her door.

"It's like eighty feet between these houses, they'll be all right," Cynthia dismissed, getting into the car.

Reign sat in the car, pulling her seatbelt on. She cut her eye at Cynthia as her sister started the car. "Put your damn seatbelt on."

Cynthia put a hand up. "Chill out, I was *gonna*." She quickly did as her sister said, then turned the music to a party station. She noticed the tight grip that Reign had on the car handle near the window. "Will you stop it?" She laughed, "*Relax* chica, you're going to have some fun tonight."

"Yeah, yeah," Reign muttered. She said a silent prayer as Cynthia pulled off.

Cynthia pulled in front of their parents' home, turning the car off.

Reign quickly snatched her seatbelt off. "I swear to God, I'm never getting into a car with you again," she fussed, pushing open the car door.

Stepping out of the car, Cynthia sucked her teeth. "That stupid jackrabbit came out of nowhere, I *had* to break hard."

"It was *nowhere near* us," Reign fussed, stomping up the pathway.

Cynthia tried her best to conceal a giggle as she jogged after Reign, but was unsuccessful. "I apologize."

Reign smoothed her hair with her hand, then knocked on the door. Cynthia appeared next to her and opened her mouth to speak, but Reign jerked her hand up. "Do *not* say anything to me right now."

Cynthia couldn't help but find her sister's anger with her amusing. "*Smile* at least," she urged.

Reign rolled her eyes as the door opened.

"Happy birthday!" Vivian bellowed, throwing her arms around Reign and squeezing her tight.

Reign hugged her back. "Thank you, Mom."

Vivian pulled back from their embrace and studied her daughter. Her brow furrowed in concern. "Why do you look so upset?" she asked.

Cynthia brushed pass them into the house, clearing her throat. "Mom, don't get me yelled at again," she quickly threw out behind her.

Reign shook her head at Cynthia's departing back. "I'm not upset. You know that my face looks like this at rest," she deflected.

Vivian giggled, then grabbed Reign's hand. "Come, dinner is ready and waiting."

As Reign was pulled into the house, she was greeted by a room full of people yelling, "Surprise!"

"What the hell?" Reign shrieked, holding a hand to her chest.

"Don't scare her to death, you know she's old," Cynthia joked from the crowd.

Vivian snapped her head in her direction. "Hush up, Cynthia."

"Happy birthday!" the guests followed up, excited.

As cheers and applause rang out, Reign eyed her mother sternly. "Mom—"

Vivian put a hand on Reign's arm, silencing her. "I know you said no party, but I'm the mother and I do what's best." She smiled, "Like I said, you deserve it."

Reign's face softened; she couldn't honestly be upset with her mother for doing something thoughtful for her.

Vivian gave Reign a kiss on her cheek. "Love you."

A small smile appeared across Reign's face. "Love you too," she said. "And thank you."

Smiling back, Vivian offered a nod, walking away to tend to the food.

Walking into the living room, Reign was immediately swarmed by people. Her father, sister, cousins, friends, even people from college whom she hadn't seen in *years*.

Reign beamed when Ava and Chase approached, accompanied by another woman.

Ava gave Reign a hug. "Don't be mad, your mother made me

call every friend we had from college," she told.

"It's okay," Reign assured, pleasant. "It's good to see everybody."

Grinning, Ava handed Reign a drink. "Here you go, birthday girl."

Reign eyed the clear liquid in the glass. She chuckled, "This doesn't look like wine."

"It's *not*, now drink up," Ava urged, dancing along to music that was playing in the background.

The other woman stood in front of Reign, tipping her liquor filled glass to Reign's. "Happy birthday," she said. "It's good to see you."

"Thank you, Sasha," Reign replied. "Likewise."

Sasha gave a nod, then gave Reign a once over. "I swear, you don't look a *day* over twenty."

"I don't know how I feel about that. I'm certainly not trying to relive my twenties," Reign quipped.

Giggling, Sasha gave Reign's arm a pat. "Girl, be *glad* for those good genes."

"She'd *better*," Ava chimed in, amusement in her voice. "Because *some* of our classmates look older than our *parents*."

Reign shook her head at Ava, amused. She then looked at Chase. "What did my mother make *you* do?"

Chase gave a nonchalant shrug. "Make a liquor store run." Reign lowered her head, shaking it briefly; he laughed slightly. "No, I *offered* to make the run. It wasn't a problem."

"Oh, *our* mother baked you a pineapple upside down cake," Ava slid in. "It's in the kitchen."

Reign's eyes lit up. "That was so sweet of her," she replied, grateful. "It's my favorite."

"She knew," Ava smiled.

Reign tilted her head, she chuckled slightly. "How did she know that?"

"*Chase* told her," Ava answered, giving her brother a nudge.

Tucking hair behind her ear, Reign's face flushed. "Chase, you remembered that?"

"Of *course* he did," Ava blurted out before Chase had a chance to respond. Chase took the drink that Ava was sipping on from her hand, making her laugh.

"You're right, I said I'd stop," Ava said.

Sasha looked around as she bobbed her head to the music. "It really *is* great to see you guys," she mentioned. She surveyed the room again, this time with concern masking her face.

"Something wrong?" Reign asked, raising an eyebrow.

"No nothing's wrong but—" Sasha looked to Reign. "We're missing somebody... Where's Marcy?"

Ava pinched the bridge of her nose, letting out a heavy sigh.

Chase shot Reign a glance, as Reign just stared at Sasha; her eyes narrowed.

"Jesus," Ava muttered. *Great, first those stupid flowers from Troy and now this heffa brings up Marcy.*

Ava wasn't surprised that Sasha had asked; the woman used to hang out with both Reign *and* Marcy in college. That didn't stop Ava from being annoyed with the question.

"I don't know where she is," Reign answered, tone becoming an octave lower. Nobody outside of her family and Ava and Chase knew everything that had transpired with Marcy. Reign was a private person; sharing something so hurtful and embarrassing with people she rarely spoke to anymore wasn't something that she was about to do. But she wasn't going to answer questions about her ex-friend either.

Sasha scratched her head. "Really, when was the last—"

Reign tensed.

"Sasha—I think the appetizers are ready. You should go get some," Ava broke in, agitation seeping through her voice.

Sasha glanced back toward the kitchen. "Ooh, I was waiting for those." She walked away from the trio, swirling the ice around in her drink.

Ava followed Sasha's departing figure with her eyes. "Let me go make sure she doesn't bother anybody else with that stupid ass question."

Reign exhaled deeply as Ava walked off.

Chase touched Reign's arm. "You okay?"

"Yeah," Reign replied, tone low. She put the glass in her hand to her lips, taking a quick sip. The strong liquid hit the back of her throat, and Reign coughed in shock. "Shit, she gave me straight vodka," she wheezed.

Chase shook his head and gently patted her back. "I don't know what her problem is," he jeered of his sister. When Reign's coughing ceased, he took the glass from her. "I'll get you some wine."

Reign patted her chest with her hand. "I think water will be better."

Reign stood outside on her parents' lit deck, enjoying the mild January night air. Though the area surrounding her was illuminated, the view in the distance was dark. Reign's eyes were fixated on the large, dark silhouettes out in front of her. The Arizona mountains, though intimidating at night, Reign found the view peaceful.

Chase stepped outside. "Your mother is looking for you," he said, sidling up next to her.

Reign glanced over at him. "I'll be in in a minute; I just needed some air." After several hours of eating, conversing, dancing and all the extra attention, Reign had decided to take a few moments to herself.

"Understandable." Chase shoved his hands into his pants pockets.

"I suddenly remembered why I've limited my communication with some of the people we went to school with," Reign jeered.

Chase laughed, "*That's* understandable *too*."

She joined him for just a moment. "No, let me stop," Reign said, laughter subsiding. "I'm enjoying myself."

"Good," he smiled, gazing at her.

She took a deep breath as a breeze brushed past her face. "I *needed* to have a good time, especially after what happened earlier."

A frown of concern fell upon Chase's face. "What happened earlier?"

Reign looked at him, almost as if she didn't want to say it. "I received some flowers at work today," she finally explained.

Chase chuckled, "What's wrong with *that*?"

"They were from *Troy*," she spat.

Any trace of amusement left Chase's face. "What?"

Reign slowly nodded, "Yup."

Chase shook his head. "He really has some nerve," he bit out.

"Yup," she repeated, disdain heavy in her voice.

Chase stared at her for a moment. "Stupid question coming," he prefaced. "How did that make you feel?"

"It pissed me *off*," Reign vented. "Like, what was the point in that? The relationship is *dead*, I can't stand his ass, what was the *point*?"

"I honestly don't know," Chase replied, calm. "But thinking from a guy's perspective, maybe he wanted to cross your mind in some way..." he put a hand up. "Trust me, it's irritating *me* just thinking about it, so I can *imagine* what you're thinking," he added when Reign frowned at him.

"Chase, the *only* thing that crossed my mind when I read that card was how much I wanted to snap his neck like I snapped those flowers." She crossed her arms. "He better leave me alone."

"I agree, he shouldn't be contacting you in any capacity." Chase's tone grew serious. "If he does it again, let me know, and I'll handle it."

"Don't waste your energy, he's not worth it."

"If he bothers you again, I'll waste all the energy that I *need* to," Chase vowed, drawing his words out slowly.

Reign smiled a bit. "I appreciate it." She turned her attention back to the view in the distance. "You ever look out at the mountains at night?" she asked, smoothly changing the subject.

"All the time," Chase answered, gazing in the distance. "I love it."

"They look so ominous, but beautiful at the same time." Her voice was full of awe.

Chase glanced at Reign, smiling to himself. One could say the same thing about Reign, he felt. When she wasn't smiling, or was intensely focused on something, she had the ability to look unapproachable—*mean* even—but she was stunningly beautiful. Even those threatened by her appearance, couldn't help but be in awe of her.

"I need to stop being afraid and go up there one of these days," she said, cutting into Chase's thoughts.

Chase's eyes widened in disbelief. "You've never been up to the mountains?"

Reign shook her head.

He folded his arms. "You're missing out," he said after a moment.

Reign shrugged slightly. "Maybe." She moved her hair behind her shoulder. "It wouldn't be the *first* thing I'm missing out on... I have *yet* to see snow."

Chase scratched his head, letting out a light chuckle. "Trust me, you're not missing much on the snow front." Reign had been born and raised in Arizona, as did he. But in his travels, both during his time in college and for work, he often saw more snow than he liked.

The back door opened, causing both Chase and Reign to turn around as Cynthia poked her head out.

"Umm Rae, were you planning on taking the rest of that pineapple cake home with you?" Cynthia asked.

Reign stared at Cynthia, who was desperately trying to avoid eye contact. Reign squinted. "You ate it, *didn't* you?"

Cynthia lowered her head but didn't say anything. The gesture alone gave Reign the answer.

"It was half a cake left in there when I came out here," Chase said, voice filled with amusement.

Cynthia jerked her head up. "Mind your business, Chase!"

Reign pinched the bridge of her nose, huffing loudly.

Chase laughed. "Little sisters," he said in an aside to Reign.

"God," Reign groaned.

Chapter Twenty

SITTING AT HIS WORK DESK in his home office, Chase adjusted his wireless earbuds as he sketched on the large sheet of trace paper. "How's that new book you're working on, coming along?" he asked into the line.

Reign left her own home office with her phone to her ear. "It's going well," she answered, heading down the steps. "I'm almost finished the first draft. It's a novella, so it's pretty short."

After working on his building sketches for some time that evening, Chase had decided to call Reign for their nightly "check-in" chat. Their evening conversations had become something that he looked forward to.

"Nice," Chase praised, sketching out a new floor. "Are you going to let me read it?"

"Sorry, but no." Reign's tone held a twinge of remorse. "I'm not allowed to let anyone read anything that I've ghostwritten before it's published; I'm under contract."

"I understand that." Chase sat back in his seat. "How does that make you feel?" he wondered. "Knowing that when people read these books that you've written, they won't know that it's actually *you* who wrote it?"

Reign adjusted a throw pillow on her couch. "I'm totally fine with it."

"Oh?"

"Yeah." She ran a hand along the back of her neck. "I like the fact that I can help bring people's ideas to life...so to speak." Her voice was filled with pride.

"Makes sense." Chase grinned. "Okay fine, I can't read the ghostwritten stories, but what about what you've actually written for *you?*"

Reign paused short of going into the kitchen, rolling her eyes to the ceiling. "Please, nobody wants to read a bunch of journal entries, and sorry poems."

Chase laughed a bit. "Anything that comes from *your* mind, I'm sure is *far* from sorry."

"Yeah well, you don't know about the horribly structured, shitty stories I wrote as a teenager," Reign threw back as she walked through the kitchen. Grabbing a container from a cabinet, she packed her leftover dinner away.

"Let's make a deal," Chase proposed. "You let me read one of your earlier poems or stories and *I'll* show *you* one of my early sketches."

Reign let out a laugh. "Oh come on, that's not fair, you've *always* been a good artist."

"Oh you haven't seen the shit that *I* drew as a teenager," he chuckled back.

"Yeah well—" She paused, glancing at the back door, frowning. "Hold on."

"What's—"

"Shhh, hold on, I think I hear something." Hearing another noise, this time louder, Reign stepped away from the door. "Yeah, I did hear something," she told him. "It's coming from the backyard."

Chase leaned forward in his seat, face masked with concern. "You heard *what?*"

"I don't know, it sounded like something was knocked over." Reign backed into the living room.

Chase jumped from his seat, pocketing his cell phone. "I'm on my way."

"What?"

Darting out of his office, Chase moved through the living room. "I'm on my way," he repeated, making no effort to mask the urgency in his voice. "Make sure your doors are locked and stay away from the windows, I'll be there in ten."

"Okay." Though Reign's voice was calm, she was nervous.

"I'll stay on the phone with you," Chase promised as he bolted out of the house. "But if you hear it again, hang up and call the police."

He jumped into his car and sped off.

Chase arrived at Reign's home in record time. He was sure he'd blown past a stop sign or two en route. Had he received a ticket, he wouldn't have cared. He jumped out of the car, adjusting his earbuds. "I'm here," he spoke into the line, voice low.

Reign, sitting by a wall in her living room with a butcher knife in hand, glanced at the back door. "Do you see anything?" she asked.

Chase slowly crept up Reign's driveway until he reached the side of her house. "I'm going into the backyard now," he whispered.

Holding a steady eye on the door, she released a deep breath. "Chase, *please* be careful."

"I've got this. You just stay put."

Chase peered around the corner into Reign's backyard, slowly scanning the area with his eyes. Not seeing anything, he quietly moved into the yard. Maneuvering around Reign's patio set, he examined his surroundings. He checked every inch, until he reached the other side of the yard.

"I don't see anything," Chase finally spoke. "Well, aside from the fact that one of your trashcans fell over—I'll pick it up."

Reign let out a sigh of relief. "Thank God." She stood from the floor, leaving the knife on the counter on her way. "I'm opening the door."

"Okay—" Chase stopped his progress. He heard a noise from the can's direction. "Hold up Reign, don't open the door," he urged.

Reign stopped, already gripping the handle. "What's wrong, what do you see?"

"I don't know, just stay inside," he urged, cautiously approaching.

Reign retrieved the knife from the counter, then posted by the door, waiting.

Chase stood in front of the can for a moment, then bent

down, peering inside.

"Do you see anything?" Reign asked him when he'd been quiet for too long.

Chase reached for the fallen lid. "No, it might've just been—" Something jumped out from behind the can, startling him. "Shit!" he bellowed, falling back onto the gravel.

Eyes widening in panic, Reign unlocked the door and snatched it open. "Chase, are you okay?"

Spotting the culprit at last, Chase stared in annoyance. "Yeah, I'm good," he huffed, picking himself up. He shook his head in their direction as he walked to Reign's door. Chase stood there, staring at Reign.

Reign stared back at him, curious and confused. "What happened?"

"I fell," he grunted.

She shook her head slightly, putting a hand up. "Why? What did you see?"

Chase kicked a pebble with his shoe. "A hare," he muttered after a moment.

Reign's face took on a blank expression. "A *what*?"

Chase ran a hand over the back of his neck, sighing in the process. "A hare," he repeated.

Reign's lips tightened as she fought the urge to giggle.

"A rabbit…a damn *bunny*," Chase further added.

Reign dissolved into laughter.

He shook his head. "A *bunny* just made me, a tall, grown ass, two-hundred-and-forty-pound man, fall on my ass."

Reign doubled over cackling at his words. Though she felt bad for Chase, it was still hilarious.

Chase couldn't help but chuckle. "That's okay, I deserve the laughter. I looked like a complete fool."

Reign touched his arm. "Aww, poor thing," she sympathized, giggles still in her voice. She gestured inside. "Come in."

Accepting the invite, Chase followed Reign inside.

Reign closed the door, locked it, then set the knife in her hand back on the counter.

Chase gestured to it. "Smart, grabbing the knife."

"Yeah, it would've been useful on the bunny," she teased.

A deep chuckle escaped him. "You got that."

Reign moved around to Chase's back, brushing the dirt from his white long-sleeved shirt. "I'm sorry, I don't mean to laugh," she said. "After all, you *did* come over here on my account."

Chase faced her. "It's no problem, I'd do it again."

Reign flashed a quick smile before putting her knife in the sink. "Did you eat dinner yet?"

"No, I kind of lost track of time while I was working and talking to you," he answered.

"Well, I made some stuffed salmon, broccoli and rice. You can go sit down and I'll heat you up some, if you want."

Chase smiled, grateful. "I'd appreciate that."

"Hold up," Reign called, halting his progress to the living room. He turned and looked at her. She grabbed a kitchen hand towel. "Turn around."

"Am I in trouble?" he chortled.

She giggled. "No silly, I'm making sure that all of the dirt is off of you," she explained, dusting the back of his shirt and jeans off again with the cloth. "Cream couches and all."

Chase nodded, "Gotcha."

As Chase headed into the living room, Reign began to prepare his plate. "Do you want water, juice, or wine?" she asked him.

Chase sat on the couch, brushing the front of his clothes off in the process. "I think I need wine after that ordeal," he quipped.

She laughed, "Wine it is."

While Reign warmed his food, Chase scanned the living room with his eyes; he smiled. This was the first time he'd been in Reign's house since she'd fully decorated it. It was bright, yet warm and inviting. He glanced at the cushy throw rug and large pillow on the floor near the fireplace. He didn't know for sure, but he was almost certain that it was one of Reign's favorite spots; she likely did most of her writing on that pillow, when she wasn't in her office that is.

Hearing her enter the living room, Chase glanced up, smiling. "Thank you, I appreciate it." He took the plate from her hands.

"You're welcome, it's the *least* that I can do." Reign removed a coaster from its holder, setting it on the coffee table, followed by a glass of white wine on top.

"Trust me, it was no problem," Chase assured.

Reign retreated to the kitchen to get her own glass of wine, while Chase began digging into his food. A moment later she returned, sitting on the couch beside him.

Chase didn't say a word as he devoured his meal while she quietly sipped on her wine.

Finishing, Chase let out a satisfied sigh. "That was so good."

She chuckled. "I would *hope so*, the way that you inhaled it just now."

"I have no shame when I'm eating." Chase wiped his mouth with a napkin. "*Especially* when it's good."

"Well, I'm glad that you liked it." She noticed that he went to get up, empty plate in hand. "You can just put it on the table. I'll get it later," she said.

Chase did as he was told, then grabbed his glass of wine, settling back against the cushions. "I'll tell you what," he began after a moment.

She fixed him with a curious gaze. "What?"

"I'm glad that your cooking has improved drastically. Because that noodle dish that you made in college was *bad*."

Reign's mouth fell open in shock, though amusement showed in her eyes. "You tasted it *one* time." She delivered a playful backhand to his arm. "And *that* was only because you happened to be visiting Ava on campus that weekend and I made it for her."

"That one time was all I needed to be scarred by it," he teased, giving his arm a rub.

Reign narrowed her eyes at him. "Oh *wow*."

He broke into laughter, "Sorry, but you had to be told."

She made a face at him. "Yeah well…it didn't taste that bad to *me* so shut up."

"Hey, at least *you* attempted to cook back in college," he said. "I can't count how much money I spent on pizza and wings back then… I wasn't a fan of the cafeteria food."

Reign giggled a bit. "The food at my school wasn't too bad. But when they were closed, and I was still hungry—noddle dish it was." She waved a dismissive hand. "Takeout money was spent on notebooks and ink pens, so…"

Chase chuckled. "Yeah, you clearing the notebook shelves doesn't surprise me," he said. "How many of them do you *have*, exactly?"

Reign looked at him. "A *lot*." She crinkled her nose when he laughed slightly. "Are you making fun of me, sir?"

Chase put a hand up. "Not at all." He smiled to himself as he glanced off to the side. "It's just funny how some things haven't changed no matter how much time has passed."

Reign took a sip of her wine, reflecting a bit. "Yeah," she agreed.

Chase was about to say something else, when something on the coffee table caught his attention. Leaning forward, his eyes zoned in on the framed photo. He pointed to it, smiling. "I remember that picture."

Reign peered at it. "*Do* you?"

"Yeah, especially because *I'm* the one who took it," he chortled, studying the picture of a teenaged Reign and Ava, standing outside of an ice cream shop. "That was the day that Ava had me drive you two around while you looked for prom dresses."

Reign laughed. "You were so mad at us that day." She lightly tapped his leg. "We dragged you from store to store, then she made you take us out to eat *and* get us ice cream."

Chase was amused as the memory flooded back to him. "I swear, my sister has always been bossy," he quipped.

"Yeah, but she always means well," Reign replied with fondness. She looked over at Chase. "So how mad *were* you when you found out you had to take me to prom?"

Chase eyed her back. "I wasn't mad."

Reign shot him a knowing look. "Come on now."

He chuckled, "What?"

"Chase you were a sophomore in *college*, all the way in *Georgia*, and you had to come home to escort your *little sister's friend* to her senior prom," Reign reminded. "I'm sure you weren't too happy."

"I honestly didn't have a problem with it," Chase assured, setting his glass back down. "And you weren't just Ava's friend, you were *mine too*... We were pretty close."

A smile crossed Reign's face. "Yeah, I know."

"I guess I should ask you, were *you* upset that you had to go with me instead of someone from your class?" he wondered.

"Please, no guy from my class wanted to ask the bookworm to prom. That's why my mom talked to your mom about you taking me." She tucked some of her hair behind her ear, then tapped her fingernails on her glass. "If anything, I was embarrassed at first because she made it seem like I was desperate for a date... I mean, I kind of *was*, but that's not the point."

Chase shook his head, amused.

"I was dead set on being the third wheel to Ava and her date," Reign added. "But Vivian said 'no, you will *not* take a prom picture by yourself' so...yeah."

Chase nodded slowly; his eyes were bright. "It was a good prom, better than my *own* actually."

Reign looked out in front of her. "Yeah, it was..." she let out a deep sigh. "I had a good time."

Chase was quiet for a moment as he pondered his next question. A seriousness fell over him. "So umm...did you ever tell anybody what happened *after* prom?" he asked.

Reign looked at him. She didn't respond, but she knew exactly what he was referring to.

"What happened between us?" he added, eyeing her intently.

Reign shook her head. "No."

"Really?" he tilted his head. "Nobody ever knew that I was your first?"

Reign turned away briefly as the full memory of her prom night flooded back to her.

Chase was right; Reign was just as much Chase's friend as she was Ava's. She and Chase had their own relationship, which she treasured. She didn't admit it to anyone then, but she'd been secretly excited that Chase was going to be escorting her to prom. She couldn't have asked for a better date. They'd laughed, danced, and partied the night away, before breaking off from the rest of the crowd and taking a long walk along the pond behind the hotel where their prom was held.

After talking for what seemed like forever, sharing their thoughts, hopes, and dreams, the pair had finally made it back to Reign's hotel room where Chase had escorted her inside. As they were saying their goodbyes, still on a high from their beautiful evening, Chase had kissed her, and Reign had eagerly kissed him back. It was her *first* kiss, and before she knew it, she was willingly experiencing *another* first.

However as beautiful as that evening was, nothing ever came of it. Chase had returned to college a few days later, and Reign had just chalked it up to a normal prom night experience. She'd returned her focus on graduating and starting her own tenure in college.

It had always been a fond memory for Reign, one that resurfaced from time to time. But it was also one that she'd kept to herself. "Who was I going to tell?" she finally asked, returning her focus to him. "Your *sister*? That would've been weird."

Chase nodded in agreement. "Good point." He blushed, "I still think about it, you know."

"Really?" she looked at him almost as if she didn't believe him.

"Of course." Noticing that her expression hadn't changed, Chase's brows gathered slightly. "You think I wouldn't?"

Reign shrugged.

"Come on Rae, I might not have been a virgin, but being with you that night *meant* something to me..." he said. "That night was special for me too."

"I didn't mean to insinuate that it wasn't," Reign replied, sincere. "I guess that's just my own—" She quickly shook her head, "Never mind."

Chase's face softened. "Say what's on your mind, Rae."

"It's nothing," she denied.

"Are you sure?"

She offered a quick nod. "Yes."

Chase offered a slow nod back. "Okay." He took a deep breath. "You don't know this, but...I had planned on asking you out...to *date* me," he revealed.

Reign's eyes widened. "Really?"

Chase nodded again. "The next day—well, honestly, I had been *wanting* to ask you out for a while, but never did... I didn't think you'd accept."

The disbelief hadn't left Reign's face. "Wait, *what?*"

"Yeah," Chase confirmed. "I actually had a crush on you from the day I met you."

"I honestly had no idea," Reign replied. "I just thought that you became friends with me because of Ava."

Chase shook his head slightly. "No, not at all."

"Oh," she breathed.

"Yeah, I mean, I figured before it wasn't the right time but after...after the night that we had—after we slept together, I felt if *any* time was the right time to ask you, it would've been *then*." He cleared his throat. "But the next day when I tried to talk to you...it seemed like nothing had changed between us."

Reign looked down at the wine glass in her hand. *That* part of the memory, she wasn't fond of. "Chase, I umm—"

"No, I'm not bringing that up to make you feel bad. It was a long time ago," Chase soothed, sensing her guilt. "It was just part of the memory, that's all."

"Yeah," she murmured, unable to look at him.

"Anyway, I just figured that what happened, happened in the heat of the moment, but you still only saw me as a friend, not someone you wanted as a *boyfriend*. So I just…I let that fantasy go and moved on." He glanced off to the side, sighing. "It was naïve of me to think dating while going to colleges in different states would've worked anyway," he shrugged. "So, it's just as well."

Reign looked at him, her mind racing a thousand miles a minute. "I'm sorry," was all that she could say.

Chase met her apologetic gaze. "Hey, if you didn't see me in that way, there's nothing to apologize for." He reached over, patting her hand. "You can't help what you don't feel, you know?"

"Right," she answered after a moment.

"I was just happy to still *be* your friend," he smiled at her.

Reign glanced away with a sigh, but didn't say anything.

Chase's smile faded after a moment as more memories flooded back. "Even though… We didn't talk as much while you were in college," he mentioned. "In fact, aside from the time when I came to see Ava, we didn't talk at *all*— We didn't start communicating again until I moved back here after finishing grad school."

Though Reign's eyes were set on the objects sitting atop a shelf across the room, she wasn't really seeing them. She wasn't focused on anything other than the intrusive thoughts pounding in her head. "I know," she quietly said.

Chase sat for a moment, joining Reign in silence. He hadn't expected the somber memory of the time when their friendship had stalled to come back to him. Or that it would *affect* him still. "Anyway, we're good *now*, and that's all that matters. No need to dwell on the past right?" he continued. When he didn't get a response, he glanced over at Reign; she had yet to make eye contact with him again. She looked deep in thought. "You okay?" he asked her.

Reign nodded, setting her glass down. "Uh hmm," she quickly put out. "I think I want to make some brownies. You want some brownies?"

Chase held a blank stare; that was out of nowhere. "Uh… sure," he replied, slightly amused.

"Okay." Jumping up from the couch, Reign grabbed his empty plate and scurried towards the kitchen, leaving Chase sitting there bewildered.

Chapter Twenty-One

AVA PULLED A LARGE PLASTIC bin from the top of her closet. "I'm thinking of getting a dog," she said to Reign, who was seated on the cream carpeted floor of Ava's walk-in.

Reign peered up at her as Ava set the bin down and joined her on the floor. "You don't *like* dogs," Reign replied.

Ava glanced up at the ceiling light fixture, tapping her finger to her chin. "I know, which is why it's weird that I'm thinking of getting one."

Reign frowned, more confused than ever. "Ava—*what?*"

Ava busted out laughing. "No, I'm joking." She paused for a second. "I *am* thinking of getting a cat though."

"Cats are good," Reign approved.

Ava removed the lid from the bin. "I'll probably get a kitten... That'll be the closest thing to a grandchild that my mom will get from me."

Reign chuckled.

"I'm going to dress it up and carry it around in a baby carrier, too." Ava joked, removing folded items from the bin. "She's going to be so pissed."

"You better leave your mother alone," Reign advised, amusement still in her voice as she too grabbed some of the folded items from the bin. "You know she doesn't play."

"Oh, I *know.*" Ava moved her hair from her face. "You remember back in high school, that time she came up for a conference because our science teacher said that I talked too much in class?"

Reign busted out laughing at the memory. "You had the nerve to show off by getting smart with her, and she smacked you right in the mouth."

"Felt like my goddamn lips swung around to the back of my head," Ava remembered. Reign doubled over with laughter; Ava narrowed her eyes at her cackling friend. "It was *not* that funny, Price."

"Oh no, what *was funny* was how you tried to play that shit *off*," Reign threw back, still laughing.

Ava held her stern gaze, trying to keep from giggling herself.

"Coming up to me holding your face talking about, 'she's always being extra, it didn't even hurt though'," Reign teased, mocking Ava's voice.

Ava shook her head. "Hurt like shit with my lying ass," she chuckled. "Ellie is a tough one, but that's my homie."

"Yeah." Reign's laughter subsided. She unfolded a shirt, holding up the faded and tattered orange short-sleeved top. "Why do you still *have* this?"

Ava's mouth fell open. "That is a vintage t-shirt from high school that I can still *fit into* by the way." She grabbed for it.

Reign held it out of reach. "It's *ugly* and raggedy, throw it out." She tossed it to the side.

Ava pouted, "Fine." She surveyed the closet space. "Thanks for agreeing to help me organize my closet by the way," she said, grateful. "I've accumulated so much crap— It was starting to get cluttered in here."

"It's *been* cluttered," Reign commented. She flashed Ava a smile. "No problem though."

Ava smiled back, before sorting through her belongings. "So, what about you?" she asked after a moment.

Reign shot a curious glance. "*What about* me?"

"Is your mom hounding *you* for a grandchild now that you're moving up in your thirties?"

Reign shook her head slightly. "Nah," she answered. "I think after the whole mess with Troy, she doesn't expect me to even *date* again, so…"

"Do you *want* children?"

"Of *course*, I do," Reign assured. "Doubt it'll happen anytime *soon*. But yeah, I still want them."

Ava nodded slowly. "So…what *about* dating?" she brought up. "I know it's been less than a year since your breakup, but do you think you're ready to start doing that again? …Do you think you'll *ever* be?"

Reign started to speak, then let out a sigh. "I don't know," she answered honestly.

"Do you think—and don't kill me for saying this," Ava prefaced. "But do you think the reason you don't believe you're ready is because you still have feelings for Troy?"

"*Fuck* no." Reign scowled. "There is nothing on the face of this damn earth that would *ever* make me take him back." She adjusted her position on the floor. "I'm over him," she shook her head, exhaling deeply. "Truth be told…that relationship should've *been* ended."

"Look, despite *how* it ended, I'm glad that it *did* end," Ava admitted. "That bastard never deserved you."

Reign ran a hand over her hair, bringing it to one side. "I know," she agreed, somber. "I only wish that I realized it sooner."

Ava fixed Reign with a sympathetic gaze.

"After a while I just became so focused on my career and my plans that I just ignored the dumb shit… I looked up and it had been six years…" Reign paused, unpleasant memories flooding back. "At that point I didn't want to walk away because…how do you just walk away after all that time?"

Ava's sympathetic gaze hadn't wavered. It hurt her to know how much her best friend had gone through.

Reign scoffed, disdain filling her. "Funny, I was hell-bent on trying to make a relationship work with a goddamn gaslighting—*fool*, who didn't even care enough about me to *break up* with me before he started fucking someone else."

Ava let out a deep sigh. "How…how did that bullshit between the two of them even *start?*"

Reign glanced away. "I never asked for details," she revealed. "The knife was already in my back, so…"

Ava reached out, rubbing Reign's shoulder. "I'm sorry luv, I shouldn't have asked."

"It's okay." Reign tapped her fingernails on the inside of the bin. "How is it that my first relationship turned out to be utter bull-shit?" She shook her head. "I successfully avoided idiots all through college and my early twenties just to wind *up* with one at twenty-seven…Just pathetic."

Ava waved a hand Reign's way. "Hell, I'll see your idiot and raise you two…*three*."

Reign managed a slight chuckle.

Ava tapped Reign's hand. "You're not pathetic sis," she soothed. "You just—loved the person you *thought* he was. It *happens* sometimes. Don't beat yourself up over it."

Reign shook her head again. Staring in the bin, she focused on the bundle of colored fabric inside. All traces of humor were gone from her face. "You know," she began after a moment. "I sometimes feel I wasted so much time with the wrong person, that maybe I missed the opportunity to meet the *right* one," she confessed. "And given that… I don't want to waste my time dating just for another relationship to go nowhere."

Ava tilted her head. "Sweetie, the *right* one…the one you're *meant* to be with…you'll *be* with," she stated. "It doesn't matter how much time you think you've wasted, he's out there for you, and you won't have to *try* to make the relationship work… It just *will*."

Reign shrugged but didn't respond.

Ava unfolded a pair of stonewashed jeans, examining them. "Ugh, what possessed me to buy these?" she muttered, tossing the item into the trash pile. She focused her attention back on Reign. "I'm about to get preachy on you right now."

Reign rubbed the back of her neck. "Okay."

Ava folded her arms on the top of the bin. "I honestly believe that everything happens for a reason."

Reign raised an eyebrow. "*Do* you?"

"Absolutely," Ava nodded. "*Yes*, you were with the wrong man for six years. But because you went *through* that, you now know what you won't tolerate again."

Reign just sat there, examining her friend's wardrobe as Ava spoke.

"You know what type of man you *do* want now. You know what you require in a relationship now, you know what you *deserve* now," Ava preached. "You'll never again be with a man who isn't everything that you need him to be... So while what happened was some bullshit...you *had* to go through it in order to get to this place."

Reign pondered Ava's words for a moment. "You know, you sound like my mother," she finally said.

"I *love* Ms. Vivian," Ava gushed. "She's always so sweet."

Reign giggled a bit, "Yeah, I know."

Ava retrieved another item. "*Furthermore*—"

Reign chuckled. "Furthermore, huh?"

"Yes, furthermore," Ava maintained, humor in her voice. "At least you met Troy's simple ass in your twenties and not your thirties—the twenties are *meant* for mistakes." She put a hand up when Reign opened her mouth to protest. "Granted, you were *thirty-two* when it *ended*, but you get what I mean."

"If you say so," Reign jeered, amused.

The humor left Ava's face. "So with that being *said*," she eyed Reign intently. "*Whenever* the right man comes into your life...you need to allow yourself to be *open* to him."

Reign frowned. "What's *that* supposed to mean?"

"Rae, I love you, but you are the most emotionally guarded person that I know," Ava bluntly stated. "You shut down and shut *off* like a pro."

Reign jerked her head back in offense. "Well damn."

Ava folded her arms. "Am I *lying*?"

"No, but still, damn," Reign threw back, making a face. Letting out a quick sigh, she threw her hands up. "Okay fine. If I *ever* meet this so-called 'Mr. Right', I will try to be more...open emotionally."

Ava shook her head in amusement. "A damn shame," she commented of the disgusted look on Reign's face. "Can't hardly get it out."

"I feel sick just *thinking* about it." Reign rubbed her stomach. "You know how I hate being vulnerable. It's never gotten me anywhere. *Especially* in the relationship department."

Ava giggled. "Trust me, I know. But for *Mr. Right*, it will." She tossed the item in her hand aside. "Ooh, just a heads up, since you, Chase and I are single, for Valentine's Day we're going to a food and wine tasting event they're having downtown," she informed. "It's next Friday. You have nothing else to do, so just say yes."

"Fine," Reign groaned, rolling her eyes.

Ava smiled in satisfaction. "Good." After working in silence for a few moments, Ava's brow creased.

Catching the look, concern crossed Reign's face. "Everything okay?"

"Yeah, I was just…thinking back to my past relationships," Ava answered, a puzzled look on her face.

"What *about* them?" Reign wondered.

"I'm trying to figure out what the hell I was *thinking* back in my early twenties."

Reign reached out, patting Ava's hand. "Didn't you just tell me not to beat myself up over my past relationship?" she reminded, sincere. "Take your own advice, luv."

Ava looked at Reign, shaking her head. "No Rae, I really fell for some sorry ass men back then," she maintained. "Hell, *one* of them had the nerve to be bad in bed."

Reign snickered.

Ava folded her arms. "I can't believe that my twenty-three-year-old *ass* was *crying* over a guy who couldn't find my clit even if I took it off and *handed* it to him."

"Oh come on Ava, he couldn't have been *that* bad," Reign said, amused.

Ava fixed Reign with a serious stare. "Reign, I would drag my bare, waxed vagina across a cactus, then masturbate with its thorns before I *ever* get into bed with a man *that* sexually dense again."

Reign stared at Ava wide-eyed for a moment, before erupting with laughter. "Wait *what*?!"

Ava tried to keep a straight face, but could no longer hold it. She dissolved into laughter right along with her.

Still laughing, Reign grabbed a shirt from the bin and smacked Ava on the arm with it. "So *stupid!*" she howled.

Chase headed out of his office building, loosening his tie with his phone to his ear. "When is this thing again?" he asked.

Ava adjusted the wireless headset in her ear, before typing on her laptop. "I've told you this several times already, but since you know I love to hear myself *talk*, I'll repeat it. The *food and wine tasting* event is tomorrow at seven," she bit out. "You have nothing to do, so don't try to get out of it."

Chase chuckled, then coughed. "I'm not, I was just double-checking."

"Um hmm," Ava grumbled. "Between you and Rae, I have a hard time getting you to agree to my little outings."

"Nobody besides *you* would decide to do this on Valentine's Day." Chase walked towards his car. He grabbed the keys from his pocket, pushing a button to unlock it. "The three of us will be there surrounded by couples," he mentioned. "Like being single isn't depressing *enough*."

"Well you know what, Valentine's Day is about celebrating the ones you love, and I love you both, so we're going." Ava continued her vigorous typing. "Wine and food make everything better anyway."

Chase sat in the car. "Whatever," he dismissed.

Ava stopped typing, a smirk appearing on her face. "*Unless…*"

"Unless *what?*" Chase sighed, pinching the bridge of his nose.

"Unless you want to just go with *Reign*," Ava hinted. "I mean, I have a bottle of wine at home. I could just order some takeout—sit this out."

Chase coughed again. "I told you about trying to be—" He paused when a coughing spell came over him.

Ava turned her lip up in disgust. "Eww, what's up with all the hacking?"

"I think I may be coming down with a cold," he answered once the fit subsided.

Ava rolled her eyes. "Not going to work. Go home, drug yourself up, get some rest, and Reign and I will see you tomorrow night," she ground out. "Love you. Bye." She disconnected the call, then went back to typing.

Hearing footsteps nearby, Ava glanced up; a familiar person was approaching Reign's office. "Reign stepped out for a moment, Dwayne," Ava said to the mail man.

The elderly gentleman turned around, smiling. "Thanks for the heads up." He held a package up. "This came in for her."

Ava held her hand out. "You can leave it with me."

"Perfect, my knees can't take another trip up the stairs," Dwayne chortled, handing the box to Ava.

"You know this building has an elevator, right?" Ava called after him as he walked away.

"The elevator isn't exercise," he threw back.

Ava just shook her head, resuming her typing. After a moment, she stopped, giving the package a side-glance. Her gaze lingered on it; she raised an eyebrow, then shook her head. "No, he wouldn't pull that shit again," she muttered to herself. She tried to get back to work, but not even a minute later, she grabbed the box. "Yeah, he *would*."

Carefully peeling the tape back, Ava opened the box to find a bouquet of six yellow roses in a vase. Reading the attached card, she sucked her teeth.

Rae,
It probably doesn't mean anything,
but Happy Valentine's Day.
-Troy

Livid, Ava's eyes widened and her jaw tightened. She tossed the card back in the box, snapping it closed.

Seeing how angry Reign was after receiving the *last* unwanted delivery from Troy, Ava was determined to keep this one from her.

Pushing back from her desk, Ava grabbed the box, then made a hasty beeline for the office kitchen. Heading straight for the large garbage can, she tossed the entire box in.

"Fuckin' moron," she grunted, sauntering back out.

Chapter Twenty-Two

REIGN GLANCED BOTH WAYS BEFORE crossing the busy downtown street. Adjusting the small black clutch under her arm, she walked up the conference building steps where Ava was waiting.

"Okay sexy," Ava praised, eyeing Reign's black, long-sleeved crop top and high-waisted knee length skirt set.

Reign chuckled. "Thanks, you look nice too," she complimented of Ava's deep purple, long-sleeved, fitted sweater dress. "But, did we really need to dress up for this?"

"Yes," Ava assured. "Tickets said, 'dress to impress'."

Reign scrunched her face. "Who am I supposed to impress?"

Ava made a face back. "*Me*, now hush and come on." She grabbed Reign's hand, pulling her along.

Heading for the entrance, Ava retrieved a small mirror from her purse, examining her reflection. "Chase is late, we'll wait for him inside."

"Okay," Reign agreed.

"You talk to him today?"

"I missed a call from him while I was getting ready, but when I called back, he didn't answer," Reign replied, moving her hair over her shoulder.

"*He* was probably getting ready," Ava chortled.

Entering the massive ballroom area, the women were greeted by an abundance of food and wine stations, all hosted by restaurants and wineries from the city and surrounding areas. The countless patrons, dressed in their best outfits, milled about enjoying the food, drinks, music and overall upscale atmosphere.

"I'm pretty excited about this." Ava beamed, walking with Reign in tow. "I've been wanting to try some of these restaurants, and now I get to sample some of their best dishes."

Reign gave a nod. "Makes sense," she looked around. "It *does* smell good in here."

"Doesn't it?" Ava mused, scanning the room. Her eyes locked on the flowers setting on one of the wine stations—yellow roses. She flashed back to the ones that Troy had sent to Reign just yesterday—the ones that Ava had discarded. Ava couldn't help but feel a wave of anger fall over her. *I still can't believe he had the unmitigated gall to send her more of those sorry ass flowers.* If he was standing before her, Ava wouldn't hesitate to kick Troy in his precious jewels. Not that they would have a chance running into him *or* Marcy at this establishment—they'd never attend an event this tasteful.

"You're quiet over there," Reign mentioned, cutting into Ava's thoughts.

"Sorry—just trying to figure out where to start," Ava sputtered, moving her hair over her shoulder.

Reign's eyes roamed the space. "Same here."

Ava looked at Reign, a seriousness on her face. "Can I ask you something?"

Reign met her eye. "Sure."

"You…you haven't seen Troy, have you?"

Reign frowned. That was certainly out of nowhere. "Huh?"

"I mean…you haven't caught him *lurking* anywhere, have you?" Ava clarified. "Following you or anything?" Though Reign hadn't mentioned anything to her, or even seemed *afraid* after receiving the unwanted birthday delivery, Ava just felt the need to ask. She couldn't help but wonder if his flowers could turn into something else; something *harmful* to her friend.

Reign tucked some of her hair behind her ear. "No, I haven't spoken to, seen, nor *felt* his presence," she assured. "Up until those raggedy flowers, I'd forgotten that his sorry ass even *existed.*"

Ava exhaled deeply. "Okay, good." *And it just better stay that way, or I've got a taser with his name on it.*

Reign squinted her eyes at Ava. She was curious as to where

the question had even come from. "Is there a reason you asked?"

Ava raised her shoulders briefly before letting them fall. "Just—just making sure you're good."

Reign smiled, giving Ava a pat to her arm. "I am. Stop being neurotic."

Ava giggled. "I'll try." Feeling a bit relieved, Ava's appetite was at an all-time high. She pointed to a station. "Come on, let's try that one."

Ava trotted up to the table, eyeing the sign. "'Rosemary seared salmon with mango rice'," she read aloud. "Ooh, I'd like to try that, please," she said to the station worker. When the man handed both Ava and Reign a helping, Ava didn't hesitate to dig in. "Oh my God, I have to make this," she praised.

Reign giggled at Ava's reaction as she ate her own helping.

"Better yet, I need to *order* this… We both know I'm not going to cook this," Ava amended. "I am *not* gifted in the culinary department."

"Awww, your *lasagna* is good," Reign pacified.

Ava chuckled, "That's because it's *Mom's* recipe." She gave Reign a playful nudge. "But thanks for not agreeing that I suck in the kitchen."

"Stop it, you don't suck." Reign placated, then hesitated for a moment. "Watch a few cooking shows, maybe," she slowly drew out.

Ava busted out laughing. "Noted." Finishing her food, Ava surveyed the room. Looking for another interesting table, she pointed to one. "Let's hit that one next."

"Very well." Reign discarded her empty dish in a nearby trashcan on the way. While Ava looked intrigued at the offerings, *she* was wary of the food sitting on the table in front of her. "What is that?" Reign asked the station worker.

"Oh, this is seared snail," the man answered.

Reign nodded. "Oh. Oh okay—nope." She turned to walk off, but was stopped by Ava clutching her arm.

Ava chuckled a bit. "Stop, we have to try this."

"No, *we* don't," Reign refused, moving her arm from Ava's grip.

Ava placed a hand on her hip, shooting Reign a stern gaze.

"Don't be rude to this handsome man, just try it."

"You know me well enough to know that I'm not eating a damn bug," Reign bit out.

"It is a *delicacy*," Ava argued.

"It is a *bug*," Reign maintained. Hearing the man snicker, both women turned to him.

Ava shook her head. "Don't laugh at her, she's rude," she jeered of Reign, before turning back to her. "Rae, come on," she insisted. "We're here in this beautiful place, to try these different foods, so let's just *try* it."

Reign stared at Ava for a long moment. Resolved, she stomped her heel covered foot on the floor, letting out a whine in the process.

Pulling Reign closer to the station by her hand, Ava let out a laugh. "Rae, don't be dramatic." She grabbed two helpings, handing one to Reign.

Reign stared at the seared snail in disgust; Ava delivered a light nudge to her arm. "Stop it," Ava demanded. "*Act* like you're in your thirties."

Reign rolled her eyes.

"On three," Ava prompted, grabbing her fork. On the count of three Ava, placed the entire piece into her mouth while Reign took a tiny bite. Ava chewed her food, savoring the taste and texture. "It's not bad actually," she said. When Reign didn't respond, Ava glanced at her. She stared for a moment, then nodded slowly once realization set in. "It's still in your mouth, isn't it?"

Reign nodded.

Ava put a hand over her face, sighing. "At least turn around if you're going to spit it out."

Reign grabbed a tissue, turned her back to Ava and the station worker, then spat the piece of snail into the napkin.

Ava shook her head. "A damn shame."

An hour later, the ladies had sampled more dishes, some desserts, and even tasted a bit of wine. Despite her earlier experience with the dreaded cooked snail, Reign was enjoying herself.

Ava checked her phone, pursing her lips in annoyance. "I think that Chase stood us up," she ground out.

"Maybe he's stuck in traffic," Reign reasoned. "The roads *are* pretty crowded tonight."

Ava rolled her eyes. "Um hmm."

Reign pushed some of her hair behind her ear. "When I spoke to him yesterday, he didn't sound that great." She sighed, recalling their brief conversation. "Said he was catching a cold."

"It's the *sniffles*," Ava mocked. "You know how men are."

Reign just shook her head. A moment later, her phone rang. Grabbing it from her purse, she saw Chase's name on the screen. "*Speaking* of your brother."

Ava glanced over as Reign answered.

"Hey Chase."

"Tell him, I don't appreciate being stood up," Ava slid in.

Reign flagged Ava with her hand. "Are you on your way?" she asked. Concern fell upon her face. "Are you okay?... Yeah, no you need to rest... Don't worry about it, you rest... Okay. Do you need anything? ...Okay... Don't worry, I'll tell her... I hope you feel better... Talk to you later."

Ava held her inquisitive gaze on Reign as she hung up. "What's going on?"

"His cold has gotten worse." Reign couldn't hide the worry in her voice. "He said that he had still planned on coming, but the more time passed, the worse he felt."

"*Man* cold," Ava nodded.

Reign flashed a warning look her way. "Stop it."

"I'm just joking, I hope he feels better," Ava amended. "I'll call him later to check on him...even though he didn't call to tell *me* that he wasn't *coming*."

Reign put the phone back in her bag. "He probably thought you'd yell at him."

"I would've," Ava admitted, humor filling her voice.

As the two women continued to stroll through the place, Ava caught sight of the far off look on Reign's face. She gave Reign a soft nudge. "You worried about him?"

Reign snapped out of her trance. "Huh?"

Ava stopped walking, standing in front of Reign and halting *her* steps. "You can go check on him. I know you want to."

Reign shook her head. "No, he needs to rest."

"I have a feeling that he'll rest better after you go check on him." Ava tapped Reign's shoulder when she opened her mouth to protest. "*Go* luv."

Reign let out a quick breath. "You don't want to come with me?"

Ava shook her head. "He's in good hands with you," she said. "I'll be fine. I drove my own car, remember?"

"Okay." Reign pointed a warning finger. "Don't drink anything else."

"Trust me, I *won't*." Ava put a hand on her stomach. "I'll probably leave right after you anyway. That damn snail is starting to mess with my stomach."

"Eww," Reign scoffed, giving Ava a hug. "Call me when you get home."

"Will do," Ava promised.

Chapter Twenty-Three

LAYING BACK AGAINST HIS COUCH cushions, Chase pulled the throw blanket up to his chest. Feeling a coughing spell coming on, he braced himself.

Chase put a hand to his chest, grimacing as it ceased. At this point, he'd been coughing so much that his chest hurt. "This is some bullshit," he grumbled aloud. Grabbing the remote, he prepared to channel surf, when he heard a knock at his door.

Shuffling over, he rubbed his chest as he cleared his throat. Glancing out of the peephole, a glimmer of surprise formed on his tired face. He opened the door, eyes widened. "Hey." He hoped that he wasn't gawking too much.

"Hey," Reign replied. She opened her mouth to say something else, but Chase turning away and letting out a cough, stopped her. "Aww, I'm sorry, I didn't mean to disturb you—"

"No, you're not, come in," Chase quickly slid in. He moved aside. "What brings you by?"

Reign faced him as Chase closed the door. "Well, I honestly didn't like how sick you sounded on the phone earlier, so I decided to stop by and bring you a care package—" She held up the plastic bag in her hand, showing him. "Care *bag*."

Chase's eyes lit up. "Wow, *thank* you."

She smiled back, giving a nod. "You're welcome." She gave the bag a quick glance. "It's just some leftover soup that I made and froze, a box of tea, a lemon and honey…" she dug her hand inside, pulling a small box out. "Ooh, and these double chocolate chip cookies that have *nothing* to do with helping fight a cold, but they're *so* good."

Chase fixed a look mixed with gratitude and admiration on

Reign as she spoke. *You're so beautiful.* "I appreciate it, Rae," he said instead.

"Good, now have a seat and I'll go heat this soup up for you." Taking his arm, Reign guided him back to his couch.

Chase sat down, getting comfy again. When Reign headed for the kitchen, Chase bolted back up. "Wait, do you need help with—"

Reign snapped her head in his direction, a stern look on her face. "Sit down."

Chase let out a slight laugh, hands up in surrender. "You got it."

It took Reign approximately twenty minutes to heat Chase's soup and make his tea. She returned to the living room, careful-ly holding both. "Sit down, I'm fine," she commanded when Chase made a move to get up again.

"You're bossy when you're taking care of the sick, huh?" he joked.

She laughed as she set the tea down on the coffee table, careful to use a coaster. She handed him the bowl. "Because you don't know how to just sit down and relax."

"I could say the same about *you*," he countered, stirring the steaming chicken noodle soup with his spoon.

"*I'm* not the one who's sick," Reign threw back, sitting down next to him.

Chase shook his head in amusement.

As Reign channel surfed on his television, Chase ate his soup. "You know," he began after finishing. "Normally I'm not a fan of soup, but *this* is really good."

"Thank you," Reign beamed. "And I *know* you don't like soup, but you needed it." She ran a hand through her curled hair. "I remember when I went with your family to visit you for family weekend your freshman year of college, and your mom yelled at you because you'd given all those cans of soup that they'd sent, to your roommate."

Chase laughed at the memory. "Cussed me out and told me I'd better not starve for being picky."

Reign giggled. "I don't blame you though. That canned mess *was* disgusting…it was even worse than my noddle dish."

"Nah, I think the soup had that dish beat." His teasing earned a playful backhand to his arm.

"*Anyway*," she continued. "Since you like it, I'll make extra for you next time, so you can freeze it just in case you get sick again."

"I hope it's no time soon," Chase ground out. "This is horrible."

Reign grimaced. "I know. I wasn't trying to wish that on you." She shot him a sympathetic look when he let out a cough. "Poor baby."

Setting the bowl on the coffee table, Chase let out a deep sigh. "I hate that I missed tonight," he said. "I know that Ava probably thought I was trying to back out of it, but I really *did* want to come." He turned to Reign. "How was it?"

"It was actually nice," Reign answered. "Aside from that nasty ass snail that Ava had me try, the food was good."

Chase raised an eyebrow. "*You* ate a snail?"

"If you call holding it between my front teeth before spitting it out, eating it then yeah, I ate it," Reign jeered.

Chase shook his head. "I don't know *why* she thought you'd eat that." Laughter filled his voice. "She should know you better than that."

She rolled her eyes. "She *does*, and that's the problem."

Chase chuckled, then reached for his mug of tea. "So, did the event end early?"

She tilted her head. "What do you mean?"

"I mean, it started at seven, it's only been about an hour and a half," Chase pointed out. "Just figured it was over since you stopped by here on your way home."

Reign hesitated for a moment. "I actually left early," she admitted. "I just…felt like I should check on you."

Chase gazed at her, adoration filling his watery eyes. No woman aside from the ones in his family had ever showed genuine concern for his well-being. At least not enough to cut their evening short just to come take care of him in his time of need. Chase wondered if she knew just how much it meant.

"Thank you," he breathed.

Reign put a caring hand on his, sincerity showing in her eyes. "You don't have to thank me."

Chase's gaze lingered on her, and their eyes met. No one said a word for a long time before Reign turned away, moving her hand from his.

Sheepishly tucking her hair behind her ear, Reign exhaled deeply. Chase was on her mind a lot nowadays; she never realized how much until now. Ever since reminiscing about their brief past a few weeks ago, Reign had to fight hard to keep her mind off of it. *Get a grip, Rae.* Turning back to him, Reign grinned. "Besides, you came to my house to fight a bunny for *me*, the *least* that I can do is heat up some soup for you," she said, trying to lighten the intense moment.

Chase nearly spat out the tea in his mouth from laughter.

She giggled, then noticed the bottle of cough syrup on the coffee table, pointing to it. "When was the last time that you took some medicine?"

Chase glanced at the bottle. "This morning."

Reigh scooped the bottle from the table, reading the instructions. "You're supposed to take some every *four hours*."

"Once is enough, it's nasty," Chase muttered.

Reign frowned at him. Not saying a word, she removed the top, pouring some into the small cup. She held the dark blue liquid to his face. "Here."

Chase moved his head back, eyeing it in disgust.

"What are you, a toddler?" Reign mocked. "*Take* it."

"Rae, I'm good, the soup and tea is already helping," he insisted. The glare that she was giving him was so intense that Chase felt like shrinking under it. Taking the cup from her hand, he quickly downed the medicine.

Reign stared at him. "You were fighting hard not to make a face, *weren't* you?" she teased after a moment.

"You have *no* idea, that stuff is disgusting." Chase rubbed his face and earned a laugh from her for his trouble.

Chase's eyes fluttered open, focusing on the images flashing on the television screen. He slowly sat up on the couch, rubbing his eyes. Judging by the preview loop, he figured that he'd fallen asleep on the movie that he and Reign were watching. He had no idea of exactly *when* he'd drifted off, but when he looked at his phone, it was after two o'clock in the morning.

Intending on moving to his bedroom in hopes of falling back to sleep, Chase noticed a sleeping Reign seated next to him. Her head was leaning on the arm of the couch. *Wow, she's still here.* Chase thought that she would've taken the opportunity once he'd fallen asleep to slip out. But while he was pleasantly surprised that she was still there—he felt bad. She looked uncomfortable.

Chase gently shook her shoulder. "Rae," he called, softly.

She stirred a bit, but didn't wake.

Sitting back, Chase struggled with whether he *should* wake her. If he succeeded, she'd leave, and he didn't want her driving home this late—even if she *was* just ten minutes away. Then he caught himself staring dreamily at her. *She's even beautiful when she sleeps.* Quickly snapping out of it, Chase ran a hand over his head. *I can at least make her comfortable*, he thought.

Gently grabbing Reign, Chase carefully pulled her to lay down on the couch. As he went to get up, Reign turned on her side, pinning Chase's arm beneath her.

His eyes widened. "Shit," he whispered, panicked; that certainly wasn't expected. He contemplated just pulling his arm from under her, but he didn't want to further disturb her. Resolved, Chase left his arm in place.

Adjusting his position, Chase laid down behind her. Pulling the throw blanket over them, he drifted back to sleep.

Chapter Twenty-Four

AVA TOOK A BITE OF her grilled veggie wrap then grabbed her glass of iced tea, taking a long sip.

Reign was steadily jotting in her notebook, pausing just long enough to take a bite of her Caprese panini.

The two women had decided to have their lunch at a nearby sandwich spot that they'd grown fond of over the past few weeks. It was becoming one of their favorite places to venture to during the work week.

Ava took another sip of her drink. "Are you ever going to let anybody read all that stuff you write in those notebooks?"

"No," Reign answered, still writing.

Ava chuckled a bit. "Why *not*?"

Reign stopped writing, glancing up at her. "Because it's private, *that's* why." She made a face. "Nosey."

Ava shrugged. "That's fine. But can I at *least* read one of those stories you write for your self-assigned writing assignments?"

Reign squinted. "How do you know that I do that?"

"Because you've *been* doing it," Ava replied, laughter in her voice. "You forget before you got your own laptop, you used to use *mine* and I'd see your writing prompts."

Reign shook her head as she went back to writing.

Reign, determined to perfect her craft, had taken inspiration from her college writing professors and begun assigning herself a variety of writing prompts. They ranged from telling a story with dialogue and with*out* it, writing stories in first person, second, and third (both limited *and* omniscient), telling a story using heavy description—the list went on.

"You're the only person I know who gives herself schoolwork after graduating," Ava teased.

"Yeah well, it helps me stay sharp I guess," Reign explained, shrugging.

"I'm not mad at that," Ava praised. "I'm actually impressed by it."

Reign paused yet again. Looking up at Ava, she tilted her head slightly. "Do you want me to give *you* a prompt?"

"Nope," Ava quickly shot down, digging back into her sandwich. "So anyway, can I read some of them—the stories, I mean?"

"I'll think about it." Reign replied, pushing her hair behind her ear and going back to completing her thought. "I might send you a few later."

Ava clapped her hands in delight. "Ooh, are any of them erotic?"

Reign threw a quick annoyed glance Ava's way. "Girl—*maybe*, I don't remember."

Ava did a dance in her seat.

"You're a freak, you know that?" Reign jeered, amused.

Still dancing, Ava winked. "Yup."

Reign glanced at her watch. "Time is up," she alerted, closing her book. Both women gathered the rest of their food and their belongings, then exited the café.

"Did you figure out what you wanted to do for your birthday this year?" Reign asked Ava as they arrived back at the office building.

Ava thought for a moment. "Nothing major, just a few of us hanging out at a fancy lounge with a top shelf bar, good music and rooftop deck—that's all."

Reign side-eyed her. "That's *all*, huh?" she chortled.

Ava shrugged. "You know I don't want much."

Reign chuckled a bit. "Okay, I'll see what I can find in the next few weeks."

Patting Reign's shoulder, Ava flashed a smile.

Once on their floor, Ava made a beeline for her desk, while Reign retreated to her office.

As Reign sat down at her desk, her cell phone rang. Glancing at the screen, she smiled at the name. "Hey you," she answered. "How are you feeling?"

Chase sat back in the seat at his office. "Hey yourself," he replied, smile prominent in his voice. "I'm pretty much at a hundred percent."

"Good to hear."

It had been a little over a week since Reign had showed up to Chase's house to check on him. Though she hadn't mentioned it, Reign remembered how she felt waking up next to Chase the following morning. Even though nothing had happened other than her falling asleep on his couch, just being there *with* him felt nice.

"I'll have to make it up to you," Chase mentioned.

"No, you don't."

"Yeah, I *do*," he insisted. "Not only for what you did that night, but for bringing me more care items the *next* day *and* for checking in on me every day."

Reign fiddled with a pen on her desk. "We're friends Chase, what *else* would I do?"

Chase was silent for a moment as a sullen look flashed across his face. The more time he spent with Reign, the less he wanted to be referred to as *just* a friend. But he'd long ago learned his lesson about fantasizing about things going further with them. "Yeah, friends," he agreed, finally. "And as your *friend*, I still owe you one."

"Very well Chase," she relented, amusement in her voice. "What do you have in mind?"

"I'll think of something." He peered at his watch. "Shit, sorry, I have to get to a meeting."

"Okay, hope it goes well."

Chase grinned. "Thanks. I'll call you later?"

"Sure."

Reign ended the call, then unlocked her laptop. She put her hands to the keyboard to type, but paused. Fingers still, Reign stared out in front of her. Her eyes weren't focused on anything; her *mind* was focused on Chase. Just within those brief minutes of casual conversation, he had managed to consume her thoughts.

Rubbing her face with her hands, Reign let out a deep sigh. "Stoooop iiiit," she groaned to herself. Her head jerked up when a tap sounded on the door.

"It's open," she called.

Ava walked in, looking at her.

Reign met Ava's eye, taking note of her friend's serious demeanor. "Why are you looking at me like that? Are you okay?" Reign charged.

Standing with one arm behind her back, Ava tensed. There were none of the smiles or jokes from just twenty minutes ago.

Growing concerned when Ava didn't answer, Reign stood from her seat. "Seriously Ava, are you okay?"

"Yeah, I'm fine," Ava slowly answered. "I umm…" she hesitated. "I'm not so sure that *you* will be in a minute, though."

Reign frowned slightly. "You care to elaborate?"

Ava stepped forward, pulling a medium, flat, gold box from behind her back. "A delivery came for you just now."

Reign eyed the delivery skeptically. "What is it?"

"It's chocolate candy," Ava told. "The *what* isn't the issue…it's the *who it's from* that's going to piss you off."

Reign took the box from Ava's hand, turning it over. Seeing the card, she quickly read it.

> *It probably doesn't mean anything,*
> *but I remembered you liked these.*
> *I miss you.*
> *-Troy*

Rage masked Reign's face, but she didn't speak.

Ava almost didn't want to say what she was about to, but she felt compelled to come clean. "He sent you more flowers on Valentine's Day too," she revealed.

Reign looked at her, expression not changing. "*What?*"

"Yeah," Ava confirmed. "I umm… I intercepted the package and…because I had a feeling…I opened it and it was from him, so I trashed the flowers and the card." She sighed, "I just felt that you didn't need to see it." Reign's silence was deafening; Ava was a little unnerved. "Look, I know that I shouldn't have looked at your mail, just like I shouldn't have done it *this* time—"

Clutching the box and card in a firm grip, Reign snatched up her purse.

Ava looked worried. "Rae—"

"I'm not mad at you, I'll be back," Reign ground out, moving towards the door.

Ava spun around, watching Reign's departing figure. "Where are you going?"

"I'll be back," Reign bit out, sauntering off.

Reign pulled into an empty parking space with a screech. Furious, she turned the car off, grabbed the box and card from the passenger's seat along with her purse, and hopped out.

She stormed to the apartment complex in front of her, snatching the glass door open. Bypassing the empty security desk, Reign turned the corner, heading down the first-floor hallway. Approaching a door, she stopped in front of it, giving it several pounding knocks.

After a few moments, the locks turned, and the apartment dweller opened the door. Face fixed with a fiery glare, Reign came face to face with a stunned Marcy.

Marcy's breath caught in her throat. The last person she ever expected to grace her apartment door again was Reign. It had been seven months since Marcy had last seen her. She eyed her former friend nervously, as Reign scowled at her. Finally letting out a breath, Marcy opened her mouth. "Rae—"

Reign held the gift box up between them, silencing Marcy. "Tell your fuckin' *man* to stop sending me shit," she barked. Dropping the box at Marcy's feet, Reign delivered one stomp on it with her stiletto boot and walked off.

Marcy stepped out of the apartment, following Reign's departing figure down the hallway. "Reign wait!" she called after her.

When Reign turned the corner without looking back, Marcy let out a sigh. Glancing down at the crushed box, she bent down and picked it up to examine it. The card was still attached; she removed it and read it.

Marcy scoffed. Rolling her eyes, she went back inside, slamming the door shut. She headed straight for her bedroom, standing in the open doorway. Folding her arms, she glared at Troy; her boyfriend was laying in her bed and looking at his phone, not paying her any mind.

"You're sending Reign gifts?" Marcy charged, angry.

Startled, Troy bolted upright in the bed. "Huh—what are you talking about?"

Furious, Marcy hurled the box at him; it hit him in the chest with a satisfying *thud*.

Recognizing the gift, Troy let out a loud sigh. "Shit."

"You're *contacting* her? Sending her gifts and shit? Saying that you *miss* her?" Marcy fumed. "What the hell are you *on*?"

"Oh relax, I only sent three gifts," Troy spat.

"You shouldn't be sending *any*!" Marcy exploded. "What is *wrong* with you?"

Agitated, he rubbed his face with vigor. "A *lot*, apparently."

"*Clearly!*"

Troy tossed his arms in the air. "Fine, I won't send her anything else." He slumped back against the pillows. "It's not like she'll ever take me back anyway, so what's the point?"

Marcy looked offended. "It's nice to know that that's what's been on your mind."

He rolled his eyes. "Yeah, so what?"

"*So what?*" Marcy challenged. "That's *unacceptable* Troy, you're with *me* now."

"Oh please," Troy scoffed. "*Now* all of a sudden you care about the sanctity of a relationship. When *before*, you were sneaking and meeting me behind the gym at five-thirty in the goddamn morning to fuck while I was still *with Reign*."

"Oh you had *no* problem leaving *her* bed to come fuck me, so don't even go there," she flashed back.

Troy frowned. "You're right, I *didn't* have a problem with it." He glanced down at the rejected gift in his hand. "But I *should've*."

Marcy shook her head, eyeing him in disgust. "You know what? I'm *sick* of your depressed, lazy ass lying around here all day," she seethed. "You're working my damn nerves. We haven't done *anything* together, you haven't given *me* any money or bought *me shit* lately. Yet you're sending gifts to your fuckin' *ex*?" She folded her arms again when he ignored her. "You can act like you don't hear me all you want, but my rent needs to be paid, where's my eleven hundred dollars?"

"I'm not giving your gold-digging ass shit *else*," Troy hurled back. "You're standing there talking about what *you're* sick of. Well, *I'm* sick of *you* looking in my damn face with your fuckin' hand out all the damn time. Get a damn job."

Marcy glared daggers at him as he ranted.

"I've given more shit to *you* in *two years,* than I've given Reign through our *entire* relationship." Troy shook his head. "Some bullshit."

"Oh is *that* why you're sending her shit *now*? Because your sorry ass finally feels bad for not doing shit for her *then*?" Marcy sneered. She shook her head at him. "Yeah well, unlike *her, I'm* not going to let that shit slide. I need *something* out of this tired ass relationship."

"It's as tired as *your* ass, so leave me the fuck alone," Troy grunted, laying back down.

Marcy ran a hand over her hair, letting out a frustrated sigh. "I don't have time for this shit, get up and take a damn *shower* at least."

Troy flagged her with his hand, yet he didn't move from his spot.

Marcy scowled at him. "You *better* stop sending shit to Reign, Troy." She smacked the door with her hand. "Get *over* her, I fuckin' *mean* it."

"All right, damn, I *said* leave me alone!" Troy snapped, placing a pillow over his head.

Marcy, over the entire conversation *and* the man occupying her space, tossed her arms in the air as she stormed out of the room, slamming the door in her wake.

Chapter Twenty-Five

REIGN SAT ON HER PARENTS' couch, staring at them while they fussed with their television. Her annoyance was obvious as she listened to them go back and forth.

"Matthew, did you turn the TV to channel three?" Vivian asked.

"I *did*," Matthew assured.

"Then why is the picture not showing?"

"Do I *look* like the satellite?" he answered, flustered. "How should *I* know?"

Vivian grabbed a pamphlet from the coffee table. "It says something about a USB. Did you turn to that?"

"What channel is *that* on?!"

Reign closed her eyes, rubbing her temples. "I swear to God," she muttered to herself.

She'd been at her parents' house for over two hours. After leaving Marcy's, she'd returned to work, and despite her angered state and looming headache had managed to push through the rest of her day. But on her way home, she'd gotten a call from her mother stating that their old television had gone out. Reign had stopped and purchased them a new one, then taken it to their house, hoping to set it up quickly and go home to unwind.

Much to her displeasure, they'd insisted on trying to set it up themselves.

"Are you two really going to do this all night?" Reign cut in.

"Hey, don't blame *us*, this thing is *clearly* defective," Matthew grunted, pointing to the fifty-five-inch flat screen television. "I've tried every channel and the picture *still* won't come on."

Reign glared at him. "Dad...you really think that USB is a

television station?" she asked, her tone condescending.

Matthew looked back at the television and started pushing buttons. "Well, *I've* never heard of it, but there are so many new stations popping up nowadays—"

"There is no channel named USB, it is a *cord,*" Reign snapped. "It is that *black cord* that you took out of the box and threw over *there* somewhere, that you plug into the port *labeled USB* on the side of the television."

Vivian looked over at the cord in question; it was sprawled over a pair of slippers in the corner. She turned to her husband. "Matthew, I *told* you about trying to figure stuff out on your own."

"Mom—*you* started yelling at him about a nonexistent antenna, so *you're* to blame as well," Reign cut in. She held her hand out. "Hand me the cord. *I'll* hook it up."

Matthew folded his arms. "I can hook up a television, Reign."

"Dad, you haven't hooked it up in *two hours,* I am not sitting here all night. I had a long day," Reign argued.

Storming over to the cord, Matthew muttered something incoherently. Grabbing it from the floor, he wagged it in the air. "I'll show you," he boasted.

Vivian covered her face with one hand, shaking her head as her husband snatched the instructions from the table and flopped down on the love seat.

"Keep flopping like that and hurt your back again," Reign ground out. She shook her head at him as he studied the instructions.

Vivian couldn't help but chuckle at the interaction. Her husband and eldest daughter were so much alike in attitude and stubbornness. She approached Reign, giving her shoulder a rub. "Go on home, we'll figure this out."

"If you leave it up to him, you won't be watching anything tonight," Reign spat.

Vivian waved a dismissive hand. "We'll be fine," she promised. "Go on and relax. We appreciate you picking this up for us. *Especially* after we had you take that *other* TV back."

Reign stood up. "No problem." She rubbed her tired eyes. "I get that *that* one was a little too *advanced* for you guys," she chuckled. "Anyway, once you get the hang of this one, I'll have a bigger one delivered."

"We are *just fine* with this size, don't waste your money," Vivian replied.

Reign shrugged, grabbing her purse from the couch. She glanced at her father, who was still reading the instructions. "Dad, make sure you plug the cable cord in once you've figured out how to set the TV up."

Matthew made a face at her. "Don't you worry, I'll have this thing working like clockwork," he boasted. "Your mother and I will be watching that dancing competition show in *no* time."

"Yeah, not sure what clockwork has to do with a television, but whatever," Reign jeered, walking over to him. She gave him a kiss on his cheek, then playfully poked his forehead. "Stop being difficult."

"Yeah, yeah," he grunted. "I'll go to the bank tomorrow and get your money back for the TV."

"Don't worry about the money Dad." Reign headed for the door. "Just don't *break* the thing."

Vivian waved as Reign walked out of the house, shutting the door behind her.

Matthew looked back down at the paper, his brow furrowed. "What the hell is a HDMI?"

Vivian covered her face once again. "Lord," she muttered.

Reign walked through her front door. Locking it behind her, she made a beeline for her couch. Tossing her purse and jacket on the other side of the sofa, Reign flopped down, leaning back against the cushion.

Letting out a long sigh, she tried to relax. After a few moments, she knew it wasn't happening. She was still annoyed from earlier. Reign had hoped to never deal with Marcy or Troy ever again, but the pair clearly weren't going anywhere.

"I should've choked that bitch again," she grumbled to herself. When her phone rang, she let out a huff and grabbed it from her purse.

"Hi," she answered, unenthused.

"Good evening...had a bad day?" Chase assumed, picking up on her tone.

"You could say that."

"Sorry to hear that," he sympathized.

"Thanks. I'll be all right though." She took off her shoes and rested her feet on the soft rug. "I'll probably watch a stupid movie or something to take my mind off of the bullshit."

"I think I have a better idea," he proposed. "Have you eaten dinner yet?"

Reign rubbed her forehead with her free hand. "No, not yet. I just got in the house," she answered. "Was going to order something."

"Nah, you can hold off on the pizza tonight," he chuckled. "I know someplace better. Can you be ready in an hour?"

Reign raised an eyebrow; she couldn't help but be a bit intrigued. "I can... Are you going to tell me where we're going?"

"Nope." Chase laughed a bit when he heard her suck her teeth.

She ran a hand along the back of her neck. "Very well."

"I'll see you in an hour." His smile could be heard through the phone.

"See you." Reign hung up. She sat for a moment before getting up and heading upstairs.

Exiting his car, Chase moved around to the passenger's side, opening the door for Reign. She stepped out onto the sidewalk, while Chase dealt with the valet.

The cool February night air brushed past her face as she eyed the restaurant in front of her. Located in the middle of a scenic block in Scottsdale, from the outside *alone* the place looked upscale. She could only imagine what it looked like on the *inside*.

Chase stood next to her, pocketing his valet ticket.

Reign glanced at him. "You really paid all that money for valet?" she chortled.

"I'd rather pay that, than drive all around the city looking for street parking. Which is *nonexistent* in this area on a Friday night," Chase reasoned.

"I hear you." Reign moved her hair over her shoulder.

He looked at her, grinning. "You ready?"

Reign glanced back at the restaurant, then at him. "This place looks like it's black tie. I think I may be underdressed," she said of her dark denim form fitting jeans, black fitted turtleneck and black stiletto boots.

Chase gave her a onceover. "No, you're perfectly fine," he assured. He'd paired his own jeans with a black button-down shirt and shoes. "It's casual."

She walked alongside him as they approached the door. "If you say so. I just thought that we were going to get burgers or something."

His eyes crinkled with amusement. "You wear heels to get burgers?"

"I wear heels *all* the time," she threw back, earning a chuckle from him. He opened the door, allowing her to enter first.

The pair were greeted by the sound of smooth R&B music and a pleasant hostess. After a few moments, she walked them through a corridor to a large, dimly lit dining area. Reign glanced around, spotting where the music was coming from. "Oh, they have live music," she beamed, gesturing to the musician and singer performing on the stage in front of the room.

"Yeah," Chase confirmed as the hostess showed them to their corner table.

"Your waitress will be with you shortly," the hostess smiled, setting two menus on the table.

"Thank you," Reign replied as the woman walked off. She sat down, fixated on the songstress performing. "This is so cool."

Chase glanced at his menu. "I love this place. The live music is always good... The food is even better." He looked up at Reign; she was bobbing a little to the music. "You've never been here before?"

Reign looked at him, tucking her hair behind her ear. "No," she answered. "I usually don't venture out of my normal spots for places to eat on my own."

"Well, this place is pretty known for the music," Chase informed. "They actually have a live jazz night on Saturday's...*that's* the time when the dress code is black tie."

Reign chuckled. "Oh, I thought I was going to walk in here and be shunned by people in gowns."

Chase laughed, "No, I would've told you." His eyes roamed over her. "You look nice in what you have on. You always *do*."

Reign glanced back at the stage in hopes that Chase wouldn't see her blush. "Thank you."

"You're welcome," he returned, eyeing her. He had to look back down at the menu after a moment; he didn't want her to catch him staring.

The waitress approached the table, interrupting their thoughts. "Hi, I'm Casey, can I start you off with something to drink?"

Both Reign and Chase looked at her. "Yes," they answered in unison.

An hour into dinner, Chase and Reign had become engrossed in the relaxing atmosphere, good food, and the music. They had left the stress of the day outside and were enjoying each other's company.

Reign took a sip of her white peach sangria. "I think I should get an order of this spicy tuna bowl to go, that was good," she said.

Chase finished his sip of soft drink. "Go ahead and order it."

She set her glass down. " If I do, that'll be on my own tab."

"No, it'll be on *mine*," Chase insisted. "*I* invited *you* out to dinner, which means that everything is on me."

She squinted at him. "Fine, I'll let you have that one."

He chuckled a bit. "I appreciate it." As he reached for his glass of bourbon, he caught Reign eyeing the lit candle on the table. He stared, mesmerized by her eyes in the flickering flame. He'd always thought that her eyes (which in his mind resembled the color of honey) were beautiful, but seeing them in this light, he was entranced. *God, I want her so*— He halted his own thought, snapping out of it. *Stop it, Chase.*

Clearing his throat, he took a quick sip of his drink.

Reign eyed the glass of dark liquid, oblivious to Chase's thoughts. "How does that taste?"

"Strong…*good*, but strong," he answered, setting the glass back down. "You want to taste it?"

Reign put a hand up, shaking her head. "No, if it's strong to *you*, it'll be death to me," she refused. "I'd prefer *not* to be laid flat on my ass tonight."

Chase laughed a bit as he ate the last of his steak. "So," he began, after finishing. "I didn't want to bring it up earlier, because you seemed a bit tense when I picked you up—"

Reign shot him a skeptical glance.

"But you mentioned that you had a bad day earlier," he finished. "What happened?"

Reign let out a sigh, looking off to the side. She was hoping to forget about the incident all together. She debated changing the subject, but she *did* want to get it off of her chest. "Well…" she folded her arms on the edge of the table. "I got another *gift* from my ex today," she reluctantly told.

Chase took a deep breath, trying to keep calm. "Is that so?"

Reign nodded. "Some stupid ass box of candy." She rolled her eyes. "Apparently he sent more flowers to me for Valentine's Day—Ava trashed them before I could see them."

Chase pinched the bridge of his nose as his jaw clenched. If Troy were standing in front of him, he'd choke him. Probably even worse. "Rae—"

"Chase, I'm not going to let you go beat his ass. I *know* that's what you want to do," she bristled.

Chase looked at her.

"He's not worth your energy," she stressed.

"He needs to be punched in the face…*again*," he seethed.

Reign ran a hand through her hair. "I *get* it, but no."

Chase rolled his eyes.

She frowned at Chase's attitude. "I'm not trying to *protect* him, if *that's* what you're thinking."

"I'm not thinking that Rae," Chase said, tone even.

"Well *good*," she fussed. "Because this isn't about him, this is about *you*. If you go fight him again, you could end up doing something that you can't take back. *Then* what?"

Chase lightly pounded the table with his fist. "He *obviously* hasn't learned to leave you alone."

"Well maybe he will *now* since I paid Marcy a little visit," Reign revealed. "Dropped that shit off to her and told her to tell him to stop sending me stuff."

Chase narrowed his eyes. "And how did *that* go?" he asked, eerily calm.

"I *literally* dropped it on the floor and left. What she did afterwards I don't know, and I don't *care*." Reign let out a quick breath; she was annoyed just talking about it. "Anyway, *that's* what was bad about my day today." She gestured to him with her hand. "So…there you go."

Chase took another quick sip of his drink. "Well…you seemed to have handled the situation." He pushed the glass aside. "You're right, maybe he'll stop with the bullshit now that Marcy knows what he's doing."

She scowled at his tone, tilting her head slightly. "Are you being sarcastic?"

"Not at all."

Not bothering to respond, Reign grabbed her drink. Taking a sip, she watched the performers in silence.

Chase sighed; he felt bad. Not only had he caused Reign to relive the incident, he'd gotten upset and as a result, now *she* was upset. That wasn't his intention; he only wanted to know what had her troubled earlier, not bring the mood all the way down.

"Hey," he called, calm.

She looked at him, agitation heavy on her face. *He better not bring this Troy shit up again.*

Chase gestured to the stage. "Do you know what song they're singing?"

Reign relaxed the frown on her face. "Yeah, I know it," she answered. "It's one of my favorite songs."

"Mine too." A smile crossed his face. "You remember, we danced to this at your prom?"

Reign's eyes lit up; she smiled bright. "Oh my God, you remember that?"

Chase nodded. "Yeah, especially since you stepped on my foot like three times," he teased.

She narrowed her eyes. "I didn't know what I was doing, leave me alone," she spat, somewhat amused.

Chase laughed. "It was rocky at first, but once you let me lead, it ended up being good."

She made a face at him. "Whatever."

He glanced at the stage for a moment, then looked back at Reign. "You want to dance to the rest of the song?"

She eyed him back, chuckling a bit. "Do you see a dance floor?"

"I see the space right here in front of our *table*," he threw back.

Reign looked around as she thought for a minute. "All right," she agreed, standing up.

Chase followed suit.

"Watch your feet, I have on higher heels this time around," she quipped, standing in front of him.

"Not worried at all, I've got this." He held his hand out.

Reign eyed it for a second, then put her hand in his, allowing herself to be pulled close to him. He wrapped his arms around her waist, and she wrapped hers around his neck as they began to sway to the music.

As the melodic sounds escaped the singer's lips, Reign and Chase focused only on each other. They were so wrapped up in the moment that it felt like they were the only two people in the room.

Reign couldn't remember the last time that she'd slow danced;

the last time that she'd been held close. The last time that she felt *this good* being in someone's arms.

Chase held Reign closer as she leaned her head on his shoulder. He wondered if the woman in his arms had any idea how hard he was falling for her. What he'd felt for Reign years ago failed in comparison to what he felt *now*. Just being with her, being in her presence, he was happier than he'd been in a long time. The way that she felt in his arms while they moved to the music, Chase wished that the song would never end.

As the singer belted out the last note, Reign lifted her head from Chase's shoulder; she looked up at him, locking eyes.

Though the song was over, and the pair were no longer dancing to the next tune, they had yet to part. They held their gazes on one another; Chase's eyes were intense and full of longing.

Reign was feeling the same way. Yet after a moment, she snapped out of it. "Umm—"

"Yeah, we look crazy just standing here, huh?" Chase sputtered, releasing her from his grasp.

Reign ran a hand along the back of her neck, laughing nervously. "Right," she agreed, sitting back down.

Chase sat down, taking a deep breath as Reign grabbed her drink and downed it. She'd hoped that it would aid in cooling her down. *Control your hormones; he's your friend... Just your friend*, she told herself.

"Do you still want to order your food to take home?" he asked, cutting into her thoughts.

"Huh?" She shook her head slightly, gathering herself. "No, I think I'm good. I think—I think I should go home and get some sleep."

Chase nodded, "Okay," and signaled for the waitress.

Chase pulled in front of Reign's house, turning the car off.

She looked over at him, removing her seatbelt; he was making a move to get out of the car. "You don't have to walk me to my door, it's right there," she said to him, gesturing to her house.

Chase eyed her back. "It's no problem—"

"No really," she cut in. If Chase walked her to her door, he might try to kiss her goodnight, and not only would she kiss him back, she'd invite him in—crossing a line that she didn't want to cross again. Especially not with someone she considered one of her best friends.

Chase held his hands on the steering wheel. It was taking everything in him not to lean over and kiss her. But he wasn't sure if she would accept it, and the last thing that he wanted to do was scare her off. "Okay. But you can't stop me from waiting until you get in the house before I pull off."

"Wouldn't expect anything else." She slung her purse over her shoulder and glanced at him; a smile crossed her face. "Thank you for tonight," she said, sincere. "I needed it and I really appreciate it."

Chase nodded. "You're welcome."

She hesitated for a moment, then leaned over, giving him a quick hug. "Talk to you tomorrow."

"Okay," Chase replied, sullen, as she practically jumped out of his car. He watched as she hurried up to her front door, unlocking it before entering. Once Reign closed the door, he looked out in front of him. Sighing, he leaned his head back against his seat. *What are you doing Chase?*

"Shit," he whispered, rubbing his face.

Glancing back at Reign's closed door once more, Chase's eyes lingered before turning his car radio on. He hoped that the soft tunes would clear his mind for the short ride home.

Chapter Twenty-Six

STANDING BY THE WINDOW IN Reign's home office, Ava grabbed a small house plant from the sill, examining it. "You know, I used to have a few houseplants in my place," she mentioned, touching the leaves. "But I killed them all."

Reign stopped short of opening her drill box, glancing up at Ava. "Put my damn plant down."

Ava busted out laughing. "It wasn't on *purpose*. I just lack a green thumb…and I forgot to water them for periods of time."

Reign shook her head, peering into the open box. "Terrible. Poor plants."

Setting the plant back in the window, Ava chuckled a bit. She eyed another one alongside it. "You're the only person I know who has a cactus plant *in their house*."

Reign removed the drill from the box, standing up right. "Well, I happen to like them," she explained. "They get such a bad rep."

Chuckling, Ava grabbed a leveler from a nearby toolbox. "Probably because those who *gave* them that rep have been pricked by them in some way, shape or form."

"Well, if one is careful in how they handle it, they won't get pricked," Reign replied, setting up a drill bit.

Ava tapped her finger to her chin. "I can't help but to wonder if that is a metaphor for something else."

"It's *not*." Reign double-checked that the drill was good to go. "I'm really *just* talking about the cactus."

That Saturday afternoon, Reign and Ava had ventured out to do some shopping for their places. While Ava had concentrated on small shelf items and new picture frames, Reign had elected to buy shelving units for her office. Now back home, Ava was helping Reign install them.

While Ava held the leveler up to the bare wall, Reign measured and marked key spots with a pencil.

"I already regret this," Reign complained, eyeing the hardware pieces laid out on the cream love seat.

Ava giggled. "It'll be fine. You'll be happy once they're up." Her eyes roamed the room, taking in the décor. "I've been meaning to tell you, this office looks better than the one at work."

Reign too giggled. "Thank you," she replied. "I'm so in love with the furniture in here, *especially* the desk that Chase bought me. The photo he showed me didn't do it justice."

"Yeah, he has good taste when it comes to wood furniture," Ava said. "The pieces are always great quality and he's not afraid to spend good money." She chuckled to herself. "When I first moved into my condo, he tried to help me pick out some pieces, but I went straight for the glass stuff."

"Yeah, you and I have that in common," Reign mentioned, laughter in her voice.

"Yup, all glass everything." Ava shook her head. "*Pretty*, but a pain in my ass to clean."

"*Tell* me about it." Reign positioned the power tool on one of the marked spots and drilled a hole into the wall. She stepped back, examining it. "Does that look straight to you?"

Ava glanced at the wall, then at her. "You're asking me if *one hole* is *straight?*" She snickered when Reign shot her a glare. "I'm *just* asking."

Reign quickly shook her head. "Whatever, smart ass," she jeered, earning another snicker from Ava. Reign moved to the next marked spot, drilling another hole.

After helping Reign measure and mark two other areas on the wall, Ava rubbed the back of her neck. "*Speaking* of Chase," she began. "Why isn't *his* ass over here doing this? He's good at this stuff."

Reign set her drill down and grabbed a hardware piece along with one of the brackets. Ava steadied it as Reign secured it to the wall. "I know, but I didn't want to bother him," Reign replied. "He already did something nice for me last night. I wouldn't feel right asking him to disrupt his Saturday just to hang some shelves."

"I can promise you he wouldn't have minded."

"Still," Reign maintained. She'd told Ava the half-truth. Yes, she didn't want to disturb him and ask for a favor after he'd treated her to a much-needed night out. But she also needed another day or two without seeing him in order for the feelings that had stirred in her to fade.

"You're so nice and considerate," Ava teased. "I would've been on his phone as soon as I got up, like 'wake your ass up and come hang these shelves'."

Reign snickered. "*You* can do that, you're his sister...*and* you're spoiled."

"Oh, you can do that *too*, trust me," Ava threw back.

Reign shook her head, grabbing the other bracket from the floor. "Did you have fun last night?"

Reign held the bracket against the wall. "I did." The pleasant memory filled her. She'd told Ava about the outing with Chase, but made sure to leave off certain details—their smoldering dance specifically. "Like I said, it was nice."

Ava squinted as she held the piece steady. "Soooo was it a—"

"No, it was not a *date*," Reign cut in, securing the bracket. "We are not *dating*, we are *friends*, who happen to hang out every so often."

"And talk *every day*." Ava threw her hands up in surrender when Reign let out a huff. "Okay," she relented. "I mean, it's not *uncommon* for two friends to eventually date each other. But okay."

"If that were true, why didn't you date *your* friend from college?" Reign asked.

Ava looked confused. "Who *Malcom*?"

Reign pointed at her, "Knew exactly who I was talking about too, look at you."

Ava waved a dismissive hand, "I wasn't trying to date Malcom, he was just somebody cool to hang out with."

"But you talked to him every day, right?" Reign mocked. "Sometimes for *hours*."

Ava made a face at her. "My friendship with Malcom was not the same as yours with Chase," she argued. "Malcom was cool, but he was sleeping with everything in a skirt—"

"*You* wore skirts," Reign teased.

Ava rolled her eyes. "Yeah, yeah, we hooked up that *one* time."

Reign fixed Ava with a knowing look. "Coming down with a case of amnesia, I see."

"Okay *twice*, but that was it," Ava admitted. "It was nice, but we both had an understanding that it wasn't going anywhere, so…it didn't."

Reign nodded slowly, "I get it." *In more ways than one*, she thought, running a hand over her hair. "Can I ask you a question, though?"

Ava looked at her. "Sure."

"Do you ever wonder if you would've made it clear that *you* wanted to be more than friends with Malcom, that maybe he would've made himself available *only* to you?" Reign asked. "I mean, from what *I* saw, he really liked you."

"No, I *don't* wonder," Ava sneered. "What *good* would it do anyway? It's been almost twelve years since then and we don't even talk anymore, so…"

Reign raised an eyebrow. "Whose fault was that, by the way?"

Ava narrowed her eyes at Reign, but didn't bother responding.

"Okay, I'll drop it," Reign relented, putting a hand up. "But you see how annoyed you got just now when I talked about you dating your friend—"

"Yeah, yeah, I *still* say that the situations are different, but I'll let you have this one," Ava ground out, earning a snicker from Reign. "You make me sick, give me the stupid shelf piece."

Laughing, Reign grabbed it and put it into Ava's outstretched hand.

Chase retrieved several bags of groceries from his car, adjusting them in his hands. "Bought the entire store again, huh?" he jeered to his mother, who was fishing in her purse for her house keys.

"Oh hush, you know I go shopping every week," Ellie threw back, finding the key. She approached the door with her son close behind.

After getting off work that Tuesday, Chase had decided to stop by for a quick visit with his parents. Upon arrival, he'd learned that his mother was on her way to the grocery store, and offered to take her.

"Besides, I'm making a family dinner this Sunday" she added, opening the door. Chase shut the door behind him.

"How much dinner are you *making* for four people?" Chase grunted, carrying the hordes of grocery bags into the kitchen. He set them on the floor by the counter, then began to unpack them.

Ellie grabbed bags of fresh vegetables and began putting them in the refrigerator. "Well…I was thinking that I could cook for *five* people."

Chase placed the other items in the pantry. "Do we have another sibling that I don't know about?"

"No." Ellie glanced over at him. "I was thinking that you could invite *Reign* over for dinner."

Chase paused his task, side-eyeing his mother. "Since when did you start extending the family Sunday dinner invites to non-family members?" he asked, raising an eyebrow.

Ellie put her hands on her hips. "Oh come on, she's like family."

"You know what I mean, Mom," Chase replied.

Ellie shrugged. "I just think that it'll be nice to have her over… It's been a while."

Chase held a skeptical gaze. "You've been talking with your daughter?"

"I talk to Ava nearly every *day*, but I don't see what this has to do with inviting Reign to dinner."

Chase rolled his eyes as he moved away from the pantry. "Yeah sure," he dismissed. "This sounds like you're inviting her as a *significant other*, so I'll tell you like I've *been* telling *Ava*, Reign and I are not *dating*."

Ellie looked at him, seriousness falling upon her face. "Chase," she began, sitting down at the kitchen table. She pointed to an empty chair. "Have a seat."

Chase reluctantly did as he was told.

"Listen, I know that you two aren't dating," she said. "I know that you've just been talking…hanging out. But I think that I know you well enough to know that that is not *all* you want from your relationship with Reign."

Ellie had always been observant when it came to her children. While Chase didn't consciously tell his mother that he was seeing Reign often, whenever she would call Chase, he'd mention that he'd just gotten off the phone with her, or that he was *about* to give her a ring. Or he'd casually state that he was going to lunch with Reign when his mother called to check on him at work—the list went on. Chase had other friends, yet he didn't devout this much time and attention to any of them *accept* for Reign. Which could only mean that Chase's feelings for her were more than he wanted to let on.

Chase glanced down at the table. "She's my friend Mom…" He played with a cloth napkin on the table. "My *best* friend actually."

"And that's great, *perfect* even," Ellie praised. "But I think you need to be honest with yourself and just admit that you want something more, and it's *okay* to want that."

Chase rubbed his face with his hand as he let out a sigh. He hesitated.

Ellie leaned forward. "Come on son, holding stuff in isn't good for you, you know that." Her tone was firm, but soothing. "Say what you feel."

Chase looked at his mother, taking a deep breath. "Okay—" he clasped his hands together. "Maybe I want to start dating her… For real."

She tilted her head. "*Maybe?*"

"I do," Chase admitted, finally, to someone other than himself. "I do…I—*care* for her…deeply, and I want to take things further."

Ellie fixed Chase with an intense stare, almost as if she were looking into his soul. "You *just care* for her?" she probed, voice soft.

Chase stared back, then after a moment, he shook his head.

Ellie nodded, then smiled. She knew what he really wanted to say, but wouldn't push him to say it to *her*. "Have you told her this?"

Chase sighed, "No."

"Why not?"

"Because it's too soon," Chase replied, somber.

"For you?"

"No, for *her*." Chase folded his arms on the tabletop. "A relationship that she was in for six years, ended on bad terms less than a year ago… I don't think after everything she's been through, that she's ready to date. And even if she *is*, I don't think she wants to date *me*." He looked down at the table. "I don't think I'll ever be more than just a friend to her."

Though Chase felt that he and Reign had shared a special moment last Friday, he didn't know if Reign felt it too. He'd spoken to her since then, yet their conversation had stayed its normal course. He feared that if he brought it up to her, he'd run her off, and the last thing that he wanted was to lose the friendship that they'd built, all because he had feelings for her that she couldn't or didn't *want* to return.

Ellie shot her sullen son a sympathetic look. "Can I give you my opinion?"

Chase gestured to her to go ahead.

"I don't think she'd be spending this much time with you, if she just wanted friendship," she said. She put her hand up when Chase went to protest. "Now, I'm not saying that it didn't *start out* that way but…I think now, it's becoming different."

Chase sighed again, pushing himself back from the table. "I appreciate you trying to make me feel like less of a fool, but I think you're wrong."

Ellie put her hands up in surrender. "Okay son, I'll leave it alone."

"Thank you." He stood from his seat, continuing with his task of putting groceries away.

"But I'd still like for you to invite her to dinner," she insisted. "She's your friend after all and I'd love to see her."

Chase placed a gallon of milk into the refrigerator. "I'll ask her."

Chapter Twenty-Seven

SITTING ACROSS FROM A WELL-DRESSED man at a desk, Reign keyed notes into her tablet.

"We're looking for a mixture of drama and a little bit of romance, no more than forty thousand words," the man stated.

"So basically, a novella," Reign concluded, looking up at him. "Yes."

Reign pushed some of her hair over her shoulder, then went back to keying more notes into the device. "Is she really *aware* of how short this book will be?" she asked.

The dark-skinned, handsome man chuckled a bit. "I sure *hope* so."

"I'm just wondering, because based on the notes that you've given me, forty thousand words isn't going to be enough for everything to be incorporated."

He rubbed his chin with his hand as she spoke.

"I mean, if I cut out the subplots, and focus only on the main character and their development, I can do it," Reign said. "But if you really want this story told the way that I think it *should* be, then it's going to have to be a full novel."

He nodded with enthusiasm. "Then a novel it shall be," he approved. "I will let my client know and I'll have a new contract and a bigger check drawn up."

Reign grinned, "Sounds like a plan." She stood from her seat as he stood from his.

"I agree with you. I initially told my client that a shorter book wouldn't cut it." He adjusted his tie. "The publisher that I'm going after for her has specific taste."

"I bet." Reign slid the tablet into her handbag. "Once you get the revisions to me and lock down a turnaround time, I'll get started."

"Perfect." He smiled, folding his arms. "I know that you've been an editor, but it's nice to see you stepping into the writing field," he added. "Figured you *would*, especially because back in school, you always stole everybody's A's in Creative Writing."

Reign giggled a bit at her fellow college alum. "Yeah, and the way that you always ran your mouth, it figures that *you'd* turn out to be a literary agent," she countered.

He laughed as Reign headed for the door. "It was good seeing you again Reign."

"You too."

"You'll be hearing from me within the next few days," he called after her.

"Looking forward to it," she threw over her shoulder, walking out of the office.

Reign glanced at her watch as she walked out of the building; her meeting had gone a little over. Hearing her cell phone ring, she grabbed it from her purse.

"Hi Chase," she answered.

"Hi," he replied. "I won't keep you, but since I didn't get to talk to you last night, I wanted to let you know that my mother is making Sunday dinner and she wanted to—" He paused, taking a deep breath. "*I* would like to invite you."

Reign slowed her stride to her car. "Really?"

"Yes," Chase confirmed. "Don't feel pressured or anything—"

Reign cradled the phone between her ear and her shoulder, then opened her purse. "No, I don't feel pressured to do anything, I'd love to come."

He smiled. "Okay, great."

She retrieved her keys. "What should I bring?" she asked, pushing the button to unlock her door.

"Just yourself."

Reign stepped into the car. "Sounds good. See you Sunday." Hanging up, she tossed her phone on the passenger seat along with her purse. Instead of starting the car, she just sat and let her mind wander. She'd be seeing Chase again for the first time in a week. Though she had talked to him, she missed *seeing* him. She shook her head briefly, trying to remove the building thoughts. "Just don't slow dance with him and you'll be fine," she said to herself.

Ava grabbed a few china plates from the cabinet, walking them over to her parents' dining room table.

"Mom, I hope you made that pound cake for dessert," she said, setting the table.

"No girl, I didn't. But not to worry, you'll have dessert," Ellie replied, tending to the food in her pots.

"Very well." Ava went back to the cabinet for glasses. She glanced over as Chase entered the kitchen.

"Chase, what is your father doing?" Ellie charged.

"Last time I checked, he was power washing the driveway," Chase answered.

Ava snickered at the annoyed look on their mother's face.

"God—*please* go tell that man that the driveway is clean enough and to go get ready for dinner," Ellie ground out. "And tell him to put on a nice shirt."

Chase chuckled. "I will," he promised, heading out front.

"Wait a minute," Ellie called, prompting Chase to turn around. "Did you pick up flowers?"

Chase looked confused. "No... Was I *supposed* to?"

"Yes, so you could give them to Reign when she gets here." She flashed a smile. "It's a nice gesture."

Chase held a blank stare on his mother for a moment. "Okay I'm going to say this now." He pointed to both Ava and his mother. "You two—"

"I didn't even say anything!" Ava exclaimed, placing a hand on her chest.

"Maybe not now, but you *will*," he amended, stern; Ava rolled her eyes in retaliation. "Now look, when she gets here do *not* start making jokes, suggestions, or innuendos about our nonexistent relationship." The authority in his tone was clear. "I know you mean well, but I don't want her to feel uncomfortable."

Both women stared at him.

"Got it?" he prompted.

Ellie put a hand up. "I understand and I will refrain from projecting my hopes and dreams for you and your love life on to you and Reign." She chuckled when Chase narrowed his eyes at her. "You have my word."

Chase shook his head.

"I promise," Ava added.

Giving a stiff nod, Chase headed out. "Good."

"Look at you being all protective," Ava teased.

"Ava!" Chase yelled over his shoulder.

His sister laughed while her mother shot Ava a stern look, trying not to laugh herself.

Chase walked outside. "Dad, Mom said to put the hose down and go get ready for dinner," he said.

Joseph Williams chuckled, "All right." He turned it off and rolled it up. "She told me to put on a nice shirt too, didn't she?"

Chase nodded in amusement, "Yup."

Shaking his head, a smile crossed his father's distinguished brown face. "Still know what she's going to say after all of these years," he commented. "Despite how much of what she says gets on my nerves—it's a beautiful thing." He pointed to Chase. "Don't tell her that I said that first part."

Chase laughed a little. "Your secret is safe." He put his hands in his pants pockets. "Hopefully one day I'll experience that," he said after a moment.

"You *will*," his father promised.

Chase shrugged. He wasn't so sure if his father was right; if he couldn't marry the right woman, he wouldn't get married at all. He'd rather be alone than not be with the one that he yearned for. He let out a sigh. "Anyway—"

Both he and his father glanced to the curb as Reign's car pulled up.

Joseph signaled for her to roll down her window when he saw that she was looking for a space. "You can park in the driveway," he said.

"Are you sure?" Reign asked, seeing both Chase and Ava's cars parked on the street. "I see their cars—"

"Yeah, they'll be all right," Joseph assured, waving his hand dismissively.

Reign did as she was told, pulling up the driveway.

Joseph moved around Chase to get to the door; in passing, he took notice of how his son's gaze was fixated on her. He gave Chase a slight nudge, prompting Chase to look at him. "Yeah, you'll experience it," he said, smiling.

He then looked to Reign as she stepped out of the car, before Chase had a chance to question what he meant. "Hello Reign."

"Hi Mr. Joe," she beamed, grabbing a small bag from her car. "Good to see you." She eyed the wetness of the driveway. "I see you cleaned the driveway."

"Yup, laying out the clean carpet for you, my dear," Joseph chortled, before going into the house.

Reign giggled as Chase shook his head at his father.

"He went through all of that spraying and it'll be dirty tomorrow," Chase jeered.

Reign laughed, "Leave him alone." She stood as Chase approached her, smiling as he hugged her. She closed her eyes, relishing the embrace.

Parting from her, Chase eyed the bag in her hand. "What's that?"

She glanced down at it briefly. "Oh, just some wine."

Chase slowly folded his arms. "You just *had* to bring something, huh?" Humor laced his voice.

"Yeah well, blame my mother. She taught me to always bring something when I show up to someone's house," Reign reasoned. "It didn't matter if it was a cookie, you just better bring something to be polite."

He chuckled, then gestured to the door with his head. "Come in."

Smiling, she followed him to the door.

Reign eyed the dishes of food set in the middle of the dining room table. The baked Bar B Q chicken, baked fish with herbs, baked macaroni and cheese, candied carrots, cabbage, string beans, potato salad and fresh dinner rolls looked *and* smelled divine, but it surely was an abundance.

"Ms. Ellie, are you *sure* you're only feeding five people?" Reign quipped.

Ava quickly pointed to her mother, the same time that Chase did. "We tell her all the time that she overcooks," Ava teased as Chase nodded in agreement.

"Look, I enjoy cooking, and it's not like you two don't take advantage of the extras and pack up the leftovers," Ellie threw back to her children.

Chase laughed, "She's right, I *do* eat for days after."

"Like *four* days, then the food just sits there because I can't take eating it anymore," Ava threw in.

Ellie shook her head as her husband chuckled at her.

"We're just playing, you know that we appreciate you Mom," Chase assured.

"I know, I know." Ellie waved her hand. "All right everybody, prayer. Hold hands." She held her arms out, locking hands with her husband and Ava who were sitting on both sides of her, then waited for everyone else to lock theirs. Bowing her head, she blessed the food, then lifted her head back up. "Everybody dig in."

It didn't take long for everyone to fill their plates. For the first fifteen minutes, no one barely said a word as they enjoyed the delicious meal that had been lovingly prepared.

"There is no better sound than *nothing* when people are eating," Ellie smiled. "It means that everything is good."

"It really is," Reign praised, breaking a roll in half. "I don't know what you put in your potato salad, but I wish that I had the recipe."

Ellie smiled at her. "I'll give it to you."

Reign's eyes widened. "Oh—thank you," she replied, grateful. Most cooks that she knew were hesitant about sharing their special recipes. She was pleasantly surprised that Ellie would offer so easily.

Ava's eyes brightened with excitement. "Ooh, since you're giving out recipes, can you give *me* the one for the pound cake?"

"No. *That* recipe stays with me," Ellie immediately declined.

Ava snickered, "Fine stingy."

The group continued to dine. "So Reign, how's the family?" Ellie asked after a while.

Reign took a quick sip of her lemon iced tea. "The family is good," she answered. "My sister is back at school, this is her last year. She's graduating in December." She set her glass back down. "My parents are well."

"I'm glad that your father recovered from his surgery. I know that some people *especially* of our age, don't always gain full mobility, so that's a blessing," Ellie said, sincere. "And your mother is such a sweetheart. I still have the 'thank you' card that she sent me for the gift basket, on my mantle."

"You mean the extra-large, glittery card?" Reign chortled. "She'll be happy to hear that and thank you for the kind words."

Ellie gave a nod as she scooped more food onto her fork. "And how have *you* been?"

Reign paused short of taking another sip of her drink. "Umm...I'm doing pretty well, I'd say," she answered. She felt like the center of attention, and had to admit that it was a little uncomfortable. Not because she didn't want to talk; she just didn't want to talk about *herself* all night. "Work is great. I still love what I do so I can't complain."

Ellie grinned. "That's good to hear." She looked at Chase. "*Speaking* of work, Chase, I'm glad that you finally decided to stay local. It's nice having you home."

Chase finished swallowing the food in his mouth, then took a sip of tea. "Yeah," he agreed. "I have to admit, traveling was getting tiring."

Ava scooped some food onto her fork. "You're saying that you're perfectly fine with not traveling again?" she asked, eyeing him. Chase hadn't left town since he'd returned from his three-week trip seven months ago. She had a feeling why, Ava just wondered if he'd ever admit it to *himself.*

Chase shrugged. "Not saying that if I absolutely *had* to in the future, that I *wouldn't* but...as of right now...I prefer to be home."

Ava smirked. "Hmm," she muttered, putting her fork to her lips. She let out a gasp, dropping the fork to her plate as she received a kick to her leg under the table. "Ouch—Mom, *Seriously?!*" she screeched, grabbing her calf.

"Oh, I'm so sorry baby—You promised—I am *so* sorry," Ellie quickly consoled. Ava held an angry, narrowed gaze on her. "Do you need some ice, my dear?"

Ava just glared, rubbing her leg. Chase, Reign, and her father were doubled over with laugher. "I'm glad that you all find Ellie's childishness funny," she spat. She sucked her teeth when her mother joined them.

Chapter Twenty-Eight

REIGN LEFT HER OFFICE, HEADING straight for Ava's desk. She slammed her hand on it. "Hey!" she belted out.

Startled, Ava let out a scream as she turned around. Reign, as well as nearby coworkers, busted out laughing. "Funny, give me a heart attack and this line edit won't get finished," Ava jeered.

Reign folded her arms. "I apologize, I couldn't resist," she said, humor still in her voice. "Actually, I *don't* apologize. That was payback for scaring *me* the other day when you barged into my office, making me spill juice on myself."

Ava snickered. "I didn't mean to, but it was hilarious."

Reign gave Ava's arm a playful nudge. "Anyway, come step into my office for a moment please."

Tracy slid her seat back, peering around her cubicle as Ava stood from her seat. "Oooh, somebody's in trouble," Tracy teased. "Perhaps you should've completed those edits *before* now, *huh* Ava?"

Both Ava and Reign shot stern side-glances Tracy's way.

Tracy laughed it off at first. But seeing the seriousness on both women's faces, she stopped and cleared her throat. "I'll just go back to minding my own business," she sputtered.

Reign tilted her head, slowly forcing a smile, "Good idea."

Ava turned away, successfully concealing a snicker.

With nervous eyes, Tracy followed Reign's progress as she walked off. "Reign—Ms. Price, I'll have those revisions done before I leave today," she called after her.

"Perfect," Reign threw over her shoulder.

Ava walked into the office behind Reign, closing the door. "I *told* her about being nosey," she chortled.

244

Reign shook her head as she sat down. "Have a seat please."

Sitting down, the humor left Ava's face. "Okay... *Am* I in trouble?"

Reign chuckled at her. "No." She pushed her hair behind her ear. "I called you in here because I wanted to discuss your career path."

Ava fidgeted in her seat. "What, *about* it?"

"Well, as great as you are at what you do, I feel that in order for you to go further in this business, you should be adding more to your skillset," Reign explained. Ava eyed her intently. "That being said, I am assigning you a developmental editing project. I want you to work on it."

Ava's eyes widened. "Rae, you *know* I can't do developmental editing," she protested. "That's never been my skill."

"I know that, *however* it's something that you *should* be doing," Reign stood firm. "And it's not that you *can't* do it, you *don't*."

"I get it, but I just feel that that type of editing needs someone who knows how a story should be *told*."

"*You know* how a story should be told." Reign gestured to Ava with her hand. "You've read and edited *enough* of them."

Ava let out a quick sigh. "You *know* what I mean."

Reign folded her hands on her desk. "Listen Ava, you are an amazing editor, and based on my conversations with management, you should be *lead* editor. But I can't promote you until you've grasped *all* forms of editing."

Ava sighed, then gave a nod.

"Plus, should I eventually leave this department to focus a hundred percent on writing, *you* would technically be next in line for the supervisor position, so you'll definitely need this skill," Reign added, folding her arms. She sat back in her seat. "And even if you *don't* want to become a supervisor down the line or even lead editor, you're still going to learn it because I know you'd be good at it, and I believe in your talent."

Ava squinted at Reign, recognizing the change in her voice; Reign was mocking how *she* sounded when she had been pressing

Reign to take on ghostwriting. Ava shook her head and tried not to laugh. "You've been waiting to get me back for that haven't you?"

Reign giggled, "Kind of. But on a serious note, you will be good at it," she said. "I want you to try your hand at this project, okay?"

"Okay." Ava crossed her arms. "You just have to promise not to fire me if I suck at it."

"You won't suck at it," Reign stated, confident. "Okay, quick non-work-related topic... I found a lounge that I think you're going to like for your birthday next week. Rooftop, good DJ and a bar full of that nasty liquor."

Ava perked up. "Heeeyyy." She danced in her seat. "We're taking a car service that night, so prepare to take some shots."

"Shots of water?" Reign questioned.

Ava glared at her. "Don't make me yell at you in the workplace."

Reign laughed.

Marcy sat on the couch with her head in her hands. She'd been sitting there for the past hour in silence. Hearing keys jingle in the door, she jumped up. Standing there facing the door, she folded her arms. Troy walked in, and she fixed him with a glare.

Troy looked back at her, annoyed. "What?" he spat.

"Where the hell *were* you?" she charged, angry.

"At work." He tossed his jacket on the couch.

He tried to make his way past Marcy to the kitchen, but she grabbed his arm, stopping him. "Don't lie to me."

Troy jerked away from her. "Marcy, don't start your shit."

"I called your office, and your ass wasn't there."

Troy spun around to face her. "What the fuck were you doing calling my office?"

"To see if *your* lying ass was *there*," she hurled. "You weren't there *today*, and you weren't there *yesterday*. So, where *were* you?"

Troy grabbed his face, rubbing it vigorously. "I swear to—why are you still *here*?" he barked.

"*First* of all, the last place I want to be right now, is *this* dirty ass house," she hissed. "You are disgusting, you know that? You're a thirty-five-year-old, grown ass man and you have *yet* to grasp the concept of cleaning up after yourself."

"*You wanted* me, so this is what you get," he bit back, going to the kitchen. She followed him. "Marcy, leave me alone for *five minutes* okay!"

"No, not until you tell me where you were!"

"I was just *out*," he snapped, tossing his arms up. "I was driving around, *sitting* around, doing not a goddamn thing. I just didn't want to be at work, and I didn't want to be in this house with *you*. Why are you here?"

Marcy stared him down. "Because in case you've forgotten, I got evicted last week."

"I'm trying to figure out how that's my problem," Troy spat.

"It's *your problem* because I can't pay my rent without *money*, money that *you promised* to give me," Marcy countered.

Troy scrunched his face. "You *do* realize that I only gave you that shit back then so you'd keep your mouth shut right?"

Placing her hands on her hips, Marcy stood unwavering. "It doesn't matter, you still promised it to me."

Troy rolled his eyes. "Well even if I *wanted* to give it to you, which I *don't*, it's not happening because I was demoted at my job," he grunted. "Are you happy now?"

"Am I happy that you're becoming a bum, who barely goes to work anymore? No, I'm not," Marcy barked back. "Am I happy that I allowed myself to get fired thinking that *you* were going to take care of me? No. Am I happy that I have to stay *here* with you because I lost my apartment, and my parents won't help me out? No. No, I'm not happy."

Shrugging, Troy searched for a bottle of liquor in a cabinet. "Well, that makes two of us," he muttered.

Marcy shook her head. "So, is that why you've been out all day cheating? Because you're unhappy?"

Troy looked at her. "I'm not cheating," he denied. "Trust me, I don't want to deal with any more chicks like *you*."

Marcy glared daggers at him. "Fuck you."

"Yeah, at this point, I don't even want to do *that*, anymore."

"Yeah, I can tell," her voice dripped with disdain. "*No* effort anymore."

Troy smirked. "I still get mine, so like your lack of a place to live, your inability to get off is *your* problem."

Marcy narrowed her eyes at him. She wanted to pick up and leave right then and there, but she had no place to go. She'd put all of her eggs into one basket when it came to Troy—chasing what she thought to be the good life—and in a matter of months, the relationship that she'd bragged about stealing from Reign had soured. Her selfish actions had costed her a good man in Chase, a friendship in Reign, and her own happiness. "Whatever Troy," she sneered, finally.

Troy grabbed the bottle of vodka and made his way out of the kitchen. "Yeah, whatever," he mumbled. "I wish I would've never started messing with your ass."

The last part wasn't low enough; Marcy had heard it anyway. She followed his progress out of the kitchen, tears filling her eyes. "Yeah, me too," she said to herself.

Chase smoothed his suit jacket and headed for the counter to retrieve his food order. As he grabbed the paper bag filled with his dinner, he caught the cashier staring at him; both eyes *and* mouth wide open. The woman was practically salivating.

He chuckled to himself. It wasn't rare; most women looked at him that way, especially when he was in a suit. He was flattered, but not interested. "Have a nice day," he smiled to the awestruck woman.

"You too," she sputtered in return, twirling some of her hair around her finger.

Chase shook his head in amusement as he walked out of the door. Looking at his watch, he trotted to his car and unlocked it. The cool air brushing by him, he paused short of getting into his car; looking up.

The orange and pink colors in the sky meant the sun would be setting soon. Having a thought, he smiled to himself. He grabbed his cell phone and made a call.

"Hi... What are you doing right now? ...Would you be opposed to taking a ride with me somewhere? ...Okay, I'll be there in a half hour. Dress comfortable...yeah, no heels." Chase chuckled at the response. "See you—oh wait, did you eat dinner yet? I can bring you something... You sure? ...Okay then, see you in a bit." Smile not leaving his face, he jumped into the car.

Chapter Twenty-Nine

CHASE PULLED ONTO THE DIRT road, putting the car in park. He glanced over at Reign; she had the roof handle in a firm grip with a stunned look on her face. He let out a laugh. "Are you okay?" he asked.

Staring out in front of her, Reign gritted her teeth. "Chase Bradley Williams, don't you *ever* do that again without giving me a warning first," she slowly ground out, enunciating each word.

He put a hand on his chest. "I'm sorry. You're right, I should've warned you," he apologized. "But we're here now, so…are you ready to get out?"

Reign looked at him, narrowing her eyes. "I *will* be…once I pry my fingers from this handle."

Chase couldn't help but laugh again as he reached over, gently prying them loose. "You're safe, don't worry. I do this all the time."

"Um hmm," she grunted as Chase got out of the car. He opened her door, holding his hand out for hers. She put her hand in his and stepped out.

"Can you walk?" he teased.

Reign curled her lip. "Shut up." She went to walk but stopped. Her legs were shaking a bit; she put her hands on her knees, taking a deep breath. "Give me a second."

"Okay." After a few moments, he tapped her shoulder. "You ready?"

Standing up straight, she nodded.

Grabbing her hand, Chase walked Reign away from the car and along a path. She glanced around. Now that she had calmed down a bit, it began to register that she was in the mountains — a place that she'd always seen in the distance but had never been to.

250

"How is it so far?" he asked her as they ambled.

Reign looked at him. "It's...*weird* being up here," she admitted. "A little eerie even. I mean, don't get me wrong it's beautiful up close, but knowing how they look in the distance... It'll take some getting used to."

"Yeah, I hear you," he agreed. "I'm used to it now, but when I first drove up here, I was a little scared myself."

Reign squinted. "I didn't say that I was scared."

Chase shot her a knowing look. "The way that you started screaming at me when I started driving up the hill, tells me otherwise."

Reign's eyed widened. "How was I *supposed* to react?" She delivered a light tap to his arm when he laughed. "Don't laugh at me," she pouted.

When Chase had picked Reign up, he hadn't told her where they were going. Thinking that they were just going for a quick drive, Reign had settled in for the ride. The further Chase drove, the more curious she'd become. When he'd begun driving up the well-traveled mountain path, she'd started freaking out.

Chase stopped laughing and put a hand on her shoulder. "I didn't mean to scare you," he promised, sincere. "I remember you saying that you'd never been, so...I wanted to bring you."

Reign smiled softly. "I appreciate it." She let out a quick breath. "But I wasn't scared...I was *unnerved*—yes it basically means the same thing, it just sounds better," she added when Chase opened his mouth to question her.

He gave a nod. "Okay then... Sorry that I *unnerved* you."

Reign giggled a bit.

Chase scanned his surroundings, focusing on something in the distance. "Do you want to see something cool?" he asked. She raised an eyebrow. "I promise, you'll love it...trust me."

Reign nodded. "Okay." She allowed Chase to lead her to a clearing. Upon sight, she gasped. Eyes wide, she stared in awe. Reign had seen the sunset in her home state countless times, but to see it from a mountain was another experience. "Oh my God," she breathed.

He walked her a few steps further, then stopped. "It's beautiful, isn't it?"

Her bright eyes sparkled. "That is a freakin' *understatement*." She patted the pocket of her jeans. "Shit, I left my phone in the car. I need a picture of this."

Chase grabbed his phone from his pocket. Snapping a picture, he looked at it, grimacing. "This camera doesn't do this view justice." He held it out for Reign to see.

Reign glanced at the screen. "My phone camera takes better photos. Can you walk me back to the car to get it?"

"Sure." They began the journey back to the vehicle. "After you take your picture, do you want to hang out here for a while?" he proposed. "I have a blanket in my trunk that we can sit on the ground for when we get tired of standing."

She smiled. "Sure, I'd love to hang out."

"Great."

It took them a few minutes to make it back to the car. They grabbed Reign's cell phone, some bottled water, a flashlight and the large, bright yellow blanket that Chase had mentioned prior, then headed back to their chosen spot.

Once the sun had fully set, the pair took a seat on the blanket covered spot on the ground. Chase glanced at Reign, who was busy scrolled through her many pictures of the evening sky.

"Do you want me to turn the flashlight on?" he asked.

Setting her phone at her side, Reign looked up at the sky. The moon was full and bright; the stars were abundant, sparkling like diamonds. The city lights from below completed the peaceful atmosphere. She shook her head. "No, it'll just interfere with the scenery."

Chase nodded in agreement. "Yeah, the light from this thing *is* pretty obnoxious," he admitted, humored.

She giggled. Bringing her knees to her chest, she folded her arms around them. "I see why you come up here often to unwind," she said, eyes still fixated on the sky.

Chase adjusted his position on the blanket, leaning back on

his elbows. "Yeah, it definitely helps to clear the mind…especially after a bad or even just *long* day."

"If I weren't so nervous to make the drive up here myself, I'd come up here a lot to write," she said. "I could see myself writing a whole book up here."

"Well, if you want, you can come up here with me as much as you want."

Reign glanced at him. "You wouldn't mind?"

He shook his head. "Not at all. I'd even let you have this spot to yourself, while you write." He gestured to a spot, just a few feet away. "I'd shut up and sit over there somewhere."

Reign peered over at the spot, chuckling a bit. "Nah, you don't have to be that far." She pondered for a second. "I *would* need the quiet though."

"You'd have it," Chase promised.

Reign took a deep breath, inhaling the fresh air and surveying the mountainous rocks around her. Smiling to herself, she looked at Chase, who was fixated on the view. "Chase," she softly called.

He looked at her.

"Thank you for listening to me," she said.

Chase squinted, confused. "What do you mean?"

"I mean… I didn't have to ask or even *mention* it over and over. You just heard me say that I'd never been up here, and you took it upon yourself to bring me," she explained, grateful. "You heard me… you *listened* to me, and you just *did* it."

"You don't have to thank me for doing something that's natural to me." Chase eyed her intently. "I've *always* listened to you; I've always *heard* you."

Reign smiled, crinkling her nose. "Say you're welcome."

Chase laughed a bit. "You're welcome," he echoed, giving her a nod. "Anytime."

Reign took another deep breath, then coughed. "Yeah, I think I just inhaled dirt particles."

Chase grabbed a bottle of chilled water, handing it to her. She opened and drank almost half of the big bottle without stopping.

He raised an eyebrow. "You know we're nowhere near a bathroom, right?"

"Hush." She screwed the top back on. "I just wanted to make sure nothing was in my throat." She set the bottle aside. After a moment, she shivered. "That was stupid because that water was cold, now *I'm* cold." She looked down at her cotton long-sleeved shirt. "I should've worn something heavier than this."

Chase changed his position. Sitting behind her, he stretched his legs out on both sides of her. "Sit back," he prompted, putting his hands on her shoulders. On instinct Reign moved back against him, leaning her head against his chest; he wrapped his arms around her to keep her warm.

"I am so pathetic in the wilderness." She covered his arms with hers. "Inhaling dust, making myself cold." She shook her head. "I'm surprised I haven't tripped over a rock and fallen yet."

Chase chuckled a bit. "It's your first time, don't be so hard on yourself," he placated. "Next time, I'll bring you a *room* temperature bottle."

A soft laugh escaped her. "I'd probably just spill it on myself."

"No, you'd probably spill it on *me*," he teased.

Reign laughed again. "Right," she agreed, glancing back at him.

Chase looked down at her, and this time Reign couldn't look away.

Reign's laughter subsided; the humor left her face. Like before when they'd shared a dance, their intense gazes were fixed on one another, each struggling with what they were feeling inside but didn't have the *courage* to say.

But *unlike* last time, there was no loud music, chattering patrons, or clinking dishes to snap them out of their trance. It was just the two of them, sitting up on a mountain in each other's arms with the moon and stars above them.

Chase wasn't going to miss his chance again; he leaned in and kissed Reign. It was soft, sensual, and accepted. They parted briefly, almost waiting for the other to get up or say something. Instead, they kissed again. This time Chase deepened it, and Reign responded with equal passion. The heat between them intensified as he moved from behind her and gently laid her back on the blanket, positioning himself on top of her.

Reign closed her eyes and let out a breath as Chase's lips moved lower. She relished the feeling of his kisses along her slender neck and her jawline. He gently touched her face as he reclaimed her lips once again. Reign wrapped her arms around his neck as his free hand roamed over her body.

He hadn't dare let his touch wander beneath her clothing, but Reign was yearning for him to. She was so caught up in the moment that she'd almost forgotten they were outside. Turning her head, allowing Chase more access to her neck, she opened her eyes briefly. Even though it took a moment for her eyes to adjust again in the darkness, they *did* eventually adjust—and focus. And widen in horror at what was moving along the brightly colored blanket within inches of her face.

She vigorously tapped Chase's shoulder. "Chase, it's a goddamn scorpion!" she belted out.

Chase jerked his head from her neck, glancing over, eyes wide. "Shit!" He quickly jumped up, pulling Reign up along with him. He guided her out of harms reach, then folded the scorpion up in the blanket and hurled it away. It landed on a rock several feet from them. He turned to Reign; she had her hand on her chest, trying to catch her breath.

Chase let out a deep, loud sigh. *I should've stepped on that goddamn thing!* That scorpion was his new worst enemy; it had ruined *the* moment. "I umm…I'd say it's time to go," he said, resolved.

Reign nodded, her breathing steadying. "What about your blanket?"

"It can have it."

Reign couldn't help it; she busted out laughing. As annoyed as she was to have their moment of passion interrupted by the poisonous creature, she took it as a sign that they should've stopped anyway.

Chase shook his head as he laughed a bit himself. "First a bunny and now a scorpion," he commented, walking to her. He took her hand and they headed back for the car.

Reign glanced at her front door as Chase pulled up to her house. She undid her seatbelt.

He looked at her. "Do you want me to stay in the car again?"

She shook her head slightly, staring back at him. "You can walk me to my door," she softly granted.

Chase turned the car off, then got out of the car along with Reign. They walked in silence up to her door. She unlocked it, stopping short of entering. She faced him.

"Thank you for today..." she fiddled with the keys in her hand. "I...appreciate it."

"It's no problem," he replied, voice lowered. "I'm glad that you enjoyed yourself."

Reign nodded, glancing down at the ground briefly. She didn't know what else to say; she'd just had an intense make out session with her friend, and she didn't know how to feel about it. She looked back at him. "I umm—"

"We don't have to talk about it," Chase slid in. His tone was sullen.

Reign let out a sigh of relief. "Okay," she said. "Okay good..." She pointed to the silhouette in the distance. "Let's just leave that, up *there*."

Chase glanced back at it for a moment, then turned back to her. He let out a sigh; he wished that he hadn't suggested not talking about it. He *wanted* to. He wanted it to go *further*. "Okay...we'll do that," he replied after a moment. Leaning in, he planted a soft kiss to her cheek.

Reign closed her eyes as his lips touched her. Just that simple gesture had heated her up all over again.

He stepped back. "Good night."

"Good—good night" she stammered, then bolted into the

house, leaving him standing there. Shutting the door, Reign leaned her back against it. She stood there, staring out in front of her, mind running a thousand miles a minute. After a moment, she closed her eyes and softly bumped the back of her head against the door.

"Shit, shit. What are you *doing*?" she huffed aloud

Opening her eyes, she let out a deep sigh, and headed straight for her staircase. There were two things that she needed: a cold shower, and her notebook.

Walking into the living room with a cup of hot tea in hand, Reign made her way over to her favorite spot on the floor near her fireplace. She'd showered and changed into her pajamas, then grabbed a notebook, her favorite ink pen, a plush throw blanket and ventured back downstairs.

While the thoughts churning in her head prevented her from getting to sleep anytime soon, they didn't prevent her from journaling. She filled half a notebook with all that she was feeling, before pausing to get her tea.

Chase had been drawing out emotions from her that Reign hadn't experienced in a long time, ones she didn't think she *could* have. She had to get them out, if she had any hope of drifting off to sleep before sunup.

She took a careful sip of her chamomile tea, setting the mug on an end table beside her. Just as she picked up her pen again, a knock sounded on the door. Confusion settling in on her face, she glanced at the clock hanging on the wall in front of her, then towards the front door. Resigned, she stood up. "Who the hell is at my house at almost midnight?"

Tossing her book on the coffee table, she headed for the door. Peeking out of the peephole, her eyes widened. She quickly pulled the door open.

Chase was standing on her front step. "H—hi," he breathed.

Reign's heart raced at the sight of him; she'd just left him mere hours ago and here he was, back at her doorstep. Though she was curious as to what he wanted, she couldn't help but be happy to see him. "Hey," she got out finally. Reign moved aside to let him in, closing the door behind him. She turned to face him. "What are you doing back here?"

Chase stood in the vestibule, staring at Reign at a loss for words. "I umm…I don't know," he sputtered.

Puzzled, Reign folded her arms. "O-kay," she drew out.

Reign wasn't upset that Chase was here at this hour; she was *concerned*. He never dropped by without calling her first, and his demeanor was different, almost as if he was in a trance.

She gestured to the living room. "Do you want to come all the way in?"

"Yeah." Chase followed Reign in silence.

He didn't know what had driven him to return to Reign's house. When he'd returned home after dropping her off, Chase had every intention of doing what he *could* to occupy his mind. He'd showered, ate dinner, then tried doing some work. Unable to focus, he'd put on a movie. He didn't even make it past the opening credits before he turned it off in favor of reading.

Chase didn't make it past the first chapter.

Nothing that he did could get his mind off Reign—off of what they had shared—what they'd almost *did*. Even when he'd attempted to sleep, he couldn't. He'd just laid there, staring at the ceiling until he could no longer take it, finally deciding to drive back to her house.

Reign stood in front of him, folding her arms. "Do you want anything?" she asked, breaking through the silence. "Anything to drink or eat or…*anything?*"

Slowly, Chase shook his head, eyes fixed in an intense stare. "No."

Running a hand through her hair, Reign moved over to where she'd been sitting before Chase had knocked on her door. "I don't understand what's—" she looked at him, worry in her eyes. "Chase, you're scaring me." His presence wasn't scary *to* her; she was just afraid that something was going on *with* him, or that something had *happened to* him.

Chase's gaze had yet to waiver. "I'm sorry, I'm not trying to."
The sincerity in his low tone was heavy.

Reign gave a nod. "Well…are you *okay*?"

Chase took a deep breath. "Yes."

He tried to form a clear thought in his head. He'd shown up to
Reign's home without an explanation, and knew that he'd owed her
one. They should talk; he should say *something*. But as he stood there,
in front of the woman he was falling for, looking even more beautiful
in the flickering light of the fireplace, Chase could no longer hold it
together—he wanted her.

Reign opened her mouth to ask another question, but Chase
closed the distance between them first. Before she could say a word,
he held Reign's face gently with his hands and kissed her.

Her initial shock quickly wore off as the kiss deepened. She
wrapped her arms around his neck, pulling him closer. He wrapped his
arms around *her*, holding her tight. His embrace was burning her up.

With her body pressed against his, his hands roamed over her.
Chase reached under her shirt, and ran his hands up her bare back.
She bared her neck for him as his kisses trailed down her cheek,
allowing him room to continue giving her soft sensual kisses until
he met the collar of her shirt. Reign ran her hand down his chest,
gripping the fabric of his shirt when his kisses turned from soft to
demanding. The feeling of his lips on her, paired with the hardness in
his pants pressing against her, sent her desires into overdrive.

Chase tugged his shirt off, then helped Reign out of hers before loosening his pants, letting them fall to the floor. He eyed her
bare breasts with hunger. Laying her down on the blanket in front
of the fire, Chase kissed her deeply, his hands caressing her body.
Reign's hands traced his chest, caressing his abs until her hands were
on his hips, uncertain if she should go further. She couldn't remember the last time her body was touched with such sensuality; the last
time she felt this much *passion*.

In that moment, it didn't register to Reign that she and Chase
were about to cross a line — one they had been diligent to maintain

since her prom night. She only knew what she wanted and what she wanted was Chase to never stop touching her.

She drew in a sharp breath when his tongue brushed over one of her erect nipples. Her back arched, pushing her chest closer to his face. Chase took his time with each one, touching, nibbling, sucking, and caressing.

The moans that flowed from Reign's throat only heightened Chase's yearning. He moved further down her body, planting kisses along her waist, moving to her stomach. He paused long enough to remove her pajama shorts, before reclaiming his position between her thighs. Reign stretched her legs for him without hesitation.

Holding her hips secure with his hands, Chase planted soft kisses along them, caressing her thighs, before finally tasting her with his tongue.

Reign clutched the throw beneath her as Chase's tongue flicked against her in a steady rhythm. She moaned deeper, louder, never thinking she was a loud lover until now. What he was making her feel was beyond anything that she'd ever felt before.

During her first time with Chase, she'd been nervous and in-experienced. This time, she was a grown woman; she knew her body, knew what she wanted and what she needed.

The pleasure Chase was giving her became so intense that Reign had to put her hand on his head to push him away. He took her hand in a firm grip instead, holding on tight, refusing to let up until he'd given her the ecstasy she deserved.

It didn't take long for Reign's pleasure to build to the point of spilling over. Crying out, her back arched and her legs shook as a strong orgasm surged through her body. Chase ran his tongue against her heated flesh once more, tasting the juices that flowed from her.

Eyes squeezed shut, Reign laid there, trying to catch her breath, as Chase retraced his kisses up her body.

Chase met her face to face, his hard body pressing down on hers. Eyeing her longingly, he touched her hair, her face, then drew his finger along her collarbone.

Reign finally opened her eyes, meeting his lustful gaze. As she touched his face, she ached for him to finish what he'd started. When he didn't move, she gazed deep into his eyes, studying them. The way he was looking at her, Chase was waiting on her consent to go further. With a nod, Reign gave it to him.

Not hesitating a moment more, Chase reached for his pants, dragging them over. Pulling out his wallet, he retrieved a condom. Reign's eyes roamed over Chase's body as he pushed himself back to put the condom on. Her eyes lingered, watched him roll the protective barrier over the length of him; something she'd never seen on prom night. There was no doubt in her mind, she wanted to feel him, *all* of him.

Reign gripped Chase's back as he repositioned himself on top of her, holding steady at her opening. Reign sucked in a breath as Chase slowly entered, filling her. Chase buried his face into her neck and groaned as he relished the feeling of her; she was tight, wet and felt better than he'd remembered. Deep inside of her, he held still for a moment, allowing her to adjust. Finally he began moving his hips. Like with his tongue, Chase's initial strokes were slow and steady, before becoming faster, deeper.

Reign wrapped her long legs around him, pulling him closer. Sounds of pleasure filled the room as they moved in sync, the feelings that they'd kept hidden coming out at last.

Deep moans came from Reign as a second orgasm overcame her. Her body trembled in his arms, sending Chase into overdrive. As much as he wanted to last longer, feeling her inner walls clench around him forced his own release.

Spent, Chase collapsed on top of her, trying to catch his breath. Lifting his head after a moment, he softly kissed her cheek, before rolling off and onto the floor. In silence, they laid side by side, trying to catch their breath and process what had just happened.

Chase reached for Reign's hand. Taking hold of it, he gave it a kiss before placing it over his heart.

Turning on her side, Reign pulled part of the blanket over her naked body. Chase turned over, laying at her back. Wrapping his arms around her, he pulled her closer. Neither one had said a word.

As Chase drifted off, Reign laid there, staring out in front of her. If her mind was loud before, it was *thundering* now.

She'd just had sensual, passionate sex with *Chas*e; a man she considered to be one of her closest friends. A man she'd never thought she'd *kiss* again, let alone have sex with.

What did we just do? Reign, what were you thinking? He's your friend, you can't go down this road.

Reign rubbed her face with her hand, trying to silence the voice in her head. Though she was unsuccessful, she could no longer keep her eyes open. Succumbing to her exhaustion, she drifted off to sleep, secure in Chase's arms.

Chapter Thirty

CYNTHIA SPEARED HER FRUIT SALAD with her fork, taking a bite. "You should give me some of this to take back to school with me," she said, chewing.

Reign stared out in front of her, focusing on the scenery in the distance. Feeling a breeze brush by, she pulled her cardigan closed and folded her arms.

"Rae, are you listening to me?" Cynthia asked, grabbing her glass of juice. She tapped the patio table with her free hand when Reign didn't answer.

Startled, Reign flinched. "Huh? What?"

Cynthia narrowed her eyes. "Did you hear what I said?"

Reign looked at her. "No, sorry. What did you say?"

Cynthia pointed to her salad, "I was saying that you should—" When she noticed that Reign's gaze had wandered off yet again, she sucked her teeth. "Giselle!"

"Calling me by my middle name accomplishes *what* exactly?" Reign ground out.

Cynthia made a face. "Look, if you're not going to engage with me, you might as well take your chilly behind back inside and leave me to eat my food in peace."

Reign shot her sister a glare, then made a move to get up.

Cynthia immediately reached over, grabbing her sister's arm. "No, no, I'm joking!" Cynthia belted out. "Sit down. Don't leave me."

Reign sat down, shaking her head.

After Chase had left earlier that morning, Reign had retreated to her room with the hopes of falling back to sleep. Instead, she wound up lying wide awake for hours. Only Cynthia calling with the news that

263

she was in town and wanted to stop by had forced her out of bed. Enjoying lunch on the patio in her backyard, Reign was trying to engage with her sister, but with so much on her mind it was nearly impossible.

Reign ran a hand through her hair. "What made you decide to come home on such short notice?" she asked.

Cynthia continued to eat her food. "I had a doctor's appointment."

Reign nodded. Folding her arms again, she leaned back in her seat. "Checkup, or issue? You're not pregnant, are you?"

Cynthia rolled her eyes. "No, *Mom 2.0*," she jeered. Reign chuckled a bit. "It's *just* a checkup."

Reign shrugged, "Was just checking."

"Trust me, I won't be making Mom and Dad grandparents anytime soon, I *keep* a condom with me." Cynthia reached for her glass of juice. "Have a stash in my bedroom drawer too."

"Smart girl," Reign approved. Reign had her *own* small stash of condoms, though she hadn't expected to *need* one anytime soon.

Cynthia sipped the chilled beverage, then set the glass aside. "Anyway, you're asking *me* if *I'm* pregnant, are *you* pregnant?"

This time *Reign* rolled her eyes. "Please," she scoffed.

"Okay fair enough, but are you *getting some* at least?"

Despite the chill that ran through her body, Reign's face remained neutral. "No," she lied. Until last night, she *hadn't*.

Cynthia squinted her eyes. "I think you're lying."

Reign squinted back. "And *I* think, you've worn out your welcome, little girl," she sneered.

Cynthia laughed, "Petty."

Hearing a beep from her phone, Reign picked it up, eyeing the message.

Hi, are you busy? Do you mind if I stop over? Chase's text read.

Taking a deep breath, she sent a reply.

Hey, no, I don't mind. Just come around back, I'm sitting outside with Cynthia.

Putting her phone down, she sighed. When the line rang, Reign peered at the ID. Smirking, she picked up.

"Hello…" she answered. "I'm good, thanks. Yourself?… Yes, Saturday at nine… Yes… Nope, not a clue." She chuckled at the response. "Great, see you then…Bye."

Cynthia eyed Reign as her sister set her phone back down. "You're popular this morning, huh?" she chortled. "First a text, now a call?" She grinned, "You *sure* you aren't getting any?"

Reign flashed an annoyed look her sister's way. "I'm *seriously* regretting answering your phone call."

Cynthia laughed, relishing Reign's annoyance. "Anyway…all annoying little sister shit aside…how are you doing?"

Reign sighed, softening a bit. "I'm good… Can't complain."

Smiling, Cynthia gave a nod. "Good to hear." Cynthia ate the rest of her fruit salad before working on the raspberry danish on the plate. As she went to bite the pastry, a male voice startled her.

"Ooh!" Cynthia belted out, jerking around in her seat. Seeing Chase laughing, she rolled her eyes. "Chase you never had to sneak up like that," she grunted.

Reign shook her head at her sister's dramatic response. "He didn't *sneak*, I saw him walk back here."

Cynthia waved a hand Reign's way, then smiled up at Chase. "Good to see you again," she said to him.

"You too," he replied.

Cynthia picked her danish back up. "Do me a favor Chase, since *you* talk to Rae all the time, find out who she's getting some from and tell *me* since she insists on lying to me," she quipped.

Reign's face turned red and her eyes widened, while Chase cleared his throat. Reign tapped Cynthia on the shoulder. "Take that in the house."

Cynthia gasped, "You're sending me away?"

"*Now*, please," Reign demanded, teeth clenched.

Sucking her teeth, Cynthia grabbed her dishes. "So bossy," she muttered.

Reign followed Cynthia's progress through the sliding door. Once it was safely shut, she shot Chase a quick glance, gesturing to the table. "You can sit."

Chase sat down in the chair across from her.

Though Chase was facing her, Reign's eyes were fixed on the iron table.

Reign couldn't help but be a bit surprised that Chase wanted to see her again so soon. She'd thought that he would need time to process what had happened, like *she* did. However, him sitting before her, told her otherwise.

Chase tilted his head, gazing at her. She had yet to make contact. "Are you okay?" he asked finally.

I just had the best sex of my life with you last night, and now I can barely look at you. No, I'm not okay, Reign thought, eyes still locked on the table. "Um hmm," she murmured.

Chase sat back in his seat, nodding slowly. "Okay...so can you tell me why you aren't looking at me?"

Reign lifted her head, finally meeting his eyes. "Sorry...I saw something crawling on the table," she lied.

Chase's eyes shot down to the table, trying to see what bug had infiltrated their space. He saw nothing. "What was it?"

"A dust mite," she quickly sputtered.

Chase looked back up at Reign, a blank expression on his face. "You *saw* a dust mite?"

Embarrassed over the silly explanation, Reign hid her face behind her hand. "Forget I said that."

Folding his arms, Chase chuckled, but the humor soon left his face. "Are you *sure* you're okay?"

Reign nodded. She tilted her head. "You?"

"*Definitely.*"

Pushing her hair behind her ear, Reign tried not to blush. "Good to hear." She let out a sigh, "Chase..." she hesitated. "Do we have to talk about this?"

Chase frowned, "You don't want to?"

"It's not that I— I just kind of need a minute to process— *that*," she hesitantly put out. "I mean, it was—"

"Reign, do you regret what happened?" he slid in.

Reign put her hand forward, shaking it in his direction. "No, no, that's not what I'm saying," she assured. "I *don't* re—I *wanted* to—in that *moment*, but I still just need a minute."

Chase rubbed his chin with his hand. He had *no* regrets from last night. It had been something that he'd wanted, what he'd *hoped* for, for a *while* now. But even though he seemed calm on the outside, Chase was nervous that history might be repeating itself. "I understand," he said after a moment. "I don't want to force you to talk about it right now… I just want to make sure that we're still good."

"We *are*," she promised. "Nothing has changed between us, I promise."

Chase looked off to the side. *Nothing has changed between us.* Those words hit him like a ton of bricks. "Right…nothing has changed." He couldn't hide the disappointment in his voice. "Good to hear." He pushed his chair back. "I'll let you get back to your company."

Reign watched him stand from his seat. "Okay."

"I have to get back to working on sketches for a presentation."

She nodded, offering him a slight smile, "Good luck."

"Thanks," Chase replied, resolved. "I'll call you later."

Walking away, Chase felt like kicking himself. He'd let Reign off the hook *again*, instead of talking about the state of their relationship. And while he couldn't help but feel that Reign wasn't being honest with him or *herself*, he couldn't bring himself to be honest with *her* either.

He sighed. *You're an idiot Chase.*

Ava held a dress up to her figure, posing with it. "What do you think? Too flashy?" she asked of the sequin gold sleeveless mini dress.

Reign looked up from her phone. "No, it's cute," she dryly put out.

Ava's arms fell, clutching the dress in her hand. "Cute?" she chortled. "Yeah, I'm not getting this. As expensive as this dress is, it has to be more than *cute*."

It was after work that Tuesday, and Reign had accompanied Ava on a shopping trip to find the perfect dress for Ava's birthday outing on Saturday. Though Reign had agreed to help, her attention span just wasn't there.

"Sorry, it's not just cute, it's a beautiful dress. You'll turn heads, you'll be killin' it, all of that." Reign's lackluster tone hadn't changed.

Ava stared at her, fighting the urge to laugh. "That was the *driest* encouragement to spend all this damn money if I've ever heard one."

Reign ran a hand through her hair, sighing as Ava sat on the cushioned bench next to her. "I'm sorry sis, I don't mean to be a downer," Reign apologized, sincere. "I just have a lot on my mind right now."

Ava adjusted the dress on her lap. "And not a notebook in sight."

Reign managed a chuckle. "It's a good thing that I *don't* have one with me." She gestured to a secluded corner in the boutique. "I'd be laid out in the corner over there, writing in it." She let out another sigh, this time heavy.

Ava tilted her head. "You want to talk about it?"

Reign looked at her, shaking her head. "No, I'm fine. Let's just shop."

Reign had no intention of telling Ava that she'd slept with Chase—*again*—let alone how it was messing with her head. As far as Reign was concerned, some things didn't need to be shared, *especially* with Chase's sister.

Ava studied her for a moment. Reign's demeanor had been off over the past few days; her best friend had become distracted and sullen. While Ava was interested in knowing what had happened to cause such a change in her, she decided not to pry.

"Okay, if you say so luv," Ava relented, standing up. She held the dress up, examining it again.

Reign stood up. "You like this dress, so get it." She touched the fabric. "Don't let my mood deter you, it really *is* a beautiful dress."

Ava held it up high. "I'd *definitely* rock this thing."

"Then you're *getting* it, so whip out the card," Reign insisted.

Ava grinned, resting the dress on her arm. "Done." She pulled the wallet from her purse. "Are *you* buying anything out of here?"

"Uh *no*, I'm not in the mood to spend five hundred dollars on a dress today," Reign refused, surveying the boutique's expensive inventory.

Ava retrieved her wallet from her handbag. "I get that...*tomorrow* maybe?"

"Maybe," Reign chuckled.

Chase emerged from his kitchen, a plate of food in one hand and a glass of juice in the other.

"Yes, I saw your email. That is the *exact* one that I'm looking for," he spoke into his wireless earpiece. "How much do you—trust me, that doesn't concern me... Perfect, I look forward to hearing back from you... Great."

Ending the call, Chase made a beeline for his office. A light tap on the door stopped him. Setting his meal on an end table, Chase headed for the door. Peering through the peephole, a scowl took over his face.

"What the hell?" Running a hand over the back of his neck, he let out a loud, frustrated sigh. "This should be good," he muttered to himself, opening the door.

And came face to face with Marcy.

Marcy stared at him in wide-eyed silence. Almost as if she didn't expect him to open the door. She finally offered a half-smile, one that Chase didn't bother returning.

Wiping the smile from her face, Marcy cleared her throat. "Hi Chase...you look good," she sputtered.

Chase folded his arms. "I'm sure you have a reason for being here, so what is it?" he sneered. "Keep in mind that I have very little time to waste."

"I'm sure, you always *were* busy." Marcy put a hand up. "I didn't mean that in a bad way, I swear—"

"The reason and your *point*, Marcy."

Marcy sighed, trying to gather her thoughts. "I umm… I was out today—running some errands and I passed by one of the restaurants that you and I used to go to and I—" She took a deep breath. "It made me think of you and I don't know why I thought it was a good idea, but I felt like I needed to see you."

The glare had yet to leave Chase's face. "You *shouldn't* have."

"I just— I know that there is no chance that we—"

"None, at all," he curtly shot down.

"I get it," Marcy sulked. "But I feel that I at *least* owe you a face-to-face apology for what I did…"

"I don't *need* it, nor do I *want* it," Chase bristled.

Marcy fiddled with the bracelet on her wrist, sighing yet again. "I *get* that Chase, but I still *owe* it to you." She stared at him. "You may not want to hear it, but I *am* sorry for what I did." She shook her head, regret filling her. "You were good to me—you're a good man… I just didn't appreciate it."

Chase smirked; he knew Marcy well enough to know that she had an ulterior motive. She always *did* as far as he was concerned. "Things aren't going so well for you, *are* they?" he mocked. "What do you need? Money? A place to stay—what?"

Marcy's eyes widened; she had almost forgotten how perceptive he was. "Things are going just *fine* for me," she lied. "I don't want anything *from* you, I just wanted to apologize to you, *that's* all."

"Marcy—it's never that cut and dry with you." Though Chase's voice was calm, the agitation in it was clear. "See, it's always *something* with you. Everything you do has a sneaky undertone to it. I saw it through our—I can't even say *relationship* because you were fucking someone else for over *half* of it."

Marcy looked down at the ground as he ranted.

"But you know what, *I'll* take the blame because I should've ended things with you a long time ago," Chase snarled. "I should've never wasted time with someone I knew for a fact I wasn't going to build a future with."

Marcy bit her bottom lip. "Wow...that's nice Chase," she spat sarcastic.

"Oh please," Chase mocked, unfazed by the defeat on his ex-girlfriend's face. "Face it, you didn't want one with *me either*. You only wanted what you *thought* I was going to *pay* for."

Chase's words smacked Marcy in the face. "Chase, I—"

"Marcy, I've given you enough of my time. More than you *deserve*," Chase interrupted. Marcy closed her mouth. "We have nothing else to discuss… Leave."

Resolved, Marcy scratched her head. "It's clear that I…I've made a mistake by coming here."

Chase gave a nod. "Yes, you did." He grabbed hold of the door. "Do me a favor, don't do it again."

Marcy opened her mouth to say something, but the door closed in her face. She stood there for a moment, fighting the urge to cry. Glancing around to make sure no one had witnessed the embarrassing exchange, she scurried off.

Chapter Thirty-One

AVA DANCED IN HER SEAT, attempting to pour the champagne.

Reign reached over and took the bottle and the glass away from her. "Give me this before you spill it all over this limo with all of that gyrating," she chortled.

Ava laughed, adjusting the volume button. "I'll be gyrating *all night* because it's my birthday!" she squealed over the tunes blaring through the speaker system.

Reign shook her head in amusement. "We're about to get put out of this limo."

Saturday night, Reign and Ava were dressed up, styled, and on their way to Ava's lounge gathering. Ava was excited to celebrate her thirty-third birthday, but Reign was *also* looking forward to having some fun. Between the long work week, late-night ghostwriting sessions, and trying to sort out her thoughts and feelings about Chase, Reign had been tightly wound. She carefully poured champagne into the glass and handed it to Ava.

Ava paused her seat dancing to take a long sip of the chilled beverage. "Ooh this is *good*." Her eyes roamed around the car's expansive interior. "This *limo* is good too. I thought we were just going to take a car service."

"Nah, I figured we can arrive in a little more style than that… at least for tonight," Reign replied. She smiled, "You're kind of amazing, you deserve it."

Ava giggled, "Thank you. You know I appreciate you."

"You *better* because this dress that you talked me into buying for tonight hurt my bank account," Reign jeered, running her hand down the front of her sleek, black cocktail dress.

Ava pointed a warning finger at Reign. "Hush your pretty face, Price."

Reign snickered.

"Now you work your ass off. So as a *rule,* you get to occasionally treat yourself to something expensive," Ava continued, adjusting her position in her seat.

"I didn't like the zero's," Reign pouted.

Ava tried not to laugh. "Stop it." She gestured to Reign. "You look amazing in it, so you already got your money's worth."

Reign just shook her head.

Hearing her phone beep, Ava checked it. "Chase is going to be late," she announced, texting back.

Reign didn't respond, but if the butterflies in her stomach at the mention of his name could talk, they'd be loud.

"Says he's still finishing up some work." Ava slid the phone in her clutch. "Damn, they had him working overtime like crazy this week."

"Yeah, he's preparing for a big presentation," Reign told.

Due to both her and Chase's hectic work schedule the past week, she hadn't seen him since he'd stopped by her house the morning after their night together. Part of her was relieved. Reign didn't know how she would handle being alone with him again.

Not more than twenty minutes later, the limo pulled in front of the lounge. Ava and Reign stepped out and were met with the admiring groups of men gathered outside.

"Hey sexy ladies, I hope you're coming to see *me,*" one man crooned, rubbing his chin with his hands.

Reign rolled her eyes as Ava politely shook her head. "We're *not,* but thank you for the compliment," Ava spoke.

He placed a hand to his chest in dramatic fashion. "Aww, you're breaking my heart."

Not bothering to respond, Ava quickly nudged Reign inside.

"*Why* would he think that we were coming here to see his ass?" Reign spat, once inside.

Ava laughed. "*This* is why I wanted to hurry up and get you in here." She fluffed her hair. "I knew you were about to hurt that man's feelings."

Reign shook her head as they approached an elevator. "I can't believe people still flirt like that."

"*Believe* it sis, and it gets worse, trust me," Ava replied, amused.

Reign shook her head again. "Terrible."

Reaching the rooftop, they were immediately greeted by loud party music, bright lights, stylish lounge furniture and a crowd of Ava's friends and family. The top floor was enclosed in glass to keep out the chilled March evening air, while offering a full view of the stars and the Phoenix skyline. Beaming, Ava greeted and shared a quick dance with her guests.

Eventually, Reign directed Ava to her personal VIP section— equipped with bottle service, a designer birthday cake, food, and signature treats.

Ava picked up a candy-coated strawberry. "Oh my God, this looks like it's *actually* covered in jewels," she beamed, twirling the gold sugar crystal covered berry. "I almost don't want to eat it."

Reign grabbed a strawberry from the tray; she chuckled. "Hell, *I* want to." She turned to Ava, giving her a hug. "Happy birthday. Have fun, tonight."

"Thank you so much for doing this, sis," Ava gushed, hugging her back.

"You're welcome," Reign replied, parting from their embrace.

Letting out a happy sigh, Ava fluffed her curly hair. "Time for a drink!" she belted out to her crowd, resulting in cheers.

"Hand me one of those strawberries."

Ava, finally taking a bite of her strawberry, spun around at the sound of the woman's voice. "Mommy!" she shrieked mouth full.

Laughing, Ellie hugged her daughter. "Don't choke girl."

Ava waved a dismissive hand, swallowing the berry.

"I'm not staying long, but I wanted to come out and support your party," Ellie smiled, carefully putting a hand on Ava's perfectly made-up face.

Ava smiled back; most women her age would have an issue with their mother being at their party, but *she* wasn't one of them. "Ooh Mom, before you leave, you have to have a drink."

"Girl no, but I *will* take a piece of that pretty cake," Ellie threw back, giving Reign a hug.

"You'll get a piece once you take a *drink*," Ava stipulated, then snickered when her mother gasped.

Fanning her face with her hand, Reign made her way to the bar.

The party had been in full swing for nearly two hours, and while Ava had yet to stop dancing with her other guests, Reign needed a break.

"A bottle of water please," she said when the bartender asked what she'd like. Grabbing some cash and her phone from her purse, Reign eyed a text message, quickly responding back. She offered the bartender the money once he'd set the water in front of her.

"Don't worry about it," the man politely declined. "Water is on the house."

Reign offered a smile, then placed the money into his tip glass. As she went to take a sip, Ava appeared next to her, fanning herself.

"These new shoes are getting a workout," Ava panted, sitting down. She glanced over. "Mom, I thought you said you were leaving," she laughed, seeing her mother attempt to smooth her hair back up into its bun.

"I *was*, but this music…"

"Reliving your partying days, huh Ms. Ellie?" Reign slid in, tone filled with humor.

Ellie dabbed her face with a napkin. "Honey, my partying days are still upon me."

Ava tapped the bar. "I need something to drink," she announced. "The bottle at my table is gone."

"You had *two* bottles," Reign reminded.

"And they're *both* gone," Ava chuckled. "Girl, you know how my cousins get down."

Reign shook her head in amusement. She held her water bottle out. "You want some water?" she offered.

"Girl—" Ava waved a hand at Reign, then looked at the bartender. "A shot of tequila please?"

Reign turned her face up in disgust. "Ugh. Have fun with that."

"Make it *two*." Ava corrected, nudging Reign, who looked at her with wide eyes. She pointed to the counter space in front of Reign. "Set it right in front of *this* one."

"What the hell, make it three," Ellie added, waving a hand.

Ava raised her arms. "*Yes* Mommy!"

Reign couldn't help but laugh.

The bartender set the shot glasses of tequila, a saltshaker, and lime slices in front of each of the women, then went to take other orders.

Ava grabbed her glass, holding it up. "On three—Rae, pick up the damn glass, you're doing this," she demanded. "It's just one, and it's for my birthday."

Reign rolled her eyes. "Fine," she huffed, grabbing her glass.

Ava sprinkled some salt on her hand, watching as her mother and Reign did the same. "On three?" Ava prompted, then counted. Once 'three' left her lips she, along with her mother and Reign, licked the salt, then quickly downed their shots. Ava coughed as the liquid poured down her throat. "Ooh, that was rough." She quickly grabbed a lime slice, sucking on it.

"Shit," Reign grimaced of the taste.

Ava pointed to the lime slices on the plate. "Take the lime."

"That won't help," Reign replied, patting her chest.

Ellie sat her glass down. "Well on *that* note, let me take my old behind home," she said. She gave her giggling daughter and Reign kisses on their cheeks. "Good night ladies, happy birthday Ava, and get home safely—*both* of you."

Reign waved to her. "Yes ma'am."

"You too," Ava called after her mother. "Call me when you get in." She shook her head when her mother kept walking, flagging Ava in the process.

Reign sipped her water as Ava ordered another shot. While Reign was in mid-sip, a hand touching her shoulder startled her, causing her to nearly spit her water out.

"Ooh, sorry," Chase said, amused. He gently patted Reign's back as she coughed. "I thought you heard me speak to you."

Reign grabbed a napkin from the bar, dabbing the water droplets from her mouth and clearing her throat. "It's okay," she assured. "The music is just loud."

He smiled, giving a nod before moving over to Ava, grinning. "Happy birthday." He enveloped his sister in a tight hug. "Are you drunk yet?"

"Nope, was waiting on *you*," Ava beamed, releasing him. "Mom was here."

"I know, I saw her on my way in," Chase replied, running a hand over his head. "I asked her where Dad was and she said, 'home being old'."

Ava busted out laughing.

Reign caught herself staring at him as Chase caught up with his sister. The smell of his cologne alone was a turn on, and he looked good in his all-black attire. Chase was already a handsome man, but when he dressed up, it just increased his attractiveness. Reign forced herself to turn away before he caught wind of it.

Chase pulled his wallet from his pants pocket. Retrieving a card, he handed it to Ava. "Get what you want, I'm going to go say hi to everybody." Before passing Reign, he touched her arm. "That card is for you too, get what you want."

Reign stared at his hand on her—it sent a tingle down her spine. A wave of heat rushed through her body as her mind flooded with the memories of what they'd done—what Chase could make her *feel*.

"Reign," Chase called when she didn't answer.

She looked up at him. "Yes?"

"Did you hear what I said?"

Reign nodded slowly. *Yes Daddy—what the fuck?* She snapped out of her lustful trance. "Um—yes, I heard you," she sputtered.

"Thank you."

"Sure," he replied, then walked off.

Once Chase was out of sight, Reign put her head in her hands. Leaning her elbows on the bar, she let out a groan. *Being in a public place isn't helping either!*

Frowning in concern, Ava tapped Reign's wrist. "What's the matter?" While Ava was focusing on Reign, someone walked over and sat in the empty seat on the other side of her, unbeknownst to her.

Reign lifted her head. "I'm fine, don't worry about it," she deflected. "Order your drink."

Ava held a skeptical gaze on Reign for a moment. "*You* look like you could use another one."

Reign shook her head as she glanced over Ava's shoulder. Her eyes fixed on the person sitting beside Ava. "Yeah, you're probably right," she agreed.

Ava signaled the bartender. "Can I have another shot of tequila? And mix *her* tequila with something fruity," she ordered, gesturing to Reign.

"You can put that on *my* tab," the male voice spoke up as Ava went to hand the bartender the card that Chase had given to her.

Ava turned around. Her eyes widened in shock as she took him in; her breath got caught in her throat. "What the—*Malcom*?!" she exclaimed, eyeing the dark-skinned, handsome man next to her.

Malcom Reece smiled bright at her. "Happy birthday Miss Ava."

Ava's mouth was hanging open. The last person she expected to see was her old college friend and former fling.

Malcom craned his neck, looking to Reign. "Good to see you again, Reign," he said. "Thanks for the invite."

"*Invite?*" Ava snapped her head in Reign's direction. "Rae what—"

"Turns out Malcom is the agent of one of my ghostwriting clients," Reign explained, successfully hiding a smile. "Small world, huh?"

Ava stared at her wide-eyed. "You—"

"Happy birthday," Reign cut in, giving Ava a pat on her back.

Ava watched Reign leave the bar in stunned silence. Though

she was shocked, Ava had to admit, Malcolm's presence was certainly a pleasant surprise. Letting out a chuckle, Ava shook her head. "I'm going to kill her," she uttered, turning back around in her seat.

Malcom moved closer. "Ah, don't be mad at her, she meant well," he spoke up. "I'm glad that she told me about tonight; it gave me the chance to see you again."

Ava looked at him for a moment, then twisted her lip up. "Boy—that smooth shit isn't going to work on me. You forget I knew you when you wore those raggedy sweats."

Malcom busted out laughing. "Funny, funny." He rubbed his chin with his hand. "I'll take that. But I ditched those sweats a while ago."

Ava eyed him up and down, taking in his clean-cut appearance. "I see."

Malcom smiled. "Let's say we have these drinks, then hit the dance floor," he proposed, holding his gaze on her.

Ava gave a nod. "Let's do it."

Reign checked herself in the bathroom mirror one last time before emerging. Heading through the lounge, she scanned the area with her eyes, looking for Ava. Seeing her on the dancefloor dancing with Malcom, Reign smiled.

Ava, catching Reign's gaze, smiled back as she pointed a warning finger at her.

Reign laughed; she knew what that meant. She'd be getting an earful from Ava about her little surprise later. Making her way to the seating area, she sat down on a vacant leather sofa. She glanced at her watch and let out a tired sigh; it was almost midnight. "My old ass needs to be in bed," she muttered to herself.

Peering at the empty cake plate, Reign chuckled to herself. She'd spent a pretty penny on Ava's birthday cake and didn't even think to grab herself a slice. Hearing Chase's voice next to her, she glanced up.

"I wanted to make sure that I announced myself louder this time," he said.

"I appreciate it," she replied, as he sat down next to her. "Did you finish the work that you had to do earlier?"

"Nope," Chase admitted. "Almost...I'll be finished tomorrow." He took a sip of the drink in his hand. "Did you finish *yours?*"

"I did," she nodded. "My *brain* and *fingers* hurt, but the manuscript is complete."

Chase's eyes were fixated on her—he hadn't stopped thinking about her; he *couldn't*. Not seeing her over the past week had been torture; he missed her and the last place he wanted to be was in a lounge full of people. If he had his way, he'd take Reign back home with him, rip the designer dress from her body and make love to her again.

"I'll be starting a new writing project within the next week or so," she continued.

Chase snapped out of his trance. Setting his glass on the table in front of him, he cleared his throat. "So..." he began. "Can we talk about what happened?"

Reign's eyes widened. "I'm sorry?" she sputtered. "You want to talk *now?*"

Chase looked at her, sternness in his eyes. "Reign it's been a week... I'd say that's enough *processing* time, don't you think?"

Reign started to speak, then stopped, trying to gather her thoughts. She didn't want to have this conversation *at all*, let alone in a public place. "Chase—I'll say this..." She put a hand up. "As great as that *was*...we shouldn't do it again."

Chase raised an eyebrow. "O-kay," he drew out slowly.

"I—for the sake of our friendship—we *can't*." She paused, letting out a quick breath. "I just—I don't want to complicate things—"

Chase studied Reign as she spoke. The way that she was stammering through her sentences, the quick breaths that she took between her words, the way that she fidgeted with her hands—Chase knew the tells; Reign was flustered. She only did those things during conversations that she deemed uncomfortable.

When she sucked in another quick breath, Chase reached out, grabbing her hand. "Breathe," he soothed.

Reign took a deep breath, calming herself. She looked down

at his hand, holding hers in a secure grip. She wanted to squeeze it, then decided against it. *Move your hand Reign!* Listening to the voice in her head, Reign moved her hand from his.

Clearing her throat, she moved her hair behind her shoulder. After a moment, she looked back at him. "Chase, can we just… Can we just chalk that up to a onetime thing?"

Chase nodded slowly, pondering her request. "A onetime thing that just happened…*again*." He squinted. "*That's* what you want?"

Reign turned away from his piercing gaze. She could tell by the tone in his voice, she'd offended him. Though it wasn't her intention to do so, she knew that this was necessary.

Sure, her *body* certainly didn't want last week to be a onetime thing. Otherwise, she would've pulled Chase away for some privacy as soon as he had walked in. But she knew that she couldn't give in to it; she had to listen to her head. And her *head* was telling her that going down that path with him could complicate their friendship, which was the last thing that she wanted.

Reign's silence gave Chase his answer; it wasn't the one that he wanted. He put a hand up. "It's fine Rae. It was a onetime thing… We'll leave it at that," he said, resolved. "I won't bring it up again."

Reign tilted her head, staring. "Are you upset?"

Chase shook his head, then grabbed his drink, taking another sip. "No. It's what you want so I'll respect it." He hoped the frustration he felt didn't come through in his voice.

Reign let out a quick sigh in relief. "Okay," she mouthed.

After a moment, she fanned herself with her hand. Grabbing her clutch, she opened it. Removing her cell phone, wallet and keys from the purse, she set them on the cushion beside her, before digging back inside. Finally pulling out the item that she was searching for—a compact mirror—she checked her appearance.

Chase watched her. "You look perfectly fine," he said.

"I feel like I look shiny." She snapped the mirror closed. "Thank you though."

He nodded. "You're welcome."

Ava walked over as Reign put the mirror back into her bag.

"No, you two will *not* sit down all night, come dance," Ava ordered.

Chase chuckled. "I just *got* here."

Ava grabbed Chase's hand. "Get your old ass *up*, let's go." She took hold of Reign's hand as well. "*You* too. You're too cute to be sitting."

"Hold up, let me put my stuff away," Reign protested, reaching for her items.

Ava grabbed Reign's wallet and keys from the couch, shoving them into her handbag. "All done, let's go."

"All right, all right girl, *God*," Reign groaned, allowing herself to be pulled from the chair.

"Still so damn bossy," Chase chortled.

Unfazed, Ava nudged them to the dancefloor. "And always *will* be, so get over it."

Chapter Thirty-Two

REIGN EMPTIED THE CONTENTS OF her purse, frantically searching through the items sprawled out on her bed. Not seeing what she was looking for, she pulled her comforter back and searched through the pale pink pile of fabric, before feeling down the side of her bed. Dropping to her knees, she peered underneath it.

"Where the fuck *is* it?" she huffed, standing up. Putting a hand on her head, she closed her eyes as she tried to think. Feeling a pain in her stomach, she sat back down and put her head in her hands.

Sunday morning, Reign had awoke with a slight hangover, a consequence of partying with Ava for her birthday the night before.

"Never drinking hard liquor again, I swear to God," she muttered to herself. Letting out a sigh, she reached over, grabbing the cordless phone from her nightstand. Dialing a number, she put the phone to her ear.

"Hello?" Ava groaned, rolling over in her bed.

"Hey, it's Reign—"

"Why are you calling me from your house phone?" Ava asked, glancing at the ID on her cell. "I haven't seen *this* number since you moved in."

"Yeah, I sometimes forget it's even here," Reign uttered, running a hand through her hair. "I can't find my cell phone, have you seen it?"

"No, not that I know of." Ava slowly sat up. "Hold on, I'll check my stuff from last night."

"Okay." Reign laid back on her bed waiting; Ava's movements and rustling sounds came through the line.

Ava returned the phone to her ear after a few moments. "Sorry Rae, I don't see it."

283

Reign let out a huff. "Shit. I hope I didn't leave it at the lounge or in the limo." She rubbed her face. "I can't believe I lost it. I'm not drinking with you anymore." Reign had initially set her drink limit to two; however after her stressful chat with Chase, she'd partook in several more.

Ava tried to chuckle, but her aching stomach prevented her from doing so. "Ugh, let me go lay back down," she grumbled. "I feel like shit."

"Hungover too, huh?" Reign assumed.

"*Unfortunately*." Ava curled into a ball on her bed. "I ended up sleeping in my damn makeup and clothes." She ran a hand over her hair, finding a red stirrer stuck in it. "What the hell?" She tossed it on her nightstand. "Anyway, I'm sure your phone will turn up."

"I hope so," Reign sighed. "I don't feel like getting another one."

"I hear you." Ava paused for a moment. "So…I'm not going to yell at you about inviting Malcom because I enjoyed seeing him last night," she said. "…*that* and if I yell, my head will likely explode."

Reign managed a giggle.

"He cleans up *well*," Ava cooed.

"Yeah, he's definitely a good-looking man." Reign raised an eyebrow. "So, did you make plans to get *together* anytime soon?"

"No," Ava chortled. "But we *did* exchange numbers so *maybe* I'll see him again."

"Does this mean that you're going to break that no dating rule you have going for you?"

Ava made a face even though Reign couldn't see her. "Let's just see how *talking* goes, okay."

"Fair enough," Reign relented, sitting back up. "I'll let you go now; I'm going to finish tearing up my house trying to find this damn phone."

"Okay and I'll just continue to lay my old ass in this bed," Ava jeered, earning a laugh from Reign.

"Bye silly." Reign hung up, tossing the phone on the bed before getting up to resume her search.

With laser-like focus and stylus pen in hand, Chase adjusted the images on his oversized electronic pad. Grabbing his mug of coffee from the desk, he took a long sip, then proceeded to set it back down. Eyes still locked on the screen, Chase accidentally set it on the edge—the mug toppled to the floor, spilling some of the warm liquid on himself in the process.

He jumped from his seat. "Come *on*, Chase," he berated himself.

Letting out a groan, he snatched up the mug from the floor, slamming it on the desk before walking out of the office. Grabbing a hand towel from his linen closet, he returned and quickly cleaned it up.

Retreating to his bedroom, Chase changed clothes, then headed to his laundry room, wet, discarded clothing in hand. He tossed the items into the machine, then began sorting through the dirty clothes in a nearby hamper.

Might as well do a whole load, he thought.

Grabbing the pants that he'd worn the night before from the hamper, he checked his pockets for receipts and loose change. Feeling something hard in the back pocket, he frowned in confusion—a cell phone. Chase examined it, scratching his head. "Whose phone is this?" he said aloud. His *own* cell phone was in his office on the desk.

Swiping the screen, he found it unlocked—and low on battery power. Scanning the lock screen's image, he now knew whose phone it was. "Shit," he muttered.

Returning to his office, he grabbed his cell and dialed a number.

"Good morning…" he said to Reign once she answered. "Yeah, I figured I'd call the house phone since it seems that I have your cell phone."

With her phone in hand, he started to remember staying at the lounge after Reign and Ava had left for the night to grab another drink from the bar. Returning to the spot on the sofa where he'd sat with Reign prior, he had noticed her cell phone. He'd pocketed it with the intention of returning it to her that evening, but tipsy and exhausted when he finally left, he had returned home, stripped out of his attire, then went straight to bed to forget all about it.

"You left it on the chair we were sitting on... Yeah, that's probably when it happened... I can drop it off to—okay... Okay, that's no problem... I'll be in my office, so I'll leave the front door unlocked for you. Just come in... See you soon."

Ending the call, Chase set the phone down and resumed his laundry.

Reign pulled in front of Chase's house, turned her car off, then stepped out. It had been over an hour since she'd received the call from him. She'd practically torn her house apart *looking* for her phone; she was relieved to learn that Chase had it in his possession.

She approached the door, giving it a knock. Remembering that Chase said that the door would be unlocked, she opened it. "Chase?... It's Reign," she called, walking in.

"I'm in my office," Chase answered from down the hall.

Reign shut and locked the door behind her. "Is it okay if I come back there?"

"Yes," he replied.

Reign walked down the hall, stopping at the office door. She stuck her head in; Chase was sitting at his desk, eyes fixed on his screen.

"Hi," she greeted.

Chase looked up; he smiled. "Hey."

"Sorry that I took so long." She stepped in. "I had to put my house back in order after the tornado I'd caused."

Chase chuckled. "It's okay." He grabbed the phone from his desk. "Your battery is low," he informed, handing it to her. "I would've charged it, but we don't have the same type of phone."

"Thank you." Clutching it in her hand, Reign let out a sigh of relief. "You have *no* idea how relieved I am."

"Oh, I can imagine." He gave her a slight nod. "But no problem. I'm glad that I thought to grab it last night...even though I forgot that I *had* up until an *hour* ago."

She giggled. "That's what I get for going over my drink limit."

She shook her head. "Won't do *that* again… I woke up stressed *and* with a hangover."

"Are you *still* hungover?" he zoned in, eyeing her.

Reign made a "somewhat" motion with her hand. "Stomach is better. Just more of a lingering headache than anything."

Chase shook his head, returning his eyes back to his screen. "I can only *imagine* the hangover that my *sister* woke up with," he said. "She was tossing those tequila shots *back* last night."

Moving next to Chase, Reign peered over his shoulder, eyeing the designs on the screen. "Yeah, I doubt she'll want to *look* at a drink anytime soon—you drew that?"

Chase chuckled at the sudden change in subject. "I did," he confirmed. "I sketched it, then with the design software, enhanced it and added all of the details."

Reign knew that Chase was a good artist; she'd seen abstract sketches that he'd done in the past. But to see his work designs up close, she was impressed to say the least. "Chase, this looks like an *actual* building."

"I'd *hope* so, since it's what I get paid to produce." His voice was full of amusement.

Reign put a hand on his shoulder. "No, I didn't mean it like that, I meant that it looks—realistic… You're talented, *that's* what I should've just said in the first place."

"Thank you." He flashed a grateful smile. "I can honestly say that I enjoy what I do."

"I can *tell*." She leaned in closer, taking in the intricate details. "I love writing, but drawing is something that I wish I could do."

Chase glanced up at her. "Do you want to try?"

Reign looked at him as if he were crazy. "What? And embarrass myself in front of a *professional*? No, I'm okay." She folded her arms. "I'll stick to creating pictures using *words*."

Chase pushed himself back from the desk, standing up. "Nope, too late," he said. "Come sit down and try."

Reign let out a heavy sigh, accompanied by a whine as Chase

guided her down in his chair. "It's going to be ugly," she complained.

"Will you stop it?" Chase couldn't help but laugh a little at her dramatics. He rolled the chair up to the desk with her in it. Leaning over her shoulder, he brought up a blank screen. "You can do anything that you set your mind to."

"Yes, I *know* that, but my mind isn't *set* to *this* Mr. Encouragement," she sneered, rolling her eyes.

"You can complain all you want, as long as you try." Chase handed her the stylus. "Here."

Reign reluctantly took it from him. "Fine," she huffed, setting both her phone and wallet down. "What do you want me to draw?"

"Let's try a simple structure," he proposed. "First, draw two straight lines."

"Can I have a ruler?"

"No." Chase placed a comforting hand on her shoulder. "You can do it without one. Just try it."

Placing the pen to the screen, Reign proceeded to draw a line. When it veered off center, she sucked her teeth, exhaling loudly. "See?!" she belted out, tossing a hand up.

Chase moved behind her, taking hold of her drawing hand. "You're overthinking it, just relax." He moved closer to get a better look at the monitor. Placing her hand back to the screen, he held it steady. "Try again."

Reign sucked her teeth but complied. She drew another line, this time straight.

Chase grinned. "See?"

She giggled. "Please, that was only because you helped me."

He shook his head. "I didn't move your hand—that was all you."

"Liar," Reign threw back, glancing up at him.

Their amused expressions faded as their eyes locked. Silence fell over them.

In just those few moments of falling back into their casual rapport, they'd allowed themselves to invade each other's personal space. Chase's hand on Reign's, his body close to her, the feelings that they were both fighting to push aside, rose up with a vengeance.

Reign's breath grew shallow and she couldn't look away. She knew that she should say something to break the sexual tension that was building, but as much as she willed herself to get up and move away from him, she couldn't. And she didn't *want* to.

Dropping the stylus, Reign touched Chase's face, relishing the feel of his beard beneath her fingertips. Eyeing his lips, Reign leaned in, kissing him.

He kissed her back hungrily.

Chase pulled Reign from the chair and wasted no time removing her shirt.

Reign returned the favor and pulled his own over his head, tossing it aside. Her eyes filled with lust, Reign sized up his bare, toned chest. She reached out. Her hand lingered on him for a moment, before following with her lips. Her soft kisses trailed along his chest, as her fingertips slowly brushed over his abs.

Chase gently grabbed a handful of her hair, guiding her head back so he could access her neck.

As Chase's lips caressed her throat, Reign's inhibitions went out of the window. She moved her hand down, reaching beneath his sweatpants, taking hold of him. Feeling his hardness, paired with his soft groan against her neck as she stroked him, made her ache for him even more.

Kicking the chair aside, Chase backed Reign against the wall. He grabbed her hands, holding them secure above her head as he slowly grinded himself against her, kissing her deep.

The feeling of him moving against her through the soft, thin fabric of her tights was electric. He reached into her pants, fingers dipping beneath her underwear, and began gently massaging her with his thumb; the heat building inside of her only intensified. His fingers slipped inside of her, and she couldn't take it anymore. Reign wanted the barrier of clothing between them gone—she wanted him inside of her.

Feeling Reign's wetness on his fingers, Chase knew that she

was ready for him, and *he* was ready to feel *her* again. Parting from her, Chase pulled his desk drawer open, frantically searching for protection. Not seeing a stash, he closed his eyes. *Shit!* He wasn't sure why he even looked there; he either kept them in his wallet or in his bedroom drawer. Before he could open his mouth to say something, Reign grabbed her own wallet from the desk. Opening it, she retrieved a foil packet. Chase eyes widened as she held it up for him; he was relieved…and frankly a little shocked.

As Chase reached for it, Reign moved it out of his reach. Holding her lustful gaze on him, she opened it, removing the barrier. Tossing the packet aside, she loosened the string on his sweatpants, letting them fall to the floor, before putting it on him. Removing Reign's tights and underwear in one swift motion, he tossed them on the floor and picked her up in his strong arms, resting her back against the wall.

Reign wrapped her arms around his neck and her legs around his waist, sucking in a breath when he entered her with one deep stroke. Unlike last time, he didn't go slow, and she didn't want him to. Moans left her throat with each deep, steady stroke. Pleasure was surging through her—ecstasy that only Chase could give her—and she didn't want it to end. But her body couldn't hold out any longer.

Feeling her climax approaching, Reign tightened her grip on him. Closing her eyes, she let out a deep moan as the orgasm rocked her body.

The sounds of her pleasure lit every fire inside of him, sending Chase over the edge. Burying his face into her neck, he groaned as he came.

Holding her secure in his arms, Chase steadied his breathing. Lifting his head, he planted a sensual kiss on Reign's cheek.

Reign opened her eyes but didn't speak, yet the voice in her head did, and it was screaming. *Why the fuck did you come over here? You know you can't be alone with him!*

Still holding Reign, Chase looked at her. Seeing the far off look in her eyes as she stared out in front of her, he grew concerned.

"Are you okay?" he asked.

Reign quickly nodded. "Put me down please," she softly requested.

Chase granted her request and slowly placed her on her feet.

Reign immediately grabbed her clothes from the floor, scurrying out of the office as Chase put his sweatpants back on.

Alone, Chase ran a hand over his head. Like last time, he didn't regret their tryst. But he couldn't help but wonder what was going on in Reign's head. Just the night before, she'd said that they couldn't have sex again. She was *adamant* about it. Yet she had willingly participated in a second encounter.

Chase leaned against his desk and let out a sigh. *What are we doing?*

⌒〜⌒

Reign turned the water off, grabbing a fresh hand towel from a nearby shelf.

Retreating to Chase's spare bathroom, she had freshened herself up and put her clothes back on. Staring at the sink, she slowly dried her hands. Even after they were dry, she continued to move her hands through the soft towel, almost as if she were in a trance.

She was disappointed in herself; she had listened to her body again instead of her head. Not even a full day after telling Chase that she didn't want to complicate things with sex, she'd done it again. Not only was she seeing him differently, but she was feeling differently *about* him. Her head was locked in a battle against her body *and* her heart—something that she wasn't prepared for.

Finally snapping out of it, Reign set the towel on the sink and braced herself over the countertop. Lowering her head, she let out a deep sigh.

After another moment, Reign mustered up enough courage to leave the bathroom.

Tiptoeing back to Chase's office, she peered inside. Finding him not there, she couldn't help but breathe a sigh of relief. She wasn't in the headspace to face him right now. To have the conversation that she was *certain* Chase would want to have—*again*. She needed to get out of there.

Eyeing her wallet and phone on the desk, Reign shook her head, cursing that damn phone for starting this in the first place. Snagging them both, Reign hastily moved through the house. Approaching the front door, she grabbed hold of the doorknob.

"You're leaving?"

Startled by the sound of Chase's voice, Reign spun around to find Chase standing near the kitchen. She fixed him with a wide-eyed stare. *Fuck! So much for not facing him.* "Umm—yes," she sputtered, trying to keep her breathing under control.

Chase fixed her with a stern stare; a stark contrast from the lust filled one from fifteen minutes ago. "You were really going to leave without at least saying 'bye' to me?" He couldn't help but be offended. While he understood that she might be feeling conflicted—he did as well—it didn't warrant her just running out on him.

"I'm sorry, I didn't—I just umm…" Reign sucked in a quick breath, holding the doorknob in a tight grip. "I really need to go." She pulled the door open with haste. "Bye."

Chase didn't get a chance to utter another word, because Reign had practically run out of the house. Moving to the front window, he watched with somber eyes as her car pulled away from the curb before speeding down the street.

Exhaling deeply, Chase ran a hand over his head. *Yeah, we can't keep doing this.*

Chapter Thirty-Three

AVA PULLED THE MICROWAVE DOOR open at the sound of the beep. Retrieving the bag of popcorn, she emptied it into a glass bowl and took it and a bottle of iced tea to the living room.

After sleeping away her hangover for most of the day, Ava had decided to spend the rest of her birthday weekend curled up on her couch watching her favorite television shows. She grabbed her remote, hitting play.

And quickly hit pause when her phone rang.

Annoyed at the interruption, Ava snatched up her phone from the coffee table. Eyeing the name, her head jerked back a little. "Hmm," she muttered, placing the phone to her ear. "Yes?" she answered.

A deep chuckle came through the phone. "Is that how you answer the phone nowadays? No 'hello'?"

"For *you*, yes," Ava coyly threw back. She smirked when he laughed. "Good evening Malcom."

"Good evening," Malcom replied. "It was good seeing you last night."

Ava took a quick sip of her tea. "You as well." She set the bottle aside. "It was an...*interesting surprise* to say the least."

He chuckled again. "Yeah, I could tell by how wide your eyes had gotten." Ava giggled a bit. "Anyway, I would've called you earlier but—"

"I'm glad that you didn't, I probably would've thrown up in your ear."

"Ahhh, curse of the hangover," Malcolm teased.

She shook her head. "I haven't experienced one that bad since my twenty-first birthday," she recalled. "It was terrible. I'm definitely passing up on drinks for a *while*."

"Understandable," he sympathized. "I'll keep that in mind when the time comes for me to take you out."

Ava tried to fight the smile that was building, but was unsuccessful. She cleared her throat, making sure that no traces of it were in her voice. "Who says that I'd even *agree* to going out with you?"

Malcom laughed slightly. "Are you saying that you'd be opposed to going out with an old friend?"

Ava twisted her lips to the side. "I don't know, you'd first have to ask me like you have some sense," she sneered. "I'm grown, subtle shit doesn't work."

"You're right. I apologize." Malcom cleared his throat. "Ava, I'd love to catch up with you more. Would you do me the honor of having dinner with me?"

Ava adjusted her position on her couch. "That depends, are you married?"

"No."

"Have any girlfriends that believe you're exclusive with them...or at *all*."

"No," he answered. "Wow, *clearly* you're still thinking of 'college' Malcom."

"Can you *blame* be? I haven't been in *contact* with you since then," she threw back. "You moved back East right after graduation."

"And *you* changed your number," Malcom reminded.

Ava opened her mouth to retort, but closed it. He had a point. "Yeah...lost my old phone in the damn ocean while I was on a cruise." She rubbed her face with her hand. "Okay, so that's on me, but the fact still remains; I don't know this *new* you."

"I understand," Malcolm replied, sincere. "Well, I'm permanently back in Arizona now, and I can see that I have some proving to do. Which I'm all for."

"Okay," Ava muttered, examining her nails.

Malcom stalled for a moment. "So...is that a *yes* to dinner?"

Ava pondered the invitation. "I'd like to catch up by phone for a bit first, before gracing you with my presence in a private setting," she answered finally.

"If that is what you want, then I'm down for it."

Ava smirked.

"But when I start calling you every day, don't get upset."

"I will try," Ava countered, then smiled. "Okay then. I look forward to engaging in conversation with you."

He too smiled. "Likewise."

She grabbed her popcorn bowl. "Now I hate to be rude, but I'm about to engross myself in this TV show—"

"Ooh, which one? Maybe I'll check it out myself," he slid in, enthused.

"It's a show about women who kill men," Ava answered. There was only silence on the other end; she fought the urge to laugh.

"Uh, yeah, I'll pass on that one," Malcom finally replied.

A laugh escaped her. "Thought so." She twirled hair around her finger. "I'll talk to you later."

"I'll hold you to that," Malcom threw back. "Enjoy your evening."

"You too." Ava ended the call, then stared at the phone for a moment. Smiling to herself, she dialed another number, adjusting her position on the couch.

"Rae, guess who just called me," she blurted into the line as soon as Reign picked up.

Reign put her cordless phone on speaker, then sat it next to her, returning to her task of writing in her notebook. "Who?" she asked, tone dry.

"Malcom," Ava beamed.

Reign looked up from her book, to the phone. "You realize that you sound like a teenage girl whose crush just called her, right?"

Ava made a face. "*Do* I?"

"Yes," Reign chortled.

"Eww." Ava shook her head slightly. "I *definitely* don't want to sound like that."

"It's okay if you do," Reign replied, even toned. "It just means that you're excited."

Ava shrugged. "I wouldn't say that I'm *excited*, but… We agreed to some casual conversation via phone, so… I *am* looking forward to *that*," she admitted.

"*Are* you?"

"Yes," Ava answered. "I mean, he wanted to take me on a *date*, but I need to feel him out a little bit more first."

"You surely felt him out *enough* the way you were dancing on him last night," Reign teased.

Ava's mouth fell open. "It was the *tequila*." She sucked her teeth at the low laugh coming through the line. "Which proves my point that the phone needs to stay between us for now."

Reign smirked. "I'm sure you can refrain from gyrating on him while on a regular date, so what is the *real* reason why you're pushing the date off?"

Ava jerked her head back. "Oh no honey. Someone who refuses to date *herself* will *not* make *me* feel a way about not dating," she threw back.

"*I* got out of a dead-end relationship less than a year ago, so I have an excuse," Reign countered. "*You've* been single for longer than I was *in* that relationship, so *again* what's the excuse?"

Ava sighed, playing with a few hair tendrils, "I've gotten comfortable with being single."

"And that's *fine*," Reign placated. "If you enjoy it, stick with it. But I know that deep down you'd like to have some sort of companionship…even if it's just for like two days out of the week."

Ava laughed.

Reign shook her head as she jotted in her book. "Yeah, I know you don't want anybody in your space."

"Breathing my air and shit," Ava agreed, laughter still in her voice. She glanced at the ceiling as she settled back against her couch cushions. "I guess, I'll give him a chance…*eventually*. We'll see how long it takes for him to get on my nerves."

"Be nice, luv," Reign said, amused.

Ava giggled. "I'll try." She let out a happy sigh, setting her popcorn bowl back on the coffee table. "You know what, I don't feel like staying in anymore. You want to go out to eat?"

Reign pulled her pen away from the page "Sorry, I need to sit this one out," she declined. "I'm writing."

"I hear that." Ava scratched her head. "I might go bug Chase or something."

Reign let out a sigh but didn't say anything.

"Before I let you go, did you ever find your cell phone?"

"Yes…Chase had it," Reign reluctantly answered.

"Oh," Ava replied. "That's good. He dropped it off to you?"

"No, I picked it up from him. Look, I have to go, I'll call you later, okay," Reign quickly put out.

A puzzled look fell upon Ava's face. "Okay…is everything all right?"

Reign rubbed her head with her hand. "Everything is fine Ava. I just have to finish what I'm working on before I lose my train of thought."

"All right Rae, I'll see you at work tomorrow," Ava said.

"See you."

Ava glanced at the phone after Reign abruptly hung up. "Huh," she muttered to herself. Dismissing the weird interaction as her friend being tired and hungover, Ava picked up her bowl of popcorn and pressed play on her TV.

Chapter Thirty-Four

CHASE EYED A MESSAGE ON his cell phone. Smiling in satisfaction, he dialed a number. "I just received the picture... It looks great; *perfect*... I'll be on the lookout for it. Thank you again." Ending the call, he set the phone on his desk, letting out a happy sigh. "Perfect," he said to himself.

Glancing at his watch, he went to stand, when a knock on his office door halted him. "Come in," he called.

"Heading to lunch?" Thomas asked, walking through the door.

Chase ran a hand over his hair. "In a minute, what can I do for you?" He'd just left a presentation meeting earlier that morning with his boss; Chase was curious as to what else he wanted to discuss.

"I know I said this earlier, but you killed that presentation. Great job as always."

Chase offered a smile. "Thank you," he replied. "Was that all?"

Thomas shoved his hands into his trouser pockets. "I actually wanted to know if you'd reconsider taking the trip to Connecticut."

Chase's stern face spoke volumes. However, he had no problem reiterating. "Thomas, I already stated that I'm not traveling right now," he shot down. "The team that I've put in place can handle the trip with no problem."

"I understand, and I *did* agree to your decision of staying here at the local office, but I just think that the presentation will go so much better with you there," Thomas shifted his feet. "The trip is in three weeks, so you still have time to consider—"

"If you *really* need my presence at that meeting, then my face can be on a screen via a virtual call," Chase propositioned. "I'd be happy to do that. But I'm not flying out there."

Thomas nodded, then pointed at him. "Compromise accepted," he laughed.

Chase squinted slightly, bewildered. That certainly wasn't a joke, nor was it funny. He thought that Thomas was a nice boss, but the man was corny, and Chase refused to entertain his nonexistent humor. "Right," Chase muttered,

Thomas cleared his throat. "Look, you make this company millions of dollars—"

"I do," Chase agreed, confident.

"Yes, so we'll keep you happy. You don't want to travel, you don't have to," Thomas pacified. "But in the event that you *do*, let us know."

Chase gave a nod. "Will do."

Thomas gave one in return before walking out of the door.

Chase smirked, shaking his head.

Reign was sitting at an outdoor table, staring at the grilled chicken salad in front of her. She'd barely touched it.

"You're not going to eat your food?" Chase asked her, grabbing his sandwich.

Reign looked up at him. "I don't have much of an appetite." She folded her arms.

"You feeling okay?"

"I'm fine." Reign almost didn't accept Chase's lunch invitation when he'd called her earlier. But just the thought of turning him down made her feel bad, especially since they hadn't seen each other since she'd left his house a few days ago. Now she wondered if it would've been better if she had; she was feeling and acting awkward.

"I ate a big breakfast, so that would explain it," Reign added after a moment.

Chase continued to enjoy his own meal, then sipped his drink. "How's your day going so far?" he asked finally.

Reign sat back in her seat. "It's going fine. Getting ready to take on a new project soon."

He gave a nod, "That's good."

"How's yours? How did your presentation go?"

Chase adjusted his tie. "It was successful." He smiled, "My design went over quite well."

Reign smiled back. "Of *course* it did," she praised. "I told you, you're talented."

He sat back in his seat. "I appreciate that, thank you."

Reign took a sip of her juice; her uneasiness began to fade. "So, your birthday is coming up soon," she brought up. "Planning on doing anything special?"

Chase shrugged, "Probably not. I tend to not make a big deal of my birthday. I like to keep it low key."

"Well, I'd like to take you to dinner," Reign offered.

Chase smiled.

"Someplace fancy of course, and I'll think of something else fun for us to do afterwards," she added, enthused. "If that's okay with you, of course."

"That would be *perfect* for me," he said, sincere. "Thank you." She smiled and gave a nod in return.

Chase continued to enjoy his meal, while Reign finally began to eat her salad. Sitting there in silence, Chase's mind began to race. Although he'd enjoyed the casual conversation with Reign, it wasn't the reason he'd asked her to lunch. He needed to have a serious conversation with her, and he wasn't sure how she'd handle it.

Taking another sip of his drink, Chase cleared his throat. "Rae…we need to talk," he began.

Reign looked at him, curious.

He hesitated for a moment. "I…I think you already know what it's about."

Great, just great. She had a feeling that Chase would eventually bring it up, she just wasn't sure when. Reign sat her fork down then pinched the bridge of her nose, sighing. "Okay."

"I guess I'm just more confused than anything," he said. "We… well, *you* agreed that us sleeping together was just a onetime thing—"

"*You* agreed *too*, Chase," she slid in, eyeing him sternly.

Chase shot her a knowing look. "Rae—come on, you really think I'd *never* want to make love to you again?"

Reign glanced away so Chase couldn't see her turn red.

"I agreed because of *you*," he added. "And I planned on honoring and respecting that decision. Then, it happened *again* and while I'm certainly not *complaining*, I just want to know what that means."

Reign looked back at him. "Meaning as in what?"

"Meaning as in *us*, and where our relationship is headed," Chase clarified. "It's clear that we're stepping out of the 'just friends' zone."

Reign put a hand up. "Look, I know that we crossed a line in our friendship, and I'll have to live with that. But I just don't want this to turn into a 'friends with benefits' situation," she stressed.

Chase jerked his head back, frowning. "You really think that I just want a '*benefits*' situation with you?" he asked, offended. "With *you*?"

"I didn't say that you *did*," she pointed out. "I'm just saying that I don't want it to *get* to that point."

Chase rubbed his chin with his hand. "Reign, if I wanted to have sex just for the hell of it, I *would*, and I'd do it with some random woman who didn't mean anything to me."

Reign caught herself frowning; the mere thought of Chase sleeping with another woman upset her deeply. Yet she shoved it down just like the rest.

"But the fact is, since my last breakup I haven't slept with any woman *except* for *you*," Chase stated, serious. "Contrary to what you may think about me, I'm not into meaningless sex."

"I didn't say that you *were*," Reign maintained.

"And *you're* not either."

Reign folded her arms as she shifted in her seat. She was becoming uncomfortable. "*Clearly* I'm not, I've only been with two men my entire life."

Chase didn't even want to think about the other man that Reign had slept with; as far as he was concerned, he still owed Troy another punch to his face. "With that being said, I am not interested in a 'friends with benefits' situation with you, nor am I interested in going back to how things *were* between us."

Shiiiiit! On the inside, Reign was panicking, but on the outside her face remained neutral. "So where does that leave us, Chase?"

Chase took a deep breath, hesitating.

Reign immediately went to the worst-case scenario. Her eyes shifted slightly as she tucked some of her hair behind her ear. "Are… are you about to tell me that you want to end our friendship?"

Chase's eyes widened. "What? *No*," he refuted. "Of *course* not— No, Rae, I want us to go to the *next* level. I want to date you, I want to court you— I want a *relationship* with you."

Reign stared at Chase, wide-eyed. She had to will herself to breathe. Chase wanted a relationship, a *romantic* relationship with her. She was a little stunned to say the least.

"You— You're saying that—"

"I'm saying that my feelings for you…have *changed* and I don't want to hide that anymore. I *can't*," he confessed.

Reign closed her eyes, glancing off to the side. "I umm…"

Chase sighed; her silence spoke volumes. "You—don't feel the same about me," he concluded.

Reign looked at him. "That's not true." Her voice, like her eyes, were sincere. "I *do* have feelings for you."

Chase smiled. That was everything he had been hoping for.

Reign looked down at the table. "But—"

The smile left Chase's face. "But?" he questioned.

"I…I'm just not ready to date again." Reign wished that she could block out the disappointment on Chase's face. She wasn't lying. She *did* have feelings for Chase, but she just wasn't in the right headspace to act on them.

"You're not ready to date again?" It was more of a statement than a question. Chase was fighting to keep his cool. "In *general*, or just *me*?"

"In general," Reign assured, eyeing him intently. "Chase, this isn't about you or how I *feel* about you. I'm just not ready to be in another relationship."

Chase looked away and took a deep breath, trying to contain his frustration. She'd admitted to having feelings for him, she'd *slept with* him, yet didn't want a relationship. He thought that he knew her pretty well, but in this moment, Chase was finding Reign hard to understand. "Why do I have a feeling that you're not being all the way honest with me?" Both his voice and face were stern as he looked at her.

A frown crossed Reign's face. "Why wouldn't I be honest?"

"Because you're good at deflecting and downplaying what's really going on in your head. You always *have* been," he ground out.

She was taken aback by his tone. "Wait...are you *angry* with me right now?"

"I'm not angry, I'm just confused, that's all," Chase bit out. "What exactly do you want from me at this point?"

"I *just* want you to be my friend, that's *all* I need from you right now."

Chase gave a nod. "Nothing more than that. Got it," he sneered.

Reign shook her head. "Now we're arguing." She sighed, "This is what I *didn't* want."

"We're not arguing Reign, its fine," Chase dismissed, tone even.

His tense tone and demeanor told Reign otherwise. "Chase—"

"We're good," Chase abruptly cut in, flashing a glare at her.

Reign eyed him back, disappointment in her eyes. She slowly shook her head at him, then glanced at her watch. "I have to get back to work."

"Yeah," he flatly returned, grabbing his drink. Chase refused to even look at her as she stood from her seat. "Enjoy the rest of your day, *friend*."

Reign rolled her eyes as she grabbed her purse. "Yeah. You too," she threw back, walking off.

⌒

Ava grabbed her donut order from the cashier as she spoke into her cell phone. "I'm just picking up some donuts for the office," she spoke, before mouthing 'thank you' to the cashier.

"Yeah, I'm feeling generous," she chortled, walking away. As Ava turned, she nearly collided with someone. "Ooh, sorry about that," Ava immediately blurted out, before she realized who the other person was.

"Appreciate the apology," Marcy muttered.

Ava frowned down Marcy's length, sucked her teeth, then moved around her to walk away. With Marcy still living in the city, Ava knew that she'd eventually see her, but that didn't mean that they needed to interact.

Annoyed, Marcy spun around to face Ava's departing figure. "Still ignorant, I see," she spat.

Ava paused but didn't turn around. "I have to call you back," she said into the phone. Hanging up, she spun around, pinning down Marcy with a glare. "What did you say?"

"That you're ignorant," Marcy goaded.

Ava raised an eyebrow. "Why? Because I didn't exchange a pleasant 'hello' with you," she scoffed. "When have I *ever* done that?"

"My point exactly," Marcy ground out.

Ava gave her a phony smile. "Yeah, I see what you're doing," she sneered. "You can't ruin Chase or Reign's day anymore with your bullshit because they no longer fuck with you, so *now* you want to ruin *mine*."

Marcy scowled at Ava.

"It won't work baby girl." Ava's lip curled in a haughty smirk. "You were irrelevant *then*, and you're irrelevant *now*. Now excuse me while I go back to my job."

Marcy took a step in Ava's direction as Ava went to walk out once again. "You know what Ava, let's be real for once. You've hated me since you *met* me and it was because of Reign."

"Girl, just buy a damn donut and shut up," Ava threw over her shoulder.

Marcy followed her outside. "No, admit it."

Ava spun back around. "If you're following me, it means that you want a problem," she snapped, facing Marcy. "I will drop these donuts in a minute. I owe you one anyway after what you did."

Marcy rolled her eyes. "I am not proud of—"

"Girl, yes you are," Ava cut in, upset. "*Please* don't forget that I know everything."

Marcy folded her arms, scoffing in the process. She shook her head. "Whatever Ava, you can call me *whatever* you want, think of me *however* you want."

"Oh I have, do and will *continue* to do so," Ava hissed. "In case it hasn't been made clear, I *don't* like you."

"And you never *did*," Marcy fussed. Ava shrugged as if she didn't care. "Before *any* of this shit happened, I got your attitude. And it started when I became friends with Reign."

Ava narrowed her gaze. "You must *really* be bored."

Marcy shrugged, "Humor me."

Ava raised an eyebrow, contemplating the challenge. "Fine." She pointed at her. "I didn't dislike you from the jump. I didn't *know* you, to dislike you. It was when I saw how you treated my friend—using her, leeching off of her energy—*that's* when I started disliking you."

"*Your* friend?" Marcy zoned in.

"I'm sorry, did I miss something?" Ava mocked. "She's no longer *your* friend."

"Yeah, that may be the case *now*, but back *then* she was *our* friend," Marcy reminded. "And the closer that *we* became, the less *you* were around and the more ignorant *you* became towards *me*."

Ava just glared at Marcy as she ranted.

"I doubt that it had anything to do with my *energy stealing powers*," she snarled. "No, it was because I was replacing you as her best friend and you were jealous of that."

"Jealous? Of *you*?" Ava couldn't help but to bust out laughing. "Oh yeah, you're *definitely* bored and might I add, *delusional*."

Marcy made a face at her. "Of me and Reign's *friendship*," she dug in. "You *hated* it. You hated that you no longer had her all to yourself. You were always so—extra with her, like you were in *love* with her or something."

Ava held an unwavering stare on Marcy; she chuckled. "Yeah,

see only narrow-minded people such as yourself would mistake being a loyal friend to someone I've known since I was *fifteen years old*, as being *in love* with them."

Marcy rolled her eyes.

"No sweetie, I am not, nor have I *ever* been in love with Reign," Ava clarified. "I love her like a *sister*. And based on that cute little theory that you've concocted among *other* things, you have *no* idea what it is to *actually be* a friend…" Ava eyed Marcy up and down in disgust. "*Clearly.*"

Marcy let out a huff, but didn't respond.

Ava, however, was far from finished. "And no, I am not jealous of your *past* friendship with her, I'm a grown ass woman and I'm secure in my friendships," she added, eyeing Marcy intensely. "But even if that *were* the case, and you *were* her *new* best friend as you so proclaim, you ruined that by being exactly who I *knew* you were from the beginning."

Marcy looked like the wind had been knocked out of her. She bit her bottom lip to keep it from quivering.

"You lost a good friend who was one of the *only* ones who stood by you no matter what, for a few designer bags, a cheap ass getaway, and a fuckin' *loser*." Ava cocked her head to the side. "So, this little trip down memory lane solved *what* for you, exactly?"

Not having anything to say, Marcy glanced away. Ava was right; it accomplished nothing. She was still hitting rock bottom and not even rehashing her petty feud with Ava would change that.

"Yeah, that's what I thought." Ava was over this conversation. "Now if you'll excuse me, I have better shit to do with my time." She turned to walk away, then stopped and turned back around. "Oh yeah, and stay your triflin', desperate ass away from my brother."

Marcy's eyes widened.

"Yeah, he told me," Ava sneered. "I told you, I know everything."

Marcy glared as Ava walked away from her for the last time. Defeated, Marcy just walked back inside the donut shop.

Chapter Thirty-Five

VIVIAN PULLED A BATCH OF brownies from Reign's oven, setting them on the stove just as her eldest daughter walked in.

"Mom, I said you didn't have to make those. You already brought me dinner," Reign said, sitting on a bar stool at her counter island.

"Oh stop it," Vivian dismissed, waving her hand. "You had a long day, you deserve some brownies."

Reign chuckled, shaking her head. She was pleasantly surprised when her mother had asked to drop by after Reign had gotten home from work. Not only had her mother brought over some dinner that she had cooked, she'd also baked dessert. "Well, all the calories that I'll soon be consuming *aside*, I appreciate you," she replied. "You're right, I *did* have a long day, so I definitely could use the pick-me-up."

"Do you have ice cream? I can make us brownie sundaes." Vivian's eyes were bright and full of excitement.

Reign smiled. "Yes Mom, I have ice cream." She sat as her mother prepared brownie sundaes with vanilla ice cream, whipped cream and chocolate syrup.

"A girl after my own heart," Vivian mused, setting a bowl in front of Reign, then setting one in front of herself. "Has every ingredient."

Reign giggled. "Yeah, I tend to just pick random stuff up when I grocery shop. Never know when I'll need it."

Proud, her mother scooped some sundae onto her spoon, holding it in front of Reign. "Cheers." She smiled.

Amused, Reign scooped the treat onto her own spoon, tapping it to her mother's. "Cheers."

It was silent for moments as both women enjoyed the dessert.

Reign let out a sigh as she swirled some of the melted ice cream around in her bowl. "Can I ask you a question?"

"Of course."

"Do you believe there's one person for everyone?" Reign asked.

Vivian's brows raised. "You mean like a *soulmate*?"

"I hate that term, but yeah," Reign clarified. "And when you meet them…would you even *know*?"

"You'd know," Vivian assured with a nod. "In *my* case, I knew your father was my one after about two years of dating him."

Reign's eyes widened. "You dated Dad for *two years* before you realized that he was the right one for you?"

Vivian nodded.

Reign's mouth fell open. "Mom!"

"He got on my nerves a *lot* when we first started dating," Vivian admitted, amused. Reign busted out laughing. Vivian smiled, fond memories flooding back. "But one day I looked at him and everything just clicked for me… I knew he was it for me…still *is*."

Reign enjoyed her sundae quietly while listening to the story.

"Now if you ask your *father* that question, he'd tell you that he knew that *I* was the one when he first met me," Vivian told.

Reign tilted her head. "Really?"

Vivian nodded again. "That man asked me to marry him three months after our first date," she chortled.

"You didn't think that was…*weird*?" Reign rested her spoon in the bowl. "Or, let me rephrase, because the answer for *you* would be yes since you barely *liked* him at that point—"

Vivian snickered.

Reign folded her arms on the countertop. "I guess my follow up question is…how soon is *too* soon to know if the person in your life is the one that you're meant to be with?"

"Timelines can vary from person to person," Vivian explained. "But I believe that the heart knows what it wants… It knows who it truly loves and who completes it."

Reign glanced off to the side, deep in thought. "Right," she muttered.

Vivian eyed Reign with concern. "Sweetie...this isn't about *Troy*, is it?"

Reign snapped her head in her mother's direction "Huh?" She frowned. "*No*, Mom this isn't about Troy," she denied. "Why would—"

"Reign, don't let that fool's inability to see what a *treasure* he had in you deter you from believing that soulmates exist." Vivian's firm tone matched the seriousness on her face. "They *do*, and *yours* won't string you along like *he* did."

Reign rubbed her face; she could have done without the reminder. "Forget I asked, Mom."

Vivian sighed. "I didn't mean to upset you darling, I just—"

"I'm not upset," Reign quickly cut in. "I appreciate what you said, and I get it, thanks." She resumed eating, refusing to say anything further.

Vivian meant it; she hadn't meant to upset her daughter. But just the thought of Reign losing faith in love—or even *questioning* it because of what she'd gone through—was saddening. She let out another sigh. "Sure...you're welcome."

Reign entered her home office and switched the desk lamp on. With her mother gone, she was free to journal in private.

Sitting at her desk, she opened a drawer, retrieving a notebook. She flipped through, searching for a blank page—there wasn't one. She'd filled it. Sucking her teeth, Reign stood, notebook in hand and went to the closet, opening the door.

Pulling a plastic bin from the mid-sized walk-in, Reign removed the top, peering at the piles of colorful filled notebooks inside. Her eyes left that bin, roaming over the entire closet. There were numerous other plastic bins filled to the brim, just like this one, stacked high and taking up the space. Each bin was a motley of notebooks, notepads, journals: everything she'd written in over the years. A label on each bin noted the year—Reign had kept every notebook starting from high school.

Shaking her head, Reign sighed. "This is crazy…you're crazy, Reign," she muttered to herself.

Letting out a quick breath, she tossed the book in her hand down in the open bin and closed the lid. Pushing the bin back in place with others, Reign glanced at the top shelf of her closet, eyeing a stack of fresh notebooks. She grabbed one and shut the door behind her.

Chase opened his front door to a box on the top step. Bringing it inside, he locked the door behind him and set the box on his coffee table. Carefully opening it, he peered inside. Chase let out a deep sigh. *Perfect timing*, he thought, somber. Shaking his head, he closed the box.

"Bro, did you put the steaks on the grill yet?" Ava asked, ambling into the room. "I'm starving."

Chase held his hand on the box, staring at it. "Not yet, I'm about to do it now."

Ava stood beside him. "Somebody got a package," she observed.

"Yeah," Chase confirmed, sullen.

She pushed hair behind her shoulder. "What is it?"

Chase squinted at her. "Are you ever *not* going to be nosey?"

"No," Ava countered, folding her arms.

Chase sighed. "It's…it's a gift for Reign," he answered. "I guess you could say that it's a late birthday gift."

"*I'd* say it's late, her birthday was three months ago," Ava chuckled. She put a hand on his arm when he glanced back at the box. "No, I'm playing. That's sweet."

"Thanks," his tone was low.

"So, when are you going to give it to her?" Ava asked. "Can I know what it is?"

Chase ran a hand along the back of his neck. "I don't know," he answered, honest. "And no, you *can't*."

Ava sucked her teeth. "Very well." She glanced away as she tried to decide if she wanted to bring up what was on her mind. "So umm… I ran into your ex the other day," she began.

He fixed her with a puzzled stare. "Which one?"

"The most recent," she clarified. "*Marcy.*"

Chase rolled his eyes. "Ava, no disrespect to you but I don't want to hear about her," he shot down. "We're not together, I don't care about her, and I *don't* need to hear about what she's doing."

Ava raised her eyebrows. "Well, okay then." She gave a nod. "Noted. I respect that." Ava wasn't offended that her brother had shot down her gossip attempt; she was impressed by it. "So, on that note, I'm going to tear up that salad you made while I wait for those steaks."

"I'm going out there in a minute," he promised.

"You said that *ten* minutes ago," she jeered, disappearing into the kitchen.

Alone again, Chase ran a hand over his head, sighing heavily. His phone rang, prompting him to pull it from his pocket. Eyeing the screen, he hesitated, finally hitting answer before it could go to voicemail. "Hello." His tone was dry.

Reign was in her kitchen, stirring honey into a cup of tea. "Hey," she replied, almost surprised. "You okay? This is the third time that I tried to get ahold of you today."

"Sorry, I was tied up earlier," he answered. "Work and all."

Reign paused her stirring; she raised an eyebrow. "And *yesterday?*" she questioned. "Were you tied up *then* too?"

"I was."

Reign frowned at his sharp tone. She'd been trying to reach Chase for days and he hadn't returned her calls. Ever since their conversation over lunch almost a week ago, Chase had been elusive. And now, he seemed bitter. Reign didn't like it or appreciate it, yet she didn't call to argue. "Okay, you were busy, I get it."

"Is there something that you need?" he curtly asked.

"No Chase, I don't need anything, I was just calling to check on you," her *own* tone filled with agitation.

Sighing, Chase sat on the arm of his couch. "I appreciate it."

Reign sighed, calming herself. "I—I want to make sure that we're okay," she said. "I know that things got a little intense and I didn't mean to hurt your feelings in any way—"

"They're not hurt, we're good," he cut in.

"Then why do you seem angry with me?"

"I'm not angry," he denied. "If I sound that way, I apologize. I'm just tired, that's all."

"Are you sure?" she pressed.

"Yes."

"Okay." Reign turned around, leaning her back against the counter. "So umm, do you still want to hang out with me for your birthday this weekend? I found a restaurant I think you'll like."

Chase took a deep breath. "Rae I umm... I don't know right now. I'm not really in the celebrating mood."

Hurt masked Reign's face even though he couldn't see it. "Oh."

"I'll let you know though, okay?"

She glanced down at her nails. "Okay, that's fine," she quickly put out. "I'll let you go. Goodnight."

Chase didn't get the chance to respond before Reign abruptly ended the call. He stared at the phone screen, her picture beneath the call time smiling back at him. "Yeah...you let me go," he grunted to himself. Tossing the phone on the couch, he made a beeline for the kitchen.

Ava knocked on Reign's office door, waiting for her friend to say it was all right before entering. "I saw your notes," she announced, standing by the desk.

Reign looked up from her laptop. "And how are you feeling?"

Ava smiled after a moment. "Good... A little surprised, but good."

Reign smiled in return. "You should be proud of yourself. I told you that you'd do a good job."

Ava had finally finished the developmental editing project

that Reign had given to her, turning it in days ago. She was on pins and needles waiting on the feedback and was pleasantly surprised when positive notes were returned.

"Thank you." Ava grinned, "It wasn't as bad as I thought it would be."

Reign chuckled. "I *told* you."

"Yeah, yeah you did." Ava rubbed her hands together. "So, when does it have to be sent back to the client?"

"Oh, the project is already closed out," Reign answered, nonchalant.

Ava squinted, perplexed. "I'm sorry?"

"Yeah, I edited that project a few months ago; I just sent you a copy of the original file to practice on."

Ava's mouth fell open. "You—you had me stressing over *nothing*?"

"It wasn't for nothing," Reign replied. "It was for *training* and if I had *told* you that it was only for training, you probably wouldn't have given it your all." She folded her arms. "You did a great job, I'm proud of you."

Ava folded her arms right back, narrowing her eyes in the process. While she was grateful for the praise, she didn't appreciate being deceived. "Are you *sure* I can't yell at you in the office?" she jeered.

Reign smirked. "No, you *can't*."

"Fine." Ava pursed her lips. "But I owe you a get back *outside* of here."

"Don't be petty, Ava," Reign chided, looking at her cell phone.

"Is your apology for lying in that phone?" Ava quipped. When Reign didn't look up, Ava snapped her fingers to get her attention.

"What did you say?" Reign asked, snapping out of her trance.

Chuckling, Ava waved a dismissive hand. "It was a bad joke, it's not important."

Reign moved her phone aside. "Oh… Have you heard from Chase today?"

"He texted me earlier, but since then, no," Ava answered. "Why, is something up?"

Reign shook her head. "Just curious." She'd texted Chase earlier to see if he'd made a decision regarding his birthday dinner with her for tomorrow. He had yet to respond.

Reign ran a hand through her hair, letting out a sigh. She glanced at the clock on her desk to think about anything else. "It's four-thirty, you guys can head home," she said. "Happy Friday."

"Ooh, a whole half hour early, look at you being generous," Ava teased.

Reign managed a chuckle. "Don't do that—on holidays I let you go an hour early," she reminded. "Sometimes, *two*."

Ava giggled, waving a hand. "I know, I'm just messing with you. I'll let the others know."

"Thank you."

"No problem, I'll call you later." Ava headed for the door. "Don't stay too late."

"Leaving right at five," Reign promised, looking back at her laptop.

Chapter Thirty-Six

AVA PUT THE FINISHING TOUCHES on her makeup before fluffing her curls. She smiled at her beautiful reflection. "Looking just like my mama."

"Were you talking to me, or to yourself?" a male voice asked through the cell phone speaker.

Ava giggled, "Sorry Malcom, that was a solo conversation," she answered. "You have my attention now."

"No problem, you forgave *me* for *my* solo conversation the other day."

Ava glanced at the phone, humor on her face. "You mean when you were complaining about the air temperature in your office?"

"They keep touching the thermostat," Malcom complained. "It was eighty degrees in there that day."

Ava giggled yet again. Sticking with her phone conversation only rule, Ava and Malcom were conversing nightly, had been doing so since her birthday weekend. "So, what are you getting into tonight?" she asked, placing a gold hoop earring into her ear.

"Nothing much," Malcom replied. "And yourself?"

She put the other earring in. "I'm going to my brother's house for a game night that he put together for his birthday."

"Nice. That sounds like fun."

Ava adjusted the gold bracelets on her wrist. Having a thought, she tapped her chin with her finger. "Do you want to come?"

"You mean you're finally okay with seeing me in person?" Malcolm quipped.

"I mean, my brother can break your neck if you try anything stupid in his presence, so there's no harm in inviting you," she countered.

A deep laugh came through the line. "I'm sure he *could*." Malcom's laughter subsided. "But yes, I would love to attend."

She peered at the phone. "You *do* remember how to play spades right?"

"Woman—yes and I bet I *still* play better than you," he threw back.

Ava busted out laughing. "Whatever," she dismissed. "It starts at eight, I'll be leaving here in a few minutes."

"Do you want me to pick you up?"

"No, thank you. You can meet me there," Ava answered.

"Sounds like a plan."

Ava smiled. "Good. I'll text you the address."

Reign pulled a throw blanket up her lap as she settled on the couch. She eyed the plate of food, bowl of snacks, and glass of wine sitting on the coffee table. Everything she needed for a night in front of the television, was there.

Grabbing the remote, she prepared to click the TV on, when a knock sounded on her door. She pushed the covers off and got up.

Peeking through her peephole, Reign opened the door.

"Hey sis," Ava beamed.

Reign chuckled at the excitement in Ava's voice. "Hi." She moved aside to let her in. "You look nice," she said, eyeing Ava's casual, yet stylish attire. "Going somewhere fun?"

Grinning, Ava gave Reign a playful tap to her arm. "Thank you, and *yes*, silly."

Reign was puzzled. "Okay," she replied after a moment.

Ava followed Reign into the living room.

"What brings you by?" Reign wondered.

"Well, I was passing by and I saw your car, so figured I'd stop and see if you were ready," Ava explained.

"Ready for what?"

Ava surveyed the tray of food; she scratched her head. "You're eating first?"

The perplexity on Reign's face intensified, yet she didn't answer.

"And why aren't you dressed yet?" Ava harped, eyeing Reign's sweatpants and tank top.

"Ava, what the hell is up with you tonight?" Reign finally asked. "Why would I be *dressed* for a night on my couch?"

It was *Ava's* turn to be confused. "Wait, you're not going?"

Reign stared at her, agitation showing on her face. She pinched her fingers together. "To *what?*"

"To Chase's birthday game night."

Reign's head jerked back. She put her hands down, but didn't say anything.

Ava glanced at her watch. "It's starting in like twenty minutes."

Reign stood there; her face was void of expression. "Chase is having a game night?" she got out after a moment.

Ava looked at Reign as if she were crazy. "*Yes* girl," she confirmed, slightly amused. "I mean he *just* decided to do this like *two days* ago, but yeah, it's going on."

Reign slowly folded her arms. "*Did* he?"

Ava nodded, oblivious. "It's just something small, a few friends and family—some of our old friends from high school. You remember Davita and 'em, right?"

Reign nodded slowly. "Yes, I do remember Davita and 'em," she put out, flat.

"Well, they're going to be there, and I even invited Malcom," Ava added. She finished talking long enough to finally focus on Reign. After another moment of picking up on her silence, realization hit. "You...you didn't know about this, *did* you?"

Reign shook her head. "Can't say that I did." Outside she was stoic, but on the inside Reign was seething. *So he ignores me, blows me off, then decides to throw a party and doesn't invite me?!*

Ava jerked her head back. "That...doesn't make any sense," she slowly drew out. "Hell, normally you'd know before *I* would," she attempted to joke.

"I *didn't*," Reign bristled.

"Well, there *has* to be an explanation." Ava scratched her head. "Or it could have been a small oversight. He *has* been a bit scatter-brained lately."

"Yeah, an oversight…we'll go with that," Reign spat.

Ava let out a sigh. *What the hell was he thinking?* "Look, I don't know what the deal is, but you're still coming right?"

Reign pondered the thought. Normally Reign would never go where she wasn't wanted, and *clearly* Chase didn't want her there, or she would have gotten an invite. But she wasn't going to let him get away with it without having to face her. "Yeah, I'm going," she answered, heading for the staircase. "Let me go get ready."

"I'll wait for you, we can leave out together," Ava called after her.

"Chase, anything on that bar is fair game, right?"

Chase laughed at the eager man standing in his kitchen. "Yes, anything on the bar, whether it's already open or not, can be consumed."

"Bet," the man rejoiced, darting from the kitchen along with a few other guests.

Chase shook his head in amusement, then went back to removing the lids from his food trays. Having made the last-minute decision to have his birthday game night, he'd elected not to cook anything. Instead, he'd ordered an abundance of takeout food, picked up snacks, and restocked his home bar.

Disappointed over the state of his relationship with Reign, or lack thereof, Chase's mood had been low; he was looking forward to having a good time. Hearing laughter and loud commotion come from his living room, he chuckled to himself. Grabbing his ice bucket from the counter, he moved to the freezer, placing it in front of his ice machine.

In the middle of filling it, he heard someone enter the kitchen.

"Happy birthday old man."

Chase laughed at Ava's greeting. "Yeah, that's funny." He turned around. Any other words that he was getting ready to say had gotten caught in his throat. Standing beside her, was Reign. The ice glare on Reign's face told him that she was far from pleased.

"Happy birthday Chase," Reign ground out.

Chase swallowed hard, clearing his throat. "Thank you, ladies." He slowly set the ice bucket down. "I appreciate it."

"Reign told me that she didn't know about tonight, so I just told her to come," Ava explained, gesturing to Reign, who had slowly folded her arms.

Reign had yet to remove her piercing gaze from Chase. Chase stared back at her, not saying anything.

"I figured it must've been an oversight or something, because you'd never intentionally leave her off of your guest list," Ava assumed.

Chase still hadn't spoken.

"Yeah, it wasn't *intentional, was* it?" Reign questioned. Her tone was calm, yet condescending.

Chase slowly shook his head, face void of expression. "It was an oversight."

"*Was* it?" Reign challenged.

His jaw tightened. "It *was*."

Reign's eyes narrowed. "Um hmm."

Ava frowned, glancing back and forth between the two. She'd never seen them this tense with one another before. "Uh, is everything okay with you two?"

"We're good," they spat out in unison, glaring one another down.

Chase gestured to the living room. "Bar is out there, food is here, and games will be played on the deck."

Ava scratched her head. "Yeah, I'm not messing with the hard stuff, did you pick up wine?"

"I did. It's out there," Chase answered.

Ava turned and proceeded to head out. "Good, I'll have a glass," she stopped, looking back at Reign. "Do you want some too?"

"No," Reign answered, finally cutting the stare down short; she looked at Ava. "But I'll come with you though."

Chase followed the women's progress out of the kitchen. Alone again, he ran his hands over his head, expelling a loud sigh.

"Shit," he huffed. He'd tried to exclude Reign out of frustration with her and it had only backfired; now she was upset with him.

This night of fun wasn't going to go as planned.

Throughout the evening, Reign stayed mostly to herself. Except for the occasional small talk that she engaged in with the other guests, she didn't say much.

She was there to make Chase feel uncomfortable. She knew that it was immature of her, but she felt he'd earned it. The fact that Chase had worked overtime to avoid her all evening let Reign know that it was effective.

Chase had directed everyone to his well-lit deck to play games. As his guests made their way outside, laughing, drinking and conversing, Reign just watched from her corner seat, face void of expression. It wasn't until Ava walked over that Reign offered a slight smile.

"Sis, every time I see you, you're to yourself. Are you okay?" Ava asked, concerned. Though Ava was enjoying her evening, she couldn't help but notice the tension between her brother and her best friend. To anyone who didn't know them and their relationship like *she* did, they would think nothing of the fact that the pair hadn't exchanged pleasantries, a hug, a funny moment. But Ava noticed, and she knew something was seriously wrong.

Reign clutched a throw pillow to her midsection. "I'm fine," she answered in a flat tone.

Ava sat next to her. "Rae, come on, you can't say that to me when I know you." She patted Reign's leg. "I know you're quiet in *general*, but something just seems off. Not only with *you*, but Chase too."

Reign didn't say anything, she just looked at Ava.

"Except for that weird exchange in the kitchen when we first got here, you two haven't spoken."

"He and I will talk," Reign promised, vague. "I can assure you of that."

Ava hesitated, adjusting a bracelet on her wrist. "The lack of invite wasn't an oversight, *was* it?" she asked after a moment.

Reign gritted her teeth as she looked away. "He said it was, so it was."

Ava glanced at the pillow Reign was holding. "The way that you're about to rip that pillow apart with your nails, I'd say that that was a lie."

Reign looked down; her nails were digging into the small, burnt orange pillow. She tossed it on a chair next to her. "How are things going with Malcom?"

Ava held her gaze on Reign, letting out a sigh. Her deflection wasn't missed, but Ava decided not to push; the more she did, the less she'd get. "Things are going well," she said. "As you know, we've just been talking, but it's nice having him here tonight."

Reign nodded. "Are you ready for that actual date yet?"

Ava giggled. "I don't know yet—*maybe*," she coyly replied. "If he makes me lose at spades, then no."

Reign laughed a little. "Petty."

"Hey, what are you two doing over there, come join the crowd!" a woman bellowed.

Ava rolled her eyes. "God Vita, do you always have to be so loud?" she muttered in an aside to Reign. She stood. "Are you coming over?"

"In a minute," Reign replied.

Ava gave a nod, then walked away.

"Reign come over here and help Chase win, because if he plays with anyone else, he's going to lose," Davita chuckled.

"She doesn't want to play," Chase assumed, tone dry.

"No, I'll play," Reign said, getting up from her seat. She sat in a chair across from Chase.

Feeling Reign's eyes burn through him like a laser, Chase kept his focus on the cards being shuffled by Malcom.

Malcom glanced at Ava. "Ava, remember how mad you'd get when you'd lose those spades tournaments we used to have in college?"

"I'd only *lose* because I had *your* non-paying-attention ass, as a *partner*," Ava threw back. "Always asking, 'what suit did we just play'?"

Malcom laughed as he dealt the cards. "Funny. But blame yourself, your beauty distracted me."

"Oh shut up, you just can't play," Ava scoffed, earning more laughter from Malcom as well as the other guests who'd gathered around. "I don't know *why* I'm even subjecting myself to being your partner *now*."

After the cards were dealt, Malcom picked up his hand. "Don't you worry, we've got this," he boasted.

Ava shook her head as she arranged her cards. "Chase, remember when Mom taught Reign how to play spades in high school?" she brought up. "Rae was nervous that she wouldn't catch on, but she *did*, and she and Mom whopped our asses every game."

Chase couldn't help but chuckle at the memory while setting up his hand. "I remember," he said. "She's always been a fast learner."

Reign had no amusement on her face as she arranged her cards, nor did she respond.

Ava eyed her cards. "Bro, Rae, how many books do you two have?"

"Four," Reign answered.

Chase stared at his cards for a moment. "Five and a possible," he answered finally. "We'll go ten."

Reign tilted her head, staring at him. "*Really?*"

Chase eyed her back. "Really," he confirmed, unwavering.

"Damn," Ava muttered. She looked at Malcom. "Malcom?"

Malcom rubbed his chin with his hand. "Six."

Ava stared at him, annoyed. "No the *hell* you *don't!*"

Malcom busted out laughing.

"I'm not about to do this with you," Ava grunted. "*I* don't have anything and it's apparent that *he* still can't count books—we're going board."

"Ava, I *have* good books," Malcom promised, animated.

"I *said* board." Ava pointed to the notepad in front of Malcom. "Write it."

Malcom shook his head, then chuckled. "That's a shame, you don't even trust your partner." He jotted down the numbers.

After a few hands had been played, Ava had begun to feel that she'd made a mistake in bidding so low. "Damn, I apologize

Malcom. You had books *after* all," Ava admitted, watching Malcom scoop up yet another book.

Chase rolled his eyes as he threw out a card.

"Maybe next time you'll listen to me," Malcom threw back, watching Ava discard too.

Ava smirked. "Maybe."

Reign tossed out a card. "Chase, you've forgotten how to count books, I see," she taunted.

Chase shot her a glare. "I *didn't*." He gave a hard shrug. "Sometimes things just don't go as planned."

"Yeah, the plan seemed to derail with every *one* of *your* books," Reign mocked.

Malcom snickered, then catching Ava's warning glance, wiped the humor from his face. Tossing out his card, he snapped his fingers. "Damn," he muttered, watching Reign pick up the book that she'd won.

Reign tossed a card out. "You sure you're focusing Chase?" she watched the table. "You sure nothing is bothering you?"

Chase took a deep breath as Malcom threw a card down. "Nope, I'm all good over here," he grunted, throwing his card out.

Raising an eyebrow, Reign looked up at Chase. "You *sure?*"

"*Yes*, yes I'm sure," Chase answered, flustered. "Why are you insinuating that I'm *not?*"

Reign pointed to the cards on the table. "Because you just cut me."

Chase frowned, looking down at the cards. Noticing what he'd done, he became frustrated. "Shit," he hissed, folding his cards in his hands. "I can't—somebody take this hand."

Reign put a hand up. "No, no. I'll remove myself." She held her cards out. "Vita, you want to take my place?"

Davita bolted over, eager. "Sure *do.*"

Reign stood from her seat, handed the woman her cards, then walked away.

Chase pinched the bridge of his nose, letting out a deep sigh.

Ava shot Chase a glance. "You want to call it a night?" she asked.

Chase shook his head. "Nope, let's keep playing." He grabbed his drink, taking a long sip.

Reign glanced at her phone; it was after one in the morning and the last of Chase's invited guests had left for the evening. She'd retreated inside the house after the spades game, sitting in an accent chair off to the side, out of sight.

There she stayed, thinking, fuming. On more than one occasion, she wanted to get up and leave, hurt and offended by Chase's behavior. But she knew that a conversation needed to be had.

Setting her phone on the arm of the chair, Reign finally got up, walking into the kitchen.

Chase, who was loading his dishwasher, spun around, eyes going wide. "I thought that you'd left."

"I'm sure you *did*." Reign folded her arms. She surveyed the mess of trays, empty cups, plates, liquor bottles and trash. "Do you need help?"

"No, I got it." Chase placed more dishes into the appliance. It was silent for moments as Chase maneuvered about the kitchen; the tension was thick. "Did you drink?"

"Nope," she answered.

"Oh." He tossed trash into the metal garbage bin. "Did you ride here with Ava? Do you need a ride home?"

"No, I don't need a ride home, but I *do* need you to be honest with me," Reign bristled.

"Honest about *what* Reign?" Chase bit out, still cleaning.

"About the fact that you *are* angry with me."

Chase exhaled sharply. "I *said* I'm not angry."

Reign put her hands on her hips. "Oh yeah?" she challenged. "Because the fact that you have been ignoring my calls, having an attitude when you *do* finally speak to me, brushing me off and not even inviting me *here tonight* tells me otherwise."

"I *said* that was an oversight, Reign."

Reign clapped her hands in anger. "It was *not* a fuckin' oversight," she snapped. "You did that on *purpose* because you didn't want to see me, and I need to know why."

"*Friends* don't always return phone calls. *Friends* don't always have time for one another," Chase sneered, wiping down the counter. "It *happens*."

Reign was taken aback. "That's not how *our* relationship is."

"Oh, *now* you care about our *relationship*," he mocked.

"Are you serious right now?" She scoffed. "You're being an asshole."

"Sorry you feel that way." Chase gestured to the door. "Feel free to vent to yourself about it on your way home."

Reign narrowed her eyes; she could've picked up one of the empty glasses on the counter and thrown it at his head. "Oh *sure*, you're not angry," she drawled, sarcastic.

Chase slammed the dishrag on the counter, spinning around to finally face her. "You know what, you're right," he snapped, glaring. "I *am* angry, but feel free to add disappointed and confused to the list."

"Okay well what is the goddamn *problem*?" Reign asked, frustrated. "What did I *do* to you?"

"You're not being straight with me."

Reign tossed her hands up. "About *what*?"

"About how you feel. About *us*," Chase argued. "You say you only want friendship from me, yet you *behave* like you want *more* than that."

Reign frowned, "Because I slept with you?"

"You don't think that's grounds for me to be confused?" he scowled. "Past prom behavior aside, we had sex *twice*, and have almost kissed on *more* than one occasion," he reminded. "You're telling me that you do that with your *other friends*? You talk to your other friends every single day, see them multiple times a week?"

Reign folded her arms, looking away.

"You don't even talk to *Ava* that goddamn much, so tell me that I'm wrong."

Reign snapped her head back in his direction. "What is it that you want me to *say* to you, Chase?" she barked. "That I have feelings for you? I *said* that I did."

"And what feelings are *those*?" His frown deepened. "*Anger* is a feeling, *sadness* is a feeling, so what are you saying?"

"You know what? You're coming down on me about not being clear about feelings, but you aren't clear either," she brought up. "You told me that your feelings for me changed."

He crossed his arms. "They *have*."

"Changed to *what*, exactly?"

"I love you," Chase answered, instantly.

Reign's mouth dropped open; her eyes widened. Unable to speak, she just stared at him.

Shaking his head, Chase let out a deep sigh. "We're being childish," he admitted, calming himself down. "This back and forth—my behavior over the past two weeks—I'm better than that... *We're* better than that... I'm sorry that I hurt your feelings. God knows that was the last thing that I ever wanted to do."

Reign couldn't think of a thing to say; she just kept replaying the words "I love you" in her head as Chase spoke to her.

He stepped forward. "Part of the reason why I'm frustrated is because I've been holding my feelings for you in, and I can't do that anymore."

Reign felt like she was holding her breath. "Chase, don't—"

"I love you," Chase cut in, sincere. "I've *been in* love with you and I can't hide that anymore. I *won't*. It's killing me."

Reign ran her hands through her hair as she tried to keep her emotions in check; the conflicted look on her face and her labored breathing was a sign that she was failing. Chase had just told her that he was in love with her, triggering all the feelings that she'd kept buried inside of her, including *fear*. "Umm...Chase I don't know what to— When did—"

"This isn't recent Reign," Chase confessed. "It—it wasn't recent. I just suppressed it. But like I said, I *can't* anymore."

Reign put a hand on her head, trying to steady her breathing.

"I don't know what to say."

Chase ran his hands over his face. Reign was flustered; he knew that telling her would bring out that reaction in her. In the past, he'd let her off the hook. He wouldn't make her talk; he'd allow her to deflect. But this time, he wasn't going to allow her to take the easy way out; he needed answers. He needed to know where they stood. "Just say what you feel…what you *really* feel," he pressed.

Chase moved closer to her; his gazed locked on her. Reign could no longer hold eye contact with him.

"Can you look at me?"

"I don't know what to say," Reign stammered, shaking her head.

"Can you *look* at me please?" he begged.

Reign let out a deep breath before looking him in his face. "I…I *do* have feelings for you Chase, but I just can't—"

"You can't *what?*" Chase's eyes were pleading.

"Relationships ruin friendships and I don't want that to happen to us," she said. "I can't go through another breakup."

"Who says we'd have to break up?"

"Chase don't be naïve okay," she hurled, upset. "People say shit all the time in the beginning, it's always good in the *beginning*… I don't want *us* to end up where my *last* relationship did."

A mask of anger formed on Chase's face. He turned away, moving back to the counter island.

Reign took a step forward. "Chase, I care about you *so* much. I truly do," she continued, standing in front of the counter. "But…I can't do the relationship thing again…at least not now."

Chase nodded slowly. "So…you spending all that time with me, the connection that I felt from you, you sleeping with me…what was that?" he questioned, eerily calm.

She sighed.

"See I took that as you perhaps feeling the same way that *I* did. I took that as you wanting to take our relationship to another level," he added. "But *clearly* I was wrong. Clearly I was being *used.*"

Reign scowled. "*Excuse* me?"

"It was fine for me to *act* like a boyfriend, but I can't actually *be* one," he bristled. "You used me to fill whatever void you had, just admit it. It wouldn't be the first time that I was used by a woman."

Reign stared at Chase with fire in her eyes. Furious, she pushed the empty ice bucket off the counter, sending it crashing to the floor. "Are you fuckin' kidding me?!" she exploded. "I have *never* used you! Everything that I've done when it comes to you has been genuine. How *dare* you say that to me?"

Chase's jaw tightened as she ranted.

Reign pointed at him. "Don't you *ever* say some shit like that to me again! Don't you *ever* compare me to another woman."

"Don't *you* compare *me* to that bastard you used to be with!" Chase yelled back, moving around the counter.

"I *never* compare you to him!"

"You did when you stood here in my face and in so many words said that a relationship with *me* would end up like the one with *him*," Chase argued, standing in her face. "I am *nothing* like him!" he stressed, smacking himself on the chest. "I would *never* do to you what he did, I would *never* treat you how he treated you. You *never* should've been with him in the *first* place, and you *know* that."

Reign saw the hurt in his face. She'd compared Chase—a man who always looked out for her, cared for her, protected her, put her feelings first—to a man who had disregarded her, cheated on her, and hurt her. "I know you're not like him." Her voice lowered. "You are... *better* in every way imaginable." Her emotions were coming to a head.

Seeing the tears fill Reign's eyes, Chase's anger melted away. He reached out, trying to touch her arm, but she moved away from him.

"I'm not lying, I care about you, but I just can't do this." Reign slowly backed away from him.

"Reign, don't—"

"You deserve to be with someone who's ready for you," she cut in, voice faltering. "I'm sorry."

Chase, feeling like he was about to break down, followed Reign as she stormed through the living room. "So, you *just care* about me?" he hurled at her back. "That's it? You don't *love* me?"

Reign kept walking towards the door, desperately trying not to bust out in a full-on cry.

Chase darted up to her. As Reign opened the door, he pushed it closed.

Reign spun around. "Let me leave!" she screamed at him.

He held his hand on the door. "I *can't*, not yet. I'm sorry."

Angry, Reign raised her hand to hit him, but he grabbed it, placing her balled fist to his chest. "You have to tell me the truth."

"I *told* you!"

"You're holding back from me, Reign." Though Reign was enraged, Chase was calm. He didn't want to argue, he just wanted the truth. "I *know* you are—"

"Can you stop?" Reign pleaded, snatching her hand from him. Tears were spilling down her face. "Just stop—can we just go back to how things were?"

Chase lowered his head momentarily, taking a few deep breaths. He felt his own emotions coming to a head. "I can't," he answered after a moment. He looked back up at her.

Reign closed her eyes at the sight of tears in Chase's eyes.

"I can't go back to how things were," he choked out.

Covering her face with her hands, Reign broke down crying. What she feared was becoming a reality—her friendship with Chase would never be the same. She felt guilty; guilty for leaning on him, guilty for allowing lines to be crossed, and mostly, guilty because she was too afraid to admit how deep *her* feelings for *him* ran. "Please?" she cried.

"I *can't*," Chase answered. "My feelings for you run too deep."

"Chase, I told you that I have feelings for you," she sniffled, removing her hands from her face. "I *do*, I just can't—"

Chase touched her face. "I know you're scared, I understand," he soothed. "You've been through a lot; we *both* have. But I know that we can make it work."

Reign tried to open the door again, but Chase's hand on it

prevented her from doing it.

Chase was desperate; Reign was trying to run from her feelings, from *him*, but he wanted to make her see that she didn't have to fear a future with him. He *needed* to.

"I need to leave," Reign pleaded.

"Baby—*please* don't run from us." The desperation was heavy in his voice. "Don't run from what we could be."

"Chase, let me *leave!*"

"You're everything that I ever wanted," Chase professed. "You make me happy. Just the sound of your voice brings me peace. Seeing your beautiful face, being in your presence—it makes everything right for me." At this point, Chase didn't care how vulnerable he was; Reign was the woman that he loved, the one he'd *always* loved. He couldn't let her walk away until she knew just how much.

Reign could do nothing but cry.

"I love *everything* about you. From the good to the *frustrating*... I've never loved anyone the way that I love you."

Reign put her hand on his chest, attempting to push him back from her. Instead he covered her hand with his, holding it in place.

"I want a life with you," he declared. "I know we can be great together, I just—I need to know that you love me." Tears spilled down his face. "You're not ready yet fine, I'll wait, but—Rae just tell me that you love me... I need to know that I have a chance." He searched her face with hope in his eyes.

Reign turned away from him; she couldn't speak.

After a long moment of silence, Chase shook his head. Releasing her hand, he stepped back from her. He wiped the tears from his face. Reign's silence told him what he didn't want to hear. Resolved, he cleared his throat. "Okay," he said after a moment. He let out a deep breath. "Okay."

She looked at him, tears still flowing.

"You don't love me, you don't want to be with me...that's fine. I'll have to accept that." Chase fixed a somber gaze. "But knowing how I feel about you and what I want *with* you, and being faced with the reality that you don't want the same… I just—I can't be around you." He shook his head yet again. "The last time I did that, I watched you end up with someone else, and I don't have it in me to do it again."

Reign stared at him. Hearing the defeat in his voice, seeing it on his face—it nearly broke her.

"This friendship Rae…it has to end," he said. "I'm sorry."

Reign finally opened the door. Face still wet from tears, she sniffled. "I'm sorry too." She bolted out of the house, and didn't look back.

Reign stormed into her house, slamming the door behind her. Grabbing her hair with both hands, she stood in the living room and belted out her cries to the empty space. She was distraught, furious with herself. She'd downplayed her feelings like she always did, and only hurt Chase in the process.

Falling to the couch, Reign cried until she couldn't anymore. Physically and emotionally drained, she just sat there, staring at the pictures on her walls. Reflecting on her choices, the choices that she made when she was younger and how they'd impacted not just her life, but Chase's as well. The guilt and regret were so heavy on Reign that it felt like the pressure would crush her.

Hearing a knock on her door, she closed her eyes and sighed, standing up. Checking the peephole, she opened it without a word, slowly backing. She watched in silence as Chase slowly entered.

Silence filled the room as they stood in front of each other. Chase reached into his jeans pocket and pulled out Reign's cell phone.

Reign could only stare at it as he held it out for her. She'd left it on the arm of the chair in his living room. Sighing, she took it from him. She didn't even have it in her to say "thank you". She hoped that he knew that she was grateful anyway.

Chase had found her phone after she'd left. While he knew that it would be hard seeing her so soon, he figured that returning it to her right away, while they were both still raw, was better than waiting. He wanted to get it over with. Yet Chase couldn't speak either. What was said, had already been said.

He didn't know why he thought that it would be so easy to drop it off and walk away. Walking out of that door would mean walking out of her life. He just wasn't ready.

Reign wasn't unnerved by the fact that Chase was still standing in front of her; his inner conflict was her own. She was forcing him to let her go, and that meant she would have to let *him* go. But in that moment, she didn't want to. Not yet.

I don't want to walk out of this door...I can't. Despite what his heart was telling him, Chase knew that he had to. Locking his glistening gaze on Reign, he felt himself getting choked up again as he slowly backed away. "Goodbye Reign."

Reign's heart sank even further into her chest. Hearing the words made the reality that much harder. Trying to keep the newly forming tears at bay, Reign opened her mouth to say the words back, but no matter how hard she tried, she couldn't. "Don't go," she choked out instead.

Stopping, Chase's heart melted; his face softened as he expelled a deep breath.

"Not yet." Reign's voice was barely audible as tears built behind her pleading eyes. "Please."

Her pleas were his undoing. Almost as if Reign had willed him to her, Chase moved in and kissed her. Wrapping his arms around her, Chase pulled Reign close to him, fusing his body to hers. She dropped her phone to the floor, wrapping her arms around his neck as the kiss grew desperate.

Chase picked Reign up in his arms and carried her through the living room and up the steps to her bedroom. He laid her on her bed, removing her clothes before she aided in removing his.

Reign held her eyes on Chase as he climbed on top of her, trying to commit everything about him to memory. She relished the feeling of his hands on her, leaving no part of her untouched. Her passion grew as his kisses traveled. Her mind filled with haze as his tongue flicked against her.

She couldn't focus on the fact that this was probably a mistake—like every other time. She could only focus on the pleasure that was building inside of her. She grabbed her covers with one hand, holding Chase's head steady with the other, as the building orgasm that he was creating with his attentive tongue reached its peak.

Reign barely had a chance to catch her breath before Chase hovered above her. Pausing just long enough to protect her with a condom from her bedside drawer, Chase entered her. With each deep, powerful stroke, Reign's emotions came to a head. She knew that this wasn't just another tryst that would result in an awkward conversation before settling back into normality. This was different; this was goodbye.

Tears filled then spilled out of her eyes as Chase moved in and out of her. She wrapped her arms tight around his back, almost as if she didn't want to let go of him. Her moans came out as cries as she climaxed again, with Chase following suit.

Lifting his head from her neck, Chase noticed Reign's tear-streaked face. Touching her face, Chase's eyes widened slightly with worry. He opened his mouth to speak.

"I'm fine," she managed to get out, in a tearful voice. "I'm fine."

Chase moved her damp hair from her face. "Are you sure?" he asked, tone soothing.

Reign didn't want to speak again; if she did, she'd just break down crying. Instead, she just nodded.

Chase let out a sigh of relief; he would've hated himself if he had hurt her. He stared into her eyes a bit longer, memorizing them. Planting a soft kiss on her cheek, he moved off of her, lying beside her.

Both laid there in silence.

Reign turned her head, wiping the wetness from her face with her sheet.

Chase sighed, then after a moment, he grabbed Reign's hand, giving it a kiss before holding it over his heart.

Chapter Thirty-Seven

REIGN ADJUSTED THE CELL IN her hand as she knocked on her parents' door. "Yeah, I can come pick you up," she spoke into the line. "Just make sure everything is packed before I get there. I'm not going to want to be there all day... Yes, I know it's next week, but I still need to remind you of that." She looked up when her mother answered the door. Offering a wave, Reign walked in. "Just remember what I said... Okay, bye."

Vivian chuckled, "Who are you fussing with?"

"Your daughter," Reign answered, putting her phone in her purse. "She needs me to pick her up for break next weekend."

"Oh sweetie, your father and I can go pick her up," Vivian offered.

"It's fine, I don't mind." Reign set her purse on the couch. "I need the distraction anyway."

Vivian shot Reign a sympathetic glance. "Still not going to tell me what happened?"

Eyes lowering, Reign shook her head.

Vivian sighed. She had visited Reign weeks ago, and was witness to Reign's emotional breakdown. While comforting her daughter, she had tried to get Reign to tell her what had her upset. All that she could get out was that Chase was no longer in Reign's life. "Well...I just pray that whatever caused the rift between you two, can be resolved so that you can go back to being friends."

Reign sighed, glancing off to the side. "It's not that simple, Mom."

"That's such a shame, you two are so close."

"We were," Reign agreed. Seeing her mother wave her hands in front of her eyes, Reign sighed yet again. "Please don't cry."

"I'm sorry, I just—after that mess with Troy, you were so broken, and…Chase made you smile again and—" Vivian wiped her tears with her hands. "I'm sorry, don't mind me."

Reign put a hand on her mother's shoulder. "Don't worry about me…I'll be okay." The lie seemed to satisfy her mother, who just gave her a hug.

Truth was that the breakdown in front of her mother wasn't the first or the last that Reign had suffered since Chase had left her home nearly a month ago. She hadn't seen him nor spoken to him since.

Vivian parted from the long embrace and watched her daughter rub her forehead. Worry set in. "You okay?"

"Just getting a headache, it's no big deal," Reign told. "Probably a hunger headache, I didn't eat much this morning."

"Well let me go get this food together." Vivian headed for the kitchen. "I'll just be a few minutes; you have a seat and relax."

Reign watched her mother disappear into the kitchen, then went to sit on the couch. Hearing her father enter the living room stopped her in her tracks.

"I thought that I heard you in here," he said.

"Yeah." Reign tucked her hair behind her ears, torn between sitting and going to the kitchen. "Mom invited me over for lunch."

Matthew nodded. "Yeah, I notice she's been doing that a lot lately," he mentioned. "Normally she spaces her smothering out for a few weeks."

Even if Reign *wanted* to crack a smile at her father's lackluster joke, she couldn't. She nodded instead. "Yeah, I know," she agreed, tone even.

Matthew tilted his head, eyeing Reign with curiosity. "Why do you think that is?"

Reign shrugged. "I'm…" she let out a sigh. "I'm having a little bit of a rough time, so I guess she just wants to keep tabs on me."

Matthew folded his arms. "*What's* rough?"

"Just *things* Dad," Reign dismissed. "But I'm dealing with them, like I always do."

Matthew rubbed his chin with his hand. "Reign…I'll never understand why you let things bother you so much." His tone lacked any emotion.

Reign frowned at him. She was not in the mood for another one of her father's lectures.

"I don't know *how* many times I have to say, stop stressing out over unimportant things." Sternness showed in his tight eyes. "There's no *point* to it."

Reign folded her arms. "Unimportant things," she repeated, bite in her voice. "Unimportant such as, my feelings. *That's* what you mean right?"

He sighed, "Reign, don't get defensive."

"Oh okay so not *only* am I not allowed to *feel* anything, I can't get defensive when you call what I *feel* unimportant," she sneered. "That's great to know." Shaking her head, she snatched her purse from the chair. "I can't do this today."

Matthew watched Reign barrel for the door. "What is so wrong about what I said?"

Reign spun around, jerking the purse strap onto her shoulder. "You know what Dad? I am so *sick* of you being so damn dismissive of everything that I feel," she snapped.

Matthew was taken aback. "Excuse me?"

"'Don't let it bother you Reign', 'don't let them see you cry Reign', 'suck it up Reign'," she vented. "Well I'm tired, I'm *tired* of sucking it up."

Reign had grown up being subjected to her father's dismissive advice whenever she'd tried to express what was bothering her. She'd always listened to it, but those times were over.

"Me telling you to get a handle on your emotions is not *dismissive*, Reign," Matthew argued.

Reign's eyes widened in anger. "Do you *know* how much shit I suppress every single day trying to keep a *handle* on my damn emotions? Do you *know* how hard it is for me to even *talk* about how I feel?!" she placed a hand to her chest. "I can't express myself, I don't know *how* to. I don't know how to even be *vulnerable* because all that's in the back of my mind is 'it's not important', and that translates to 'what *you feel* is not important'." She shook her head at her father, pain in her eyes. "Do you have *any* idea what you've done to me?"

Matthew's eyes widened. "You think that I—"

"What is all of this yelling about out here?" Vivian interrupted, entering the living room. She looked back and forth between her husband and daughter. The obvious tension concerned her. "What happened?"

"It's nothing Mom," Reign dismissed, going for the door.

Vivian took a step forward. "Wait honey, are you okay? What—"

"I'm fine, like *always*," Reign spat, walking out of the house and slamming the door in her wake.

Vivian spun around, facing her husband. "What did you say to her?" she charged, upset.

Running a hand over the back of his neck, Matthew exhaled deeply.

Stepping off the treadmill, towel in hand, Troy scanned the gym as he wiped his brow. He surveyed the wide-open space, eyeing its patrons. Hearing chatter from the entrance, Troy craned his neck to get a better look. Not seeing who he was looking for, he sucked his teeth. Snatching his gym bag from the floor, Troy sprinted towards the exit.

Stepping outside, Troy paused, eyeing everyone who passed him on the sidewalk. His eyes lingered on each passerby, disappointment growing as each person and each minute passed.

After a moment, he let out a sigh, rubbing his face in the process. Troy had been to the gym nearly every day and at the same time, early evening—the same time that *Reign* used to go. He'd hoped to get a glimpse of her just once, but she never showed.

Resolved, he made a beeline for his car.

The fifteen-minute drive home was filled with glum silence; Troy couldn't even bring himself to turn on the radio. Pulling into his garage, he turned the car off but hesitated to get out. Glancing at his house, he rolled his eyes. "I don't feel like dealing with this shit."

As he finally made a move to get out of the car, his phone beeped. Grabbing it from the gym bag, he eyed the text message from Marcy.

What time are you coming back?

Troy once again rolled his eyes, before promptly deleting the message. "Leave me the fuck alone, will you," he huffed. He might have cleared the message from his phone, but it was only a matter of time before he had to see her; the woman still lived in his house after all.

Still holding the phone in his hand, Troy pulled up Reign's phone number, staring at it. Something he'd been doing often—he'd refused to delete her number. Clicking off her contact, Troy went to his pictures. He scrolled until he came to one in particular: a picture of he and Reign taken in the beginning of their relationship. They looked happy; *he* looked happy.

He knew that he should click out of the app, but he couldn't. He couldn't stop staring at Reign's picture; just like he couldn't stop *thinking about* her. He wasn't over her and at this point he didn't think he'd *ever* be.

As a wave of sadness fell over him, Troy touched her image with his finger. *I miss you so much.*

A loud smack to his driver-side window startled him. So much so that he let out a yelp, dropping his phone in the process. Wide eyes shooting up, he saw Marcy's angered face staring back at him.

"Great," he muttered. Sucking his teeth, Troy snatched his phone from the floor. Closing the photo, he shoved the device back into his bag.

Marcy stepped back, arms folded, a scowl frozen on her face. "Funny, you had your phone in your hand, but couldn't answer my *text*," she barked, as Troy exited the car.

"There was no *need*, I was already home." Troy moved past her to the door.

Marcy following him into the house. She watched him bolt for the stairs. "Troy—"

"Marcy, if you're about to argue, complain about something, or ask me for shit, I'm *pleading* with you not to right now," Troy blurted out still en route up the steps. "I'm not in the mood."

Marcy gritted her teeth. "You know what, screw you, I just wanted to talk," she bit back. Troy stopped in his tracks but didn't turn around. "You know, contrary to what your narcissistic ass *thinks*, every time I open my damn mouth, I'm not trying to argue or *ask* you for shit. Sometimes I *just* want to *talk*."

"You don't want to talk, you want *attention* Marcy, just like always," Troy grunted, still not bothering to face her.

"And what's so *wrong* with that?!" Marcy tossed her arms up. "God—it's been the same shit with you day after day," she vented. "The *same* fuckin' arguments over and over for *months*. The same disregard, the same *disrespect*—"

"Then why do you *insist* on sticking around?" Troy hurled, back still facing her.

Marcy opened her mouth to yell, but hesitated. Eyes lowering, she slowly shook her head. "Because..." she sighed. "I'm trying to make this—*thing* with you, *work* Troy."

Troy finally turned around. Staring at her, his face was void of emotion. "Why?" he asked finally.

Marcy frowned, though she didn't respond. She *couldn't* because...she didn't have the answer. At least not one that would make any sense.

Tired of this conversation and Marcy's presence all together, Troy continued his progress up the steps. "Do me a favor, don't follow me up here," he threw over his shoulder.

Hearing the door shut, Marcy slumped down to the couch. Covering her face with her hands, she let out a long, deep sigh. "Fuck my life."

Chapter Thirty-Eight

CHASE WALKED OUT OF THE café. "Yes, that's fine," he spoke into his cell. "How long is that trip?... Okay, and the next one?... I'll do that one too... Great, I'll be on the lookout for the travel information... Thanks."

Ending the call, he stuck the phone into his back pocket. Letting out a sigh, Chase took a careful sip of his coffee.

Since walking away from his friendship with Reign, Chase had immediately dove back into traveling for work. Without her to look forward to at the end of each work day, there was no longer a reason to restrict himself to local clientele.

As he sipped his coffee, Chase stared at the mountains in the distance. The memory of his last trip up there with Reign flooded back to him. It took everything in him not to grab his phone and call her. As much as he missed hearing her voice, seeing her face, he knew that to make a clean break and protect his heart, he couldn't talk to her.

Though he was convincing himself that he'd made the right decision, Chase felt the void she'd left behind every day. Shaking his head, he turned away and began walking down the sidewalk.

Standing in Reign's office, Ava slung her purse on her shoulder. "Do you want to go grab some dinner?"

Reign shook her head. "No thank you," she declined, tone low. "I'm feeling a little run down. I just want to go home and rest."

Ava's head tilted. "Are you coming down with something?"

"No, I don't think so, I'm just tired."

"Understandable," Ava nodded. She folded her arms; Reign's somber mood had not been missed. The woman hardly ever smiled or laughed anymore; it made Ava a little uneasy. "Are you going to tell me what's been going on with you?" she asked, straight to the point.

Reign rolled her eyes. "There is nothing *going on* with me, I'm just tired."

"*Every* day you're tired?" Ava countered. "Because that's the excuse that I get *every* time I inquire about why your mood has been off."

Reign huffed. "I really don't know what you want me to say to that."

Ava tossed her arms up, then let them drop. "I swear, *you're* acting weird, *Chase* is traveling every five minutes again—"

Reign felt a chill go through her at the mention of Chase's name. "He's traveling again?"

Ava raised an eyebrow. "You didn't know?" she questioned. "I figured that's why you two haven't been hanging out."

Reign didn't answer as she looked at her laptop. She hadn't shared anything about what had transpired between Chase and herself with Ava; Reign didn't need the meddling or the opinions. "You should probably head home before traffic gets bad," she deflected.

"Yeah, I'm going, but seriously, are you two—"

Reign's eyes shot up at Ava. "Ava, there is nothing for you to be concerned with," she interrupted, agitated. "*I'm* fine, I'm sure your *brother* is fine, just leave it at that okay?"

Ava frowned at the attitude being thrown her way. However, instead of harping, she decided to let it go. "Okay fine."

"Enjoy your evening," Reign dismissed.

"You too," Ava muttered, walking out.

Reign sauntered out of the office building, adjusting the purse on her forearm. She couldn't wait to get home and unwind—or *try* to at least.

She was so preoccupied with her thoughts that she didn't notice the person she was passing by. Someone grabbed her arm, and Reign screamed. Spinning around, she launched her fist at her attacker.

341

"Whoa!" Troy grabbed her hand before it had a chance to collide with his face. "It's me, it's me," he quickly explained.

Shaken, Reign stared at Troy as if he were crazy. Taking several deep breaths, she gained her composure. "Oh…okay," she got out.

Troy let out a sigh of relief.

With Troy's defenses down, Reign jerked her arm. Still in Troy's grasp, it pulled him forward while she kneed him in the groin.

"Shit!" he bellowed out, releasing her. He barely had a chance to grab his groin before Reign smacked him across the face with her handbag. It connected with his face, making Troy yell out. "*Shit Reign!*"

"You must've lost your fuckin' mind," Reign seethed, moving around him to storm away.

Pushing past his injuries, Troy grabbed her wrist again. "Wait—"

Reign spun around, delivering a punch to his face. "Stop fuckin' grabbing on me!"

Troy stumbled back onto the sidewalk. He grabbed his aching groin with one hand, his face with the other. "I'm sorry, I didn't mean to—"

"Shut up! I don't want to hear it." Reign jerked her bag back on her wrist. "I told you before to leave me alone."

Troy pulled his hand from his face. Eyeing the blood, he closed his eyes. He was almost certain that she'd just split his lip. But he couldn't focus on that right now. "Reign, I'm not stalking you, I just wanted to see you," he groaned, tone pleading. "I know you don't want my gifts, or *me*, I just—I just wanted to see you."

Reign's eyes widened in fury. "Are you drunk?!" she belted out. "Why would you think that I would *ever* want to see you again?"

"I know you don't, I—"

Reign stepped towards him. "Then leave me *alone*," she fumed through clenched teethed.

Troy sat up, putting a hand out in caution. "I just miss you," he choked out.

"That is *your* problem." She yanked her car keys from her bag.

"Because I *certainly* don't miss *you*. I don't want you, I don't love you, I don't *like* you, I don't give a damn *about* you."

Troy's emotions came to a head, but Reign left him no room to get a word in.

"Stay away from me or I swear to God, you'll be sorry," she warned, walking away.

Troy's breathing became heavy as he watched her leave. "Reign, I made a mistake!"

"Live with it!" she threw over her shoulder as she got in her car, leaving him sitting on the concrete.

"Are you serious?!" Ava exclaimed, glass of wine in hand.

Reign nodded. "Yup."

"What the hell is his goddamn *problem*?" Ava was fuming.

Rolling her eyes, Reign shrugged as she took a quick sip from her own glass.

Reign had called Ava as soon as she was safe; her friend didn't hesitate to invite Reign over to her place for a glass of wine and a listening ear.

Sitting on the couch with Ava, Reign gave her a rundown of the entire ordeal.

Ava took a sip of her wine, then shook her head. "What the hell did he think that was going to accomplish?"

"It accomplished *nothing*," Reign sneered. She set her glass on the coffee table. "*Clearly* his simple ass wasted his time, *and* mine. Which, given our history, isn't surprising."

Ava shook her head. "Well, at least you got to knee his pathetic ass in the balls…and punch him in the face."

Reign couldn't help but chuckle. "That was the *only* upside to the entire encounter."

Ava laughed a bit herself, then let out a deep breath; the humor leaving her face. "In all seriousness, do you think you'll need a protective order against him?" she asked. "I mean, he *did* show up at the job."

Reign scoffed. "Please." She waved a hand. "While what happened today *startled* me, I'm not afraid of Troy. Never *have* been."

"Are you *sure?*" Ava pressed. "You already know your father will have the *entire police force* posted in front of your house."

Reign let out a deep sigh. "Troy is—a *lot* of things…violent isn't one of them," she maintained. "I'm not worried."

Ava tilted her head, holding her concerned gaze.

"I'm *annoyed,*" Reign clarified. "But I'm not worried about my safety."

Ava put a hand up. "I hear you. I just wouldn't have felt right not asking."

Reign flashed an appreciative look Ava's way. "I get it… Thanks."

Ava gave a nod, sipping more wine. "*Speaking* of running into irrelevant people…" she began after a moment.

Reign eyed her with curiosity.

"I ran into Marcy a while ago," Ava told. "At a damn donut shop of all places."

Reign raised an eyebrow. "I'm sure that made your day," she jeered.

"*Hardly.*" Ava's lip turned up at the memory. "Ol' girl tried to get under my skin with her bullshit." She swirled the remaining wine around in her glass. "Started going on about how I never liked her because I was jealous of your friendship with her, and how I'm in love with you and shit."

Reign frowned in confusion. "Oh, come on."

"I know." Ava laughed, "I'm *not* in love with you by the way."

"I *know* that, crazy," Reign assured, amused. "I wouldn't even dwell on that mess, the girl is delusional."

Ava set her glass down. "Hell, I'm still trying to figure out what made you befriend her in the *first* place."

"I don't know." Reign sighed, "Clearly, I'm not a good judge of character."

Ava shot Reign a sympathetic look. "I didn't mean it like that."

"It's fine," Reign uttered, shrugging.

Ava pushed some of her curls from her face. "Anyway, I tried to tell Chase about my run-in a few days after it happened but he, in so many words, told me not to bring her ass up to him again," she said. "Then I figured *you* wouldn't want to be subjected to hearing about her *either*, so I just kept it to myself...until *now* obviously."

"Nothing wrong with keeping some things to yourself," Reign replied after a moment. She let out another sigh. "Listen, I know that I caught an attitude with you earlier and I didn't mean to."

Ava just looked at her.

"I just—had a long day," Reign added. "But that's not an excuse... I'm sorry."

"It's fine." Ava patted Reign's hand. "And I know that I can pry a lot, I'm just worried about you, you know?"

Reign stared at Ava as she spoke.

"For a while you seemed happy again, and now you're just..." Ava tilted her head. "You have a sadness to you."

Reign glanced off to the side as she played with a ring on her finger. "I just have a lot on my mind nowadays," she admitted. "I'm reflecting on my life and I'm questioning a lot of my past decisions...that's all."

"That's *all*?" Ava zoned in. "That seems like a *lot*, luv."

Reign shrugged slightly. "It is what it is," she downplayed. "You know me, I'll fill up like eight notebooks with my mental bullshit, then I'll be back to normal."

"Notebooks aren't people sweetie," Ava pointed out, sincere. "Sometimes you need to *talk* about what you're feeling."

"It works for me," Reign maintained. Hearing a knock at Ava's door, both women glanced at it. "You're expecting company?"

Ava waved a hand in nonchalance. "Yeah girl, it's just Malcom."

Reign shot a wide-eyed look Ava's way. "Why didn't you tell me that he was coming? I would've taken my ass *home*."

"Because you needed me, and because it doesn't *matter*, Malcom and I are not doing anything," Ava justified. "He cooked dinner and offered to bring me some, that's all."

Reign rose from the couch. "Yeah okay," she quipped. "Get up and get the door for your man."

Ava stood up, heading for the door. "He's not my man, we're still *just talking*."

"Full of shit, you're *dating*." Reign grabbed her purse.

Ava laughed as she opened the door. "Hey," she greeted Malcom, smiling.

Reign went to the door. "Showing every tooth," she joked of Ava. Ava playfully tapped her arm. Reign looked at Malcom, who stood there, bag in hand. "Hi Malcom, bye Malcom." She hurried out of the door.

"Call me when you get home," Ava called after her.

"Sure Mom," Reign chortled, heading down the hall.

Malcom chuckled as Ava shut the door. "Was I interrupting something?"

Ava hugged him. "Just girl talk."

"Sweetie, are you out here?" Ellie asked, walking around the back of Chase's house.

Chase looked up from the book that he was reading. "Yes," he answered. Watching his mother walk over, he smiled slightly.

Smiling back, Ellie leaned over, planting a kiss to his cheek. She took a seat at the patio table across from him. "Am I disturbing you?"

Chase closed his book. "No, was just reading a little bit." He set the book on the table. "Do you want anything to eat or drink?"

Ellie put her hands up. "No, I'm perfectly fine." She folded her arms on the table. "I appreciate the invite to come visit."

"Yeah well, you threatened me enough. I figured I'd better extend one," Chase chuckled.

She laughed a little. "You're damn *right* I threatened you." Her tone grew more serious. "I haven't seen you in a while, so I was beginning to worry."

Chase nodded slowly. "I understand that… I definitely don't mean to worry you."

"I'm your mother, I'll *always* worry." She delivered a light tap to the table after a moment. "You've been out of town often over the past weeks…traveling for work again?"

Chase nodded. "Yeah, figured I'd jump back into it." He took a deep breath. "There's talks about a umm…a transfer."

"A transfer where? And for *whom*?"

"Not far," he alluded. "To Vegas…and, for *me*."

Ellie let out a sigh as she adjusted a bracelet on her wrist. "True, Vegas isn't far… But you *love* Arizona, and your career has been great here—"

"It's just in talks Mom… They're opening a new office out there and I'd run it, if that's what I want," Chase cut in. "It's just a thought."

She sighed again, nodding. "Well, you *know* I'd prefer to have you *here*… But if that's what you want to do, then I support it."

Chase looked down at the table, not saying anything.

Ellie studied her son's demeanor; it was sad, just like his voice when she'd spoken to him on the phone. She'd noticed the difference in him for a while, but had yet to question what was wrong. Now that he was mulling over the possibility of moving from his beloved home, that curiosity had turned to concern. "It *is* what you want to do, right?" she carefully asked.

Chase glanced off to the side.

She tilted her head. "I mean…*is* it?"

Chase looked at his mother. He'd been successful in deflecting and avoiding telling anyone what was going on with him, including his sister. Yet when it came to his mother, he found it hard to lie to her. After a moment, he shook his head. "No…it's not," he confessed.

"Then why are you considering it, my love?"

Chase shrugged slightly. "Things have just…*changed* for me here and as of right now it's the last place that I want to be."

"*What's* changed?"

Chase almost didn't want to answer, but keeping his feelings bottled up was eating at him. "My reason for wanting to settle down and be home…is no longer part of my life so…"

Ellie eyed him intently. "Are…are you talking about Reign?"

Chase lowered his eyes, nodding in the process. "Yeah, we're not umm…we're not talking at the moment."

Ellie let a gasp slip. "What? You two are so close."

Chase was fighting to keep a handle on his emotions; the memory of their friendship and everything that he and Reign had shared had come to a head. "I know. She was—*is* my…everything."

Ellie put a hand to her chest as the air caught in her throat. "You're in love with her," she breathed.

Chase closed his eyes, pinching the bridge of his nose—an effort to keep the tears from surfacing. "Yes." He fixed his mother with a somber gaze. "But she doesn't feel the same and I'm not going to lie, it hurts. So…as of *right now*, I can't handle being around her."

A deep sigh left Ellie. She was trying to find the words to say to her son to offer him some comfort. She felt terrible for what he was going through. "You know…I knew for a long time how you felt about her," she began. "You could hide it from other people, but I picked up on it." She glanced up at the sky for a long moment. "Do you remember how you were at fifteen?"

"I do," Chase answered. "A *mess*."

She looked at him. "Yes, you were," she agreed. "Was always *smart* as hell, but you just stayed in trouble… Hanging with the wrong people…those fast ass little girls."

Chase shook his head.

"You stopped *drawing*—" she paused, sighing. Ellie had recognized Chase's passion and talent for sketching at an early age. She and Chase's father had always encouraged and nurtured him. When he'd quit in favor of unproductive activities, it had broken their hearts. "Your father and I didn't know what we were going to do with you," she admitted. "With your behavior—we were terrified that you'd end up in jail. Hell, do you remember when you were *actually arrested*?"

Chase grimaced, then nodded. "Yeah. For vandalizing a wall behind school."

Ellie narrowed her eyes at him. "And *why* did you do that again?"

"I was dared," Chase told. "A stupid excuse, I know."

"Thank *God* you were let off with just a warning." She shook her head. "Then you got into that fight—"

"Let off with another warning," Chase finished.

"I swear, just *thinking* about how the police chief looked out for you—I need to send a *dozen* gift baskets to that house," Ellie said, reflective.

Chase nodded in agreement. "Yeah." He let out a heavy sigh. "I was terrible, I know... I put you guys through a lot."

Chase's brief time as a troubled teen was something that he and his family rarely brought up; for he was no longer that person. Yet at times Chase reflected back on it when he needed a reminder of how far he'd come in life.

"Uh huh," Ellie muttered. She then smiled as another memory flooded back. "Then when you were seventeen, you were introduced to Reign, Ava's new friend...a quiet, intelligent, pretty little bookworm."

Chase smiled, remembering his first encounter with Reign as a teenager. "She always had a stack of books with her," he recalled. "And never let anyone borrow them."

Ellie laughed. "I don't blame her, you wouldn't have appreciated them." Her laughter ceased, but her smile remained. "I swear, from the moment you met her, you started changing for the better," she remembered fondly. "The closer you two became as friends, it was like she had a positive influence over you that no one else had... You went from skipping assignments and failing tests, to being on the *honor roll*. You stopped hanging with the wrong crowd, you started drawing again and you just..." She began to fill with pride. "You went to college, graduated with honors, got your master's degree—you have an amazing career... You became the you that's sitting in front of me right now."

Chase let out a deep sigh. "From the moment Reign came into my life, I fell for her," he confessed. "She affects me in ways nobody else can, and even after everything we've both been through, I just..." He sighed again. "I thought she would be *it* for me...I *felt* it."

"Chase, I believe that it's still possible—"

"It's not," he broke in, resolved. "That's one dream that just won't come true, and I'll have to get over it."

Ellie reached for Chase's hand, placing it into hers. "I'll say this," she began. "I don't know why this is happening. I don't know why she's feeling how she is, but in my heart, I don't believe that God would bring her in to your life, would have you love her for all of these years, to fall *in* love with her...just to keep her as your friend. I don't believe that." She squeezed his hand. "So, I don't want you to give up hope...not yet anyway."

Chase glanced down. "I appreciate your words Mom, but...I have to."

Ellie sighed. Releasing Chase's hand, she stood from her seat and enveloped her son in a long hug. *Please let everything work out how it's destined to,* she thought.

"Mom, do me a favor and don't tell Ava about what we talked about," Chase requested, parting from their embrace.

"I won't," she promised. "I know how protective she is over you."

Chase ran a hand over his head. "Yeah. She'll just get mad and go off on Reign... I don't want *their* friendship to be affected by what's going on between us."

Ellie gave a nod. "You have my word."

Chapter Thirty-Nine

GLANCING AROUND THE CLUTTERED DORM room, Reign ran a hand through her hair. "I remembered hearing myself say that I needed for you to be *packed* before I got here," she ground out.

Cynthia looked up from the hordes of clothes on her bed. "I *know* you did, but I can explain—"

"You can *try*," Reign spat, folding her arms.

Cynthia put a finger up. "I…procrastinated, *but*—"

Reign huffed. "I swear to God."

"Finals were *brutal*," Cynthia explained. "That's the *real* excuse, I was driving myself crazy studying for those. So packing had to be pushed to the backburner." She caught sight of the glare on Reign's face. "Do you want an apology donut on our way back?"

Reign rolled her eyes at the smile on Cynthia's face. "No," she grunted. "Keep your donut, just hurry up."

Cynthia shrugged, continuing with her task of packing.

Reign removed Cynthia's clothing from a chair, tossing the items to the floor.

"Hey—"

"Shut up, girl." Reign sat down. Putting her head in her hands, she groaned.

Cynthia tossed some items into a nearby bin. "Groaning kind of loud over there, you okay?"

"Not really. I'm tired and you're irritating me," Reign muttered. She lifted her head, surveying the space. "*And* this room is disgusting."

Cynthia rolled her eyes. "Whatever, it's only *slightly cluttered* in here."

"I beg to differ," Reign bristled, rubbing her temples. "Your only saving grace is that it smells *good* in here."

Cynthia made a face. "Well…that's my peach blossom air freshener." She tossed more items into her bin. "I have a body spray that smells just like it."

Reign sat back in her seat. "Good to know Cyn, *please* hurry up."

Cynthia shook her head. "Okay cranky," she mumbled.

In the middle of her task, Cynthia glanced over at Reign; she was staring out of the small window in silence. Normally Cynthia would continue to pester or make jokes, but her sister looked like something heavy was on her mind. "Hey," she called, softly.

Reign shot an agitated look Cynthia's way. "What?"

"You okay?"

Reign rolled her eyes slightly. "You asked me that already."

"I know and you said that you were tired among that *other* ignorant thing." Cynthia fiddled with the shirt in her hand as a seriousness came over her. "But I mean, are you okay…*mentally*? Like, is everything okay…in your life?"

Confusion fell over Reign's face. "Why are you asking?"

Cynthia stood upright, tossing the shirt into the bin. "I don't know, you just seem *down*," she answered. "And aside from that—*ordeal*—you almost *never* look like that…like you've mastered stone face well, so this thing you got going on right now—" She gestured her hand in Reign's direction, "is concerning me."

Reign waved a dismissive hand at her sister. "Girl, I'm fine, get back to doing what you're doing."

Ignoring the demand, Cynthia grabbed a stool. Positioning it in front of Reign, she took a seat on it. "I'm not packing shit else until you start talking."

Reign frowned. "You are *stalling*."

"And you're *avoiding*, which one is worse?" Cynthia threw back. She put her hand up when Reign went to protest. "Aht, my room, my rules, avoiding is worse."

Reign narrowed her eyes at Cynthia.

Letting out a sigh, Cynthia's expression turned serious. "Fore-al...what's going on with you?" she pressed. "And I don't mean just *today*...The past few times I've talked to you, you seem different."

Reign exhaled deeply. The pressure of everything she was feeling was suffocating. "I'm just dealing with some stuff right now," she alluded.

"Like what?" Cynthia probed. "Work?"

Reign shook her head. "No, work is fine."

"Relationships?"

Reign shrugged slightly. "I guess you can say that." She took a deep breath. "It's...it's complicated. You wouldn't understand."

Cynthia put a hand up. "Hey, I may not understand *your* situation, but both of my boyfriends' think they're the only one, so *complicated*, I *get*."

Reign stared at Cynthia wide-eyed for a moment. "*What?*"

"Ignore that last part," Cynthia dismissed, waving her hand. "Back to *your* situation."

Reign folded her arms.

Cynthia tapped her arm. "Come on, talk to me," she urged. "You'll feel better."

"I doubt it," Reign muttered.

"*Try* it." Cynthia leaned forward. "I know you get tired of holding stuff in. Hell, *I'm* tired just *watching* you do it... It can get to be too much."

Reign glanced away. Hesitating for a few moments, she finally spoke. "Chase and I...we're not speaking." Sadness filled her eyes. "We're not friends anymore."

Cynthia's eyes widened in shock. "What?" she belted out. "What *happened*? You two were so close. *Especially* after all that mess with your stupid ass ex."

"I know," Reign agreed, somber. The words "you two were so close" were like a broken record playing in her head. "We were."

Cynthia couldn't believe her ears. She never would've thought that Reign and Chase would fall out. "You have to help me understand what happened that drastically to end your friendship."

Reign struggled with whether she was going to say anything. "We…had a difference of—" She huffed; her sister was right, Reign was tired of downplaying. "Chase told me that he's in love with me," she revealed at last.

Cynthia's eyes could've popped out of her skull. "Really?"

"Yeah." Reign sighed deeply. "And…he wants—*wanted* for us to be in a relationship."

Cynthia put a hand over her heart. "Awww. I love him for you," she gushed.

Reign glanced out the window again as everything she'd been hiding came to the surface. She felt tears prick her eyes. "I love him for me *too*," she admitted, finally. "I…I'm in love with him." Tears spilled down her face; she wiped them away with her hand. "But I didn't tell him that… I got scared and I didn't tell him and—I told him that we needed to just remain friends. He said that he couldn't *just* be that anymore so we're not."

Cynthia pouted at the sight of her sister crying. "Don't cry."

Reign wiped her eyes again, sniffling. "I'm so fuckin' stupid."

"No, you're not," Cynthia consoled, touching her arm.

"I am," Reign insisted. "*This* time, I really am… I let the best thing that ever happened to me go, because I'm too damn scared to get into another relationship…" she shook her head.

Cynthia tilted her head. "You need to talk to him, sis."

"And say *what*?" Reign glared through her glassy eyes. "Sorry I hurt your feelings? Sorry I downplayed how I felt, how I've *always* felt? No…it's been over a month and I'm sure he's moving on… I'd deserve it."

"Rae, that man has *not* stopped loving you," Cynthia replied. "That's not how the heart operates."

"Doesn't matter."

"It *does*." Cynthia let out a huff; she wasn't sure why she was even surprised that Reign was being stubborn, it was how she'd always been. "You know what your problem is?"

"Besides what I just said?" Reign jeered.

"Yes, you overthink things," Cynthia replied. "You always *have* and it's fine most times but, in this case, you need to just relax and go with the flow."

"It's not that simple."

"It's not because you're *making* it that way," Cynthia threw back. "You need to tell him how you feel…how you *really* feel. If Chase is the man that I believe he is, he'll understand."

Reign just shook her head. Cynthia was wrong, and talking about the situation had only made Reign feel worse.

Cynthia exhaled deeply. "You need to allow yourself to be happy, sis," she said after a moment. "You *deserve* to be."

Wiping the remaining wetness from her face, Reign sighed. "Yeah."

Cynthia gave Reign's hand another soft pat. She let out a chuckle after a moment of silence. "You know what I just realized?"

"What?" Reign asked, unenthused.

"You're in love with your ex-friend's, ex-boyfriend."

Reign frowned. "That sounds like a damn novel."

Cynthia snickered, "*I'd* read that."

"Yeah, I'm sure you *would*," Reign chortled. "Finish packing so we can get out of here."

Ava was on her couch hunched over her coffee table, typing furiously on her laptop. "I need part two of this book like yesterday," she said to herself.

Hearing a knock on her door, she bolted from the couch. "Coming." Yanking the door open, she grinned. "Hey you," she said to Chase, hugging him. She stepped back, eyeing the paper bag in his hand as he walked in. "Did you bring trash to my house?" she joked.

"No, crazy," Chase replied, tone dry. "I bought too much food for *my* house, so figured I'd drop some off here." He set the bag on an end table.

"Oh okay." Ava scratched her head. "I appreciate you. Do you want the money back for it?"

"No," Chase declined. "It was just going to go to waste anyway. In a few days I'll be leaving out again, so I don't need it."

Ava's face fell. "Damn man, you just got back *home* a few days ago."

Chase rolled his eyes. "It's the job, don't start."

Ava folded her arms. "Fine, whatever." She gestured to the couch. "You want to chill with me for a bit?"

He pointed to the open laptop. "Aren't you working?"

"I can take a break," Ava dismissed. "I'm just proofing a novel. The book was so good, I brought it home to finish it." She adjusted a bracelet on her wrist. "I *swear* it's one of the ones Rae ghostwrote but of *course* she won't tell me."

Chase's heart jumped at the sound of her name. "No, she won't tell you," he muttered.

Ava flagged the laptop with her hand. "Anyway…are you two going to hang out before you leave?" she asked, oblivious.

"Umm, no," Chase slowly drew out.

"Oh…" Ava shrugged, then chuckled. "Honestly, I'm surprised that you haven't been posted up at our job every day."

A puzzled look flashed across his face. "Why would I do that?"

"Because I'm sure you'd want to see if Troy shows his stupid ass back up."

Chase frowned. "What are you talking about?"

All traces of humor left Ava's face. "Troy was waiting outside of our office building, waiting for Reign to get off of work about a week ago," she told.

Chase stood there; the emotion had drained from his face. "Say *what?*"

"Yeah," she confirmed. "He was talking some mess about how he just wanted to see her…being an idiot as usual." Ava folded her arms yet again. "She said that he grabbed her arm as soon as she walked out, and she had to hit him."

Chase was quiet for a moment; he took several deep breaths. "I had no idea about that," he finally said.

Ava was baffled. She was sure that Reign would've mentioned

it to Chase. She knew that they weren't hanging out like they had before, but she thought that they were at *least* talking. "Okay—"

"I have to go," Chase interrupted.

Ava sighed. "Fine." She placed her hands on her hips. "Well, at least tell me where you're going *this* time."

"Vegas," Chase replied.

"Damn, does your company own stock in the city or something?" she quipped. "Or do you like going there, *that* much?"

"I don't," Chase's tone was flat. "But my company does a lot of business in the city. Plus, they'll eventually open an office out there… Once that happens, I'll probably be spending *more* time there."

Ava shook her head. "That's crazy," she charged. "Having you go back and forth like that, when they can just have someone work out there *permanently*."

Chase cleared his throat; he hadn't planned on telling Ava about the possibility of him moving. He had asked his mother to keep that secret, but it was only a matter of time. He ran a hand over the back of his neck. "Look, I already told Mom. I might as well tell *you too*."

His sister eyed him in anticipation. "Tell me what?"

"I'm considering moving to Vegas to run the new office once they open it."

Ava squinted, "But you're practically running the office *here*, so why would you want to move?"

Chase shrugged, "A change of scenery."

Ava fixed Chase with an intense stare. "A change of scenery?" she repeated.

Chase stared back at her. "You've never heard those words paired together before?" he sneered. "You're an editor, so that's a bit concerning."

Ava scowled. "Catching an attitude, I see," she ground out. "Is there something you want to talk about?"

Chase rolled his eyes. "No. I'm good," he spat. "I'll see you later."

"Oh no, clearly you're *not*." Ava moved around to face him. Chase let out a groan. "You already know I don't care about that, I

lived to annoy you when we were kids," she threw back. "But seriously, what is going on with you? You've been acting miserable lately—"

I'm definitely not acting, Chase thought as Ava ranted.

"You're traveling again when you said you no longer *wanted* to,
and *now*, you're thinking about *moving* just for a *change of scenery*,"
she harped, counting the items on her fingers. "To *Vegas* of all places,
a city that you *just* said you don't even *like*. So *something* happened."

Letting out a deep sigh, Chase glanced at the floor. "Nothing
happened," he lied.

Ava searched his face for the truth. "Chase—you forget I
know you." She held a hand to her chest. "What's the matter? What
happened?"

Chase rolled his eyes; he shouldn't have brought up the move.
Ava was never going to stop interrogating him, and while he understood her concern, he didn't want to discuss it. Yet he knew that
he had to give her *something*. "Things…things that I thought were
going to happen here, *didn't*," he alluded finally. "So, I just don't want
to be here right now."

"So because something didn't go as planned, you're about to
run?" She stepped forward. "That's not like you. What's going on?"
His sister's eyes were pleading. "Chase, come on talk to me."

He opened his mouth to speak—then decided against it. "You
know what, forget I said anything," Chase said instead.

Ava jerked her head back. "*Forget?*"

"Yes, forget it," Chase stressed.

Ava's frustration was quickly turning into full-on anger. She
opened her mouth to argue, but paused. After a moment, she pointed at him. "This…this has to do with Reign, *doesn't* it?"

Chase looked at her but didn't say anything.

"That's *it* isn't it?" Ava assumed. "*She's* the reason why you're so
depressed; *she's* the reason why you want to leave here."

Chase shook his head. "Let it go, Ava."

A loud gasp erupted from Ava, a deep frown forming on her
face. "You *both*… are you two even *friends* anymore?"

Every conversation Ava had had with both Reign and Chase over the past few weeks flooded back to her. Every time Ava had mentioned their names, neither person wanted to comment. It was as if the sound of them alone brought each one sadness.

"We're giving each other space," Chase said. "That's it."

Ava's angered eyes burrowed through him. "Chase… What did she do to you?"

Chase was over this conversation; he tried to go for the door, but Ava blocked him again. "She didn't do anything, now move."

"For you to want to uproot your life, just to avoid *her*, she had to do *something*," Ava fussed. In that moment, Ava's only concern was for her brother. For him to be this hurt over Reign, Ava could only imagine what she'd done.

Chase was trying his best to keep calm, but his sister was pushing it. The last thing he wanted was for her to blame Reign. "I *said*, let it go," he barked, teeth clenched. "You're jumping to conclusions when you have none of the damn information."

"I know that you *love* her," Ava hurled back. "Yeah, I'm not blind, I see it," she added when Chase's eyes widened. "I've *always* seen it."

Chase ran his hands over his face, sighing deeply.

Ava took a deep breath, an attempt to calm herself. "I know how you feel about her so I know that for things to get to *this* point… where you can't even be in the same *city* as her—"

"Get away from the goddamn door Ava," Chase warned.

Ava stared at him, almost challenging him. But after a moment she relented. Rolling her eyes, she moved aside.

Chase grabbed the doorknob. "Now like I said, things didn't work out how I'd hoped. It is what it is." His eyes blazed with anger. "That is all I'm going to tell you. That is all you need to *know*. So, stay *out* of my damn business and don't you go running your mouth to Reign."

Ava glowered at him but didn't respond.

"I mean it. Stay. Out. Of. It." He punctuated his stern warning by walking out, slamming the door in the process.

Ava flinched at the loud *smack*.

Chapter Forty

CYNTHIA HURRIED OUT OF THE house. "Oh my God, you are a life saver," she breathed, darting for Reign, who was standing by her parked car holding up an electronic tablet.

Reign handed the device over. "It was wedged between the back door and the seat."

Cynthia grabbed it, hugging it to her chest. She'd been back home for days and had torn through her bedroom looking for her tablet. She was relieved when Reign had called to let her know that she'd found it in her car and would be dropping it off after work.

"I could've come picked it up from you," Cynthia said.

Reign rubbed her eyes. "It's fine. I was already out."

Cynthia studied Reign; her sister looked lethargic. "You look kinda sick in the face."

Reign shot a narrowed eyed glare at her. "Whatever." She turned to get in the car. "I'll see you later."

"I didn't mean that in a bad way," Cynthia explained.

"What other way *is* there?" Reign sneered. She sneezed.

Cynthia turned her face up as Reign sniffled. "Eww, bless you," she scoffed. "I was right. You have a cold, *don't* you?"

"No."

Cynthia waved a dismissive hand. "Still downplaying, I see," she mumbled. "Anyway, you're not going to go say hi to Mom and Dad before you leave?"

"I talked to Mom earlier," Reign said.

Cynthia opened her mouth to say something else, then hearing her father's voice, turned towards the door. "Hey Dad. Rae was just leaving."

Matthew stood in the doorway, arms folded. "I see that," he replied. "Reign, can I talk to you for a minute?"

Reign, back turned to him, rolled her eyes. She hadn't spoken to him since she'd blown up at him almost two weeks ago. "Can this wait, Dad?"

"No, it *can't.*" His tone was even, yet stern. "I'll be out back."

Cynthia winced, watching their father disappear back into the house. She glanced to Reign. "Shit...what did you do?"

Reign turned around, an annoyed look frozen on her face; she didn't answer. Letting out a huff, she shut her car door, then headed around the back of the house. Seeing her father seated at the patio table, Reign approached. Pulling out a chair, she sat down and folded her arms, leaning back in her seat. "Yes, Dad?" she said, unenthused.

The sternness left Matthew's face; a small smile replaced it. "How are you?"

Reign gave a hard shrug, not bothering to return his smile. "I'm *fine,*" she ground out. She was still irritated with her father's behavior towards her. As far as she was concerned, she could've gone a bit longer without having this sit down.

Matthew's smile faded. He placed his hands on the tabletop. "I uh... I've done a lot of thinking about our... *conversation.*"

Reign just fixed him with an indifferent stare.

He took a deep breath. "Your late grandfather always instilled in me, the importance of not letting things or people affect me..." he said. "I didn't understand it at first, but as I got older, I did... I thought that it made sense. If you don't let people's behavior—their *actions*, affect you, they can't hurt you."

"It's impossible to go through life without being hurt at some point, Dad," Reign bristled. "I'm sure even *Granddad* realized that at some point."

"To be honest, I don't know whether he did or didn't, but I know what *I* was raised to believe," he explained. "I honestly thought it was good advice, and I just wanted to instill the same in *you*... I thought that if I could in some way prevent you from being hurt, then I was doing my job as a father."

Reign raised an eyebrow. "Do you realize that by constantly *instilling* that in me, you made me feel like—*feeling* was a weakness? Or *pointless* I should say."

Matthew glanced down at the table. "Reign—I never wanted to make you feel that what you *felt* didn't matter. That you weren't *allowed* to be sad or angry." He sighed heavily. "But knowing that that's exactly how I made you feel...*I* feel *horrible*."

Reign let out a sigh; she didn't agree with her father's methods, but she loved him, and he appeared to realize the error of his ways. "Dad—I understand what you were *trying* to do... I get your logic, and most of the time, it worked for me. I've found ways to get out what I *need* to without people knowing what's bothering me. Then I'd just go about my day like normal... But sometimes that's not enough," she confessed. "I've gotten so used to keeping things to myself to protect myself that when it comes to expressing what I feel—what hurts me, what scares me or *whatever*—it's like I can barely *talk*... And on the rare occasion that I *do* show vulnerability, I feel like shit afterwards."

Matthew held his somber gaze on the table.

Reign shook her head. "I'm thirty-three years old and I still feel like I have to hide my feelings between the pages of a notebook."

Matthew ran his hands over his face, trying to keep his emotions contained. "Sweetheart I—I *sincerely* apologize for how I made you feel all of these years." The remorse in his voice was heavy. "If I could change things, I'd do so in a heartbeat."

"I'm not entirely blaming you, Dad," Reign placated. "I mean, yeah you started it, but I just let it keep going... It's something that I have to change about myself, and telling you how I feel...*finally*, is a start."

He nodded. "I promise you that whatever you feel, whatever is bothering you—you can come talk to me and I won't shut you down." His voice cracked. "I'll never shut you down again, you have my word."

Reign stared at him.

Tears glassed over his eyes. "I'm so sorry,"

Reign tilted her head. "Are you crying?"

Matthew chuckled a bit as he wiped his eyes. "Yeah, it appears that I am."

"I never knew you had tear ducts," she quipped.

"Okay, you got me," he threw back, laughter in his voice. He held his arms out for her.

Reign rose from her seat and hugged him.

"I love you kid. *So* much," Matthew professed. "Always have, always will."

"I love you too, Dad."

Matthew parted from the embrace, looking up at her with hopeful eyes. "Can you forgive a cranky, stubborn old man?"

Reign smiled down at him. "Of course I can."

Ava sat at her desk, staring at her laptop. Though her eyes were fixed on the open document, she wasn't reading anything. She couldn't focus. All she could think about was the conversation she'd had with Chase two days ago.

Chase had told her to stay out of it, and she'd obliged. She'd barely spoken to Reign for fear of what would come out of her mouth.

Even though Reign was her best friend, her brother was clearly upset over her, and that was something that Ava couldn't overlook.

Tapping her heel-covered foot on the floor, she eyed Reign's closed office door, scowling. Hearing her cell ring, Ava gave a quick glance at the ID, then answered.

"Hey, I'll have to call you back," she spoke into the line.

"Is everything okay?" Malcom asked, picking up on the agitation in Ava's voice.

"It *will* be after I have a conversation with someone."

Malcom was silent for a moment. "Ava…honey, don't do something you'll regret." Malcom had been a listening ear while Ava had vented her frustrations to him the night that Chase had left her condo. "Now, remember what your brother said—"

"I said I'll call you back," Ava spat, abruptly hanging up on him.

Reign sat with her elbows on her desk, head buried in her hands. She'd been like this for the past half hour. What had started out as a simple scratchy throat and a few sneezes earlier that morning, was turning into a splitting headache, stuffy sinuses, and watery eyes throughout the day.

The heat radiating from her skin finally forced her to lift her head from her hands. When a knock sounded on her door, she took a deep breath, smoothing her hair from her face to pull herself together. "Come in."

Ava walked through the door, closing it behind her.

"Hi," Reign spoke.

"Hi." Ava's tone lacked pleasantry, just like her face. She approached Reign's desk. "You look sick."

"Thank you," Reign replied, sarcastic. "I'm pretty sure I'm coming down with the world's worst cold." She grabbed a water bottle from her desk, taking a sip. She cleared her throat. "What can I do for you?"

Ava folded her arms. "I need to talk to you about something."

Reign eyed her, taking notice of Ava's furrowed brow. "You seem upset, is something wrong?"

"I *am*, and there *is*." Ava's tone dripped with disdain, her eyes fixed with a piercing glare.

Reign looked puzzled. The way that Ava was speaking *at* her, the way she *looked* at her—Reign was almost certain that Ava's issue wasn't with anyone outside of that room. "Are...are you upset with *me*?"

Ava stared Reign down. "You could say that."

Raising an eyebrow, Reign shot Ava a challenging look. "Is this reason work related?"

"Nope," Ava spat out.

"Then we're not going to talk about it now," Reign shot down.

Ava jerked her head back. "Oh no, we *are*," she demanded. "Because it's about *Chase*."

"We are *not* going to talk about this."

Ava's temper was nearly at her max. "Hold up." Stepping forward, she put a hand up. "I know *damn* well you're not sitting here trying to *dismiss* me like I'm your child. You've got the *wrong* one, sweetheart."

Reign frowned. "You might want to calm that down *just* a bit."

"Don't tell me to calm down." Ava pointed at her. "You can pull that dismissive, deflective shit with everyone *else*, but you're not doing it with me, not *this* time."

Reign slowly rose from her seat as Ava ranted on. "Ava," she warned.

"I'm not playing with you Reign, you're going to tell me what the hell you did to—"

"Hey, hey!" Reign snapped, clapping her hands.

Ava immediately ceased her verbal attack, though she was still fuming.

"Now look, I don't know what possessed you to come in here on ten and hurl accusations at me, but I suggest you stop for *just* a moment and remember where the hell you are," Reign fumed. "While we are in this *building*, on this *clock*, I am your boss, and you will *not* talk to me crazy."

Ava's breathing became heavy; she looked as if she was fighting the urge to explode, yet she remained silent.

"Now take that negativity *back* to your desk," Reign dismissed, staring Ava down.

Ava's jaw clenched; she was furious. But she knew that Reign was right. This was not the time nor the place to hash things out; she'd hold her tongue, for *now*.

"Sure thing *Ms. Price*," Ava bit out through clenched teeth. Turning on her heel, she stormed out of the office, closing the door behind her.

Alone, Reign took a deep breath and slowly let it out. She was so upset that her hands were trembling. She ran them through her hair. "Shit."

Reign let out a sigh as she jotted in her notebook. Her food sat on the table in front of her. Between her looming sickness and bad mood, Reign's appetite was nonexistent. Determined to stick out the rest of the workday, but needing to get out of the office, Reign had decided to spend her lunchbreak at her favorite café.

She wondered why she'd even decided to go there; it might have been her favorite lunch spot, but it was a spot that she frequented with Ava. After their confrontation earlier, Ava was the last person she wanted to be reminded of.

When a wave of fatigue hit her, Reign blinked several times then closed her notebook. "To hell with this, I'm going home." As she wrapped up her uneaten meal, the café door opened, then shut. It wasn't unusual; the place had patrons walking in and out all day. It wasn't until Reign felt a presence at her small table that she looked up.

"Figured you'd be here," Ava sneered, staring down at her.

Reign took a deep breath. "You don't want to try this again tomorrow?"

Ava jerked the chair in front of her out, plopping down. "No, this conversation happens *now*." She fixed a bitter stare. "And we're not in the office so talking down to me isn't going to fly this time."

"I didn't want to do that, but I had no choice, Ava," Reign replied, rolling her eyes. "You were showing your ass."

"Yeah, whatever," Ava dismissed, waving her hand. "Back to what the hell we need to talk about."

Reign was not in the mood for Ava's meddling; she put her hands over her face, huffing loudly. "I can't *do* this with you right now girl, I don't feel well."

"*And?*" Ava folded her arms on the table. "What the hell did you do to my brother, Reign?"

Reign folded *her* arms, staring daggers at Ava. "I don't know what you're talking about."

"You know *exactly* what I'm talking about," Ava accused. "First he's depressed and *now* he's talking about moving out of the state just to not have to see *you* again."

Reign felt her heart sink into her stomach. "He's moving?"

"He's *talking* about it." Ava's temper rose just *thinking* about it. "But that's not the point, the *point is* that he's trying to *run* from *you*, so what the hell did you *do* to him?"

Reign couldn't focus on what Ava was hurling at her; she could only think about Chase leaving town for good. Just the thought of it was devastating. Reign didn't know what she would do if he left, especially if it was because of her. Yet she wasn't about to give Ava any of that information, or the satisfaction. "You know what?" she began, eerily calm.

Ava's eyes thinned. "What?"

"You need to learn to mind your goddamn business," Reign spat out.

Ava slammed her hand on the table. "My brother *is* my business, and *you* seem to have forgotten that." She scowled. "I know—"

"What the *fuck* do you know?" Reign stomped her foot on the floor. "You don't know shit. You're just running back and forth trying to piece together information about *nothing*."

"I know more than you *think* I do."

"*Please* enlighten me," Reign challenged.

"I know that you two were sleeping together." Ava smirked at the stunned look on Reign's face. "Yeah, it didn't take a rocket scientist to figure that out. You both were acting funny around each other for a while, and I *know* that's the reason." She leaned forward. "Are you going to lie and say it's not true?"

Reign clenched her jaw, but didn't speak.

"All those words you know, and you've got nothing?" Ava goaded.

Reign glanced away.

Ava nodded. "Okay, you don't want to admit that you were sleeping together recently… That's fine." She tilted her head, eyeing Reign intently. "How about *prom night?*"

Reign's head snapped back in Ava's direction, eyes bulging. "How the *hell* did you know about that?!"

"We shared a hotel room that night, remember?"

Confusion masked Reign's face. "Yes, but *you* spent the night in your *boyfriend's* room, so I had the room to myself."

Ava tossed her arms in the air in frustration. "And his ass pissed me off so I ended up coming *back* to our room in the middle of the night and imagine my surprise when I tiptoed in there, trying not to wake *your* ass up, and find you and Chase in the bed asleep." She leaned back in her seat. "The clothes on the floor, the way you two were hugged up—it didn't take a rocket scientist *then* either." Ava had never told a soul about it, until now.

Reign was horrified. "If you knew all this time, why didn't you *say* anything?"

"Because I didn't feel the *need* to," Ava answered. "You were grown, and I honestly thought that you two were good for one another."

Reign just eyed Ava in disbelief as she spoke.

"I knew Chase had a crush on you, even though he never said anything. I knew how much he wanted to be your boyfriend," Ava confessed. "I figured that you felt the same *considering*, but *obviously* that turned out not to be the case."

Reign took a deep breath to calm herself. "Look, I care about Chase, I always have—"

"Oh, you *care*?" Ava cut in. "*Just* care, huh? That's fuckin' cute."

"What the hell do you *want* from me?!" Reign didn't care that she was sitting in a café with onlookers; she was fed up with Ava's probing. "What do you want me to *say* to you?"

Ava scoffed. Shaking her head, she eyed Reign with disgust. In that moment, she didn't see her best friend; she only saw yet another woman who had hurt her brother. "I am *so* sick and tired of you bitches taking advantage of Chase."

Reign's head jerked back. "Oh, I'm a *bitch* now?" she questioned. "That's nice *sis*."

"Right *now*, you are," Ava flashed back.

Reign looked Ava up and down. "Don't disrespect me," she warned. "*Please* don't make me forget that we've been friends for eighteen years."

Ava rolled her eyes. "Yeah, like time, history, and *loyalty* mean anything to you." She scoffed. "You just use people for your own damn convenience, then when someone full of shit comes along, you toss the good ones aside like they don't mean anything to you."

Baffled, Reign's face scrunched up. "What are you even *talking* about?"

"You used Chase as a fill in before you got with Troy. Then when Troy fucked you over, you went right *back* to using him."

Reign's eyes widened.

"Even *me*. You used me as your 'best friend' fill in, then when Marcy's triflin' ass came into the picture, you tossed me aside like I was nothing," Ava spat. "Then when *Marcy* started fucking you over, you came right back to *me*."

Reign stared at Ava almost as if she didn't know her. Offended and hurt, tears glassed over Reign's eyes. "Really Ava?"

Ava shrugged, unfazed. "Really."

Reign gathered her purse. "You know what?" she began, fighting to keep both the tears from falling and herself from exploding. "It's nice to know how you *really* feel about me after all these years."

"It's nice to know how you really *are* after all of these years," Ava bristled.

"That's fine." Reign stood from her seat. "Another *friend* bites the dust. Don't know why I'm even surprised."

"Oh, don't worry you won't be friendless for long. I'm sure your naïve ass will end up with another Troy or Marcy in no time," Ava spat at Reign's departing back.

Reign stopped and turned around, eyes blazing.

Ava, seeing her approach the table, rose from her seat. She stood, unwavering, as Reign came face to face with her.

"Just going to keep pressing that knife in further, huh?" Reign seethed.

"Oh, did I strike a nerve? Are you mad?" Ava mocked. "Go write about it in your fuckin' notebook."

Reign's upper lip curled in disgust as she stared Ava down. "You're being so goddamn evil."

Ava folded her arms. "I'll take that. Do *you* want to take this outside?"

Reign smirked through her glare. "We *both* know how that would play out." She scanned Ava up and down once more. "Lucky for *you*, I don't have the fuckin' energy." She punctuated her response by turning and storming out of the café.

Chase sat in his car in front of the gym, staring at the entrance. He'd been sitting in that same parking spot for a little over an hour in silence, just watching and waiting. The sports watch on his wrist read eleven-thirty in the evening. Glancing back at the large window, he watched a group of late-night fitness junkies prepare to exit.

Eyeing one gym-goer in particular, Chase stepped out of his car and walked up to the building. Approaching a brick wall near the door, he leaned against it. As he stood there, a group of women walked out. Noticing him, one of the women smiled.

"Waiting for someone, sexy?" she crooned, much to the embarrassment of her friends.

Chase returned a smile. "Yes," he replied, polite. He found it almost amusing. Here he was dressed in black sweatpants and hoodie, standing by a wall alone at almost midnight, and he was *still* being hit on.

"Dani, leave that man alone. You're sweaty and look gross, *and* he might be a serial killer," one of her friends scoffed, grabbing her grinning friend's arm.

Chase chuckled. "I promise I'm not a serial killer but you're right, you should be more careful talking to strangers at night."

"Ooh, fine *and* gives good advice," Dani squealed. "Want my number?"

"I'm flattered but no thank you. Get home safely ladies," Chase said. He shook his head as the girls made their way down the street. Glancing at the door, he saw who he was waiting for. As soon as the man stepped out, Chase grabbed his arm with force, twisting it behind his back.

"Ahhhh, what the fuck?!" Troy yelled, dropping his gym bag to the ground. He tried throwing his elbow back to strike his attacker, but it was blocked. Before Troy could try another method, his assailant wrapped an arm around his neck.

Chase forced him to move along the sidewalk, then around the side of the building. It was dark, it was desolate—it was perfect.

Chase pushed Troy's arm further up his back, causing him to yell out. Chase thought about *breaking* his arm, but decided against it. Releasing Troy from his grasp, Chase moved in front of him, standing face to face.

Shaken and in pain, Troy grabbed his arm, staring at Chase wide-eyed. "Yo—what the hell is your problem man?!" He made a move to throw a punch, but Chase put a hand up, halting him.

"I wouldn't do that if I were you," Chase warned, tone menacing. "I don't want to have to bash what little brain you have, against that brick wall behind you."

Thinking twice, Troy put his hand down. He'd lost a fight to Chase before; he had no confidence that the outcome would be different this time around. He grabbed his sore shoulder instead.

Chase eyed Troy with disgust. "I swear to God, I'll never figure out what Reign ever saw in your bitch ass."

Troy frowned. "What the fuck were you *doing*? Waiting for me or some shit?"

"Yeah," Chase answered without a qualm.

Chase had finished his workout, when he'd caught a glimpse of Troy entering the building, just as Chase was walking out of the locker room.

Ever since Ava had told him about the run-in Reign had with Troy, Chase had been hoping to have his *own* run-in. Seizing the opportunity that night, Chase had waited patiently in his car while Troy completed his mediocre workout.

"Figured I'd allow you to experience what *Reign* experienced when you waited for *her* outside of her job like a fuckin' stalker," Chase added, furious.

Troy's eyes widened. "Man—I didn't *assault* her!"

Chase clenched his fists at his sides. "Doesn't matter, you *scared* her, and you *touched* her and I damn sure wasn't about to let that shit slide."

"What, are you her *protector* now?" Troy scoffed.

"Always *will* be," Chase replied. It was the truth; he might have been upset with Reign, but that didn't change how he felt about her or what he'd *do for* her. "See, I didn't break your neck when we came to your house that night because I was just happy that Reign was finally done with your stupid ass. But you seem to have not gotten the message that she wants *nothing* to do with you. Sending shit to her job, ambushing her—you don't think that's an issue?"

"I just wanted to *see* her, there's nothing wrong with that," Troy argued.

Chase was growing tired of Troy and this entire conversation. He took another step forward, causing Troy to back up. "I see that you really *are* as stupid as I always thought you were." His dark eyes bore through Troy like a laser. "So let me make this clear for you... If you send her anything else, if you walk up on her, touch her, contact her, *look* at her again...I *promise* you, you'll regret it."

Troy cleared his throat, trying not to let it show just how intimidated he was. "What? You gonna kill me or something?" he tried to laugh off.

Chase just stared at him, unwavering, unamused.

The humor left Troy's face; a scowl replaced it. "So, you're telling me you would go to *jail* for *Reign*?"

Chase smirked, "Absolutely." He put his finger close to the side of Troy's head. "Trust me, you don't want to test me." He delivered a hard pat to Troy's injured shoulder. Troy let out a yelp in pain. "You should probably go back and get your gym bag before somebody steals it...you know there's crazy people out here this time of night." Leaving a shaken Troy still standing there, Chase walked off, disappearing around the corner.

Chapter Forty-One

REIGN TOOK A CAREFUL SIP of her tea and set the mug on the coffee table. She sniffled, coughing a few times before leaning back against the couch cushions. She'd been laid up in her living room for the past few hours that evening with the television on, trying to focus on the movie playing on the screen and not on how sick she was feeling.

Her worsening cold had forced her to stay home from work for the past two days. She hadn't spoken to nor seen Ava since she'd stormed out of the café. She couldn't remember the last time she'd had an argument with Ava; the situation both angered *and* saddened her. However, she was trying to focus her energy into getting better.

When her cell rang, Reign let out a sigh, picking it up. "Hey Mom." Her voice was tired, stuffy.

"How are you feeling?" Vivian asked, tone soothing.

Reign rubbed her forehead. "Miserable," she complained. "And that's an *understatement*."

"Aww, my poor baby," Vivian sympathized. "You hardly ever get sick and when you do, it hits you like a ton of bricks."

"A *brick* is what I feel like I've actually been hit with." Reign rubbed her watery eyes.

"Did you take any medicine? Have you been drinking tea? Have you actually been *resting*?"

"Yes, yes, and I'm *trying* to." Reign winced as she adjusted her position on the couch; her body aches made her not want to move at all. "It's hard to sleep and nothing is working."

"Do you have fresh ginger for your tea?" Vivian asked. "You know ginger helps."

Reign let out a cough, then groaned as she ran a hand over her forehead. "I do, but I don't have the energy to peel, cut and boil that mess right now."

"Do you want me to come over?"

"No Mom, come on, it's like ten-thirty," Reign shot down. "And I don't need *you* getting sick." She exhaled deeply, "I'll be okay, I'm just going to take more medicine. Hopefully it'll knock me out this time."

Vivian sighed. "Okay my love, well I'll let you go," she said. "Try to get some rest. I love you."

"Love you too."

Reign ended the call, letting the phone drop to the floor. Grabbing the bottle of cough syrup from the coffee table, she quickly downed a serving and gently laid back down. Pulling a throw blanket over her, she closed her eyes in hopes of falling asleep.

Until her phone rang once again.

"What the fuck man?" She snatched it from the floor. Seeing the name on her screen, Reign's brow furrowed in confusion. "The hell?" she said, putting the phone to her ear. "Hello?"

"H—hi Reign," the woman on the other end sputtered.

Reign slowly sat up. "Tracy," she replied, tone unenthused. "Is there a reason why you're calling me at this hour?" Reign had given her number to her editing team when she'd become supervisor; in case they needed her for any reason during the day and she happened to be out of the office. She never had, nor expected any of them to call her after hours, except Ava.

"I know that it's late and I apologize for calling."

"Tracy, *why are* you calling?" Reign tried to remain calm. She was literally sick and tired and well off the clock. "Are you okay?"

"I'm here with Ava," Tracy explained, nervous.

Reign frowned.

"After work, a bunch of us decided to stop at Marty's Pub for happy hour," Tracy told.

Reign's patience was nearly exhausted. "*And?*"

"And umm, well… Ava is *really* happy right now."

"That means *what* Tracy?" Reign spat, rubbing her face. Tracy was sweet, but the woman could drag out a conversation like no other.

"She's drunk," Tracy blurted out. "Like *extremely* drunk. Like she can't drive at *all*, drunk."

Reign's annoyance quickly shifted to worry. It didn't matter how upset she was with Ava; she was still Reign's friend and Reign was concerned. Ava had gone to happy hour a few times in the past, but past birthday behavior aside, she'd never gotten drunk in public.

"I was going to take her home, but she can't find her house keys, and I know she wouldn't want to come to *my* house," Tracy further explained. "I'm sorry, I know you're her friend—I didn't know who else to call."

Reign stood from the couch. "No, that's okay, where is she now?"

"Sitting here at the bar," Tracy answered. "I'm trying to stop her from ordering more drinks."

Reign grabbed her keys from an end table. "Stay with her, I'm on my way."

"Do you need the address?"

"No, I know where it is," Reign assured, before hanging up. With haste, she put her sneakers on and bolted out the door.

The drive from Reign's house to Marty's Pub in downtown Phoenix took twenty-five minutes. Pulling into a parking spot, she turned the car off, then put her face in her hands as another coughing spell came over her. Her chest hurt so badly, she felt like crying. Willing herself to keep going, she emerged from the car and entered the bar.

Scanning the space with her eyes, it only took a few seconds to zone in on Ava and Tracy sitting at the bar. Reign walked over, tapping Tracy's shoulder.

Tracy spun around, a sigh of relief escaping her. "Thank God," she breathed. "Ava cursed me out four times already."

Reign glanced over at Ava, who was staring out in front of her, trying to keep her head from falling forward. Reign looked back at Tracy. "You can go, I'll take it from here," she said.

"You sure?"

Reign nodded. "I'm sure, get home safely."

Tracy stood up, allowing Reign to sit down in her place. "Here's her purse." She handed Ava's tan satchel to Reign.

"Thank you," Reign replied, sincere. "Really, thank you for calling me."

Tracy smiled, then gave a nod before walking off.

Reign watched her walk out of the door before turning to Ava. She waited to see if Ava would turn around, to give *any* indication that she was aware of Reign's presence—but Ava just sat there. Reign tapped her shoulder. "Hey."

Ava slowly turned to her; her half-lidded eyes widened slightly. "Where the hell did *you* come from?" she slurred.

Reign shook her head; Tracy was right, Ava was clearly drunk. "My house."

Ava held her lazy stare "*Why*?"

"Tracy called me."

"For *what*?" Ava spat.

"Because she was concerned," Reign answered. "Had one too many, huh?"

"*No*." Ava made a face. "I'm good."

Noticing something in Ava's hair, Reign stared at it. "Yeah?" Reign challenged. "Can you get that straw out of your hair?"

Head swaying, Ava sucked her teeth. "Is it *bothering* you?"

"It is," Reign ground out.

Rolling her eyes, Ava moved her hand over her hair. "Fine," she huffed. She touched every part except where the red straw was stuck.

Frustrated, Reign moved Ava's hand down, quickly snatching the straw herself and tossing it on the counter.

"Thanks," Ava muttered. She turned to the bartender. "Hey!" she slapped the counter. "Another tequila shot."

Reign fixed the bartender with a stern look, shaking her head. "Don't bring her another thing."

The bartender nodded at Reign before turning his attention

to the other patrons.

Offended, Ava tossed her arms up. "Did you not hear me?" she snapped at him.

Reign stifled a cough as she stood from her seat. "Come on, it's time to go," she said. "I'm taking you home." She searched through Ava's bag. "Where are your house keys?"

Ava gave a hard shrug. "I don't know."

Reign let out a loud huff. "That's great," she grumbled. "Whelp, I guess you're coming to *my* house."

Feeling Reign's hand on her arm, Ava jerked away. "I'm fine, I can sleep *here*."

"Ava—" Reign took a deep breath, trying to calm herself. "You are *not* sleeping at a bar. Now come *on*."

When Reign reached for Ava's arm again, Ava put her hand up. "I'm not ready to go yet!" she wailed.

Frustrated, Reign flopped back down in her seat. She didn't have the energy to argue, nor the physical strength to drag Ava out of the bar. "Fine, we'll sit here until you're ready."

Ava folded her arms on the counter, leaning her face in them. After a moment, she popped her head back up. "Okay, I'm ready."

Shaking her head, Reign slung Ava's purse over her shoulder as she stood. She carefully helped Ava out of her seat, wrapping an arm around Ava's waist to steady her.

Eyes practically closed, Ava slung her arm over Reign's shoulder, leaning her head against Reign's.

Please don't pass out right now, Reign thought, grabbing the hand that Ava had hanging over her shoulder for extra support as they slowly made their way out to the car.

Somehow Reign managed to get her front door open while still holding on to Ava. Maneuvering inside, Reign kicked the door shut with her foot.

Head hanging, Ava muttered something incoherently.

"You're in the house," Reign answered, unsure of what Ava

had said. "Come on, let's get you to bed."

Reign carefully moved with Ava through the corridor to the living room. As Ava took another step, she tripped over her own foot, falling.

"Oh shit!" Reign shrieked. She attempted to hold on to Ava, but her efforts were in vain. Ava's drunk weight pulled Reign down to the floor with her.

Reign groaned, struggling to sit up. She peered at Ava, who was sprawled out on the floor, eyes closed. Reign shook her; there was no response. "Ava!" she called, shaking her again.

Panic took over her as Reign inched closer; she had no idea if Ava had hit her head when she'd collided with the hardwood floor. Examining her, she saw that Ava was still breathing. After a moment, she heard a snore.

Reign rolled her eyes. "Great," she muttered. Still sitting on the floor, she slid back, leaning against a small table. Running a hand through her hair, she tried to take a deep breath, but all that came out were coughs.

There was *no* way that Reign was going to get Ava off the floor; she'd used her last bit of energy just getting Ava from the car to the house. She sat there exhausted, staring at her sleeping friend.

Reign grabbed her phone from her pocket, resigned to her fate. Scrolling through her contact list, she landed on Chase's name…and struggled to hit the call button. She was afraid to face him, but this wasn't about her. She pressed the little green icon, put the phone to her ear, and waited.

The line picked up. "Hello?" Chase answered, his voice was a mixture of shock and confusion.

Reign hesitated. She realized how much she missed the sound of his voice. "Hi," she finally spoke.

"Hey…what's up? Are you okay?"

Reign scratched her head, clearing her throat. "I'm fine," she replied. "Sorry to bother you, but your sister is at my house… She's drunk and while I was trying to get her upstairs to bed, she fell and

I can't get her up."

There was a pause on the line. "What?" he asked, baffled.

"Yeah, I know how it sounds." Reign scratched her head yet again. "I can't get her off the floor and I don't want to leave her down here, so I was hoping that you could come help me."

Chase paused again.

"Chase?" she asked when he didn't respond.

"I'll be there in ten."

"Okay." Reign looked at the phone when he hung up. Hearing Ava stir, she glanced over in hope. But all Ava did was mumble something before drifting back off.

Reign rolled her eyes. "Lord have mercy."

Ten minutes later, Reign heard a knock. Slowly, she pushed herself to her feet then headed for the door. She opened it without even bothering to look.

Chase stepped through.

"Thanks for coming," Reign said, closing the door.

"No problem." Chase caught himself staring. *God, I've missed you.* In those few short seconds of seeing Reign's face, Chase had almost forgotten why he was there. Clearing his throat, he snapped out of his daze. "Where is she?"

Reign pointed to the floor a few feet away.

Chase looked over, shaking his head at the sight. He knelt at his sister's side.

"She's alive," Reign promised. "She's just asleep."

"Yeah, the snoring gave it away." He gave Ava a light nudge. When Ava didn't wake, Chase scooped her up in his arms, then rose to his feet. "Thanks for calling me, I'll take her to my house."

Reign stood in front of him as he made a move for the door. "No, it's fine that she stays here," she insisted. "It's too much to get her in and out of the car, trust me." She offered a tired shrug. "She can have the guest room."

Chase adjusted Ava's weight in his arms. "Are you sure?"

Reign nodded. "Yeah, I'm sure." She gestured to the stairs. "You can take her up. I'll be there in a second."

Chase hesitated for a moment. He took notice of the stuffy, scratchy sound to Reign's voice. "You sound funny, are you okay?"

"I have a cold, it's fine though," she quickly dismissed. "Take her up, I'm sure the dead weight is heavy."

"Nah, I bench press more than this," Chase said, walking towards the stairs.

Reign had a flashback of how strong Chase was, wrapped in his arms while they'd had sex against the wall of his office. Shaking the memory away, she grabbed Ava's fallen purse and her own phone from the floor.

Chase nudged open the door to Reign's guest room, heading straight for the bed. He gently placed Ava on it, then turned on the bedside lamp. Eyeing his snoozing sister, he shook his head. "I'll be sure to throw this in your face as soon as possible." He chuckled to himself. Hearing Reign walk in, he turned around.

"I brought her some of my pajamas. Those work clothes can't be comfortable to sleep in," Reign said of Ava's form-fitting tan pencil shirt and black button-down blouse. She set them on the bed.

Chase flashed a grateful smile. "Thank you, I know she'll appreciate it."

"Maybe," Reign muttered. She wasn't sure if Chase knew about the argument that she and Ava had had about him, but she knew that *she* wasn't going to bring it up.

Reign loomed over Ava, examining her face. Her chin was wet with drool. "Can you grab a washcloth? I want to wipe her face."

"Sure." Chase walked to the door.

"The linen closet is—"

"I know where it is, Rae," he cut in, looking back at her.

Reign glanced at him. "Right," she uttered. She followed Chase's progress out of the room, before turning back to Ava, who'd begun to stir. Reign watched as Ava opened her eyes.

"Hey," Reign spoke. "You okay?"

Ava just stared up at Reign, not saying anything.

Reign sighed. "Well since you're up. You might as well change before you go back to sleep." She grabbed Ava's arms, slowly helping her sit up.

Ava's head hung as Reign began to unbutton her blouse. As Reign undid another button, Ava hiccupped, then her head jerked up. Before Reign could react, Ava leaned forward and vomited. Reign caught a massive amount of bile on her chest.

"Are you fuckin' *kidding* me?!" Reign erupted, shoving Ava back down to the bed.

Letting out a groan, Ava grabbed her stomach, turning on her side.

Chase bolted into the room. "What happened?" he charged, wet washcloth and hand towel at the ready.

Completely disgusted, Reign stiffly stood, hands raised. "Ava just fuckin' threw up on me."

Chase walked over. "Shit." He grimaced, eyeing the substance on Reign. "Damn Rae, I'm sorry."

"Just wipe her face, I need to get out of this shirt," Reign bit out, leaving the room.

As Reign headed for her bedroom, she felt a wave of fatigue come over her. Leaning against a wall, she stood there for a moment, taking several labored breaths. *I need to get to bed before I pass out.*

After discarding her soiled clothing and taking a quick, hot shower, a pajama clad Reign returned to the guest room.

Chase was adjusting a pillow under Ava's head. "She fell right back to sleep," he quietly said. He'd cleaned his sister's face, and removed her shoes, electing to leave her in her work clothes.

Reign rubbed her throat with her hand. "Not surprised."

"Hopefully she doesn't throw up again." Chase pulled a blanket over Ava. "There was a little bit of it on the floor; I cleaned it up."

"Thanks." Reign stifled a cough. "Figured most of it got on *me* anyway."

Chase looked at Reign, letting out a sigh. "I apologize again on her behalf." He shook his head. "That was disgusting."

"You don't have to." Reign cleared her throat as she ran a hand through her hair. "Anyway umm…you can head home, I'll watch over her."

Chase rubbed the back of his neck. "No, you should get some rest, I'll stay for a bit and keep an eye on her," he insisted, glancing at his watch. "I don't have to leave for my trip tomorrow until—"

"Oh my God, you have to travel tomorrow?" Reign cut in, stunned. "I feel terrible, you should be asleep right now."

Chase placed a gentle hand on her arm. "It's no problem." Heat was radiating from her skin; a look of concern appeared on his face. "Rae, you're burning up."

"Of *course* I am." She ran a hand over her forehead. "Because a cold just *wouldn't* be complete without a goddamn fever," she drawled, sarcastic.

Chase removed his hand from her arm, eyeing her sympathetically.

Reign let out a quick sigh. "I'm sorry," she apologized, sincere. "I didn't mean to snipe at you."

"Don't be sorry, I understand," he replied, caring. "Go get some sleep. Don't worry about Ava, she'll be fine. Like I said, I'll chill for a bit to watch her." He pointed to the lounge chair in the corner of the room. "I'll be right over there."

Reign was too tired to argue. "Okay." She glanced at the chair. "The chair reclines so hopefully you'll be comfortable… I'll bring you an extra blanket and—"

"I'll be fine, go." He gave her a gentle nudge.

She gave a nod. "Okay." Sighing, she walked off.

Chase followed Reign's progress until she disappeared out of the room. He peered over at Ava once more, then headed for the chair. Sitting down, he leaned his head back and pulled the side latch, activating the recliner. He stared at the wall in front of him until his eyes became heavy.

Chase adjusted his position on the recliner in an effort to get comfortable. Glancing at his watch, he read the time: two in the morning. Though he was able to close his eyes for a bit a while ago, he couldn't drift into full slumber. He peered at Ava; she was sprawled out across the bed, snoring.

Sitting up, Chase stretched his back. Hearing a muffled noise coming from the hallway, he sat up, listening to see if it would cease. When he heard it again, he got up, following the disturbance to Reign's bedroom door. It didn't take him long to realize that the sound was her coughing.

The door was cracked; Chase opened it a bit more, peering inside. Reign was laying on her side, hand over her mouth, suffering a severe coughing spell. Chase eyed her sympathetically. He was also *empathetic*; he remembered exactly how that felt. He raised his hand to knock on the door to ask if she needed anything, but paused. Instead, he went downstairs, heading straight for Reign's kitchen.

Finding the coffee and tea station on Reign's counter, Chase grabbed a tea bag and a jar of honey. He opened the refrigerator, quickly scanning its contents. After a moment, he retrieved a lemon, and some fresh ginger. Locating a small pot and tea kettle, he filled both with water, placing them on the stove. Peeling and cutting the ginger, he placed the chucks into the small pot.

Once both pots came to a boil. Chase grabbed a mug, rinsed it out, placing a tea bag inside. He filled the mug most of the way with the piping hot water, then filled the rest with the ginger liquid. He finished the concoction off by adding honey and fresh squeezed lemon juice. Grabbing the mug by the handle, he carefully walked back upstairs. Approaching Reign's bedroom once again, he gave the door a light tap.

He intended on waiting for her response, but when all he heard was coughing, Chase decided to just go in. Reign was laying in the same position he'd left her in. The only change was that she was now clutching a pillow to her chest.

Chase moved to her bedside, setting the mug on the nightstand. Sitting next to her, he gently took hold of Reign's arm. "Come on, sit up," he softly said, guiding her upright.

Still holding the pillow, Reign leaned forward, coughing again.

Chase rubbed her back. He hoped that the cough would pass soon; judging by the sound coming from her, he could only imagine how badly her chest was hurting. He held his hand on Reign's back even after she stopped. "When was the last time that you took medicine?"

"Before I laid down," Reign whined, slowly lifting her head.

Through the moonlight peering in between the curtains, Chase could see that her face was streaked with tears. He felt terrible for her.

Putting a hand over her face, Reign sniffled as more tears fell. "I can't sleep."

Chase slowly guided his hand up and down her back. "Yeah, it's always worse at night." He grabbed the mug from the nightstand. "I made this for you."

Reign wiped the wetness from her face, then glanced at him with tired eyes. "What is it?" she croaked.

"Tea," he answered.

Turning away, Reign shook her head. "I don't want any, it's not going to help."

"It *might*, just drink some." He held it out in front of her.

Relenting, she took the cup from him, blowing away the steam for a bit before taking a careful sip. The liquid was soothing. Feeling heat in the back of her throat after a moment, she cleared it.

"I boiled some ginger and put the liquid in there, so it's probably a little spicy," Chase spoke up.

"It's fine," Reign replied. After drinking a good amount of the tea, she handed the mug back to Chase, who set it on the nightstand.

Pulling the cover over her, Reign laid back down on her side.

Chase sat there, staring at her. He knew that he should go, but he couldn't just leave her to suffer alone.

Following his instincts, Chase laid down beside her. He gently pulled her close to him, wrapping his arms around her.

Reign, eyes closed, folded her arms over his, pulling them tight around her waist. She felt comfortable, safe.

Chase planted a kiss on the top of her head and closed his eyes.

Chapter Forty-Two

REIGN FLIPPED A FEW PIECES of turkey bacon in a frying pan, pausing long enough to sip on her tea. Up for two hours already, she'd bathed, thrown on some comfortable loungewear, then proceeded to make breakfast for herself and her unexpected houseguests.

Satisfied with the crispiness of the bacon, Reign turned the stove off. Removing the pieces from the pan, she divided them between three plates, alongside scrambled eggs, pancakes, and fresh strawberries.

Hearing commotion in the living room, she turned around to see Chase entering the kitchen.

Running a hand along the back of her neck, she stared at him. Waking up in his arms, even if it was simply to comfort her, had felt good.

"Morning," she greeted, finally.

"Morning," he replied. "How are you feeling?"

She grabbed a plate of food, walking it over to the counter island. "Honestly, I feel a little better." Her voice cracked; she touched her throat. "Sorry, my voice is going in and out."

"Don't apologize," Chase said, sincere. "How does your throat feel?"

"Despite how I sound, it feels better." She folded her arms. "That tea you made for me…it helped."

Chase offered a warm smile. "I'm glad." His smile faded. "Honestly, seeing you suffering like that…" he paused for a moment. "I'm just happy that you're feeling better."

Reign eyed him with adoration, trying to find the words to express exactly how appreciative she was. She fiddled with her hands. "I umm…I made breakfast. Do you want some?" were her words of choice.

Chase put a hand up. "No thank you, I have to get going." He checked his watch. "I'm already late…overslept."

Reign glanced down at her hands. "I'm sorry."

Chase put a gentle hand on her arm. "*Don't* be." He'd oversleep a *million* times if it meant that he could wake up next to Reign again. "I checked on Ava, she's still asleep."

"Okay." She met his eye again. "I'll take care of her, don't worry."

"I'm not worried."

Reign tucked her hair behind her ear. "Thank you for last night," she said after a moment. "I should've *lead* with that… I appreciate it."

"Rae, you don't have to thank me," Chase replied with sincerely. "It's the *least* that I could do. After all, you stayed with *me* when *I* was sick."

Reign glanced at the floor, sighing. Inside, she was screaming. She wanted to say more than "thank you"; she wanted to tell him how much she missed him, how hard this past month had been. She wanted to tell him what she'd told her sister— that she loved him. But she couldn't bring herself to say the words.

Reign's silence wasn't new to Chase; he didn't expect her to say much else. "Well…I should get going."

Feeling tears sting the back of her eyes, Reign prayed that they wouldn't surface. "Okay," she choked out.

Oblivious to Reign's building emotional breakdown, Chase wrapped his arms around Reign and hugged her.

Hugging him back, Reign couldn't stop the tears from surfacing. She held him for a long moment, then discreetly wiped her eyes with her hand before parting. "Can you do me a favor and shoot me a text letting me know when you get to your destination?" She wiped her hands down her black shirt. "Just for my peace of mind."

Chase smiled then gave a nod. "I can do that." He stood there for a moment longer; he didn't want to leave, but he knew that he *had* to. "Take care of yourself."

"I will," she promised. "Drive safely."

"I will," he replied, before walking out of the kitchen.

Reign stared at his departing figure as it disappeared through the corridor. Hearing her front door open and close, tears filled her eyes yet again. Sitting on a nearby stool, she put her face in her hands and cried.

Chase jumped into his car, starting it. Eyeing the fog on his window, he pushed a button, activating his windshield wipers. He rolled his eyes. "Of *course* it's out of wiper fluid," he muttered to himself.

He popped the trunk before stepping out of the car. Walking around to the back of his car, Chase peered into the trunk, but something else caught his eye. Chase let out a heavy sigh. "Damn," he whispered to himself. With Chase's hectic travel schedule the past month, it had been a while since he'd looked back there; he'd forgotten all about it.

Retrieving the box, he closed the trunk.

Hearing a knock, Reign lifted her head. Grabbing a napkin from the counter, she dried her face and went for the door. She gave the peephole a quick glance before opening it. "Hey, did you forget something?" she asked Chase.

He stood there with a box in his hands. "Yeah, kind of."

Reign moved aside to let him in.

Chase faced her as she shut the door. "I forgot to give this to you."

Reign glanced at the white box. "What is it?"

Chase looked down at it, letting out a sigh. "It's a…late birthday gift for you," he answered. "At this point it's *beyond* late." He looked back up at her. "I put it in my trunk a while ago and it umm… it slipped my mind."

Reign put a hand up. "I wouldn't feel right accepting that from you," she protested. "Not after everything—"

"That doesn't matter, I still want you to have it," he cut in. "So please take it."

Reign nodded after a moment. "Okay...thank you."

"You're welcome." He shifted the box in his hands. "It's a little heavy, do you mind if I take it up to your office for you?"

She shook her head. "No, I don't mind."

As Chase headed upstairs, Reign went back into the kitchen. When Chase came back downstairs, he said his goodbyes once again and left. Wrapping up the extra plate of food, Reign put on a pot of coffee, then made herself another cup of tea. Hearing a noise come from upstairs, she glanced up at the ceiling before leaving the kitchen.

Rolling over in bed, with one hand over her stomach and the other over her face, Ava let out a groan. The hangover that she'd experienced after her birthday was a cakewalk compared to *this*. Between the severe nausea and the splitting headache, Ava regretted opening her eyes.

Peering over the side of the bed, she eyed the small clock radio that she'd accidentally knocked to the floor while stretching.

"Shit," she muttered, slowly sitting up. Painstakingly, she bent down to retrieve the fallen, item, placing it back on the nightstand. Afterwards, Ava just sat there, slumped over. She ran a hand over her hair, pushing the wild curls off her face, then peered down at her wrinkled clothes—the same clothes she'd had on the night before.

Putting a hand on her head, Ava tried to remember what exactly had *happened* last night. Looking around, she at least knew where she was: Reign's spare bedroom. She'd been over enough times to recognize it.

It wasn't long before Reign appeared in the doorway, items in hand. Ava slowly looked up at her.

"Morning," Reign greeted, monotone.

It took a moment for Ava to speak. "Morning," she finally croaked out.

Reign walked over, placing the items at the end of the bed. "You probably feel like shit right now."

Ava slowly nodded.

Reign folded her arms. "I brought you a change of clothes." She gestured to the black folded pile of fabric. "Just some tights and a t-shirt of mine. We wear around the same size so you should be able to fit into them." She pointed to the other items on the bed. "There's also a washcloth, towel and a spare toothbrush—you can get yourself together whenever you feel up to it."

Ava tucked some of her hair behind her ears, averting Reign's gaze. Like the hangover—her regret over their argument—was overwhelming. She knew that she needed to say *something*, but didn't know where to start.

Taking Ava's silence as just her not feeling well, Reign headed for the door.

"Rae," Ava called.

Reign turned around. "Yeah?"

Ava eyed her. "Thank you," she softly spoke.

Reign gave a slight nod. "Sure." She walked out, shutting the door behind her.

Alone again, Ava rubbed her face with her hands and sighed.

Reign sat at her counter island, eating her breakfast at a leisurely pace. Taking a sip of tea, she gazed into her backyard through the glass doors, fixating on the mountains in the distance. She smiled softly as pleasant memories from her trip up there with Chase flooded back. But just as quick as the smile and pleasant memories had appeared, they faded. Hit with the reality of how badly she'd messed up, tears clouded her eyes.

Reign shook her head. *Yeah, keep crying, Rae, that's going to solve your problems,* she berated herself.

Hearing Ava enter the kitchen, Reign quickly sucked up her tears, dabbing her eyes with a napkin. She eyed Ava, who was inching her way to the island.

Reign folded her arms on the countertop as Ava pulled out the seat beside her, sitting down. It had been nearly forty-five minutes since she'd left Ava upstairs. "How are you feeling?" Reign asked after a moment.

"Like shit," Ava groaned, arms folded over her midsection. "I had to practically *drag* myself to the shower."

"Figured."

Ava adjusted her wild ponytail. "Thanks for the clothes by the way." She smoothed the fabric of the top. "That damn skirt was cutting off my circulation."

Reign chuckled slightly; the humor quickly left her face. "It's no problem." She pointed to a covered plate on the other side of the counter. "I fixed breakfast, but I'm guessing you don't feel up to eating it right now."

Ava slowly shook her head. "No, not yet. But thank you."

Watching Ava fold her arms over her stomach yet again, and noticing the nauseas look on her face, Reign stood from her seat. "I have ginger ale. Do you want some?" she offered. "It might help settle your stomach."

"Yes, please," Ava replied.

"Sure."

Ava slowly rocked herself in her seat as Reign poured a tall glass of the cold beverage. "I can't believe I drank so much." Reign set the glass in front of her. Ava offered a grateful half-smile in return.

"Me either." Reign returned to her seat. "You normally reserve that amount of alcohol consumption for your birthday."

Ava wanted to chuckle, but couldn't.

"Even *then*, I don't think I've ever seen you drunk to the point where you practically passed out," Reign added.

"I know," Ava agreed. She took a long sip of her soda. "I was...I had a lot on my mind."

Reign nodded slowly. "You should thank Tracy. *She's* the one who called me last night."

Ava set her glass down. "I will... I owe her lunch or—*something*."

"That would be nice."

Both women sat in silence for a few moments. Almost as if one were waiting for the other to speak.

"You want to talk about it?" Reign asked, breaking the silence. Ava took a deep breath, looking at her. She nodded. "I'm sorry."

Reign tilted her head, staring back.

"I hate that this fight even happened," Ava added remorseful. "...I wanted to call you, but I didn't know what to say...I guess that's why I drank so much. I was upset."

"It's okay." Reign shrugged slightly. "Friends fight sometimes."

"Not like that." Ava said. "At least not when it comes to *us*." She ran a hand over her arm. "I've never had a reason to be nasty towards you...and the fact that it was over something that wasn't even my business, just makes it worse. So...I'm *genuinely* sorry."

"Ava, I accept your apology. Like I said, it's okay," Reign replied sincere. "And while I didn't like *what* was said, I understand why you said it. Chase is your brother and naturally you're protective over him. I'm the same way with my sister, so I get it."

Ava let out a heavy breath.

Reign glanced off to the side. "Besides...it's not like I've been behaving the best when it comes to him." She shook her head, returning her eyes to Ava. "You were within your right to be upset with me so like I said...we're good."

Ava looked down at the counter, tapping her fingernails against her glass. "Listen...I know that you say that we're good—you brush things over to keep the peace, but I *know* that I hurt your feelings." She shook her head in shame. "And those comments that I made..." Tears formed in her eyes. "You're not a user; I know that. Your friendship—*you* have *always* been genuine. You have a good heart, Rae. I don't know where I pulled that accusation from."

"Probably from your ass," Reign quipped.

Ava managed a small chuckle. "Yeah, you're probably right." The humor immediately left her face. "You're not naïve either; I don't—"

Reign put a hand on Ava's arm to calm her. "It's *okay*," she soothed. She grabbed a napkin, handing it to Ava. "*We're* okay, I promise."

Ava dabbed the spilled tears from her cheeks, nodding. "I appreciate you looking out for me last night…and even *now*." She sighed heavily. "But…I don't want you to think that this will become a habit."

Reign shot a puzzled look Ava's way. "I don't," she replied. "Why would you think that?"

"It's just that I know that when you were friends with Marcy, she was problematic and that was draining for you," Ava explained. "The last thing that *I* want to be is a burden to you."

"Ava you got drunk, it *happens*." Reign consoled. "That doesn't make you problematic, or a burden… You're nothing like that, nothing like *her*, so don't be hard on yourself."

"Even though I threw up on you?" she brought up, grimacing.

Reign too grimaced. "You remember that?"

"Just barely." Shame masked Ava's face. "I'm so embarrassed."

Reign chuckled. "It's okay." She rubbed Ava's shoulder. "It was just a t-shirt."

Ava opened her mouth to speak, but instead she put her head in her hands, letting out a groan.

"Headache?" Reign assumed.

"Yeah," Ava nodded. "I took an aspirin. It just hasn't kicked in yet."

Reign shot a sympathetic look as Ava massaged her temples with her fingertips. After a moment, Reign let out a deep sigh. Though they had made up, there was something else that she needed to say to Ava.

"Ava…about what you said regarding you feeling like I replaced you—"

Ava lifted her head, putting a hand up. "No Rae, don't even bring that up, that was childish and irrelevant," she protested. "I was just upset with you."

"It's how you felt."

Despite her pain, Ava vigorously shook her head. "It was stupid."

"It's how you *felt*." Reign eyed her intently. "I didn't know that I made you feel that way. I just figured that since you had other friends, it didn't *matter* that we didn't hang out as much when I became friends with Marcy."

"Rae, you don't have to—"

"Just let me finish," Reign cut in, tone calm.

Ava closed her mouth, giving a slight nod.

"I know what it feels like to have my feelings brushed aside and that's the last thing that I want to do to you." Reign placed a hand to her chest. "I never wanted or meant to make you feel like you were being replaced in my life… It may be childish to *you*, but I acknowledge that you felt that way and for *that*, I'm *so* sorry," she continued, sincere. "You're my best friend. Always have been, always *will* be."

Ava wiped the newly formed tears from her eyes, then poked her lip out. She truly appreciated Reign's words. After a moment, Ava smiled at her. "See?" she playfully poked Reign's arm. "Good heart."

Reign smiled, yet it quickly cleared from her face. "I wish you would've told me, then."

Ava shrugged slightly. "I guess… I guess I took a page from *your* book."

Reign nodded slowly. "That's fair," she said. "I'm sorry…for everything."

"Me too." Relieved and happy to put their feud behind her, Ava embraced Reign. "I love you, sis."

Reign hugged her back. "I love you too."

"I promise not to fight with you anymore," Ava said, parting from the embrace.

"Don't make that promise," Reign joked, moving her hair behind her shoulder. "You might feel differently after you catch this cold I have."

Ava laughed. "Hell, I'd deserve it anyway." She folded her arms on the tabletop, letting out a light exhale. "Was this the biggest fight we've ever had?"

"It was," Reign answered, nodding.

Ava giggled as a memory flooded back to her. "I think our first argument was freshman year in college." She tapped her chin. "It was over what? A book?"

Reign chuckled. "You mean the time you borrowed one of my books and returned it to me with a broken spine and pages that you folded because you were too lazy to find an actual bookmark?"

Ava let out a laugh; she gave Reign's arm a playful shove. "Your head nearly exploded."

"I don't play about my books, you know that," Reign countered, voice laced with laughter.

"Yes, I know." Feeling lighter, Ava took a deep breath. "I think that my appetite has returned."

"Good." Reign stood from her seat. "I'll heat up your plate."

Ava made a move to get up. "You've done enough, I can get that."

"Sit your ass down," Reign commanded, pointing at her.

Ava's mouth fell open; amusement resonated on her face. She put her hands up in surrender. "Okay, geez," she said. "Good heart *and* bossy."

Reign shrugged as she grabbed the plate from the counter. She placed it into the microwave, starting it. Waiting, she tapped her nails on the counter, letting her mind wander.

Ava sipped on her ginger ale.

"Do you remember Chase being here last night?" Reign asked.

Ava nodded. "Briefly." She set her glass down. "My memory is in and out, but I *do* remember hearing his voice after I threw up." She chuckled, "He's going to curse me out later. He had to drive to Vegas today; I know he'd planned on going to sleep early last night."

Reign stared down at the counter, lightly pounding her fist against it. She heard the microwave beep but didn't move. "He's not going to curse you out." She sighed. "He stayed with you because he wanted to."

Ava scratched her head. "Yeah," she murmured. "I know that I get on his nerves sometimes, but he'd do anything for me...for *anybody* that he loves. That's how he's always been."

"I know," Reign agreed, tone low. She paused for a moment. "You were right."

"About what?"

Reign glanced up at the microwave. "You were right to question me when I said that I just care about Chase...because it's not true."

Ava tilted her head, fixing Reign with a curious glance. "What are you saying Rae?"

Reign took a deep breath. "I love him."

Ava frowned, unsure if she'd heard her. "What did you say?"

Reign didn't answer as she pulled Ava's food from the microwave. She walked over, placing it in front of her.

"Rae, what did you say?" Ava pressed.

"I said that I love him," Reign repeated, looking up at her. She didn't know what had made her say it to Ava, but there was no turning back. "I—I'm in love with him."

Ava's mouth was gaping open. "Seriously?" she managed to get out after a moment.

Reign nodded. "Seriously."

Ava was trying to figure out what to say. She always felt that Chase and Reign would be good together—*great* together. Now that she knew that they both felt the same way about each other, she couldn't help but be excited. "You *just* realized this?"

Reign shook her head.

The excitement left Ava's face. Though she wasn't sure, she had a pretty good idea of what had caused Chase to fall out with Reign. She knew Reign and her ability to hide her feelings all too well; she sighed after a moment. "You don't have to give me details...it's not my business," she said. "I just hope that whatever is keeping you from telling him..."

"I know," Reign slid in, somber.

Ava eyed the plate of food in front of her for a long moment. "I will say *this* though," she began.

Reign braced herself. "Okay."

"I know that being vulnerable scares you," Ava said. "But...if it's *one* person who you should be—*need* to be completely open and honest with, it's *him*... Especially if you truly love him. He deserves that."

Reign closed her eyes for a moment, exhaling deeply. "I know." It was the truth; she *did* know, but exactly when she'd get up enough courage to do so, was an answer that she didn't have. Just thinking about it made her feel anxious. She gestured to the plate of food. "You should eat that before it gets cold again."

Chapter Forty-Three

CHASE TOOK A SIP OF coffee, eyeing the drawings on his tablet. Setting the cup down on the desk, Chase scrolled to a blank page with his stylus. He began to sketch, but paused in the middle of drawing a straight line.

He sat, staring at the page, thinking back to when Reign had attempted to draw a while back; the pleasant memory brought a smile to his face. Before he knew it, his mind was bombarded with thoughts of her. Her smile, her laugh, their time spent together, their conversations both deep and lighthearted, the way that she made him feel, the love that they made; it consumed him.

Chase had been in Las Vegas for three days, and he could barely focus. Just being in Reign's presence for mere minutes had brought every feeling that Chase had been trying to suppress over the past month flooding back with a vengeance. Sitting back in his seat, he tossed his stylus on the desk. Rubbing his face with both hands, he let out a deep sigh.

Grabbing his cell, he scrolled to Reign's name, opening the text history. He read their last exchange from three days ago.

Chase: Hi, just letting you know that I made it to my destination. Just checked into my hotel.

Reign: Hey, good. How was the drive?

Chase: Not as bad as I thought it would be.

Reign: That's good. Do you have a full itinerary this trip?

Chase: Unfortunately. As a matter of fact, I have to get ready to log on to a meeting now.

Reign: Okay, good luck with your meeting.

Chase: Thank you. Take care of yourself, get some rest.

Reign: You're welcome, and I will.

He'd reread the brief, casual exchange later that same evening, fighting the urge to call her. Though Chase was still hurt, he missed talking to her—he missed their friendship.

Fuck it, call her. Listening to his inner voice, Chase dialed Reign's number, holding the phone to his ear as the line rang. When the call went to voicemail after several rings, Chase couldn't hide the disappointment on his face.

"Hey Rae, it's Chase," he spoke once prompted. "I'm calling to check in on you...to see how you're feeling..." Closing his eyes, he sighed. "I umm...I wanted to hear your voice." He pinched the bridge of his nose. "...I guess I'll talk to you later. You can call me anytime... Bye."

Hanging up, he set the phone back down on his desk. Shaking his head after a moment, he picked his stylus back up.

Reign picked up a book, reading the back of it. "This seems like it'll be good," she said, placing it in a small hand basket.

Ava shook her head. "And just *where* are you going to put more books?" She chuckled, pushing her hair behind her ears. "Your bookshelves are *full*."

Reign was already eyeing another. "I'll find room."

"You can always send some home with *me*." Ava took a sip of her mocha latte.

"Not happening 'spine breaker'," Reign jeered.

Ava nearly spat out her drink. "Funny." She delivered a playful tap to Reign's arm.

That Saturday afternoon, feeling nearly back to normal, Reign had decided to meet up with Ava for lunch. But first, Reign had stopped at a bookstore in search of new fiction titles to add to her collection.

Ava grabbed a book from a shelf, peering at it. "Huh," she

uttered, then showed the cover image to Reign. "I looked *exactly* like this demon after my drunk episode last week."

Reign busted out laughing, "Cut it out."

"No, I was a hot, disgusting mess." Ava placed a hand on her stomach, making a face. "My stomach *still* hurts whenever I think about liquor," she groaned. "*Speaking* of that drunk night, remind me to give you back the spare key to my place... I can't believe I actually left my house keys at work that night."

Reign giggled, giving Ava's arm a light rub. "Don't be hard on yourself, you were depressed."

Ava shook her head in amusement as she reshelved the book that she was holding. "If only Malcom was that sensitive when he came over my house later that weekend," she recalled, slightly humored. "His disrespectful ass clowned me for like two hours straight."

"He's still a jokester after all of these years."

"That man has *never* been funny," Ava bristled, earning another laugh from Reign. Ava laughed a little herself. "No, I'm joking, he's pretty funny when he's not on my nerves."

"How is that going by the way?" Reign probed, picking up another book. "You two still talking or are you finally going to admit that you're dating him?"

Ava waved a hand Reign's way. "Okay fine, as you already know, we *have* gone out a few times already, so yes, I'd say that we're dating."

Seeing Ava's smile come through, Reign flashed a grin of her own. "Now how hard was that?"

Ava's eyes became slits. "Oh shut up."

Reign giggled. "I'm happy for you."

Ava put a finger up. "That doesn't mean that we're in a full-on relationship. I'm still feeling him out. I haven't even *slept* with him—"

"Either *way*, I'm still happy for you," Reign cut in.

"Thank you." Ava replied, sincere. "He's a good man. He understands that I want to take my time, and he's fine with that. For *now*, anyway." She chuckled as she adjusted the purse strap on her shoulder. "I just want to be careful with my heart, you know."

"I understand, trust me," Reign replied.

Taking another sip of her drink, Ava glanced at Reign.

Reign, catching her stare, squinted her eyes. "You want to ask me about Chase, *don't* you?"

Ava tossed her head back in dramatic fashion. "Oh my God, I *do*." She raised a hand. "*But*, I promised that I would stay out of it, so I will."

Reign shook her head in disbelief. "Yeah, sure."

"I'm serious," Ava chortled.

"Uh huh."

Ava laughed, "I'm *trying* anyway."

Reign placed a book into her basket; she sighed. "I still haven't told him," she confessed.

Ava tilted her head. "You haven't spoken at *all* since last week?"

"We've texted, and talked for a little bit a couple days ago, but…"

"At least you're communicating with each other again," Ava pointed out, hopeful. "*That's* something. It's a *start*."

Reign just offered a solemn shrug. After hearing Chase's voicemail, Reign did not hesitate to return his call; they had talked briefly before Chase had to finish his work. While Reign was happy to see him—to talk to him—the interaction wasn't the same. It *wouldn't be* until Reign came clean to him. "Yeah," was all that she could say.

Ava put a caring hand on Reign's shoulder. "Well, he's home *now*, if you want to skip lunch and go visit."

Reign quickly shook her head. "No, we're not skipping. I'll deal with my mess later." She eyed more books. "I should probably be in the *self-help* section, instead of fiction," she muttered. "Lord knows I have issues."

Ava chuckled, then placed an arm around Reign's shoulder. "The only thing you *need* to do is bare your soul," she teased. "Stop being a punk."

Reign made a face in retaliation. She grabbed the book that Ava had previously shown her. "Here, you forgot your mirror," she ground out, pushing it in Ava's direction.

Eyeing the demon, Ava erupted with laughter. She snatched the book. "You make me sick."

Bowl of soup and cup of ginger ale in her hands, Reign entered her home office late Sunday evening. Setting the items on her desk, she sat down and turned her laptop and monitor on, waiting for them to power up.

Glancing down at the pink keyboard on her desk, she chuckled to herself. Of all the rooms in her house, her office was the one place where she allowed her love of pink to be displayed: from the lamp on her desk, to her chair, to the art on her walls.

Not many people knew that it was her favorite color. It wasn't something that she broadcasted; aside from a few subtle accessories, Reign hardly wore it.

Shaking the wandering thoughts from her head, Reign ate her soup, pausing when her phone vibrated. She picked it up; there was a text message from Ava.

At my parents' house. Found these in Mom's photo album. Thought you'd enjoy them.

Puzzled, Reign stared at the screen. "You didn't send anything, crazy," she said aloud. Another text came through.

She won't let me take them out of the album, so I'm trying to get some good pictures on my phone so I can print them out later. Hold on.

Reign giggled at the message. She could imagine the bantering that was taking place between Ava and her mother over the possession of the photos. After another moment, an influx of photos came through her phone.

She scrolled through them, smiling as she scanned through pictures of her and Ava through high school, and college—pleasant memories from those frozen moments in time flooded back. Coming across a photo of her and Chase taken the night of her prom, her smile faded.

She couldn't look away as memories of Chase began to fill her thoughts. She even touched the image of his face. In that moment, she wanted nothing more than to call him and tell him the truth. Closing the texting app, she pulled up Chase's phone number. Her finger hovered over the call button, but for the life of her she couldn't press it.

Frustrated, Reign tossed the phone on the desk. Running her hands through her hair, she let out a deep sigh. "Shit, shit, shit," she huffed. Lifting her head, she reached for a tissue, and knocked the cup of ginger ale off the desk.

"Come the fuck *on!*" Jumping from her seat, she darted to the hallway. Snatching a hand towel from her linen closet, she marched back into the office, heading straight for the mess. The cup and its contents had fallen onto a box that was nestled on the side of the desk. She retrieved the cup and set it back on the desk, then began dabbing the liquid from the box. It was the late birthday gift Chase had placed in her office a week ago.

Not working, *or* journaling while recovering from her illness, Reign hadn't been in her office until that evening. It had slipped her mind entirely.

"Nice Reign," she berated herself aloud, pushing hair behind her ear. "He probably thinks that I didn't like it." Reign pulled the box from the corner and sat down in the middle of the floor. Grabbing a small pair of scissors from her desk, she carefully slit the tape, tossing the scissors aside.

Opening the box, she was met with a small pink card sitting atop an assortment of pink tissue paper. She smiled to herself; Chase had remembered her favorite color. Taking a deep breath, she picked it up and read the handwritten message.

Reign,

I know that this will never replace the piece of your heart that's missing, but I hope it at least brings back pleasant memories for you. Happy birthday.

Love Chase.

Reign held the card to her chest, clutching it there for a few seconds. She had no idea what was hiding beneath the tissue paper, but whatever it was, Chase had put thought into it. She set the card aside, pulling tissue paper from the box. Then Reign let out a loud gasp.

Overcome with emotion, tears filled her eyes and spilled down her cheeks. She couldn't believe her eyes: sitting inside the box was her grandmother's typewriter. The very one she'd loved, the one she'd wrote so many stories on, the one she wished she could've taken when her grandmother had passed away. She ran a trembling hand over the typewriter, touching the "special" key that her grandmother so lovingly named after her. Reign busted out crying. Holding one hand on her precious gift and the other to her face, she bawled.

The extent that this man had gone to show Reign how much he paid attention to her, how much he cared for her, how much he *loved* her—she knew that she couldn't go on like this for another day.

Tears still spilling down her face, Reign finally rose from the floor. Heading for her closet, she opened the door, and began searching through her bins. Rifling through stacks of journals, she grabbed several and headed downstairs.

Chase had finished washing the last dish in his sink, placing it into the drying rack. Wiping the counter down, he hung the dishrag and headed straight for the living room.

Arriving back in town yesterday, Chase had spent the remainder of his weekend resting, trying to mentally decompress from the hectic week. With dinner finished and the kitchen cleaned, he planned on capping the evening off with a movie. But as he prepared to sit on the couch, he heard a knock.

He glanced at the door, eyeing it with suspicion. He wasn't expecting anybody, nor did he want any company.

Sighing, he got up. Peering out of the peephole, his eyes widened. With haste, Chase unlocked his door and opened it. "Rae," he breathed. She was standing there with too many notebooks clutched in her arms.

"Hi," Reign spoke. She hesitated for a moment. "May I come in?"

"Of course." Chase stepped aside, closing the door behind her.

Clutching her books to her chest, Reign turned around. Though she was facing Chase, her gaze averted to the side. Shifting her weight from one foot to the other, she bit her bottom lip. She knew that she needed to speak… She just didn't know where to start.

Chase tilted his head, focusing on her. Reign's unannounced visit filled him with mixed emotions. While he was certainly *happy* to see her, given how things were now, he couldn't help but wonder *why* she was there. "Umm—"

Reign's eyes shot up at him. "I opened my birthday gift," she abruptly cut in, a soft expression on her face. "Thank you…*so* much."

Chase smiled. "You're more than welcome."

Reign couldn't help it, she had no words; she was still in disbelief. "It's the most beautiful— How— Where did you even *find* it?"

Chase dropped his chin to his chest, thinking back. "I asked your mother if she had a picture of it…she *did*, and I just searched through pawn and antique shops online…" he shrugged. "Turns out, it was in an antique shop in Tucson." He looked up at her. "After hearing how much you cherished it…I just wanted you to have it."

Reign stared at him, eyes bright and glossy with subtle tears that built as he spoke. Chase had done the sweetest thing that Reign had ever experienced in her adult life, and the fact that he was speaking about it with such humility—she wanted to jump in his arms right then and there.

"Is that why you came over?" Chase asked, cutting into her thoughts. "To thank me in person?"

Reign tucked some of her hair behind her ears, clearing her throat. "Yes and no," she answered after a moment.

Chase raised an eyebrow. "Okay…well, what's the *other* reason?"

Reign took a deep breath, trying to form her thoughts. "Umm…first…I miss you."

A look of relief appeared on his face, as Chase exhaled deep. She felt the same as *he* had. "I miss you too." he replied. "More than you know."

Reign wanted to smile, but couldn't, at least not yet. She took another deep breath. "I..." she glanced down at the journals in her hand. "I know you've seen me write in one of my notebooks ever since you've known me," she began. "Truth is, I've been writing in these things since I was a child... I was never good at talking—expressing my feelings. So, I just wrote... I wrote everything."

Chase held his gaze on her as he listened intently.

"Every dream that I had, every aspiration, every fear, everything that I felt but couldn't say, or was *afraid* to say or didn't *want* to say...I wrote it down." She sighed, "I have a *ton* of these that I've kept over the years, that nobody has ever read." She placed a hand over them. "*These* are some of the ones that include how I feel about *you*. How I've *always* felt about you." She paused.

Chase took a step towards Reign; she backed away.

"No, I need you to stay there," she softly protested. Reign knew that if Chase came any closer to her that she might just abandon her mission and kiss him. She needed to finish what she wanted to say. "You thought that I didn't see you as being more than my friend...I *did*. I *always* did... I felt something for you since I *met* you, I just didn't think that you felt the same."

Chase went completely still, his mouth falling open. He couldn't believe his ears; he always thought that *his* feelings were one-sided.

"After we slept together prom night—" she shook her head. "The reason why I gave you the cold shoulder is because I had convinced myself that *you* didn't see *me* as more than a friend," she poured out. "I knew what *I* wanted—I knew that I wanted to *be* with you, I just didn't think you wanted the same thing... The fact is, until you *told* me... I honestly thought that you slept with me because it was the—*prom* thing to do."

Chase's eyebrows gathered, though he didn't speak. *All these years, she thought that what we did didn't mean anything to me... I can't believe I made her feel that way. I should've told her then.*

"I had convinced myself that someone as great as you, would never want to be tied down by someone as complicated as me." She let out a heavy sigh. "So, I did what I've *always* done... I suppressed what I felt." She glanced down at her hand; it was shaking. Trying not to focus on it, she used it to cradle the journals to her chest. "And...I closed you off."

Reign remembered crying in her hotel bathroom in the middle of the night, while Chase slept soundly in bed that night in high school. She didn't give herself to him because of a prom night tradition; she'd done it because she *loved* him, and by convincing herself that he didn't feel the same—she'd broken her own heart.

Chase let out a sigh. "You know...I didn't know exactly *why* you stopped talking to me," he finally spoke. "...I thought you were upset with me, and that hurt because upsetting you was the last thing that I ever wanted to do."

The pain in Chase's voice nearly broke her. Tears welling in her eyes, Reign squeezed them shut in hopes that they'd go back down. Opening them, she met his gaze with glassy eyes. "Chase, I was never mad at you; I was mad at my*self* for creating a—*fantasy*, that I never expected to actually come true," she lamented. "I shut you out because I needed to get a handle on my feelings for you."

Chase stared at Reign, taking in everything that he'd just heard with care. He understood her; he understood *why* she did what she did, why she felt what she felt. "I understand," he softly spoke.

Shifting her weight again, Reign let out a deep breath as she wiped the tears from her eyes. Tapping her journals with her hand, she struggled to find the next words to say.

Chase could tell by her constant movement, the shakiness in her voice, tears in her eyes that confessing this to him—being this vulnerable—was hard for her. Chase wanted so badly to comfort her.

Reign stepped forward before Chase had a chance to move. She held her books out for him. "Here."

Chase didn't speak as he retrieved them from her.

"You can read them if you want. I don't care anymore." More

tears spilled down Reign's cheeks. "I don't want to hide how I feel anymore. Not from you."

Chase looked down at the books he held, then back at her.

Reign wiped her eyes as she backed up. "I loved you then, and I'm in love with you now, Chase."

Chase let out a breath; he almost couldn't believe this was real. He'd convinced himself this would never happen, just like she had. She was even willing to allow him into the depths of her mind, letting him read her private notebooks, which she'd never shared with another soul. Except for his.

Setting the books on a nearby table, Chase stepped forward. "I'm in love with you too," he professed. "That hasn't changed... It'll *never* change."

Reign folded her arms across her chest. "I *hate* myself for not telling you the truth after you poured your heart out to me."

Chase reached for her hand. "*Please* don't," he begged.

Overcome with guilt, Reign moved her hand from his reach. "No because, I just walked out on you." She was trying her best to keep from busting out crying.

"It's okay," Chase soothed, taking another step forward.

"It's *not* okay." She hid her face behind her hands. "I confused you, and hurt you, and I'm sorry."

Chase closed the distance between them. "Baby, *I'm* sorry too." He gently moved her hands from her face, holding them secure in his. "*I* didn't handle my feelings the best way either... I should've *never* cut you off. It wasn't right—*especially* since I knew how it felt." Tears began to build in his eyes. "I handled it immaturely, and it was torture for me...not having you in my life has been torture."

"It was for me too," Reign sniffled. Squeezing his hands, she braced herself as she prepared to say the other thing that was holding her back from him. "Chase...I want to be with you, but I just need you to understand that I'm a little scared."

Chase put a loving hand on her face. "What are you afraid of, baby?"

Staring at him with tear-filled eyes, she went to speak, but hesitated.

"Tell me," he prompted. "Whatever it is, I can handle it."

"My last relationship…it scarred me." She regretted the words as soon as they left her lips. "It made me realize how easily someone can go from loving me to not even *caring* about me… I don't want that to happen with us… I don't want you to one day look at me and realize that I'm not enough for you. Or *too much* for you."

Those words made Chase's heart sink into the pit of his stomach. The fact that Reign could ever believe that she wouldn't always be what Chase wanted, unnerved him and saddened him. "That'll never happen," he promised after an agonizing moment. "Reign, I'm not him."

Reign let out a heavy breath, fighting to contain a full-on cry. "I *know* that," she choked out. "I *promise* I do, and I *hate* that I feel this way…"

Chase wiped the tears from her cheeks. "You can trust me." He gazed into her eyes. "You mean everything to me. I won't hurt you, baby, I promise."

His words floored her. She'd finally bared her heart to Chase—the man she loved as a teenager, and had fallen deeply *in* love with as a grown woman. For the first time in her life, Reign was letting herself be vulnerable, and Chase was unwavering in his love for her.

Reign had known that Chase was the one for her, but this moment solidified it. She buried her face into his chest, sobbing as Chase wrapped his strong arms around her.

Burying his face into her neck, Chase, held onto her tight. "I love you," he said, his voice almost breathless.

Reign squeezed him tight. "I love you too."

Chase pulled back and Reign lifted her head. Their eyes met, love and longing pulling them in. Passion sparked between them, igniting a deep, intimate kiss. Chase clutched at her desperately as the kiss went on, turning from sweet to intense, fueling their desire—something neither one thought they'd ever feel again.

Chase tugged his shirt off as Reign removed hers; they tossed them aside at the same time, in opposite directions. Reign eyed his chest, caressing it gently with her fingertips. Chase reclaimed her lips with his, carefully backing her down the hallway towards his bedroom.

Leaving a trail of clothing along the floor, they slowly made their way inside. Hands roaming each other's bodies, they moved towards the bed.

Reign guided Chase back, pushing him gently onto the mattress before straddling him. She could feel his erection as she moved against him; paired with his hands touching her body, it sent her arousal into overdrive. She didn't need foreplay, she was ready for all of him *now*.

Lifting up slightly, Reign gently took hold of him, stroking him just once before shifting her hips where she needed to be. A deep groan escaped Chase as Reign guided herself down onto him. Her wetness bathed him; her tight walls gripped him.

Chase gripped her waist as she began moving her hips in a steady rhythm. The pleasure that Reign was bringing Chase was insurmountable. He loved this woman with everything in him, and finally she was his.

Hands on Chase's chest, Reign closed her eyes and moaned in exquisite pleasure as she rode him. He filled every inch of her, hitting spots that she didn't know she had. This man beneath her not only stimulated her body, but he stimulated her mind, her heart. Feeling her climax nearing, Reign sped up her rhythm until she was finally forced to let go.

Before she had a chance to come down, Chase sat up right. Wrapping his arms around her back, he pulled her closer to him, as if he could fuse their bodies together. Holding her firmly, Chase began to thrust up inside her even deeper than before.

Reign gripped Chase's back as their pace quickened. When he kissed her neck, she could no longer contain it. "Chase," she moaned as another orgasm shook her.

Hearing her call his name so breathlessly, feeling her contract around him, was Chase's undoing. "Reign, baby," he breathed as he came.

Still holding one another secure in each other's arms, they caught their breath. Looking up into Reign's eyes, Chase moved the tousled hair from her face, resting his hand on her cheek.

Reign put her hand over his. Gazing back into his eyes, she smiled at him.

He smiled back. "I love you Rae," he crooned.

Reign placed a sensual kiss on his cheek. Meeting his gaze, she placed a hand over his heart. "I love you too."

Chapter Forty-Four

REIGN GLANCED OUT OF THE passenger side window as Chase opened her door. She stepped out of the car, adjusting her jacket in the process.

"Are you *sure* you're okay with being here?" Chase asked, shutting the car door. "I know you're tired from the flight."

Reign pushed some of her hair over her shoulder. "I'll be fine. I'll sleep when I get home," she answered. "Besides, you know I can't pass up your mom's cooking. I'm starving."

Chase smiled. Taking hold of her hand, he gave it a kiss. "Well, I promise we won't stay long."

Reign gently grabbed his chin, giving him a quick kiss on his lips. "Okay."

Approaching his parents' door, Chase gave it a knock. As they waited for someone to answer, he glanced at Reign. She wasn't looking at him, but that didn't stop him from keeping his gaze on *her*. He smiled to himself; he still felt like he was in a dream.

Six months ago, Reign had come to his house as just a friend. After a night of heartfelt confessions and passion, she'd left his *girl-friend*. Chase couldn't have been happier.

The door opening snapped him out of his blissful thoughts.

"Hi! Come in, come in," Ellie beamed, moving aside to let them in. As Reign stepped inside, Ellie wrapped her arms around her. "It's so good to see you."

Reign hugged her back, smiling. "You too."

Chase shook his head in amusement. "Mom, you act like you didn't just see her two weeks ago."

Parting from Reign, Ellie flagged Chase with her hand.

"Hush." She hugged him. "How was your vacation?"

"Perfect and *much* needed," Reign replied, removing her jacket. "I can't remember the last time I took two weeks off."

Chase grinned. "Same here." He placed his hand on the small of Reign's back, giving it a rub. "Turks and Caicos is absolutely beautiful; I can't wait to go back."

Reign flashed a glowing smile Chase's way. She was floored when he'd surprised her with the two-week trip in celebration of their six-month anniversary.

"Well, you *both* look well-rested." Ellie smiled, glancing back at the kitchen. "Ava, your brother and future sister-in-law are here!"

Reign giggled as Chase put his hand over his face, shaking his head. He wasn't surprised. Ever since he'd announced that he and Reign were a couple, the flood gates to marriage comments had opened. "Don't start Mom." he warned.

Ava darted out of the kitchen with Malcom in tow. "Hey," she squealed. "I thought you two weren't going to make it." She gave Reign a hug as Chase shook Malcom's hand. "You *just* got back in town."

"She's hungry," Chase chortled, gesturing to Reign.

"I *am*," Reign agreed, laughter in her voice. She rubbed her stomach. "We dropped the bags off, freshened up, and came straight here."

Ellie took hold of Reign's hand. "Well, let's get you fed sweetheart." She pulled her along. "For dessert, I made pineapple upside down cake *just* for you."

Reign let out a light gasp. "Oh my God, you're the best."

"Mom, *I* asked you to make your pound cake," Ava said, feigning hurt.

"Girl, I already told you that I wasn't making it, now hush," Ellie dismissed as she and a giggling Reign disappeared into the kitchen.

Ava's mouth fell open. "Rae is already replacing me as Mom's favorite daughter," she joked. She squinted at Malcom, who had one hand over his mouth. "You're laughing a little too hard over there, sir."

Malcom planted a kiss to Ava's check. "I apologize, but it was funny." He rubbed his hands together in anticipation. "Now that Reign is here, maybe your mom will let me sample the cake."

"Go ahead and try," Ava said. She followed Malcom's progress as he practically ran to the kitchen. "He's going to get hit with a spatula, watch," she said to Chase, who erupted with laughter.

"You just set him up." Chase laughed.

"I know, and surprisingly, I feel a little badly about it," Ava admitted, amusement filling her voice.

Chase laughed again, then the humor left his face. "All joking aside...are you happy with him?"

Ava smiled warm. "Yes, I *am*." After consistently dating Malcom, Ava had finally decided to commit to a relationship. "I mean, it still feels weird to say that I have a *boyfriend* again after damn near ten years—"

Chase chuckled.

"*However*," Ava continued, humor lacing her voice. "He's proven himself thus far, and I can't complain... It's been a great two months."

"Good to hear, he's a good man." Chase folded his arms. "And he better *stay* that way."

Ava smirked. "I'm confident that he will."

Chase gave a nod. "Just saying, I would hate to have to step to him the way *you* stepped to *Reign* about *me*."

Ava's eyes widened. *Oooh shit.* "She told you about that, huh?"

"She did," her brother confirmed. "It slipped out recently. I had to practically drag the rest of the details out of her."

Ava fiddled with the bracelet on her wrist. "So...how do you feel about that?" she slowly drug out. "Are you about to yell at me?"

Chase tilted his head, fixing her with a stern stare. "I remember telling you to stay *out* of it." His face softened after a moment. "But, I appreciate you looking out for me."

Ava smiled back. "No problem," she replied, sincere. "But that was the first *and* last argument that she and I will be having over your ass, trust me."

Chase chuckled and shook his head.

Ava gave his arm a light tap. "Besides, I don't even have to ask if *you're* happy because I can see it all over your face." She pushed her hair over her shoulder. "*Both* of you just walking around glowing."

Chase's smile was so bright, it could have lit the entire cul-de-sac. "I *am*. Happier than I've ever been."

"I knew you *would* be, and I'm happy *for* you." Ava smirked. "I take it that the move to Vegas is off the table."

"That shit was off the table after I went to Rae's house the night that you got drunk," he chuckled. Ava giggled. "No, my home is *here*."

Ava nodded in approval. "Glad to hear it." A loud yelp from the kitchen interrupted anything else she had to say. Reign darted out, doubled over with laughter.

"What just happened?" Chase asked.

Reign took a moment to compose herself. "Malcom just tried to cut a piece of cake because your dad told him that he could, and your mom smacked his hand with a spatula," she told.

Chase busted out laughing, while Ava put her hand over her face, shaking her head in amusement.

Reign opened her front door, walking in with Chase following behind her. "That was fun," she said.

"Yeah," Chase agreed, closing the door behind him. Plastic bag in hand, he followed Reign into the kitchen. "Mom overcooked as *usual*." He set the leftovers on the counter island.

"I'm not complaining, I'll be eating on those leftovers for the next few days." Reign grabbed a container from the bag; removing the lid, the delicious aroma hit her nose. "Hell, I'm heating some of this up *now*."

Chase laughed. "Hungry again, already?"

"Yup." She headed for the microwave. "I'm going back to the gym tomorrow, so I might as well get all of my overeating in now," she joked, placing the container inside. "I feel like I've gained ten pounds over these past few weeks."

Chase chuckled. "You haven't," he said. "Even if you *did*, you'd still be beautiful."

Reign glanced at him, smirking. "Yeah, you just had *better* said that."

He laughed, "It's the truth."

Reign pulled her food from the microwave when the beep sounded. "Do you want me to heat you up some?"

Chase looked at his watch. "No thanks, I'm still full actually." He let out a sigh. "I should probably get going."

Reign's face fell. "Okay." She'd just spent two weeks straight with Chase. Sleeping beside him every night, waking up to him every day, it was something that she had gotten accustomed to. Though she was happy to be home, she was going to miss him the moment he shut the door behind him.

Her voice dropping an octave wasn't missed by Chase. He shot her a questioning gaze. "Do you want me to stay over?"

Reign waved her hand. "No, it's fine. We both need to be up early tomorrow."

Chase nodded. "Yeah, if I stay over, we won't get much sleep."

"Yeeeaaaah," she slowly drew out. Making love every night was *another* thing that she had gotten accustomed to.

Chase folded his arms, eyeing her intensely. "Are you going to give me your *real* answer?"

"Stay over," she blurted out.

A laugh escaped him; she'd read his mind. "You got it." He tapped the countertop with his hand. "I'm going to go home and grab my work clothes for tomorrow, and I'll be back."

"Okay." She watched him walk out of the kitchen.

"Want anything while I'm out?" he asked, poking his head back in the kitchen. Reign shook her head. "Okay. Love you. See you in a bit."

"Love you too—wait, cookie dough ice cream!"

"I *knew* it," Chase hurled back, walking out of the door, earning a giggle from Reign.

Marcy ambled to Troy's door, holding her phone to her ear. "You want me to come in at *what* time?" She rolled her eyes. "Sure, that'll be no problem… Yeah… Okay, got it. See you then. Bye."

Sighing heavily, Marcy tossed her phone in her bag. As she retrieved her key, Marcy stared down at the red designer bag; the one Troy had gifted during their secret affair. All at once, she realized how much she hated it and everything it represented. Shaking her head, she stuck the key in the door.

Troy glanced up from the couch as Marcy walked in. "Back I see," he sneered.

"Yeah, no shit," she bit back, closing the door. "Where *else* do I have to go?"

Rolling his eyes, Troy turned back to his TV show.

Marcy tossed her purse on a chair. "Before you fix your disrespectful ass mouth to say anything, I still plan on leaving as soon as possible."

Troy ran a hand over his head. "You've been saying that shit since you moved *in* here."

Marcy put a hand up. "Look, I *just* started my job two months ago," she reminded. "Despite me working at a damn *hospital*, the job doesn't pay that damn much… I still need to save up."

"How much did you think a medical coder would *make* Marcy? A *doctor's* salary?" Troy mocked, standing from the couch.

"Whatever Troy," Marcy bristled.

Troy put his hands up. "Look, I'm not knocking the job. I don't care if you were working at a *bar*, just make your money and get the hell *out*." Troy was over his unwanted houseguest. "Like a fuckin' fly that can't seem to find the goddamn open window," he grunted. "Just *go* already."

Marcy glared as Troy walked by her. She and Troy had officially ended their doomed relationship six months ago, but with nowhere else to live, no job and no safety net, Marcy had no *choice* but to stay with Troy.

She spun around to face his departing back. "You know what,

you've been a complete and utter *asshole* through this *entire* relationship."

"So what?"

Marcy jerked her head back. "*How* is it that you treated me *better* when we were sneaking around?" she snapped. "Did you *ever* plan on *being* with me in the open? *Damn* Troy, I thought you loved me."

Troy stopped walking. Facing Marcy, he eyed her with disdain. "Not *once* did I say that I loved you." His tone was nasty. "Not *even* when we were fucking."

A loud gasp escaped Marcy; her eyes were bulging. "You son of a—did you treat *Reign* like this?!" she erupted. "I mean, did she *really* put up with this shit for *six years*?!"

Troy scowled. "I told you to keep her name out of your goddamn mouth."

"Or what? You're going to hit me?" Marcy challenged; she pointed at him. "I wish the fuck you *would*. I'll wear your ass out."

He pointed back. "No, I won't hit you. But I *will* put your broke, useless ass out *sooner*."

Marcy scoffed, shaking her head. "It's been over a year and you're *still* not over her?" she realized. "Seriously? You're pathetic."

"You know what? You're right, I *am* pathetic." Troy sighed. "I'm *this* close to losing my job because I don't put the effort in anymore. I spend most of my days sulking around this dirty ass house and I've basically become a shell of my former self and guess what? Unlike *you*, I know that I deserve *all* the shit that's happening to me because I'm a *shitty* ass person."

Marcy glared at him. "So, you let your whole life go to shit over *her*." she fumed. "Someone who can't even stand the *sight* of you."

Resolved, Troy shrugged. "Yeah well, I realize exactly how special Reign was, and I know how much of a mistake I made neglecting her and fucking around with *you*." He shook his head. "I fucked up and I'll just have to live with that." However, it didn't mean that he had yet to move on from that regret, or his thoughts *of* her.

Marcy stared at Troy with pain in her eyes. "I can't believe you could just stand in my face and say that to me." She folded her arms.

"You're deliberately hurting me."

Troy ignored her words; he couldn't care less about her feelings. "Too bad *your* ex doesn't give a shit out *you*."

Marcy was taken aback; she had no idea what he meant.

"Yeah, I was ambushed by Chase a while ago," Troy explained. "He heard that I waited for Reign outside of her job and he practically threatened to *kill* me if I even so much as *looked* at her again."

Marcy narrowed her eyes; this was the first that she'd heard of this. "Hmm…so *that's* what it took for you to be reminded that your relationship with her is dead, huh?" she mocked. "You couldn't move on like a *normal* person, you had to get punked." She let out a laugh. "By *my* ex, who by the way, is better than you in *every* aspect."

Troy smirked. "That's fine," he dismissed. "But me being *punked* can't take away the fact that I've never seen him go hard for *you* like that." He folded his arms. "Guess it's clear that she's special to *him too*."

Marcy rolled her eyes, "Chase and Reign are just *friends*. You know that."

Troy shook his head. "Nah, I'm almost certain that not *only* is he fucking her, but he has feelings for her," he said, digging the knife in further. "And to keep it a hundred…I don't blame him."

Marcy tried to hold a neutral expression, but she couldn't. She glanced down at the floor, eyes tight, jaw clenched. *That can't be true.* Just the mere *thought* of Chase and Reign being together made her see red.

"Thinking about how the two people we hurt have more than likely found happiness with each other, while *we're* miserable?" Troy wondered, cutting into Marcy's thoughts.

Marcy looked up at him, unable to speak.

"Yeah…me too," Troy finished.

Marcy glanced off to the side as Troy headed for the staircase.

"Hurry up and find a damn place to live." He bolted up the steps. "I'll *give* you the damn deposit if it'll get you out sooner."

Feeling tears beginning to build, Marcy covered her face with her hands.

Chapter Forty-Five

REIGN REMOVED THE CLEAR PLASTIC wrap from her sandwich. Raising it to her mouth, she paused short of taking a bite. Frowning, she put the sandwich to her nose, sniffing it. She dry-heaved.

"Eww, what the hell?" she tossed the sandwich on the wrap. "Come in," she called, hearing a knock.

Ava strolled in, smiling bright. "Guess who just killed another developmental editing project?"

Reign looked up at her. "Are you going to do this *every* time you finish one?"

Ava laughed. "Probably." She took a seat.

Reign chuckled. "It's good to know that you love your job."

"I do," Ava affirmed. She eyed the glass vase full of fresh, blooming pink and white orchids on Reign's desk. "Gorgeous flowers," she grinned. "From Chase?"

Reign squinted at her. "You *know* they're from him, you intercepted the delivery," she reminded, earning a giggle from Ava. Reign shook her head, slightly amused. Ava's excitement over Reign and Chase becoming a couple had yet to wane. "But thank you, they *are* beautiful...my favorite flowers."

Ava leaned forward, grabbing a silver picture frame from Reign's desk. "How is that book you're working on, coming along?" Eyeing the five-by-seven photo of the happy couple from their vacation, she smiled. "Awww."

Reign reached over, snatching the frame from Ava's grasp. "Will you stop it?"

Ava laughed, raising her hands. "Okay, okay."

"But to answer your question, it's *going*." Reign set the picture down. "It's a fantasy novel, so it's pretty long. But it's a six-month contract so I have time."

"Are they still talking about moving you to full-time writer?"

"That's the plan," Reign nodded. "*Speaking* of which, Dennis asked me to start giving you more responsibility."

Ava tilted her head. "Okay."

Reign looked at her. "You okay with that?"

"Stop making it seem like I have a choice," Ava chortled, prompting a giggle from Reign. "But yes, I'm okay with that. Like you said, I love my job."

Reign gave a nod. Picking up her uneaten sandwich, she proceeded to rewrap it.

Ava pointed to it. "Not hungry huh?"

Reign paused short of tossing it in the trashcan. "I *am*, but the turkey in this sandwich is spoiled," she spat. "If I weren't so tired, I'd take it back."

"Where did you get it from?" Ava asked.

"The deli around the corner."

Puzzled, Ava frowned. "Seriously? Their food is usually on point." she held her hand out for the sandwich. "Let me smell it." Reign handed it to Ava, who pulled aside the plastic and took a whiff. "Rae, there is nothing wrong with this sandwich."

Reign took it from her. "Ava, it's spoiled. You don't smell it?" she sniffed it again, handing it back to Ava after she nearly gagged.

"*No* crazy, it smells like a *regular* roasted turkey sandwich," Ava maintained, humored.

Reign grabbed her bottle of water, taking a sip. "Well, I'm not eating that," she refused. "You can have it if you want it."

Ava shrugged. "Do you want the sushi that *I* brought for lunch?"

Reign scrunched her face in disgust.

"I'll take that as a no," Ava teased when Reign refused to answer.

Reign shook her head and stuck to her water.

Ellie turned on the kitchen sink; she'd decided to pay her son a visit that afternoon. "You know what I think would be nice?" she asked Chase, washing a dish.

Chase glanced over at her from the refrigerator. "Mom, put the bowl down."

Ellie let out a laugh.

"Stop trying to find something to clean every time you come over." Chase shook his head. "One dish in the sink won't kill you."

She set the bowl down. "Okay, fine," she relented, amused.

Chase chuckled as his mother took a seat at the island. "So, what do you think would be nice?" he asked, going back to the original topic.

She folded her arms on the countertop. "I think we should have a big family dinner."

Closing the refrigerator, lunch meat and cheese in hand, Chase eyed her, trying to suss out what she had in mind. "You mean with our extended family?"

"No, I mean with us and *Reign's* family."

Chase raised an eyebrow. "And just *when* do you plan on doing this?"

Ellie shrugged. "I don't know…Thanksgiving maybe?" she answered. "It's what, a month away?"

Chase began to prepare himself and his mother a sandwich. "Uh huh," he muttered. "Do you plan on inviting *Malcom's* family?"

"For your information, I *did* ask Ava about it, but she said no." She chuckled. "I don't think she's reached the 'meet the family' stage of her relationship yet."

Chase moved to the island, setting a plate in front of his mother. "Oh okay."

Ellie studied him as soon as he sat down. "You don't think it's a good idea?" she assumed, picking up on his lackluster response.

"I didn't say that," he denied.

"You don't think she would agree to it?" she followed up.

"I didn't say *that* either."

Noticing the look that Chase was giving her, his mother frowned. "Why are you looking at me like that?" she asked. "Like you think I'm being sneaky?"

"I'm just wondering if there's a bigger reason why you want to get both families together so soon." He leaned back in his seat. "Are you expecting something to *happen*?"

Her mouth fell open. "Son, are you accusing me of plotting to get everyone together in hopes of a *proposal*?"

Chase pointed at her. "Knew *exactly* what I was talking about."

She let out a laugh. "Chase, that's not what I'm trying to do," she promised. "I just think that it would be nice to have Thanksgiving with them. After all, they're family too."

Chase shook his head in amusement. "You almost sound convincing."

"I'm *serious*." Ellie gave his arm a light tap. "I know that you two have only been together six months, and though I know where your heart is, I don't expect you to *propose* that soon."

Chase looked at her, tilting his head. "You think that six months is too soon to propose?"

"Absolutely not," Ellie answered, honest. "If you know it's right, it doesn't matter *how* soon you do it."

Chase nodded as his mother took a bite of her sandwich. "I agree." He paused for a moment. "Which is exactly why I already bought a ring."

Ellie's eyes nearly popped out of her head. She took a sip of water to push the rest of her food down. "Wait, you *what*?"

Chase smiled, "I bought an engagement ring."

Ellie clasped her hands together in delight, tears of joy filling her eyes. "Oh my God," she gushed. "I'm so proud of you."

He chuckled. "For *what*?"

"Just for…being a good man." She dabbed her eyes dry with a napkin. "I would say *more*, but I'll just embarrass you."

"Thank you," Chase replied, sincere. "I have no idea *when* or *how* I'm going to propose, but it won't be on Thanksgiving…sorry."

"Son, you do it whenever and *wherever* you feel is best." Ellie grinned. "Just make sure you call me *right* afterwards."

"I will." He sighed after a moment. "*Plus*...I want to make sure that *she* doesn't think it's too soon." He broke eye contact, staring off to the side. "Part of me wonders if she might think it's a bit crazy to get engaged already. I mean *yeah*, we've been friends for *years*, but a *relationship* is another level, so...I don't know."

Ellie fixed her son with a serious gaze. "Honestly Chase, I don't believe that she would," she said. "After being with someone who didn't know what they had—someone who wasted her damn time, I'm sure she *appreciates* being with someone who knows *exactly* what they want and is not afraid to *show* it."

Chase just nodded, though he was still unsure. He knew that Reign loved him; he had no doubts about that. But he wasn't sure if she'd be ready for *marriage* after only six months. Would she feel that it was too fast? Would she believe that *he* was ready? "Thanks Mom," he answered, despite the questions swirling in his head.

Ellie smiled.

"I'll talk to her about Thanksgiving," he promised.

"Ooh, they have pumpkin cheesecake," Vivian beamed, picking up a box. She showed it to Reign. "You want to try this?"

Reign glanced at it. "Not really, but don't let me stop you from getting it." Her voice was tired.

Vivian set the pie box back into the freezer. "Eh, no need in buying this big ol' cheesecake if I'm going to be the only one eating it." She peered at the items in her shopping cart. "Your father doesn't like pumpkin and Cynthia hates cheesecake."

"Makes sense, I guess," Reign replied, unenthused.

Reign's quick visit to her parents' home had turned into an impromptu trip to the grocery store with her mother. "How much stuff do you need?"

"Not much," Vivian answered. "Am I holding you up? I can take a cab home if you have to go."

"Mom don't be silly, I'm not leaving you." Reign patted her mother's shoulder. "I wasn't trying to rush you."

Vivian glanced at Reign while she pushed her shopping cart down the aisle. Her daughter was rubbing her face with her hands. "Are you okay?"

Pulling her hands away, Reign pushed her hair behind her shoulder. "I'm not going to lie, I don't feel good today."

Concern fell upon Vivian's face. "What is it? Are you coming down with another cold?"

"I don't think so, I'm just feeling…off," Reign tried to explain. "Like, physically just *off*."

Vivian grabbed a few items from a shelf. "It's not stress, is it?"

Reign shook her head. "No, I don't have anything to be stressed *about*. My job is great, my *relationship* is great…" she shrugged. "I don't know, maybe I'm just having an off day or something."

Vivian nodded slowly. "You just started feeling like this *today*?"

"I doubt you're going to figure out what the issue is, so you can stop the twenty questions," Reign chortled.

Vivian twisted her lips. "It hasn't been *twenty*, smarty pants," she threw back; Reign smirked. "And I'm not trying to be nosey, I'm just *concerned*."

"Okay fine." Reign sighed. "It's not just *today*. I've been feeling weird for about a week or so."

"Or so?"

"Mom— Yes, *or so*," Reign huffed. "I'm sure I'm fine, so can we drop the subject please?" Grabbing a bottle of syrup from the shelf, she skimmed the label before turning to her mother, "Hey, have you ever had—" She paused; her mother was eyeing her skeptically. Reign frowned. "Is there something on my face?"

"No," Vivian answered.

"Then *why* are you looking at me like that?"

Vivian took the syrup from Reign, placing it in the cart. "We should stop by the pharmacy section."

Puzzled, Reign squinted. "Why?"

"To get you prenatal vitamins."

The confusion had not faded from Reign's face. "*For?*"

Her mother grinned. "For your baby."

Reign's eyes widened. "Mom—" She put a hand up, "It's cute that you're no longer hiding your desire for a grandchild, but you're crazy. I am not pregnant."

"You're sure about that?" Vivian questioned.

"Yes, I am *sure*," Reign ground out. "Just because I don't feel well, doesn't mean that that is the case. Relax, okay."

Vivian put her hands up in surrender. "Okay." A hint of a smile remained on her face.

Reign narrowed her eyes. "What are you smiling for *Vivian?*"

"No reason," Vivian answered, innocently.

Reign folded her arms. "Um hmm."

"So moody," Vivian teased. "You should stock up on ginger tea too, it helps with morning sickness."

Reign rolled her eyes. "Yeah, okay, don't make me rethink leaving you here," she bit out, earning a loud snicker from her mother.

Reign rubbed her tired eyes before returning her hands to her keyboard. Her fingers moved at high speed as she focused solely on the words on the screen. She glanced at the time on the monitor; eleven-fifteen PM. Reign had been in her home office writing for approximately three hours. Hearing her cell phone ring, she grabbed it, smiling at the name on the screen. "Hey baby," she crooned, cradling the phone between her ear and shoulder.

Chase smiled at the endearing greeting. "Hey your*self.*"

"Why are you still up?" she asked, typing.

"I guess I should ask *you* the same thing." Amusement laced his voice.

She smirked. "I'm writing." she told. "I couldn't sleep, so figured I'd get some work done." She leaned back in her seat, stretching. "You?"

"Well, I'm definitely not *writing*," Chase chortled, earning a giggle from Reign. "But I couldn't sleep either, so I'm just sitting out on my deck." He grabbed his glass of iced tea, taking a quick sip. "Figured I was taking a chance by calling at this time, but I wanted to check on you to see if you were feeling better from earlier."

Reign rubbed her forehead; Chase was aware that she had been feeling a bit run down.

"A little," she answered. "That nap I took after I left my parents' house, seemed to help a bit…which would explain why I'm still up."

"Well, that's good." He breathed a sigh of relief. "I'd hate to think that you were coming down with another cold or something."

"No, I doubt that's what's going on." She sighed. "I probably just need another vacation or something. I've been writing nonstop on this new project these past few weeks."

"We could go to Colorado for a few days next month… You want to see snow, right?" Chase proposed, excited.

Reign smiled. *God, I love how he listens to me.* "Yes, I want to see snow."

"Then it's settled, I'll make the plans." He ran a hand over his head. "Do you plan on going to sleep *any* time soon?"

Reign saved her document. "Probably *not*, but I *do* need to give the imagination a rest for the night," she replied. "Sitting out on the patio sounds like a good idea, I'll probably go sit out on mine. It's about time that I give that fire pit that I spent all of that money on, a test drive."

Chase took another sip of his tea, chuckling in the process. After a moment, he sighed, the humor leaving his face. He knew the real reason why he was having trouble sleeping; he wasn't sleeping next to Reign. It was getting harder for him to not wake up next to her every day.

"Would you like company?" he offered.

Reign tucked some of her hair behind her ear, a smile building. "Yes, I would."

Beaming, Chase stood from his chair. "Okay, I'll be there in ten."

Reign wrapped a small fleece blanket around her shoulders as she watched Chase set the fire pit alight. She smiled at the flames rising up.

Chase glanced at her. "I take it by the size of that smile, that you're pleased with your purchase?" he asked, amused.

Reign giggled. "Yes."

Chase walked over, taking the cushioned seat next to her. Reign grabbed a mug of hot chocolate from the table, handing it to him.

"Thank you, baby," he replied, taking a careful sip.

"You're welcome." Reign picked up her own mug; it tasted perfect. "It's nice out."

"I know right," Chase nodded, setting his mug down. Inhaling the fresh night air, he surveyed Reign's backyard.

Over the past few months, she'd traded her metal table and chair set for a cushioned patio sofa with matching chairs and table, plus a larger patio umbrella. She'd also added a grill, the fire pit, outdoor lighting, and had landscaping done.

Reign caught his eyes roaming. "Are you looking for that rabbit?" she teased.

A deep laugh erupted from Chase. "Still won't let me live that down, will you?"

"Nah," she laughed back. "At least not for the next fifty years."

He leaned back, putting his arm around her. "Well, at least it's nice that you're still planning on *putting up* with me for the next fifty years."

She leaned her head on his shoulder. "Give or take," she joked.

Chase shook his head in amusement.

They sat in comfortable silence for a while, relishing each other's presence.

"Can I ask you a question?" Chase began.

"Of course."

He hesitated for a moment "How do you feel about timelines?"

"Timelines?" Reign questioned, adjusting the cover over her chest. "As in what?"

"As in relationships?" he clarified. "Do you believe there is a standard timeline for things to progress between a couple? Proposal, marriage, children?"

"I *used* to," Reign admitted. "When I was younger, I thought that the norm was date a year or two, be engaged for a year, then get married and have children." She shrugged. "But *now*...I don't believe that there *is* a standard timeline—well, there is a such thing as waiting *too long* to progress, but..."

"Do you believe that those things can happen... too *soon?*" Chase wondered when she trailed off.

"As long as the couple is sure that they want to build a life together, no," Reign answered.

Nodding slowly, a look of relief set on his face. He placed a kiss to the top of Reign's head. "I agree."

Reign lifted her head, looking at him "What made you ask me that?"

Chase eyed her back. "Just...getting a feel for what you consider normal or not," he answered. "Want to make sure we're on the same page."

Reign raised an eyebrow. The topic was so random, she couldn't help but wonder if he was leaving something out. "Oh."

Chase chuckled; the skeptical look that she was giving him wasn't missed. He leaned in, planting a tender kiss to her lips. "It's nothing to worry about, I promise you."

Reign smiled softly, nodding. "Okay...I believe you."

Chase grinned back. "Good."

Chapter Forty-Six

MARCY STOOD ALONE IN THE middle of a small living room, plastic cup in hand. "This is pathetic," she uttered. Shaking her head, she surveyed the boxes strewn about the furniture-less space that had become her new home.

Going from her own spacious two-bedroom apartment, to Troy's house, to her *current* tiny studio apartment—Marcy felt as if she was moving backwards.

Unable to put up with Troy any longer, Marcy had sold many of her prized possessions— including her precious designer bags— in order to come up with the deposit. With the previous eviction on Marcy's credit report, the only apartment complex that would rent to her was *Reign's* old building. Desperate, Marcy had taken the first available, albeit *smallest* apartment there.

If walking into that building everyday wasn't sad enough, having her apartment right down the hall from where Reign used to live, was torture. It was a constant reminder of all that she had lost.

Grabbing the half-empty bottle of port wine from atop a cardboard box, Marcy filled her cup then plopped down to the floor. Feeling the hard floor under her behind, she grimaced. "Freakin' thin ass carpet." Setting the bottle on the floor beside her, she took a sip, making a face at the bitter taste. "Drank damn near this entire cheap ass bottle and it *still* tastes no better."

Letting out a deep huff, Marcy sipped her drink. Finished, she set it aside, dragging a box in front of her.

She pulled the tape off, then paused, examining her nails. Gone were the long, sculptured nails with the extravagant colors. Her nails were short, brittle and clear. She couldn't remember the last time that she'd had a manicure.

Running a hand over her hair, smoothing wayward strands up into her messy bun, Marcy opened the box. Eyeing the bathroom accessories inside, Marcy rolled her eyes, pushing the entire box aside. *Everything in that damn box is going to clash with that ugly yellow paint in the bathroom*, she thought.

Scanning the space with her eyes, Marcy tried to figure out how she would arrange the furniture that she still had in storage. How would it even fit? Better yet, how she would be able to *get* it from storage in the first place. She had no car, and no friends; Troy had made it clear that he wanted nothing to do with her. Worse, she didn't have money for a moving trunk and movers.

Huffing loudly, Marcy reached for a refill. But there wasn't a drop left to drink. Marcy slammed the empty bottle to the floor, then threw the empty cup across the room in a fit of frustration. Folding her knees to her chest, she put her head down, letting out a deep sigh. *Fuck my life.*

Sitting on a stool in front of Chase's counter island, Ava twisted the bottle opener until it tightened. "If there's *one* thing that I can count on when I come to your house Chase, it's that you always have a good bottle of wine," she said, popping the cork.

Positioned at the stove, Chase glanced at her. "Nice to know how important that is to you," he jeered.

Ava giggled, pouring herself a glass of red wine. "I feel like I should be helping you with dinner." She took a quick sip. "Instead of sitting here being useless."

Flipping a piece of breaded fish in the pan, Chase shook his head. "No, you *don't.*"

"You're right, I don't." Ava swirled the wine in her glass. "You know how much I love having people cook for me. Which is yet *another* reason why I like Malcom… He can cook."

Chase let out a chuckle as he tended to the fish frying in the skillet. After work that Tuesday, Ava had dropped by for an unexpected visit while Chase was in the middle of preparing dinner for himself and Reign; Chase had invited her to stay and join them.

"The other day, he made a Cornish hen that was better than *Mom's*," Ava boasted. She pointed her finger at her brother. "Don't tell her I said that."

"I won't," Chase promised, amused. "Rae and I took a 'date night' cooking class a while ago and we learned how to make Paella. It turned out pretty good." He checked his fish. "You and Malcom should come over next Saturday, I'll make it."

Ava gave a nod of approval. "Sounds good to me. I'll let him know." She took another sip of wine. "*Speaking* of Rae, what time is she coming over?"

"She's *been* here," he told. "Poor baby was exhausted. I told her to go lay down until the food is finished."

Ava grimaced. "Yeah, she seemed pretty lethargic at work today." She set her glass down. "I told her that she should've stayed home today but…well, you already know how she is."

"Yeah." Chase removed the filets of golden-brown fish from the pan. He set them on a paper towel covered plate to rest. "To be honest, Rae hasn't been feeling well for weeks…" He let out a sigh, "It's worrying me."

"Has she been to the doctor?"

"No." He looked at Ava. "I suggested that she go, but she insists that it's just due to lack of sleep."

Ava shook her head. "That girl isn't going to go get checked out until she *passes* out," she huffed.

A stern frown crossed Chase's face. "Don't even speak that into existence."

"You're right, I'm sorry," she agreed, putting a hand up. "Positive thoughts only… I'm sure she's fine."

Chase sighed again, staring down at the pot of rice in front of him. "Yeah," he uttered.

Taking note of Chase's worried state, Ava tilted her head. "Do you want me to change the subject?"

Chase nodded. "Please." He couldn't bear the thought of something being wrong with Reign. His sister was right; he needed to keep positive.

"Okay then." She drummed her nails on the counter. "I'm thinking of buying a house within the next year or so."

Chase glanced at her. "Yeah?"

Ava nodded, reaching back for her glass. "Yeah... Don't get me wrong, I love my condo, but I could use more space."

Chase nodded slowly. "Would you want to buy *this* house?"

Ava nearly choked on the wine that she'd just sipped. Grabbing a napkin, she dabbed the droplets from her chin. "You're planning on selling?" she asked, regaining her composure. "I thought you loved this house."

"I *do* like my house, but I'd have no problem parting with it." He turned the stove off. "I mean, I have to start thinking about the future and if things go how I *hope*, Reign and I will be living together eventually and..."

"You don't think she'd move in *here* with you?" Ava jumped in. "Or even to a *new* house?"

"Reign loves her house," Chase declared. "She worked hard for it, she's *proud* of it—" He folded his arms, leaning against the counter. "I'm sure she'd move for me, but...why should I *make* her? Like I said, I can part with my house."

Ava nodded, smiling. "True," she said. "And you wouldn't have a problem moving into *her* home?"

"Not at all," Chase answered.

"Have you talked to her about this?"

Chase shook his head slightly. "Not yet."

Ava placed a hand on her chest. "Well, *I* for one, think you're a sweetheart for taking her feelings into consideration." She rose from her seat. "But, the way that your relationship is progressing, you'll be moving in together sooner than I'd be ready to buy, so don't wait on me."

Chase chuckled, "Noted." He followed Ava's progress as she walked away. "Where are you going?"

She flashed an innocent look his way. "I'm going to wake Rae up."

Chase glared. "Ava, don't bother her," he warned. "She'll get up when she's ready."

Ava waved a dismissive hand. "Hush and make sure you don't burn my food."

"Yeah, burning food is *your* thing," Chase hurled at her departing back.

"Oh shut up!" Ava belted out.

Reign laid on her side, clutching a pillow to her chest. Though she had been in Chase's bed for at least a few hours, she'd only closed her eyes for approximately fifteen minutes. Despite her energy being nonexistent, she just couldn't seem to fall asleep.

Hearing a light tap on the door, Reign rolled on her back and let out a sigh. "*Yes*, Ava?"

Ava busted through the door, amusement showing on her face. "How did you know it was me?"

"Chase wouldn't have knocked," Reign pointed out, voice tired. "Plus, I heard you come in earlier."

Sitting on the bed, Ava looked down at Reign, who stared back up at her, perplexed.

"What?" Reign questioned.

"Sis, you look miserable," Ava blurted out.

Reign couldn't help but laugh a little. "Shut up," she rolled back on her side.

Ava leaned on Reign, tapping her arm. "Dinner is almost ready, you might as well get up."

Letting out a groan, Reign put a hand over her face. "*God* Ava, go somewhere, will you?"

Ava playfully poked Reign's shoulder. "Get up best friend. Get up, get up, get up," she sang.

Reign nudged the laughing Ava off her. "You are fuckin' insufferable," she bit out, sitting up.

Ava adjusted her position as Reign leaned back against the

pillows. "My *insufferable* behavior aside...what's going on with you, luv?" All traces of humor were gone. "You've been sick for a while—"

"I am not *sick*, I am just not feeling *well*," Reign cut in, voice filled with annoyance.

Ava raised an eyebrow. "Explain the difference to me."

Reign opened her mouth to flash back, but couldn't. "I *would*, but my brain is on pause right now." She ran a hand through her hair, sighing. "I'm fine sis, I've just been a bit tired. A few headaches here and there— Nothing major."

"You don't think you need to go to the doctor?" Ava probed. "I mean, this isn't normal for you."

"No, I *don't*."

"Okay." Ava moved her hair over her shoulder. "A *pregnancy test* maybe?"

Reign frowned at the suggestion. "Have you been talking to my mother?"

Intrigued, Ava's brows raised. "Oh, *she* suggested the same thing?"

"She did." Reign folded her arms. "I don't understand *why* it is that when a woman says that she's not feeling well, *pregnancy* is automatically the assumption."

Ava chuckled. "Yeah, your hormones must be on ten right now, because that was an asinine statement," she countered. Reign rolled her eyes. "It's not an assumption of *all* women, it's *you* and the circumstances."

"Yeah, yeah," Reign grumbled. After a moment, she brought a hand to her face, examining her nails. She exhaled deeply. "I actually *did* buy a test," she confessed.

Ava tilted her head, eyeing her intently. "Did you take it already?"

Reign shook her head. "I'm still trying to psyche myself up to do it."

"Have you told Chase?"

"Not yet," Reign answered, meeting Ava's inquisitive gaze. "Again, still trying to psyche myself up... We haven't been together that long, so if it's positive—I'm not sure how he'll react."

Ava pointed at her. "Him or *you?*"

Reign squinted her eyes. "I *hate* that you can read me."

Ava giggled. "*Most* of the time anyway." She put a caring hand on Reign's arm. "The sooner you take it, the sooner you'll know."

"Duh," Reign spat, earning a snicker from Ava. "Now move so I can get up. I'm starving."

Ava's lip curled. "Ugh, I hope that it *is* pregnancy that's causing this unbecoming rude behavior of yours." She crossed her arms. "I'd be okay dealing with it if it means that I get a niece or nephew out of the deal."

Reign flung a dismissive gesture Ava's way. "*Move.*"

While Chase wiped the kitchen table down, Reign was taking care of the dishes.

Chase looked over at her. "Baby, I said that I would take care of those," he said. "You need to rest."

"Doing a few dishes isn't going to hurt me, Chase," she ground out, still washing. Immediately feeling bad for her curt reply, Reign closed her eyes, letting out a sigh. "I'm sorry. That was uncalled for." She placed a clean dish into the rack. "I know that you're just trying to look out for me."

"It's okay," Chase assured, going back to tidying up.

Ava had gone home nearly an hour ago, leaving the couple alone once again.

Chase glanced at Reign once again as she continued with the dishes. He chuckled a bit. "You know, I don't understand why you don't just use the dishwasher," he mentioned. "The one in *your* house still has the plastic on it."

She shrugged slightly. "I guess I'm just used to washing by hand," she reasoned, even toned. "I didn't *have* one until I moved into my house."

"Makes sense, I guess." Chase approached the sink; Reign moved aside to allow him access to the water. As he ran the dishrag under the warm water, he kissed her cheek. She turned her head, allowing him another peck on her lips.

She offered a half smile. "Was that for the great job that I'm doing on these dishes?" she joked.

A small laugh escaped Chase. "No, that was for that *brownie sundae* you made for dessert," he joked in return.

Reign shook her head in amusement, but didn't respond. As Chase went to put the leftovers away, the traces of humor left Reign's face. She was glad that her back was facing him, or he would have seen the worry on her face.

Reign wasn't sure how she was going to bring up the fact that she could be pregnant. She had mulled over the idea of just taking the test and telling him only if it came out positive. But when they'd become a couple, she had promised herself *and* him to be honest about everything that she was thinking and feeling.

"What movie should I put on?" Chase asked, breaking through Reign's thoughts. "It probably doesn't matter; we're going to fall asleep on it anyway."

She turned the water off. "I bought a pregnancy test."

Chase regarded her with a questioning look. "What did you say?"

Reign dried her hands on a towel. "I brought a pregnancy test," she repeated, looking at him.

Chase stared at her, wide-eyed. "You—you think that the reason why you haven't been feeling well is because you're *pregnant*?"

She shrugged, "I didn't at *first*, but now..." Reign sighed, "I don't know...maybe."

Chase rubbed the back of his neck. "Well...it's not like we've been *entirely careful* every time we've—"

"I know," Reign slid in. She stared at him as a brief silence fell between them. "What are you thinking?"

Chase let out a deep breath. On the inside, he was excited at the possibility of becoming a father; it had been something that he had been thinking about. Sure, it would be ideal for them to be *married* first, but he would be happy either way. "I'm thinking that...you should take it now so that we can find out for certain," he answered finally.

Reign took a deep breath. "Like *right* now?"

"Yes," he chortled. "You seem nervous."

"A little," she admitted.

Chase closed the distance between them and took her hand. "No matter the outcome, everything will be fine."

She nodded. "Okay."

Chase stood outside of the bathroom waiting. Shifting his weight from one foot to the other, he ran a hand over the top of his head. "You okay in there?" he asked through the closed door.

"Chase, I do *not* want you standing by the door listening to me pee. Go somewhere," Reign spat.

Laughing, Chase put his hands up. "Okay, okay." He backed away. "I'll be in the bedroom, just call me when you're ready."

"I will."

Chase walked into his bedroom, taking a seat on the edge of his bed. Running his hands down his pants, a deep sigh escaped him. After a few moments, Reign entered. Chase jumped up, "Is it—"

Reign put a hand up. "It takes five minutes," she interrupted, tone calm. She gestured for him to sit back down. When he complied, she took a seat next to him.

"Okay." He rubbed his hands down his legs again. Growing restless, he looked at her. "Should we do something to take our minds off of waiting?"

Reign stared at him; humor crossed her face. "It's *five minutes*, baby," she said. "It's not much that we can get done in that small amount of time." In a way, she felt a bit of relief; he seemed to be as nervous as *she* was.

"Right," Chase nodded, then scratched his head. "I guess this is a good time to tell you that my mother would like for you and your family to have Thanksgiving with us this year."

Reign nodded slowly. "That's nice of her."

"I meant to mention this before now, but I got sidetracked."

"It's okay," she assured. "I'll see what my parents say, but in all honesty I don't see them turning down the invite."

Chase nodded. "Cool…if they *do* accept, please let Ms. Vivian know that she doesn't have to worry about bringing anything."

"Yeah, that's not going to happen," Reign chortled. Chase chuckled himself.

Hearing the phone alarm beep from the bathroom, she stood from the bed just as Chase bolted up. "You can wait here," she offered.

Chase vigorously shook his head.

She shrugged. "Very well." Reign walked out of the room with her boyfriend following close behind her.

Chase stood at the door while Reign went inside. She glanced at the stick on the sink. Picking it up, she fixated on it for a moment before throwing it in the trash.

Exiting the bathroom, she stood face to face with Chase, who was leaning against the wall, face full of anticipation.

His eyes lit with hope. "Well?"

Reign opened her mouth to speak, then closed it. Opting instead to just shake her head no.

Chase's face fell. "Negative, huh?"

"Yeah," she confirmed, tone low.

Chase took a deep breath, "Okay… at least we know."

Reign held her gaze on him. "I'm sorry," she said after a moment.

His brow furrowed in confusion. "Why are you apologizing?"

"Judging by the look on your face," she began, gesturing to his face. "You were hoping that it was positive."

Chase immediately regretted his facial reaction. "Baby, I didn't mean to make you feel like—"

"It's okay," she cut in, sincere. "I'm not going to lie… I wouldn't have been upset if it were positive either."

Chase reached out, enveloping Reign in a loving hug. He planted a kiss on the top of her head. "When the time is right, it'll happen," he consoled. He hoped that it offered her some comfort, although it didn't offer *him* any.

She held on to him, burying her face in his chest. "I know."

Chapter Forty-Seven

SEATED IN A SMALL OFFICE, Marcy scanned through pictures in her phone while she ate her lunch. She'd just taken another bite of the microwaved pasta dish, when the office door opened; Marcy peered up at the visitor.

"Marcy, I need you to call the insurance company and find out if these ICD9 codes are covered for these patients," the woman curtly demanded, placing a folder on Marcy's desk.

Marcy fought the urge to roll her eyes at the middle-aged woman standing before her. *Damn, can't even bother to say "hi" before you start barking demands?* she thought of her supervisor.

Marcy moved her food aside, then pulled the folder to her, opening it. Flipping through the pages of patient's names, she frowned. "It's like fifty codes per *patient* in here."

The woman flashed a cold, stern stare Marcy's way. "Is that going to be a problem?"

Marcy snapped the folder closed, stifling a snide remark. "No, it won't be a problem Ms. Grace, it'll get done."

"Good." Ms. Grace made her way out of the office. "Oh and just a reminder: you get thirty minutes for lunch, *not forty-five,*" she threw over her shoulder. "And those codes need to be verified before you leave for the day."

Marcy gritted her teeth. *Oh my God, I went over my lunch break one time, why are you still making a big deal of it?* "Got it," she managed to get out. Once the door closed, Marcy sucked her teeth, pushing the folder aside. "Fuckin' bitch," she grunted to herself.

Like every job she'd had before this, Marcy hated *this* one too. But unlike before, getting fired wasn't an option. She had no backup plan that didn't include crawling back to her parents in San Diego. She'd work *four* jobs before letting that happen; the judgment *alone* would destroy her.

Marcy glanced at her watch, then let out a huff—her lunch time was up. When the office door opened again, Marcy braced herself for more demands from her boss. Seeing her coworker and another woman walk in instead, Marcy feigned a smile.

The young women offered a wave before engaging in their side conversation.

"After we clock out for the day, let's go get some drinks," one woman proposed.

"I'm down," the other agreed, excited. "Want to go to dinner first?"

"Yup."

Back facing the chatty women, Marcy rolled her eyes as she once again opened her folder. *God, will y'all take that noise elsewhere?* Another thing she hated: sharing the small space with her fellow biller, who often had visits from other coworkers.

"Marcy."

Exhaling deeply, Marcy rubbed her temples. "What's up Tara?" she answered, unenthused.

"If Ms. Grace comes in, can you tell her that I ran to the bathroom?"

"You *just* got back, but *sure* Tara," Marcy agreed, tone not changing.

As Tara and her friend scurried out of the office, Marcy grabbed the office phone, preparing to make her phone calls, but paused short of dialing.

Marcy couldn't help but replay the conversation that she'd overhead. Sure, it only consisted of plans for dinner and drinks between friends, but it reminded Marcy that she didn't *have* friends to go out with. Though Marcy had hung out with other people in the past, Reign had been her only friend.

Letting out a sigh, Marcy set her office phone back in the cradle, picking up her cell instead. Scrolling through her photos once again, she began deleting pictures of Troy—another person who was no longer in her life.

As her photos began to dwindle due to multiple deletions, she happened across one of her and Reign—taken the night of Reign's thirtieth birthday. Marcy's eyes lingered on the picture, her finger hovering over the delete button. But no matter how much she willed herself to erase it, she couldn't. Tears filling her eyes, Marcy clicked out of the app.

She couldn't help it, she missed Reign. Pulling up Reign's number—yet another thing that she couldn't delete—Marcy stared at the screen. Tears spilled down her face as she fought the urge to press dial.

God, I just want to talk to her, but would she even be willing to talk? Has enough time passed? How would I even start the conversation? Could she ever forgive me?

With so many questions pounding in Marcy's head, she cleared the number from her screen. Tears still clouding her eyes, she slid the phone aside. With a heavy sigh, she made her first work call.

Sitting on an accent chair in Cynthia's bedroom, Reign rubbed her temples as her sister danced around the space. "Cyn, can you please turn the music down? I have a headache."

Cynthia sucked her teeth, but did as she was asked. "Fine," she huffed. "Is this better, bossy?"

"I'd prefer that it was *off*, but I guess I'll settle for this," Reign jeered.

Cynthia waved a dismissive hand her sister's way.

Reign had stopped by to pick up Cynthia from their parents' house so that Cynthia could run some errands. But as always, her sister wasn't ready. "I swear this is like déjà vu, can you *please* hurry up?"

"Okay, okay." Cynthia pulled a sweatshirt over her head. "If I would've *known* you were going to be so damn *cranky*, I wouldn't have asked you to take me."

Reign frowned at her. "What other option do you *have*?" she gestured to the car keys laying on her sister's dresser. "Your car is out of commission and Mom and Dad won't let you step foot in *theirs.*"

Cynthia put a hand up. "My car just needs a little TLC."

"It needs a new *engine!*" Reign belted out, exasperated. "I *told* you not to buy that old piece of crap."

"Yeah well… I thought it had potential," Cynthia mumbled, adjusting the high, naturally coiled puff atop her head. She placed a pair of earrings into her ears, then grabbed a bottle of body spray from her dresser, giving herself several sprays from head to toe.

Reign covered her nose and mouth as the pungent fruit smell filled the air. "What scent is that?"

Cynthia examined the bottle in her hand. "'Peach Blossom'," she read aloud. She turned to Reign, puzzled. "You don't like it?"

Holding her hand in place, Reign did not respond.

Cynthia shrugged, then went to spray some more; she stopped when Reign put a hand up, vigorously shaking her head.

"Please don't spray anymore," Reign begged.

"What the hell is wrong with you?" Cynthia huffed, tossing her arms in the air. "This is the *same* scent as that air freshener I had in my dorm room. The one that you said you *liked.*"

As Reign went to speak, she felt her stomach turn. She placed a hand to her stomach as the nauseous feeling intensified. "Shit," she panicked, grabbing the nearest trashcan.

Cynthia's eyes widened. "Oh hell no!" she screamed as Reign threw up in the can. "Eww, are you *serious*?!"

The door flew open, Vivian bolting in. "What is all of that yelling—" Her eyes zoned in on Reign—face in the trash can—vomiting sounds coming from her. Eyes widening, she darted over. "Oh my God, what happened?"

"She puked in my damn room, is what happened," Cynthia fumed.

Vivian snapped her head in Cynthia's direction, fixing her youngest daughter with a stern look. "Your mouth."

Cynthia tossed her hands in the air in frustration.

"Now go and get your sister some water," Vivian demanded, pointing to the door.

Rolling her eyes, Cynthia stomped out of the room.

Reign lifted her head from the can, a hand over her mouth; her eyes were glassed over with tears.

Vivian carefully took the can from Reign's trembling hand. "It's okay sweetheart," she soothed. "I'll take care of this."

Not uttering a word, Reign stood up, then scurried out to the bathroom.

After lingering in the bathroom for nearly fifteen minutes, Reign left feeling worse than when she'd ran in. Between the worsening headache, the newly formed stomachache, and lingering fatigue, Reign just wanted to curl into a ball.

Reign reentered the bedroom and was met with a not-so-pleased Cynthia. Sitting on her bed, arms folded, she frowned up at Reign. "Mom got rid of your bile," she bit out.

Reign ran a hand through her hair, sighing in the process. "I'm sorry." She glanced down in shame. "I don't know what just happened."

Cynthia's face softened. Reaching over to her nightstand, she grabbed a glass of ice water. "I guess you're forgiven." She handed the glass to Reign. "At least you got it in the can and not on the floor."

Reign sat next to Cynthia. "That doesn't make me feel any better," she muttered, taking a sip.

Cynthia adjusted her position. "I guess a 'your name' check on this errand run is in order, huh?" she teased.

Reign shook her head. "It's not even spelled the same."

Cynthia giggled, then gave Reign's back a light pat, the bit of humor dissolving from her face. "What's up with you, are you sick or something?"

Reign stalled as she tried to think of an explanation for why her health was taking a downward turn; she had none. "I—I don't know," was all that she could say.

Both women glanced at the door when Vivian walked in, mug of tea in hand. "Rae sweetie, I made you some ginger tea," she announced. "It will help settle your stomach."

Reign put a hand up. "No thanks, Mom. I'm okay for now."

Vivian held the mug in front of Reign. "I'm not trying to hear that, I want you to *drink* it," she insisted, stern.

Reign didn't have the energy to argue with her mother; she set her water on the nightstand, then carefully took the mug.

"Can *I* have some tea?" Cynthia asked, grinning.

"You know where the stuff is," Vivian threw back, pointing to the door.

Cynthia turned her lip up, but didn't respond.

Vivian shook her head at her youngest child, before turning her attention back to Reign who was taking a slow sip of her tea. "Reign... Did you ever—"

"I'm not pregnant Mom," Reign cut in, sullen. "I took a test last week; it came out negative."

Shocked, Cynthia snapped her head in Reign's direction. "Wait, you thought you were pregnant?"

"For like five minutes," Reign answered.

"Why am *I just* hearing about this?" Cynthia harped.

"Girl—" Reign decided not to engage with Cynthia. She looked back at her mother, who was failing to hide her disappointment. "Yup, that's the *same* face Chase had when I told him that it was negative."

Vivian sat down on the bed next to Reign. "No, sweetie, this isn't—" She shook her head. "If the reason why you've been feeling sick isn't because of *pregnancy*, I just wonder what's causing it." A heavy sigh escaped her. "I'm just concerned."

Reign let out a deep breath. "Me too," she admitted. "I finally made an appointment with my doctor to get some tests run, but I'm scared to even *go*."

Cynthia stared at Reign; her mouth open. "Wait...did you just admit that you were scared?" she zoned in. "Like, you *actually* admitted that, without us having to drag it out of you?"

Reign slowly turned and looked at her, eyes narrowed.

"What?" Cynthia shrugged. "I'm just shocked, that's all. What happened to the queen of 'I'm fine'?"

Vivian pinched the bridge of her nose. "Cyn... Go make your tea."

Not saying another word, Cynthia slid off the bed.

Vivian followed Cynthia's progress out the door, shaking her head before turning her attention back to Reign. She gently moved some of Reign's hair behind her shoulder. "When do you go to the doctor?" she asked.

"Next week."

"Do you want me to go with you?"

Reign shook her head. "No, I'd prefer to find out that I'm dying with*out* an audience."

Gasping loudly, Vivian delivered a tap to Reign's arm, startling her. "Don't you even speak that out loud, do you hear me?"

"Okay, I'm sorry." Reign's eyes widened at the sight of tears in her mother's eyes. "Mom, I'm *sorry*," she stressed. "It was a poor joke, don't *cry*."

"I swear, you or your sister are going to give me a heart attack one of these days," Vivian blubbered, jumping up from the bed.

"What happened to not speaking that into existence?" Reign called after her.

"Hush," Vivian threw over her shoulder.

Reign shook her head and took another sip of her tea.

Chapter Forty-Eight

CHASE TOOK A SIP FROM his water bottle and set it down on the bench. He glanced at his sports watch, eyeing the time, his brow knitted. Grabbing his phone from his gym bag, he quickly made a call. "Rae, where are you?" he spoke into the voicemail. "It's been almost an hour, call me to let me know that you're okay. I love you." Hanging up, he let out a sigh.

It was early Saturday morning, and the couple had planned on working out together. Chase had been at Reign's gym, in the secluded training room, waiting on her.

Chase breathed a sigh of relief when she finally walked in.

"Hey, sorry I'm late," Reign spoke.

Chase set his phone down. "It's okay. Did something happen? I called you."

Reign plopped her gym bag to the floor. "No, nothing happened, I'm just moving slowly today," she huffed. "And I forgot to take my phone off silent."

"Okay," he muttered. Chase studied her; like the days prior, his girlfriend looked drained. "Babe, are you sure you want to do this today?"

Reign rubbed the back of her neck. "Don't see why not."

Chase ran a hand over his head, exhaling. It was clear by the shortness in Reign's tone that she was irritated. Like her health, her mood had taken a dive. "Rae—I *told* you that you should take it easy until you see your doctor." He had tried to talk Reign out of their workout earlier that morning, yet she was unwilling to listen. "You need to stop being stubborn."

Reign glared up at him. "Chase, *please* don't annoy me any

more than I already am," she bristled.

Chase shook his head. "I'm not *trying* to, but you need to listen to me."

She rolled her eyes. "Look, there's no need in sitting around worrying myself. I'd rather keep busy."

"Keeping busy doesn't have to include *working out*," Chase argued. "Just write like you *always* do."

Reign pinched the bridge of her nose. *I love him, but I'm about to kill him.* "Chase—let's just get this over with okay?" she flashed back. "I promise to go sit my ass down somewhere afterwards."

Chase let out a sigh. He raised his arms then let them fall to his sides. Arguing with Reign wasn't going to change her mind; it was just going to upset her more. "Okay," he relented, moving towards her. "Listen, if you feel like you need to stop at any time—"

She flicked her hand at him. "Got it, just start."

He hesitated for a moment. "Fine... Let's start with twenty jumping jacks." He put a hand out toward her. "*Slow* ones."

Reign stood next to Chase in front of the mirror. They both did their twenty jumping jacks with ease. As Chase prepared to announce the next warm-up move, he glanced over at Reign. She had one hand on her hip, shifting her weight back and forth from one foot to the other, and fanning her flushed face.

"You okay?" he asked, concerned.

Reign took several deep breaths as she continued moving. "I need to stop," she panted.

Chase closed their distance, placing a hand on her lower back. "It's okay, sit down." As he went to guide Reign towards the bench, her eyes rolled into the back of her head and she collapsed in his arms.

Chase's breath quickened as fear shot through him. He shook her. "Baby!—"

Reign's eyes snapped back open, bringing Chase's pleas to a sudden halt. She looked up at him. "What just happened?" she asked, shaken.

Chase's eyes were wide as he stared at her. "Hello no," he panicked, scooping her up into his arms. "I'm taking you to the emergency room."

Reign held on tight as Chase carried her out to the car.

Chase paced the hospital room, as Reign laid in the bed.

Reign followed him with her eyes as he moved back and forth across the small space. "Can you stop moving please?" she begged, throwing her arm over the top of her head.

Chase did as she requested. He rubbed his face with his hands and took a deep breath.

He had brought Reign to the emergency room nearly two hours ago. Helpless, he'd stood there as they checked her vitals, took blood, and asked countless questions of her. Unlike Reign, who seemed calm, he was a nervous wreck. Just the thought of something being seriously wrong with her terrified him.

Reign slowly sat up, resting her back against the wall. "Come sit down," she softly urged.

Chase walked over and sat on the bed beside her. He smoothed her hair out of her face. "How are you feeling?" he asked.

She put a hand over her face. "I'm tired, and I'm starting to get a headache." Her voice trembled.

Taking hold of her hand, Chase desperately tried to keep his emotions contained. He knew that he needed to be strong for Reign. "Are you scared?"

Looking at Chase with tear-filled eyes, Reign nodded. The calm had disappeared, dread taking its place. "Yes."

Chase pulled her into a hug. "Everything is going to be okay," he soothed, rubbing her back. He didn't know how true that was. Hearing a knock, Chase stood from the bed.

"Come in," Reign called, wiping the tears away on the back of her hand.

They held their gazes on the doctor that walked in. "Hi, I'm Dr. Brown," the polite young woman greeted; Chase and Reign greeted her in return. "How are you feeling Ms. Price?"

"I don't know yet," Reign answered, honest. "That depends on what you're about to tell me."

"I understand your concern." Dr. Brown glanced at the file in her hand. "So, we ran some tests and from what we can see so far, you seem to be suffering from a bit of dehydration and exhaustion."

Chase frowned. "So, what is causing that?" he probed. "This isn't normal for her."

"Yeah, I mean, I know that I don't get a lot of sleep, but it's never been to the point of *exhaustion*," Reign chimed in. "And de-hydration—"

"You mentioned that you've been throwing up quite a bit over the past few days, correct?" Dr. Brown reminded.

Reign shot a skeptical look her way. "Yes," she replied. What Reign had thought to be a onetime reaction to Cynthia's unflatter-ing peach body spray just a few days ago, had turned into full-on stomach sickness. She could barely keep anything down.

Dr. Brown nodded. "*That* can cause dehydration," she said. A smile crossed her face. "All of this—including headaches—are pretty normal for your condition, especially this *early*."

Reign stared at the doctor in disbelief; how could she be smil-ing while delivering this devastating news? Reign glanced over at Chase; he had the same look on *his* face.

"*What* condition exactly?" Reign drew out slowly.

Dr. Brown gave the chart a quick glance, then looked back at Reign. "You're pregnant."

Reign's eyes expanded to the point where they looked like they were going to pop out of her head. Chase's mouth fell open in shock.

"I'm *sorry*?" Reign managed to get out.

"You're pregnant," Dr. Brown confirmed.

"Are you sure?" Chase jumped in.

Dr. Brown gave a nod. "Yes, I'm sure."

Reign put a hand up. "Hold up, hold up, wait." She put the other hand to her chest. "That's not possible. I just took a test over a *week ago* and it came out *negative*."

"The pregnancy hormone can take longer to show in some women than others. So, when you took your test, depending on how diluted your urine was and how sensitive the test used was, it didn't pick up on your hormone because it was too low," she explained. "But according to your numbers, you are in fact pregnant, and I'd suggest making an appointment with your OBGYN to get an ultrasound."

Reign sat there staring at the doctor, unable to speak another word.

Chase's shock had been replaced by a huge smile. *I'm going to be a father.* He turned to Reign, who was still staring at the doctor, silent. He chuckled, "Dr. Brown, can you please give us a minute?"

Dr. Brown smiled, "Of course."

Chase watched as she left the room. Once the door closed, he sat back down next to Reign, touching her shoulder. "Rae," he called.

Though the doctor had left the room, Reign's wide eyes were still fixed on the spot where she'd once stood.

Chase laughed. "Baby." He gave her a slight shake. When she didn't answer, he put his hands on her face, gently turning it towards him. "Reign."

"Huh?" Reign answered, finally snapping out of her trance. "Did—did you hear what she said?"

Chase chuckled, still cradling her face in his hands. "Yes," he nodded. "Did *you?*"

"I—I think so," Reign sputtered, still in disbelief. "She said that I was pregnant right?"

Chase smiled bright. "She did."

Reign opened her mouth to speak, but her breath caught in her throat.

Chase put both hands on her shoulders. "You need to breathe," he urged, calm.

She took several deep breaths. "I'm pregnant," she resolved. "We're going to have a—*baby.*"

Chase laughed a little. "I can't believe that I'm taking this more calmly than *you* are."

"Yeah well you have to understand, I was expecting her to say that I was *dying*, not that I was carrying a *baby*." Reign ran a hand over the back of her neck, exhaling again. "I just need a minute to let this reality sink in, okay."

Chase kissed her lips, then hugged her. "Take all the time you need." Parting, he let out a light sigh. "Wow."

"Yeah, *wow*." She scratched her head. "This is...crazy."

Chase shrugged. "Well, you *did* say that you wanted to have my baby, so..."

Reign narrowed her eyes at him. "Do *not* throw things said in the bedroom, up in my face right now," she bit out.

Chase busted out laughing. "You're right, I apologize."

She held her annoyed gaze on him. "I should throw up on you."

Amused and unfazed by her threat, Chase planted a kiss to her cheek. He then placed a hand to her stomach, holding it in place, beaming. "Wow," he breathed.

Letting a smile come through, Reign placed her hand over his. "Yeah...wow."

Marcy slammed the phone back into its cradle. "I can't believe I spent all that goddamn time on the phone just to find out I have the wrong fuckin' codes," she huffed. Rubbing her face with her hands, she yawned. *Why did I ever agree to come in here on Saturdays?* Reaching for her coffee cup, she shook it. Finding it empty, she sucked her teeth. *I need more coffee.*

Pushing herself back from the desk, Marcy stood up and left her office. Making her way down the hall into the employee kitchen, she set her sights on the coffee machine. Turning up her nose, she scoffed. "I refuse to drink another cup of this nasty hospital coffee." She walked out. "I don't *care* if I'm broke, I'm splurging on a caramel macchiato."

Being in desperate need of both the caffeine *and* fresh air, Marcy elected to take a shortcut to the exit through the emergency room.

Rounding a corner, she stopped short. Her eyes widened as

she stood in stunned silence.

Reign was standing in the waiting area.

"Oh my God," Marcy whispered.

Eyes focused on the cold white walls in front of her, Reign was silent as she tried to process the day's events. *I'm pregnant...I'm actually pregnant.* Nearly seven months into her new relationship with Chase, and they were about to become parents. Feeling someone touch her shoulder, she glanced to see Chase standing there.

"You left your paperwork in the room," he said, handing the stack to her.

Grimacing, Reign put a hand over her face. "God, I'm already becoming scatterbrained."

Chase put a comforting arm around her. "You're allowed to be," he soothed. "Don't worry about anything, I'm focused enough for the both of us."

Reign offered him a tired smile. She could already tell that Chase was going to dote on her; she would expect nothing less from him. Burying her face in his chest, he wrapped his arms around her, rubbing her back. "I need a nap," she whined.

"I know baby, let's get you home and in bed. I'll pull the car around."

Reign could only nod against his chest.

Pulling back, Chase gave her a quick peck on the lips. "Sit for a minute, I'll be right back."

Reign opened her mouth to respond, but hearing her name called, she paused. Chase stopped moving. Reign recognized the voice. Turning around, she was met with a wide-eyed Marcy, staring at them from several feet away.

Reign fixed her with an icy glare. She had no idea what Marcy was doing there, or how long she had been *standing* there.

Marcy didn't know where she'd gotten the courage to call Reign's name. She had been watching her interaction with Chase—seeing them together, the way that he'd hugged her before they'd shared a kiss. *Troy was right.*

But she couldn't focus on the rumored relationship, she could only focus on Reign; the friend that she had lost and desperately wanted back. "Reign... Can I—"

Chase frowned in Marcy's direction. Seeing Marcy did not faze him, but he knew that Reign hated Marcy. The last thing he needed was his pregnant girlfriend getting herself worked up over a woman who wasn't worth either of their time.

He took hold of Reign's hand. "On second thought, come with me now," he said to her.

Reign didn't say anything, she just turned away, walking with Chase towards the exit.

"Please wait Rae, I just want to talk to you!" Marcy wailed after her. "*Please,*" she begged when Reign ignored her. Seeing them disappear through the sliding doors, Marcy put her hand on her head, fighting back the tears that were building behind her eyes. Her quest for caffeine long forgotten, Marcy scurried back to her office.

Sitting up in bed, Reign adjusted the blanket over the bottom half of her body and returned to writing in her notebook.

Since coming home from the emergency room with Chase, Reign had spent most of the day sleeping while Chase ran errands. With the sun low into the evening, Chase was preparing dinner while Reign was wide awake, journaling.

Hearing footsteps outside of her room, she looked up to see Chase sticking his head through the cracked door. She offered him a smile. "Hey you."

Chase returned her smile with one of his own. "Are you okay in here?" he asked. "How are you feeling?"

"I'm okay." Reign closed her notebook, setting it on the end table next to her, along with her pen. "You can come in, you know," she chortled when he neglected to move.

Chase entered, taking a seat on the bed. "Are you ready to eat yet?"

Reign sighed a bit. "I *should*, right?" She placed a hand to her stomach. "I'm not that hungry, but I'll try."

Chase nodded, exhaling deeply.

When Chase stared off into space after a moment, Reign tilted her head, eyeing him. "What are you thinking, baby?" she probed.

"What a difference a few hours make," he answered, looking back at her. "I woke up this morning thinking about our next vacation, and now I'll be going to bed thinking about baby names."

Reign grinned. "You've thought of some already?"

"I did, but you're not going to like them," he replied, voice laced with humor.

Reign shook her head in amusement, giving her stomach a rub. She glanced up at the ceiling as the amusement left her face. "You know it's funny… People always say that when the time is right, or when something is *meant* to happen, it will," she began, reflective. "Would never have expected it to happen at this *moment*, but—"

Chase tilted his head. "Are you worried?"

She looked back at him. "I wouldn't say that." Reign shrugged, "I guess…it's all still sinking in."

Chase grabbed her hand and held it. He felt like he had an idea of what was bothering her, even though she wasn't saying it. They weren't living together, they weren't married—he hadn't even *asked* her. She had no idea that he intended to do so. He just worried that if he did it right now, she'd think that it was only because of the baby—that was the last thing that he wanted Reign to feel. "Like I said earlier, everything will be fine," he promised. "I don't want you to worry about anything, you hear me?"

She squeezed his hand. "I'll try."

"When is your appointment?"

Reign rubbed the back of her neck. "Wednesday at nine AM." She eyed him. "Do you want to come with me?"

"Of *course*," Chase confirmed, eager. "Wouldn't miss it." He chuckled, "I need to find out exactly which brand of prenatal pills you need, because when I went to the store earlier, I picked up eight different ones."

Reign let out a laugh. "I don't think it matters, but it's sweet that you almost cleared the shelf for me."

Chase laughed in return. "Anytime." A seriousness fell over him. He almost didn't want to ask his next question, but since they hadn't spoken of it since they'd left the hospital, he felt that he needed to. "So umm...how are you feeling after seeing Marcy today?"

Reign's brow furrowed. "Are you asking if I'm still upset over it?" she questioned. Chase nodded. "Did seeing her, annoy me? Yes," she answered honestly. "The woman will *always* be deplorable in my book, but honestly, until you brought it up just now...it wasn't on my mind." She tucked some of her hair behind her ear. "I have so many great—and a few *unexpected* things happening in my life right now... Marcy, is the *last* thing I'm thinking of."

Chase gave an approving nod. "Good to hear." As far as Chase was concerned, he and Reign's despicable exes never had to be a topic of discussion again. He only wanted to focus on their future— together. Chase gave her hand a kiss. "When do you think we should tell the family?" he asked, smoothly changing the subject.

Reign put a hand over her face. "God Chase, you have to give me a minute." Chase let out a laugh. "I need to prepare myself for the smothering I know I'll endure from both of our mothers... *and* sisters."

"I'll follow your lead," he said, humored. "Whenever you're ready, just let me know."

Reign nodded. "I believe my appetite is returning," she said after a moment.

Pleased, Chase stood from the bed. "I'll get your plate."

Reign watched him leave the room, before picking her notebook back up. Letting out a light sigh, followed by a smile, she returned to where she'd left off.

Chapter Forty-Nine

OPENING THE OVEN, AVA PEERED inside. "Mom, come over and check to see if this is done, please."

Ellie looked up from her task of sprinkling powdered sugar atop a pound cake. "Ava, I told you when you first said that you wanted to try your hand at that berry cobbler, that you were on your own with it," she reminded. "You said that you could handle it."

Ava's head snapped towards her mother, her eyes wide. "Ma'am, you *knew* that was a lie!"

Ellie chuckled a bit. "Why did you insist on *doing* it?"

"Because Chase is making a dessert, so *I* wanted to contribute too," Ava explained.

Ellie shook her head. Thanksgiving was finally upon them, and she couldn't have been happier. She always enjoyed having her family together and now this year she would not only have hers but Reign's family too. Everyone she cherished around one table.

Ellie went to the oven, eyeing the ceramic dish of bubbling, golden-brown cobbler. She gave an approving nod. "It looks fine, take it out."

Lips curled in a satisfying grin, Ava grabbed potholders, then carefully pulled the dessert from the oven, setting it on a cooling rack.

"You *did* taste the contents before you put them in the oven, right?" Ellie questioned, moving back to her pound cake.

Ava was so excited about her finished product, that she hadn't answered right away. "Yes, I did," she assured, finally.

Ellie raised a skeptical eyebrow. She knew her daughter's cooking abilities all too well, yet she didn't want to be discouraging. "Okay good."

Ava stood at the counter island, surveying the dishes of roasted turkey with homemade stuffing, candied yams, baked macaroni and cheese, fried cabbage, corn on the cob, rice and gravy, mashed potatoes, collard greens, potato salad, pot roast, deviled eggs, pasta salad and fresh dinner rolls on the counter. She rubbed her rumbling stomach in anticipation. "Are you ready to move this stuff to the dining room?"

Ellie opened her mouth to speak, but paused when Chase walked into the kitchen. She beamed. "Right on time."

Chase set his sweet potato pie on the counter before greeting his mother and sister with hugs.

"Is my sis here?" Ava asked.

"She's on her way." Chase removed the foil from his pie. "She had to pick up her family."

Ellie gave Chase a once over, smiling to herself; happiness resonated from him. She grabbed a dish. "Okay you two, let's move all of this stuff to the dining room."

Pulling into a parking space in front of the Williams' house, Reign turned the car off. Resting her head on the steering wheel, she waited as her family gathered their belongings.

Cynthia let out a shriek loud enough to startle the whole family.

"God," Reign muttered, rubbing her forehead.

"Girl, what is the problem?" Vivian barked from the front seat.

Cynthia grimaced. "I left the wine sitting on the coffee table." Her confession earned a sigh from her mother and groan from her father.

"You had *one* job," Matthew grunted.

"What about *yours* Dad?" Cynthia flashed back. "*You* forgot that pecan pie on the counter."

Reign snickered while Matthew shot his wife a stunned look.

Vivian's gaze thinned into a glare. "Are you serious?"

Matthew and Cynthia glanced at one another. "We apologize," they muttered in unison.

"Okay guys behave yourselves…and when I say guys, I mean *Dad* and *Cyn*," Reign interjected.

Vivian giggled, while Cynthia and Matthew mumbled something incoherent. "They will," Vivian promised. "And luckily for you *both* back there, *I* grabbed the wine and the extra cake that I baked."

Reign opened her car door, sighing in the process.

Vivian looked on in concern as Reign slowly got out of the car. "Are you okay sweetie?"

"Yes, I'm fine." Reign held her hand out for her purse. "Just trying not to jerk myself around so much," she continued as her mother handed it to her.

She and Chase had yet to tell their families that she was pregnant. They'd successfully kept the secret for nearly a month; yet, Reign wondered how much longer she could contain it. As her pregnancy progressed, so did her symptoms, including the fatigue which was currently taking its toll.

Reign approached the Williams' door with her family in tow. She raised her finger to ring the bell, but paused when Cynthia let out a loud gasp.

Reign side-eyed her. "What *now*?"

"Nothing, I just wanted to get my shenanigans out before we go in," Cynthia joked, shrugging. Cynthia's giddiness ceased when her mother plucked the side of her head.

The loud thud of Vivian's fingers connecting with Cynthia's hard head, paired with the dramatic shriek that escaped Cynthia's lips—Reign couldn't help but laugh.

Even Matthew joined in.

"Cynthia, act like you're a grown woman, for the love of God," Vivian chastised.

Pouting, Cynthia rubbed her head. "Yes ma'am."

Shaking her head, Reign rang the doorbell. Not more than a few seconds passed before Chase was welcoming Reign and her family inside.

While the Price's greeted the Williams', Chase and Reign exchanged a loving hug and kiss. Placing a hand on Reign's stomach, Chase gave it a rub. "Did they work your nerves?" he chuckled.

Smirking, Reign gave his hand a soft pat. "As always."

Chase glanced over at their families; hugs, chatter and laughter filled the room. He smiled; he couldn't have asked for a better family dynamic. Taking hold of Reign's hand, they joined the rest.

"Rae, you *have* to let me hang out with you and Ava one of these days," Cynthia bubbled. "Ava says that she knows where the best lounges are."

Reign shook her head. "No, I'm *old* remember?" she mocked. "Surely you wouldn't want to hang with *me* and my geriatric *friend* over here."

Cynthia narrowed her eyes at her sister, then at Ava who was snickering. "She's so petty," Cynthia ground out.

Reign laughed, wrapping her arm around Cynthia's shoulder. "Cut it out, you know I love you."

"Yeah, yeah, love you too," Cynthia muttered, trying to hide a building smile as she leaned her head on Reign's shoulder.

Ellie and Vivian clutched each other's hands as they spoke. "Thank you for inviting us," Vivian gushed.

"Oh, no need to thank me, I'm happy to have you," Ellie beamed. "I've always considered your family, *my* family and now that those two have finally gotten it together—" She gestured to Chase and Reign, "We can be family *for real*."

Laughter erupted from Vivian. "*My* sentiments exactly," she agreed. "I can't *wait* to help plan their wedding."

Chase glanced over at them, gently nudging Reign. "They're already planning our wedding for us babe."

Reign folded her arms. "Not surprised."

Both women focused their attention on their children, amused. "No pressure, we're just saying," Ellie clarified.

Ava laughed. "That is a bold-faced lie, and they *know* it," she slid in. "'No pressure' my behind."

Reign pointed at Ava. "Do *not* put that all on them," she

hurled to a shocked Ava. "*You* were showing me destination wedding spots just *last week*."

"That was for *me!*" Ava exclaimed. She shook her head, tossing her hands in the air in the process. "Yeah, I couldn't even commit to that lie. I'm not getting married anytime soon." She pointed to Reign. "But for *you* luv—spring wedding in Aruba—perfect, just saying."

Reign shook her head in amusement. She glanced up at Chase, giving him a knowing look. Chase grinned, but didn't say anything. "*Anyway*," she began, turning back to the group. "You should probably put your wedding plans for us, aside for a moment," she alluded.

"What, why? What happened? Chase, what did you do?" Ellie charged.

Reign snickered, while Chase shot a wide-eyed look Ellie's way. "Huh? I didn't do anything," he sputtered, confused.

"He didn't do anything wrong, we're good," Reign assured, amused. She put a hand on Chase's cheek. "He's perfect."

Chase glanced at Reign, eyeing her adoringly.

"Oh…okay good." Ellie breathed a sigh of relief. "Because I was about to say."

Chase squinted. "*About to?*" he threw back.

Reign tucked hair behind her ears. "I *said* that, because I figured you'd have your hands full planning something *else*," she slid in.

Ava looked intrigued. "Like what?"

Reign hesitated for a moment. "A baby shower," she finally answered. The room fell silent—all eyes were on her.

"Reign is pregnant," Chase added. When the stunned looks had yet to leave the faces of their family, he looked over at Reign. "I think we might have given everybody a stroke," he joked.

"Yeah, I can see that." Reign waved her hand in front of her father's stunned face. She giggled. "Dad, breathe."

"Hold on, are you *serious?*" Ellie blurted out, while Vivian put her hands over her mouth in shock.

"We're serious," Chase confirmed. He chuckled as they stared in disbelief. "I swear. I wouldn't lie about something like this."

"So wait, I'm actually about to be an *aunt*?" Ava jumped in, brimming with excitement. "Meaning, I get to spoil a baby that isn't *mine*?"

Reign giggled again. "Yes." She grabbed her purse, retrieving two items from it. "See? A note from my doctor *and* the ultrasound picture." Reign handed both to her mother.

Everyone gathered around Vivian to see.

Chase shook his head, amused at the scene. "A damn shame that we have to even *go* through all of this for you to believe us."

Overcome with emotion, Vivian threw her arms around Reign. "My baby," she gushed, tears flowing. "My baby is having a baby. I'm so happy."

Reign patted her mother's back, smiling. "Thank you, Mom."

"Wait, how far along are you?" Ava asked as a delighted Ellie enveloped Chase in a hug.

"Ten weeks," Reign answered.

"*Ten weeks*?!" Cynthia bellowed. "Rae—you and these secrets."

"Listen, we found out almost a month ago, but we both agreed to wait to share the news," Chase jumped in, parting from his mother. "Figured with everybody here together, *now* was the best time to tell you."

Ava waved a dismissive hand. "You don't owe them an explanation." She hugged Chase tight. Pulling back, she poked him in his chest. "You should've told *me*, though," she said through clenched teeth.

Chase chuckled, "I'm sorry."

"It's fine. I forgive you," Ava grinned. "I'm so happy for you both." Vivian still had Reign clutched in her embrace. "Ms. Vivian, can you *share* her?" Ava teased.

"God please, she's about to squeeze the vomit out of me," Reign grumbled.

Vivian let go. "Oh stop it," she chided, wiping her eyes. She then put a hand on Reign's face. "Are you okay? How are you feeling?"

Reign shrugged slightly. "Physically I'm a little run down, but I know it's normal," she admitted. "I'm *happy* though. You don't have to worry."

Vivian placed a hand to her chest. "I'm sure Chase is taking great care of you, but I'm coming over tomorrow to look after you for the day."

"Okay," Reign nodded.

As Vivian stepped aside, Matthew approached Reign. He didn't say anything, he just hugged her. His first-born daughter, his pride and joy, was making him a grandfather. He didn't want to speak out loud for fear of blubbering. "Congratulations. I love you so much," he whispered to her.

Squeezing him, Reign smiled. "I love you too Dad and thank you."

"I'd say this is a good time to eat," Ava brought up.

Ellie gasped. "Oh Lord, yes," she clasped her hands together. "Let's head to the dining room everyone."

As everyone made their way to the feast, Joseph stopped Chase with a tap on the shoulder. Chase faced his father.

"The women were all over you, so I figured I'd wait my turn," Joseph chortled before hugging his son. "Congratulations. You're going to make a great father."

Chase squeezed his father tight. "Thank you," he breathed. "I hope to be *half* the father you are."

Beaming with pride, Joseph patted his son's back. "You'll be *better*."

"I swear, it did *not* taste like that when I put it in the oven!" Ava belted out, annoyed as she pointed to her plate of cobbler.

Reign poked at the substance on her plate. "It's not *bad* Ava, it's just…"

"Tart," Chase muttered, setting his plate down.

With dinner over, most of the family were seated around the fireplace in the seasonably decorated den, enjoying a few of the desserts.

"It's *terrible*." Ava crossed her arms in a huff. "Terrible *and* embarrassing."

Ellie leaned over and gave her daughter's arm a pat. "Ava honey, it's not that bad," she placated. Ava shook her head in disbelief. "Would it make you feel better if I gave you my pound cake recipe?"

"No, I'd probably ruin *that* too," Ava sulked.

"Sweetie, nobody has the perfect 'first time baking' experience," Vivian tried to consol. "The more you do it, the better you become."

Ava grabbed her glass of wine, taking a sip. "I appreciate that, but I'll stick to contributing store bought items from now on." She chuckled to herself. "Those poor berries were picked for nothing."

Ellie shook her head in amusement. "Well my love, if it makes you feel any better, you're perfect in every *other* way." She winked at Ava. "And I'm proud of you—*both* of you," she added, gesturing to both of her children.

Ava smiled at her mother. "It does, and thank you."

"Thanks Mom," Chase replied, grateful.

Ava looked at Chase. "Oh Chase, I'm going to need you to bake me one of those sweet potato pies of yours like ASAP."

Chase chuckled. "I knew that was coming," he said. "Very well."

As the room became filled with chatter, Ellie sat back observing. After a moment, she approached Reign, who was quietly observing the room herself. "Sweetie, can I talk to you for a minute?" Ellie whispered.

Reign looked up at her. "Sure," she obliged, following Ellie into the living room.

Safely out of earshot of the other guests, Ellie faced Reign.

"Is everything okay?" Reign wondered.

Looking down, Ellie nodded. Taking a deep breath, she met Reign's gaze. "Reign, I wanted to take a moment to say, thank you."

Reign squinted, perplexed. "You're welcome," she drew out. "Though I'm not sure what you're thanking me for."

Ellie smiled. "Just…for being who you are, and for loving my son."

Reign's face relaxed as she stared at Chase's mother.

"You have *no* idea how much you have impacted his life," Ellie expressed. "I don't know where he'd be if he hadn't met you—"

Reign put a hand on Ellie's arm, stopping her. "Ms. Ellie, I know about Chase's past and as much as I appreciate you giving me credit for how he turned out—I won't take it," she said, sincere. "I honestly believe that if he *hadn't* met me, he still would've turned his life around."

Ellie eyed Reign with adoration. *She* knew how much of an impact Reign had on Chase's life, even back then. However, she admired Reign's modesty. "Well, if you won't take the credit for then, take it for *now*," she insisted.

Reign smiled as Ellie took hold of her hand.

Tears of happiness glassed over Ellie's eyes. "My son is the happiest that he's ever been," she gushed, squeezing Reign's hand. "And I *know* that's all because of *you*. So...thank you."

Reign felt tears fill her *own* eyes at the outpouring of love from the woman she considered a second mother. She gave a nod, "You're welcome. He does the same for me."

Smiling through her tears, Ellie pulled Reign in for a hug, squeezing her tight.

Chase made himself a drink before walking out to the patio. Seeing Matthew sitting by himself with a glass of his own, Chase exhaled deeply.

"I thought I saw you come out here," Chase said.

Matthew glanced back at him. "Yeah, I always seem to find myself outside by the end of the night," he chortled.

Chase stood by an empty chair. He pointed to it. "Do you mind if I join you?"

Matthew gestured to the seat. "Not at all." He eyed Chase as the man sat down. "I know that I didn't say much to you back there."

Chase looked at him while taking a sip of his drink.

"But I've already expressed to Reign how happy I am about the baby...and I want to say it to *you too*." Matthew smiled. "Congratulations. We're *all* excited about the new addition."

Chase smiled back. "Thank you sir... I—*we* appreciate all of the support," he replied, grateful. He took another sip, then a deep breath. "Um...I want you to know that I don't intend to *only* make Reign a mother."

Matthew tilted his head, eyeing Chase intently.

"I also intend on making her my *wife*," Chase clarified. "That's *been* my intention and I have the ring to prove it." He set his drink down and rubbed his hands together. "I just want to ask for your blessing... I know how important you are to Reign, and I wouldn't feel right about asking her to marry me without doing this."

Matthew went quiet for a moment. He glanced up at the cloudless, star-filled sky, a light sigh escaping him. "You know...I remember the first time you were brought into my precinct," he began. "Vandalism...the second time, a *fight*."

Chase lowered his head. "Yeah," he sighed. "I got into a lot of trouble back then."

"You did," Matthew agreed, nodding. As the chief of police for many years in their city, he'd witnessed the trouble Chase used to get in to back when the young man was still a teenager first hand.

Chase sat back in his seat, a cloud of shame hovering over him. "You know, I'm not *proud* of my past actions," he said. "I've always regretted—"

"I wasn't bringing that up to shame you," Matthew promised, putting a hand up. "You made mistakes; we *all* have...and even though you made a few more than I would have liked to *see*, I knew *then* you had potential... I knew in my gut that how you were *then*, wasn't how you were going to turn *out*." He swirled the dark liquid around in his glass. "Which is *why* I let you off with *just* a warning those two times... I prayed that I wouldn't see you in cuffs a third time and... I *didn't*. You proved me right."

Chase let a small smile come through. He remembered the embarrassment and fear he'd felt when he'd first found out that the police chief whom he'd encountered during his brief arrests was in fact Reign's *father*. He had no idea if the man would approve of him even *looking* at his daughter. However, he was pleasantly surprised that Matthew had never held his past against him; he had never stopped Reign from hanging out with Chase or his family.

"I appreciate that, then *and* now." Chase's eyes expressed his gratitude. "I'm not going to lie, a big motivation for me wanting to change in the beginning *was* your daughter."

Matthew smiled warmly.

"She deserved someone better and I wanted to *be* better." Chase added, sincere. "She is *everything* to me and I want you to know that you never have to worry about her. Her well-being, her happiness—I've got her."

Matthew sat up in his seat. "You know…I've been perfectly happy being a father to my beautiful daughters, but I am equally happy to be gaining a son." He held his hand out. "Of *course*, you have my blessing to marry Reign."

Overjoyed and relieved, Chase shook Matthew's hand in a firm grip.

"Welcome to the family, Chase," Matthew beamed.

Chase smiled, "Thank you."

Chapter Fifty

MARCY PACED HER LIVING ROOM floor, cell phone in hand.

She'd been pacing for nearly an hour, and Reign's phone number was still on the screen. Marcy had been trying to gather the courage to call. She'd been trying every day since she'd spotted Reign at the hospital a month ago.

Reign had been on Marcy's mind heavily, so much so that she couldn't concentrate on anything else—not even her apartment—which she had *yet* to fully unpack. Her motivation, just like her happiness, was gone.

Finally taking a break, Marcy plopped down to the floor. Gathering all of the courage that she had, she pushed the call button, putting the phone on speaker.

Marcy's face fell when the call went straight to voicemail. She tossed the phone aside. "Yeah, she blocked me," she sulked.

Putting her face in her hands, Marcy took several deep breaths. Bringing her knees to her chest, Marcy folded her arms around them, resting her chin on her kneecaps. She stayed that way for a long time until she finally gave in.

Shaking her head, Marcy jumped from the floor. "I can't take this anymore." Darting to her door, she slipped on her shoes and bolted out of the apartment.

"Are you sure we shouldn't just take the cars to the car wash?" Reign asked, standing in the doorway of her house.

Chase grabbed the hose, placing it into a soap-filled bucket. "It's a nice day out, I don't mind washing the cars by hand." Seeing how both his and Reign's cars needed a good scrub, Chase had decided to take advantage of the spring-like weather on that November Sunday and wash them both. "When I finish, I'm going to take your car to fill your gas up, so let me know if you need anything while I'm out."

Reign nodded. "Okay… I can help you wash—"

"No way, I'll handle this." Chase gestured inside. "*You* go put your feet up."

"Chase, I'm *tired* of sitting on my ass," Reign huffed, folding her arms. "At *least* let me make us some lunch."

Chase chuckled. He wasn't surprised that Reign wasn't a fan of lounging all day. He only hoped that she would start to feel more energetic once her first trimester was over. "If you insist, I'll take lunch."

"Good." Reign walked inside the house, closing the door behind her.

Turning the hose off, Chase grabbed the sponge from the bucket, and got to work, starting with Reign's car first.

He'd been washing and polishing the outside for twenty-five minutes, before opening the car door. As he sat in Reign's car, wiping down the interior, he heard a car pull up. He ignored it. He even ignored the sound of the car door opening and closing. When he heard it pull off, he shrugged to himself. *Maybe they had the wrong house*, he thought.

"Hey Chase."

Frowning, he looked up to see Marcy standing by the curb. He slowly got out of the car. "What are you doing here?" Chase bit out.

Marcy shoved her hands in the pockets of her jacket. "I guess, I should ask *you* the same thing."

Chase smirked, "You *shouldn't*, because I doubt you'd like the answer."

Folding her arms, Marcy's eyes lowered momentarily. "Yeah… figured." she said, resolved. She met his stern gaze. "Of *all* the women in this city—"

Chase stood unfazed.

"It had to be *her*, huh?"

469

Chase squinted. *She's got a hell of a nerve.* He shrugged, "It always *has* been."

Marcy nodded slowly. "Right…given everything…I'd say that I deserve it."

"None of this is about *you*," Chase spat. "You should go."

"I'm here to see Reign."

"She doesn't want to see you," Chase argued. "You only upset her and I'm not going to allow that to happen."

Marcy took a step forward. "You know, you can threaten *Troy*, but that shit isn't going to work on me," she ground out. "I came to *Reign's house* to talk to her and that's what I'm going to *do*."

Chase's patience was wearing thin with Marcy. "You know what—" He halted when he heard the front door open.

"Baby, lunch is ready." Reign paused when she took in the scene. Reign stared at Marcy, speechless, a neutral expression on her face.

Marcy gazed at Reign, hesitating for a moment. "Rae…I— I was hoping that we could talk," she stammered finally.

Chase looked back at Reign, regret on his face. "I'm sorry, I tried to get her to leave, but—"

"It's okay, go take a break," Reign cut in, gesturing for Chase to come to the house.

Chase shot Marcy a glare, before walking over to Reign. "Just ignore her."

"No, I should probably deal with this," Reign said to him. "Go in, I'll be fine."

Chase opened his mouth to protest, but decided against it, "Okay," he agreed, before disappearing inside.

Once Chase closed the door behind him, Reign stepped forward, folding her arms in the process.

Marcy stood still as Reign walked towards her. "Hi—"

"Let's walk," Reign abruptly broke in, standing face to face with Marcy.

Marcy grinned. "Come on Rae, you know that I'm not the walking type," she attempted to joke.

There were no traces of humor on Reign's face. "That was not an opening for a joke, nor was it a request. I said let's walk."

Marcy swiftly wiped the smile from her face, nodding. "Okay."

They walked down the street in silence; Marcy was on edge. She'd taken a chance showing up to Reign's house unannounced, demanding a conversation. She figured that Reign wouldn't invite her in, but she would at least think that they would talk on the lawn, not two blocks down.

Having had enough of the silence, Marcy spun around, standing in front of Reign. "Okay umm…why are we walking?" she asked.

"I don't want you near my house," Reign bluntly replied.

Marcy looked down. "Oh…you sure that's the *only* reason?"

Reign raised an eyebrow. "Meaning?"

"You umm… Do you want to…"

Reign held an icy glare on Marcy. "I'm not going to beat your ass again, if *that's* what you're stumbling to get out."

Sighing in relief, Marcy met Reign's eye. "I'm glad. I— I definitely didn't come here to fight—"

"What is it that you want to say to me Marcy?" Reign jumped in.

Marcy took a deep breath. She'd spent months rehearsing this exact moment, what to say and how to say it. Standing in front of her, Marcy found it hard to find the words. Reign's cold demeanor wasn't helping. "You umm…you look good," she began, nervous. "Then again, you always *did*."

Reign rolled her eyes. "That *can't* be it."

Marcy took another deep breath. "No—no, that's not—" She ran her hands through her lifeless hair, scratching her scalp. "I just want you to know that I've been doing a lot of thinking… *Reevaluating* and I know how shitty of a person that I've been…that I've *always* been," she said. "I… I ruined every good thing that I had going on in my life and now I'm miserable and I know that it's what I deserve."

Reign stared at her, not saying anything.

"I know how good of a friend you were to me, and—I know how badly I hurt you," Marcy stammered. "You didn't deserve what

I did to you and even though I didn't act *alone*...as your friend..."
She shook her head in shame, "I was wrong...*so* wrong and I'm so
sorry and I miss you."

Reign had yet to speak or waiver from her glare.

Her silence spoke volumes; it unnerved Marcy. She fiddled
with her fingers. "Umm...Troy and I broke up." She gave a solemn
shrug. "The relationship was a mess from the start... He was everything that I realized I *didn't* want, and vice versa."

"Aww, your relationship that was built on lies and deception
failed," Reign mocked, sarcastic. "Shocking."

Sighing, Marcy shifted her weight from one foot to the other.
"Yeah, well I didn't expect you to care, I just felt that you should know."

"You could've kept that shit to yourself," Reign spat. "You're
right, I *don't* care. I don't care about either *one* of you."

Marcy's eyes lowered. "Yeah, I know."

"*Do* you?" Reign challenged. "You must *not*, if you thought
that showing up here was going to change anything."

Marcy continued to stare at the ground as Reign ranted.

"See, you want a reaction out of me. You want me to scream
and cry and tell you how much you hurt me," Reign said. "You want
to feel that I've been as miserable as *you've* been."

"That's not true."

"It *is*." Reign's gaze thinned. "Misery loves company and you
always wanted me to feel as bad, if not *worse* than *you*." She pushed
her hair over her shoulder. "But the thing is, I'm grateful to you, hell
you *and* Troy. Both of your worthless asses successfully eradicated
yourselves from my life, and I feel *so* much lighter now."

Marcy looked at Reign, sadness in her eyes.

"I, unlike *you* am *truly* happy now."

Marcy nodded slowly. "Yeah, I can see that you're happy," she
replied. "You're happy with *Chase*."

Reign shrugged. "I saw him first." A slow smirk crossed her
lips. "He *was* my first."

Marcy's eyes widened. Not only had her own words been

thrown back in her face, but Marcy now knew just how deep the history between Chase and Reign ran. Yet she didn't deserve the right to be upset *or* jealous, so she closed her eyes. Letting out a sigh, resolve finally came over her. "Well... I'm happy *for* you."

Reign shook her head. "I don't need your well wishes. Goodbye Marcy."

Seeing Reign turn to walk away, Marcy sucked in a quick breath. "I started a new job," she blurted out. "You were right, I needed to find something steady, and I *did*. I work at the hospital now."

Reign turned, shooting Marcy with an unimpressed stare.

"I mean, I'm a biller, and I don't like talking on the phones, but it's a paycheck," Marcy rambled. "I even got a new apartment, in your old building..." She fiddled with her hands once more. "The point is that I'm making strides...*trying* to anyway."

"Bye Marcy," Reign sneered, making another attempt to walk away.

But Marcy took one more step forward. She knew that if she let Reign walk away, she would never get the chance to see her again. "I know that you're pregnant!"

Reign abruptly stopped, spinning around. "*Excuse* me?"

Marcy put her hands up. "I umm... When I saw you at the hospital that day—I didn't know if you were okay or not so after you left, I snuck and looked at your file."

Reign frowned. "You *do* realize that you broke a law, right?"

"I don't *care*, they can throw me in jail." Marcy's emotions were coming to a head. Tears filled her eyes. "I *had* to know that you were okay. You can tell whoever you want, I deserve anything that happens. I just wanted to make sure that you were okay."

Shaking her head again, Reign turned away.

Marcy pushed her hair behind her ears. "Anyway, congratulations," she sputtered. "I'm happy for you... You and Chase are going to have a beautiful baby."

Reign narrowed her eyes, then scoffed. "Yeah, thanks, bye."

Tears spilled down Marcy's face as her best friend kept walking away. "Reign— Please, you *have* to forgive me!"

Reign halted once more but didn't turn around.

"*Please*," Marcy begged. "I am *so* sorry for *everything*. You can't begin to understand *how* sorry I am. How much I *hate* myself. I hurt my *best friend* and I can't take it back… I know that we'll never be friends again, but I just ask you to please find it in your heart to forgive me."

Reign still wouldn't face her.

Marcy kept moving forward. "You remember what your mother said the day that she visited you in college our junior year?" Marcy brought up. "It was after we had that silly argument and she lectured us on forgiveness? She said that forgiveness is good for your heart and soul… She said that it brings peace to you…" Marcy wiped tears from her cheeks with the back of her hand. "I want you to have peace. I know you hate me, but you deserve peace, so I am begging your forgiveness Reign…*please*."

Reign finally turned around, but it was with a scowl. "I'm not my mother."

Marcy's face fell, her cheeks were wet with more tears than she could ever wipe away.

"And you're not fooling anybody. Those fake ass *tears* aren't fooling anybody." Reign fumed, taking a step closer. "You forget I *know* you; you don't do *shit* unless it benefits *you*."

Marcy stood there sniffling, trying to hold in her sobs.

"You don't give a fuck about my *soul*, this is for *you*." Reign pointed her finger at Marcy. "You want me to forgive you, for *you*. *You* want to be able to sleep at night, to be able to look at yourself in the mirror without feeling like the scum of the goddamn earth; *that's* what you want."

Marcy busted out crying. "It's not true," she denied between labored breaths.

"Oh it *is*." Reign stood in Marcy's face, piercing her with a fierce stare. "Let me tell you right now, so there isn't a single doubt in your fucked-up mind…I will *never* forgive you. *Ever*."

Covering her face with her hands, Marcy wailed.

"I want you to remember what you've done, every single day

and *live* with it," Reign dug in. "*My* soul is good; *mine* is at peace... *Yours* doesn't *deserve* to be."

Marcy felt her knees buckle when Reign walked off. She kneeled on the sidewalk, clutching her stomach. "I'm so sorry, boo!"

"My name is *Reign*, and don't you *ever* bring your ass back to my house again," Reign flashed back. She sauntered down the street, leaving Marcy in a blubbering heap on the concrete.

Chase peered out of his open car door. Seeing Reign approach, he got out.

"Did you eat?" Reign asked, standing in front of him.

Chase shook his head no.

Reign shot him a knowing look, tilting her head. "You were standing out here the entire time watching me, weren't you?"

"You know me so well." He reached out, rubbing her arm. "Are you okay?"

"Oh, I'm *great*," Reign boasted.

Chase nodded. "You didn't *kill* her, did you?" he joked. Reign snickered. "I mean, I have bail money, but I'd rather not have my pregnant lady in jail."

Reign shook her head. "*Physically*, she is unharmed." She rubbed her stomach. "I don't think we'll be seeing her again."

Chase gave an approving nod. "Same for Troy."

Reign smirked, "Did you kill *him*?"

He returned her smirk with one of his own. "Almost." Chase hadn't mentioned that he'd ambushed Troy on Reign's behalf, until now. It seemed that Troy had heeded his warning, so Chase was satisfied.

Reign shook her head in amusement. "My hero."

Chase chuckled as he put an arm around her. "Come on, let's go eat," he said, guiding her towards the door. "And I don't care *what* you say, you're going to put your feet up."

She rolled her eyes. "Whatever you say, Daddy." Her saucy reply earned a playful tap to her behind from Chase as they walked inside and shut the door behind them.

Chapter Fifty-One

REIGN SHOT A GLARE AT Chase when he finally approached the passenger door. "Where *were* you?" she charged.

"I was setting the blanket down," he answered.

Reign narrowed her eyes. "For a *half hour*?"

"It's a *big* blanket." His eyes shifted under the angered gaze of his girlfriend. "Uh—I was checking for scorpions," Chase stammered. Holding his hand out for hers, he grinned. "Are you upset?"

Rolling her eyes, Reign put her hand in his. "No, I was *worried*." She stepped out of the car. "I didn't know if a coyote got you or something."

Chase planted a kiss to her forehead. "Sorry for worrying you," he placated. "I just didn't want you to have to stand while I set our spot up."

Finally getting a break from the January rain (which had engulfed the city over the past few days), Chase had brought Reign up to their favorite spot in the mountains.

"It's okay." Reign let out a light breath, calming herself. "And I appreciate it." She glanced down at her stomach, giving the bulge a rub with her free hand. "*We* appreciate it," she giggled. "I may not be lethargic anymore, but I *have* gotten used to not being on my feet for too long."

Chase smiled down at her hand and covered it with his. It had been a little over three months of being expectant parents. Now out of her first trimester, Reign was finally feeling better. Chase couldn't have been happier that both Reign and their baby were healthy and progressing. "Exactly," he agreed, lightly squeezing her hand. "Let's go."

Slowly, they ambled along the path hand in hand in comfortable silence. Craning his neck to peer ahead, Chase glanced over at Reign. "Hold up. Before we go further, I need you to close your eyes," he said.

Reign shot him a confused look. "*For?*"

"Just trust me." When she complied, Chase gave her a gentle tug. "Okay, I'm going to walk you—"

Reign's eyes shot open. "Wait, you want me to *walk* with my eyes closed?" she shrieked. "What if I fall?"

"I won't let that happen baby, just trust me," Chase soothed.

After a bit of reluctance, Reign shut her eyes once again. Squeezing Chase's hand with hers, she clutched his arm with the other as he carefully guided her.

"Okay stop," Chase alerted after another moment.

Reign stood still, eyes squeezed shut and awaiting Chase's next words.

"Open your eyes."

Reign had to blink a few times to adjust them. Glancing ahead, she let out a gasp. Laid out before her was their large white blanket, surrounded by rose petals and gold pillar flameless candles. He'd laid out a small tray holding two champagne glasses, an ice filled bucket with drinks, and a small, covered basket.

Her head snapped in Chase's direction; he was beaming. "You had *all* of this wrapped in the blanket?" she asked, wide eyed.

Chase let out a laugh. "Most of it," he replied. "The rest was in my bag." He pointed to the oversized camping bag lying next to the setup.

Reign glanced back at the romantic setting, staring in awe. She placed a hand to her chest. "What's all this *for?*"

Chase shrugged. "We haven't been up here in a while, so I just wanted to make this trip up a little special."

Glancing back at him, Reign's eyes were filled with love and appreciation. She touched his face, then kissed him tenderly on his lips. "Thank you."

"You're welcome," Chase smiled back.

She gave his cheek a soft pat. "I could get used to this."

"As you *should.*"

Chase guided Reign down on the blanket, taking a seat next to her. While she looked on, Chase retrieved his cell phone from his pants pocket. He hit a few buttons, before the sound of smooth R&B rose gently through the speaker. Removing the cloth from the small basket, Chase retrieved a container of decorated chocolate strawberries, followed by a container of brownie and strawberry cheesecake bites.

Reign eyed the treats with anticipation. "Do I have to wait for you to finish before I take one?"

Chase let out a small laugh. "No." He opened the container of brownies, allowing her to take one. As she ate it, Chase pulled a bottle of chilled sparkling cider from the ice bucket, then filled both champagne glasses. Adjusting his position in front of Reign, he handed her a glass.

Finishing her bite, she held the glass in hand, staring into his eyes.

"To an amazing nine months together," Chase said, holding his glass up; Reign smiled at him. "To our unexpected *gift...*" he smiled himself. "And to many more amazing *years* together." He punctuated his words by lightly tapping his glass to hers.

"Cheers." She took a quick sip of the carbonated beverage, relishing the sweet taste.

The rest of the world seemed to fade away as the couple sat, relishing the peaceful and romantic atmosphere, sweet conversation, and each other's presence.

Peering at the sky, Chase exhaled lightly. "The sun is setting."

"My favorite part," Reign beamed, tucking her hair behind her ears.

Chase stood up. Looking down at Reign, he held his hand out for hers.

She looked up at him, curiosity in her eyes. "What's wrong?"

"Nothing, we normally watch the sunset while standing," he explained. "Just figured we might as well keep with tradition."

Reign chuckled a bit. "Okay silly." She took his hand so he could pull her to her feet.

With Chase at her side, Reign watched the natural beauty unfolding in front of them. Standing next to the man who'd stolen her heart as a teenager, and rekindled her suppressed feelings and passions less than a year ago on this very spot, Reign couldn't help but feel blessed.

She was so preoccupied with her pleasant thoughts, she didn't notice Chase moving.

"Baby," he called.

"Yes?" Reign glanced in his direction; not seeing him standing there, she frowned. Feeling him touch her hand, she looked down. He was kneeling on the blanket, smiling up at her; Reign tilted her head. "What are you doing down there, my love?"

Chase stared up at her. "Something that I dreamed of doing for a long time." Taking a deep breath, he pulled a small box from his pocket.

A small gasp escaped Reign's lips; her eyes widened. *Oh my God!*

"You already know how I feel about you," Chase began, sincere. "But I have *no* problem saying it again… You are my best friend, my confidant, my lover…my *everything* and I love you more and more every day and I want to spend the rest of my life showing you just how much."

Tears filled Reign's eyes. She put a loving hand on his face, wiping away his own tears from his cheeks.

"Reign Giselle Price," Chase choked out. "The love of my life…will you marry me?"

Reign was glowing. She loved him more than he could ever know, and she couldn't imagine a day without him. She sniffled, "Yes."

With shaking hands, Chase opened the small box to reveal a three carat, sparkling round diamond in the center of a diamond platinum band. Carefully, he placed the ring on Reign's delicate ring finger.

Mouth gaped open, Reign stared at it, shining in the last rays of the sunset.

Still kneeling before her, Chase stared at her with hope in his glistening eyes. "Do you like it?"

"*What?*" Reign reacted in disbelief. She looked at him. "I love it, and I love *you so* much."

Rising to his feet, Chase cupped Reign's face with his hands. He'd meant every word; Reign was everything to him. She was his world, and he'd spend every day making sure she knew that. "I love you too," he crooned, kissing her until the sun went down.

Epilogue

CHASE STOOD IN LINE AT the pastry shop, awaiting his order. The shop was crowded, typical for a Saturday afternoon. His phone rang, and he grabbed it from his pocket.

"Hey," he answered. "Yes, I'm here now, waiting... No, I *asked* you what you wanted—I ordered already... You always do this and I feel like I need to teach you a lesson today." He laughed at the caller's bitter response. "Yeah, love you too. See you in a bit."

Hanging up, he heard his name being called by the cashier.

"Your order is ready," the woman smiled as Chase approached.

"Thank you," Chase replied, grabbing his drink order. "Can I please add two slices of lemon pound cake to this order? Sorry about that."

"It's no problem." The bubbly woman eagerly rang up the addition, placing the items into a small paper bag.

Retrieving the purchase, Chase stepped away from the counter.

Chase was nearly out the door when someone called once more—and this time it wasn't the cashier. He halted his departure.

Turning around, Chase spotted Troy standing a few feet from him. Chase stared at him, his face devoid of pleasantries. He hadn't seen Troy in years—*four* to be exact.

"It's been a while, huh?" Troy began.

"It *has*," Chase agreed.

Troy gave a nod. "Yeah, I moved out of Phoenix a while ago." He shifted his feet. "Just back for a little bit. Doing some business."

Chase shrugged. "Okay." He wasn't sure why Troy felt the need to share that bit of information with him, or call his name in the *first* place.

481

"I just want to say that…as much as I hated our last interaction…I respected it," Troy said.

"Lucky for you," Chase replied, tone even.

Troy nodded. He hesitated for a moment. "How *is* she? … *Reign*, how is she?"

Chase smirked. "Reign is great."

"I'm glad." Though Troy had moved on, he couldn't help but think of Reign from time to time. He hadn't expected to run in to Chase, however he had to seize the opportunity. "I had a feeling *then* that something was going on between you two… Not when she and I were *together* I mean, I—"

"Do you have a point, Troy?" Chase abruptly cut in.

Troy sighed. "Yeah…Just make sure you cherish her. *That's* all."

Chase fixed Troy with an intense stare. "I *married* her."

Troy stared back; his eyes widened. After a moment, he gave Chase a nod. "Respect," he said.

Chase smirked again and walked out of the shop, leaving Troy behind.

Reign sat in the car, holding her phone to her ear. Listening to the voice message, she smiled to herself, and saved it before placing the phone in her purse. After a moment of gazing out of the window, she dug into her bag, pulling out a small notepad and pen.

Jotting a few quick words, she stared at the writing, her eyes gleaming. Seeing Chase approach the driver's side door, she tossed the pad and pen back in her bag.

He got in, handing the drinks and cake slices to Reign.

"You were in there a while," she mentioned. "Crowded, huh?"

Chase shook his head, amused. "*Too* crowded," he chortled in return, before pulling off.

Chase parked his car in the driveway of what was once only Reign's house.

Before they'd married two years ago, Chase had sold his home and moved into hers. Together, they'd remodeled a few things until they were both comfortable and happy.

Drinks in hand, Reign stepped out of the car. As they approached the door side by side, Reign stopped. "Take these," she ordered, handing Chase the drinks.

Taking them, Chase held a worried gaze on Reign as she placed a hand on her forehead, closing her eyes. "You okay?"

Opening her eyes, Reign nodded. "Yeah." She ran a hand through her hair. "I just got a little winded... It's hot."

He grimaced. "Yeah, let's get inside," he agreed, guiding her to the door.

Reign was immediately greeted by cool air, and Ava's voice bellowing from the living room. "Chase, I know you better not had left that shop without my cake!"

"Damn, *hello*," Chase threw back, closing the door behind him.

Reign laughed. "He got it," she assured, entering the living room. A bright smile crossed her face.

"Mommy!" a smiling toddler cooed, gazing up.

"Ooh, that was loud," Ava giggled, patting the top of the little brown skinned girl's curly-haired head.

Bending down, Reign held her arms out. "Come here baby girl."

The little girl bolted from Ava's side, and Reign scooped her up into her arms. "How's Mommy's baby?" she cooed, standing up.

The little girl rested her head on Reign's shoulder. "Good," she spoke.

Ava stood from the floor, toy blocks in hand. "You know Rae, Sierra *definitely* takes after you."

Reign kissed her daughter on the cheek. "What makes you say that?"

"She's only three and she loves these damn word blocks," Ava replied; Reign giggled. "That's all she wants to play with. I asked her 'do you want to watch a movie?' she answered with 'no, blocks'."

Entering the living room, Chase laughed. "Yeah, that's not

surprising." He handed Ava the cakes. "Thank you for babysitting while we were out. It was too nice of a day for us not to take a drive."

"Oh please," Ava dismissed with a wave of her hand. "I don't need thanks for watching my niece. I love her to pieces."

Reign grinned. "She loves you too." She adjusted her daughter in her arms while the little girl played in her hair. "*Both* of her crazy aunts."

Ava laughed a little. "No, *Cynthia* is the crazy one." She tossed the colorful blocks in a nearby basket. "At least *I* don't tell everyone she's *my* child when I have her."

Reign giggled again. "Yes, I know."

Ava glanced at her watch. "Well, let me get out of your hair." She grabbed her purse from the couch. "I need to finish some work before meeting up with Malcom later." She pushed her hair over her shoulder.

Reign smiled at the diamond ring twinkling on her best friend's finger. "Have you set a date yet?"

Ava glanced down at her hand. "Ooh girl, I keep forgetting that's there."

Reign busted out laughing, while Chase shook his head. "A damn shame," Chase commented.

Ava chuckled. "I'm thinking in another year maybe… I've only been engaged six months."

"Tell *Mom* that, so she can stop hounding *me*," Chase cut in. "She seems to think that *I* can talk you into setting one *now*."

"I already told her to relax, you know she doesn't listen," Ava dismissed.

Reign opened her mouth to reply to Ava, but her daughter's voice cut her off.

"Mommy?"

"Yes?" Reign answered, eyeing her.

"May I go pick flowers?"

Chase walked over, holding his hands out in front of Sierra. "Yes Muffin, I'll take you out back," he promised.

He smiled when his daughter reached for him, letting out an

enthused, "Yay!"

Reign passed the excited little girl to her father.

"See you later Ava, text when you get home," Chase said, walking off.

"Will do." Ava followed her brother's progress towards the backyard. "See you later, Sierra," she said, waving.

Sierra's little hand waved back. "See you later, Auntie Ava."

Ava placed a hand over her heart as the backdoor closed. "Ugh, I just *adore* her," she gushed.

Reign chuckled, "You sound like a woman whose ready for her *own* children."

Ava shrugged. "Eh, I'm perfectly happy being Godmother to that angel out there for now," her voice was laced with humor. "Neither Malcom nor *I* are in a rush for children."

"And there is nothing wrong with that, take your time," Reign approved. She tilted her head, eyeing Ava.

Noticing the stare, Ava squinted. "What?"

"Just observing how much your eyes light up when you mention his name," Reign teased. "It just means that he makes you happy," she added, amused, when Ava flagged Reign with her hand. "It's beautiful."

"Yeah, yeah." Ava glanced at her ring finger once again; a large grin crossed her face. "He *does*, though," she admitted. She let out a light sigh. "Life is good."

Reign nodded, smiling. She couldn't have agreed more.

Ava adjusted the purse strap on her shoulder. "Oh and *work*—"

"You like being a supervisor, don't you?" Reign jumped in.

"Girl, *do* I?" Ava boasted, "I'm so good at it." With their company finally moving Reign to a full-time ghostwriter over two years ago, Ava had successfully taken over Reign's old position of editing supervisor.

Reign gave Ava's arm a pat. "I knew you *would* be."

Ava nodded. "I know I've said this before, but thank you for believing in me, and for *pushing* me."

"You don't have to thank me for that," Reign replied, sincere.

"But since you *did*, you're welcome… Anytime."

Smiling, Ava reached out and enveloped Reign in a warm hug. "Love you sis."

Reign hugged her back. "Love you too."

"I'll see you later," Ava said, parting from the embrace.

"Okay." Reign watched Ava head for the door. "I'll call you later." Ava blew a kiss to her and shut the door behind her.

Reign ran a hand over the back of her neck, stretching it from side to side before letting out a happy sigh. Heading for the kitchen, she grabbed her drink from the counter, preparing to take a sip. But the back door opened, followed by an abundance of laughter coming from her child, stealing her attention.

Reign giggled as Sierra walked in, pink flowers clutched in her little hand; Chase was following behind her. "What's so funny, Muffin?" she asked.

Sierra pointed to Chase, who just looked down at her. "A bunny scared Daddy," she told.

Reign's eyes widened. She glanced up at Chase, who just stood there with a silly look on his face. She broke into laughter. "*Again?*"

Chase put a hand over his face in embarrassment, shaking his head. "It just came out of nowhere while she was picking flowers from the garden."

Reign's laughter subsided; though the humor was still prevalent on her face. "Awww," she soothed.

Chase chuckled. "It's fine." He gently nudged Sierra toward her mother. "At least she got to pick flowers for you, like she wanted."

Reign kneeled down to meet Sierra's height. Smiling, she held her hand out for the flowers as her daughter gave them to her. "I love them, they're perfect," she beamed and put her finger under Sierra's chin. "Just like *you*."

Sierra smiled back, jumping into her mother's arms.

Chase stood there, watched the loving interaction between his wife and child. He smiled as his heart swelled with pride. He couldn't have asked for anything more.

Reign put the last of the dishes into the dishwasher and closed it. She hit start, then wiped the counter down. Hearing Chase enter the kitchen, she glanced over.

"She's asleep already?" she asked him.

"Surprisingly, yes," Chase chortled, baby monitor in hand. "She must've been worn out." With dinner finished and their daughter sound asleep for the night, the couple was ready to relax.

Chase folded his arms as he moved further into the kitchen. "Which would explain why she didn't hound me for that bedtime story she loves."

Reign giggled as she rinsed the dishrag out in the sink, hanging it on the faucet. "No, *that's* probably because I had already read it to her four times while you were making dinner." She faced him, trying to stifle a yawn.

Chase tilted his head. "Tired?"

She shrugged. "Not tired as in I want to *sleep*, but tired as in I need to sit down and relax," Reign chuckled softly. "Like our *child*, I am worn out."

Chase reached his hand out for hers. She crossed the area and took it. He placed a kiss right beside her ring. "Well, how about we *both* sit down and finish that movie that we started last night," he suggested.

Reign nodded. "Sure." She put a finger up. "But before we do that, I have something that I want to show you."

Chase watched with curiosity as Reign made a beeline for her purse; it was on an accent chair in the living room.

"Oh?" Chase questioned, following her.

"Yes." Reign retrieved her notepad, then pointed to the couch. "Have a seat."

Chase's curiosity was quickly turning to worry. Raising an eyebrow, he complied. He held a steady gaze on Reign as she joined him on the couch.

She held the pad tight, glancing down at it. "I journaled something today—while you were in the pastry shop, and I think that you should read it."

Chase's gaze had yet to waiver. "Now?"

Reign nodded, "Yes."

Chase swallowed hard. "Oh, okay…"

Reign flipped to a page, then looked at her husband. Noticing the worry on his face, she snickered. "Baby, why do you look scared?"

"You seem so serious," he explained. "Like something is wrong."

Reign planted a soft kiss on his cheek. "I'm sorry. It's not bad, I promise." She handed him the notepad. "Here. What I want you to read, is circled."

Holding the pad in his hand, Chase adjusted his position in his seat. Hesitating for a moment, Chase cleared his throat, then looked down at the paper. Reading the two words, enclosed in a circle, Chase's eyes widened:

I'm pregnant.

His gaze shot up, meeting Reign's. She was smiling back at him. He pointed to the paper. "Wait…you're serious?"

Reign nodded. "Yes," she confirmed, almost breathless. "I received the voicemail confirmation from my doctor earlier today."

Holding a loving gaze on his wife, Chase smiled bright. "Wow," he breathed.

"Are you happy?"

"Absolutely." He touched her face with his free hand. "Are *you?*"

Reign crinkled her nose. "Absolutely."

Setting the notepad on the coffee table, Chase leaned in and placed a sensual kiss to Reign's lips, enveloping her in an embrace. "I love you so much."

She held him tight. "I love you too."

Reign sat in her favorite spot on the floor by the fireplace, writing in her notebook. The last page had been filled.

Reign finally looked up, letting her eyes roam the space. The house was quiet—Chase had retreated for bed a few hours ago.

Reign's eyes were beginning to get heavy too. She paused short of closing her book, eyeing the last words she'd just written:

> *A few years ago, I asked myself if it was possible to be completely happy. If one could be content in every aspect of their life—love life, family, friendships, career—I wondered if true happiness was attainable.*
>
> *I didn't have the answer then—I didn't want to know the answer then.*
>
> *But…I have it now.*
>
> *Yes, it's possible.*
>
> *How do I know?… I'm living proof of that truth.*
>
> *I, Reign Price-Williams, am completely and utterly happy in every single aspect of my life.*

Reign held her left hand up, eyeing the diamond wedding band that rested beneath her engagement ring. Smiling to herself, she took the same hand and placed it on her stomach, giving it a slight rub.

Finally closing her book, Reign stood from her spot. Turning the fireplace off, she paused, lingering on a picture frame sitting atop the mantel—the wedding photo of her and Chase. The memories of her beautiful outdoor, destination wedding flooded back to her.

The next frame beside it was Sierra's baby picture. She would never forget the day she'd brought her daughter into the world. Holding the life that she and Chase had created in her arms for the first time was one of the best days of her life. She was looking forward to experiencing it again with their second child.

Tucking the notebook under her arm, Reign turned the lights off and headed upstairs.

She stopped at her daughter's room first. Approaching her bed, Reign lingered over her sleeping child, adjusting the cover over Sierra while watching her dream.

As Reign planted a soft kiss to the little girl's forehead, she made a promise to herself that she would instill in her children:

the ability to express themselves without fear. It was something that Reign had to learn the hard way.

Leaving the room, Reign made another pit stop to her home office. Turning the lamp on, she headed for her closet. Pulling the notebook from under her arm, Reign removed the lid from a bin. She tossed the completed book inside, and closed the bin tight, pushing it back in place before stepping out of the closet.

Reign turned around, glancing back at the space that had become a vault—holding her inner most thoughts—Reign smiled to herself yet again, before closing the door.

Acknowledgements

This story and its characters hit me like a ton of bricks out of nowhere during one of the toughest years of my life. Somehow, between everything that was going on, including working on the final book of my *college life* series, I was able to write this novel. Writing this book gave me something to be excited about. It brought back the joy of starting something new. I didn't think that I would or *could* write a new book so soon after completing my series, but I did. I absolutely love this story, and I am grateful to everyone who supported me through this process.

My family, I am thankful for each and every one of you. Your love and support mean the world to me. I wouldn't be who I am without you.

A big thank you to my husband, Stephen. Being a writer often includes long nights, much-needed space, and when paired with the publishing process—a bit of crankiness. You've been supportive through all of it. I love and appreciate you.

A special shout out to my biggest supporter. My sister, Jawhara. Thank you for the constant encouragement, your listening ear, always having my back, and for staying on me about the "documents." You already know.

My beta readers, Jawhara, Nikki, and Aja, thank you for reading my rough, unedited work and providing not only your feedback, but your hilarious commentary. Oh, and even though I complained about how much you rushed me for these chapters, I loved the enthusiasm.

A huge thank you to my editor, Suzanne L. You are *amazing* at what you do. You not only did a tremendous job, you pushed me to dig deeper in certain areas. Which only made this book that much better. You totally get my way of storytelling, and it's always a joy working with you.

Last but *certainly* not least, I'm truly thankful for my readers. Thank you for not only buying and reading my books, but for recommending them to others, posting about them, etc. Your messages, reviews, comments, and overall support mean the world to me. I appreciate each and every one of you.

ALSO BY J.B. VAMPLE

NEW ADULT FICTION

The College Life Series

About the Author

J.B. Vample is an author who fell in love with the written word at a young age. While in her final year of high school, she came up with the concept of her new adult fiction series *The College Life Series*. After years of writing only for herself, J.B. published her debut novel *College Life 101: Freshman Orientation* in 2015. Since then, she has written and published the other eight installments of *TCLS*. Currently residing in Philadelphia, J.B. continues to write while managing her career as an indie author. *Right as Reign* is her tenth novel.